What Becomes of the Broken Hearted?

Claire Allan

POOLBEG

This novel is entirely a work of fiction. The names, characters and incidents portrayed in it are the work of the author's imagination. Any resemblance to actual persons, living or dead, events or localities is entirely coincidental.

Published 2012
by Poolbeg Press Ltd
123 Grange Hill, Baldoyle
Dublin 13, Ireland
E-mail: poolbeg@poolbeg.com
www.poolbeg.com

The moral right of the author has been asserted.

1

A catalogue record for this book is available from the British Library.

ISBN 978-1-84223-514-0

Typeset by Patricia Hope in Sabon 11/15
Printed and bound by CPI Group (UK) Ltd, Croydon, CR0 4YY

About the author

Claire Allan lives and works in Derry. She is married to Neil and is mammy to two very delightful children, Joseph and Cara. When she is not writing books she works as a reporter and columnist at the *Derry Journal*. And if she ever finds any spare time, she enjoys singing with Encore Contemporary Choir, reading, watching *Grey's Anatomy* and spending time with family and friends. She is permanently fighting her chocolate addiction.

You can read more about Claire at www.claireallan.com, find her on Facebook or follow her on Twitter at @claireallan.

Acknowledgements

First and foremost, and once again, I want to thank my family for supporting me during the writing, editing and emotional meltdowns involved in putting this book together. To my mammy, who read as I wrote, thank you for all your feedback. To my daddy, sisters and brother, thank you. Most of all thanks to Neil, Joseph and Cara who live with my multiple personalities as my characters find their way. I love you all very much.

Thanks to my wider family circle, in particular my granny, Auntie Raine, 'Mimi' and Auntie Marie Louise for their faith, support and practical help. (Cupcakes gratefully accepted, choir stress relief much needed, baby-sitting very much appreciated.)

To my lovely colleagues at the *Derry Journal* and in particular Erin, Bernie, Catherine and Mary for listening on a sometimes daily basis to my writing woes – thank you.

To Vicki – you simply rock.

For those writer friends who know exactly what it is like and who make me laugh – thank you. Special thanks for their words of encouragement go to Fiona Cassidy (aka the Galbally One), Sharon Owens and Anna McPartlin.

To my Twitter friends, especially the #tayswillinweemin – thank you again for your loveliness. #youareamazing

And to my 'real world' friends, especially my Encore choir 'family', thank you.

Special thanks as always go to all at Poolbeg – especially Paula Campbell for her vision, support and friendship, and Gaye Shortland for her never-ending enthusiasm and keen eye.

Thanks also to my agent Ger Nichol, who is always there

when I need her and who should be available on the NHS to neurotic authors everywhere. I could not do this without you, Ger. Much, much love x

Finally to the booksellers and readers who make this possible and worthwhile – thank you, thank you, thank you.

For 'the babies'

Abby, Joseph, Ethan, Cara, Darcy Bo and Arya

May no one ever break your heart, and if anyone does,

trust that I will always be there to help make it all better.

Love you all so much

x

1

Kitty

The bomb dropped at 4.17 p.m. on a Thursday. It had been a fairly ordinary kind of day before then – maybe even a good kind of a day. The shop had been busy and I had made two mammies and two bridesmaids cry with joy. Two brides-to-be had left feeling like the most beautiful girls in the world.

I had been planning on making celebratory lasagne to mark the general loveliness of the day and had developed a craving for a very nice bottle of Merlot that I knew they sold at the off-licence two doors down from Mark's office. I had tried to call him to ask him to pop in and get it but, rather unusually for a man whose Blackberry even went to the toilet with him, he hadn't answered.

So I did something I never, ever do because I didn't ever want to seem like one of those needy wife types who calls her husband at work. He didn't have a direct line, you see, and I would have to go through the gatekeeper, aka the harridan of a receptionist, who worked at his building. I chewed on one of my false nails, balking at the slightly plastic taste while I contemplated just picking up a bottle of wine from the supermarket. But no, even

1

though it was only a Thursday, I decided we should treat ourselves. A bottle of wine. A nice feed of lasagne. Maybe an early night? I smiled as I dialled his office number and asked for him.

It was then, in the second between me asking "Hi, can I speak to Mark Shanahan, please?" and the receptionist answering, that something shifted forever in my world.

That's all it took – the time it took her to breathe in and start to speak – for things to shatter. I kind of wish I'd known. I can't help, when I look back at it now, but feel like a bit of a stupid bitch for smiling so brightly as I spoke to her. If I had known, my voice would have been more sombre, doom-laden . . . I might even have sobbed.

"Mr Shanahan doesn't work here any more," she cheeped. "Can anyone else help you?"

It was the strangest thing. I heard what she said and it did register – and a weird floating feeling came over me – but I felt kind of calm and maybe even a bit giddy.

"No, no, it's fine," I said.

"Okay then. Can I ask who's calling?" she cheeped back.

I suppose a part of me wanted to just hang up, but another part of me was thinking of the lasagne which probably wasn't going to get eaten and the bottle of wine that I had really been looking forward to and I knew things had changed – and changed utterly.

"Kitty Shanahan," I replied. "His wife."

There was a pause, and I could hear her sharp intake of breath. I could almost hear her brain ticking over and as she spoke, softly and slowly, all hints of the cheerful but very guarded gate-keeperness gone, I almost felt sorry for her. She must have felt in an utterly awful position, to be honest.

"I'm sorry," she said. "Mr Shanahan left last week. I'm sorry."

I thought of Mark, doe-eyed and smiling as he fixed his tie that morning and turned to kiss me as I left to open the shop. He had looked at his watch and declared he was running late and wouldn't be long leaving after me and had rushed downstairs and into the kitchen. He had shouted to me if I knew where his keys were and I had replied that, yes, they were on the worktop.

It had been ordinary, absolutely ordinary, and now it really wasn't. I put the phone down, resting the old-fashioned cream Bakelite receiver on the hook and I sighed.

Her sense for scandal piqued, my stepmother Rose peeked at me over the rim of her glasses and raised one eyebrow. "Everything okay?"

"*Hmmm*," I replied, not quite sure what was going on. I didn't want to say my husband had been going out to a fictitious job for the last week and I had known nothing about it, so I sat back on the cream-covered stool behind my desk and looked at my hands.

"*Hmmm* good, or *hmmm* bad?" Rose asked, putting down the delicate lace she had been hand-stitching in her armchair in the corner of our workroom and looking at me again.

I couldn't lie to Rose, especially not when she was giving me her full and unadulterated attention.

"Mark's not at work," I mumbled, lifting my mobile phone and walking absentmindedly down the spiral staircase to our dressing room and on through the French doors to the garden. I knew Rose would follow me, and I would let her, but now I had to try Mark again even though I knew he already had at least four missed calls from me logged on his phone and that if he wanted to call me then he would have done. I supposed, then, if he had wanted me to know he had – for whatever reason – left his job a week before, he would have told me.

His phone started to ring and I tried to keep my breathing calm even though there was a distinct increase in the volume of adrenalin coursing through my veins.

It went to answer-phone and I listened to his voice jauntily telling me he couldn't take my call right now but would get back to me if I just left my number. As the message beeped to a halt, heralding my turn to start talking, I heard a strangled squeak spring forth from my lips.

"It's Kitty! Your wife! Call me!" And for effect I added the number of the shop, even though he knew it or at least had it in his phone and would easily be able to find it. I hung up and turned, nodded to Rose who looked utterly confused – but not as confused as I felt – and dialled his number again. He would answer this time. I felt it in my water. It would be fine. There would be two Mark Shanahans working in his office and the other one would have left – or the gatekeeper had just been feeling extra-vicious and gate-keeper-y and had decided to tell me a big fat lie. No. Everything was fine.

My waters were wrong, as it turned out. He didn't answer. He didn't even answer when I rang back a third time and shouted *"Answer the shagging phone!"* at the handset in my hand. Rose walked towards me and very calmly said, "I think maybe we should close the shop early."

She had a point. No bride-to-be would want to walk in on this. This was not what anyone needed when they were contemplating their Big Day – a rather pale and shaking wedding-dress salesperson screaming into her iPhone for her husband to talk to her.

I nodded and watched as Rose left the garden to go and lock the door while I stared at my phone and willed it to burst into life. There was still time for this to be okay.

"A cup of tea will do the trick," Rose said, bustling back through towards me. "I'll just go upstairs and put the kettle on."

A cup of tea sounded nice. It sounded soothing, even, so I followed Rose up the stairs and through the office into our kitchen – clutching my phone to me as I went and I sat down and watched as Rose boiled a kettle and put two mugs out, making her tea.

Rose was like that – an oasis of calm. Nothing phased her. She was the kind of person who, if she developed a slight case of spontaneous combustion, would simply douse herself with some cold water and mutter "Ah well, never mind" before getting on with her day.

"Mark wasn't at work," I said, as she mixed milk into the china mug and stirred it gently.

"Yes," she nodded. "Custard cream?" She reached for our biscuit jar and offered it to me.

"He hasn't been at work in a week," I said, raising an eyebrow and challenging her to look surprised. "And he hasn't told me. He hasn't mentioned it to me at all."

She looked at me and bit on a custard cream before taking a sip from her mug.

"The receptionist had to tell me," I said, willing her to agree with me that it was a Very Big Deal Indeed.

She nodded, and polished off her biscuit.

"And he's not answering his phone. I've tried, seven or eight times. He left a week ago but he's been getting dressed every morning and heading out as usual and coming home his usual grumpy self."

She nodded again.

I fought the urge to snatch the biscuit from her mouth and give her a good shake. "When I say 'left' I don't mean just, you know, left. I mean he doesn't work there any more. I phoned and the receptionist said, very clearly, that Mark Shanahan doesn't work there any more."

Rose sipped from her tea before setting her mug, slowly and carefully, back on the worktop.

"I'm not sure I like the sound of that," she said. Which was bad. Rose saying she didn't like the sound of something was akin to us mere mortals running around screaming hysterically that we were all doomed, doomed, I tells ya.

2

If 4.17 p.m. marked the bomb dropping, 5.43 p.m. marked a full-on nuclear implosion which made the initial bomb look like the charge from a Christmas Cracker snapping. A very small Christmas cracker with a very, very small charge.

Rose drove me home – she said I couldn't be trusted to drive safely and she was probably right. My hands were shaking as were my legs, and my arms, and my head slightly. In fact I was one big shaky wreck and that was no good for driving in rush-hour traffic.

Rose drove a Smart car, which was an exceptionally bright pink. The steering wheel had a Hello Kitty cover on it, and the seats were covered with lurid pink-nylon seat covers. There was a veritable sweetshop full of treats in the glove compartment which normally would have sent me into raptures but even the smell of the chocolate was making me feel slightly nauseated as Rose drove full pelt back to my house, listening to her Andrew Lloyd Webber collection and warbling along to 'Could We Start Again Please'.

Mark should have been home. He had been back as usual

6

every night for the last week, pulling into the driveway at 5.35 and walking through the door a minute or so later with a smile on his face as if nothing at all was wrong or different.

But as we pulled up the driveway was strangely empty, and I was smart enough to realise that this was probably not a good thing. Even Rose looked mildly perplexed which sent me rocketing to a whole new level of anxiety – one which I never knew existed.

"Do you want me to come in with you?" Rose asked, sucking on a Werther's Original and nodding her head towards my house as if it were a crime scene, which I suppose it could well turn into before the day was over.

"Could you? Please?"

"Sure what else have I to do with my time? Go home and cook your dad his tea? He can make himself beans on toast or a tuna sandwich. I bought some of that lovely brown bread in the baker's this morning."

She was talking in the way she always did but she reached over and gave my hand a squeeze and I had to swallow hard. It would be fine. Rose would come in and her calming presence would wait with me until he came home and then she might just stop me from killing him which, I figured, was probably a good thing in the long run.

She followed as I pushed the key into the lock and turned it and walked down the hall and looked into the kitchen where I saw the note he had left for me pinned to the fridge. She watched as I took it down, opened it and read it to learn that my husband had not only walked out of his job a week before but he had also walked out on our marriage and he absolutely and completely and totally did not intend on ever coming back.

The swimming, slightly numb sensation eased off a fair whack at that stage, it had to be said. It was as if my brain suddenly switched itself back on and started screaming.

"He's not coming back," I stuttered in a half-whisper, the words sounding strange in my throat.

Rose looked at me and there was a momentary hesitation in her reassurance which I didn't miss.

"Of course he's coming home," she said.

"He's really not," I said, handing her the letter and walking to the sink and switching the tap on. Shaking, I looked at the water spill into the sink and wondered where the holy hell we kept our glasses? I looked at our cupboards but they all just swam in front of my eyes like they didn't really exist, like nothing really existed any more.

I could hear Rose's voice fading in and out as the screaming rose and fell in my head. She was on the phone to my father, calmly telling him there was tuna in the cupboard and that she had bought some Bourbon creams which she had stashed in the biscuit barrel. "You can have two," I heard her say before telling him that everything was fine and that she would be home soon but she needed to be there for me just now. As I slammed my fourth cupboard door in a row and finally found a glass, I also found myself wishing I had an ounce of my stepmother's calm in a crisis. I sipped from the glass, hoping it would steady me – it didn't. I choked and looked at Rose. She was reading the letter again and shaking her head.

Part of me began to doubt myself. Had I read it right? Mark. Leaving. "Not working" and "nothing personal". Nothing personal? We'd been married for four years. How the hell could it not be personal? I grabbed the letter from Rose and read it again. He had typed it. The bastard. He had sat down and switched on the computer and opened a file and typed it.

Kitty,

I'm sorry to do this. You will never know how sorry I am. But you must have known. You must have felt it too. We've not been working, have we? Not for a long time.

I have tried. I've tried to make it better but I don't know – something in me has changed. It's not you, Kitty. It's not personal. I changed. I wanted more and I just can't go on pretending what we have is good for either of us any more. I know you won't understand that and that you are probably angry but, believe me, you will understand. One day. One day you won't be angry any more. One day, you will feel relieved that one of us had the guts to admit this before we went any further. At least we have no children to complicate things. It would have been worse then, for sure.

I've left work. It wasn't working either. You know I hadn't been happy for a while. I just need to be me for a little bit – to try more and to do more. I just feel as if I've not lived and I want to live a little. Please don't try and find me – even Mum and Dad don't know where I am. But I'm safe and I think I'm going to be happy.

Don't hate me. I'm not a bad person.

I'll be in touch when things have calmed down a little and when you have had the chance to realise this is a good thing.

I'm sorry.

Mark

PS There is no one else.

The words were no easier to read the second time around. If anything it just seemed a little more absurd.

"A breakdown," Rose declared, switching the kettle on and lifting two cups from the cupboard (which she got right the very first time). "It's a breakdown. I wouldn't be convinced he means it."

"It sounds to me like he means it."

"That's because you're in shock."

"No," I said, shaking my head. "It's because he pretty much says it in the letter."

"Your dad had a mini-breakdown you know, about ten years ago. You know, that time we went to Vegas and he came back with a goatee."

"Facial hair is hardly on the same level," I answered, lifting the letter and glancing over it again. It sounded so . . . well . . . wanky. So "I want to live a little" . . . what the frig did he think we had been doing over the last eleven years? It felt like living to me – falling in love, getting married, setting up in business, buying this house . . . choosing names for the babies we'd not even conceived yet. It felt pretty damn real to me.

That was when I cried, when I felt my eyes prick and my chest tighten. This was awful, there were no two ways about it. And no, I hadn't felt things were wrong between us. Things were right between us. They were always right between us. We were one of those sickening couples who finished each other's sentences and spooned together in bed every night and he would ask "What would I do without you?" Damn it, he'd asked me that last week. Little did I know he was plotting exactly what he would do without me, and not hoping we would never be parted.

I sat down, there and then, on the floor. I sat down before I fell down and I felt the numbness which had surrounded me for the last hour ebb away totally and the screaming that had been in my head screeched forth from my lungs until I actually felt as if I might stop breathing altogether. It wasn't possible to feel this much pain and still be. Was it? I scrambled on my hands and knees for my bag and fished my phone out and hit the redial button again as if he would suddenly answer now. Surely he would know that I needed to talk to him. He was my go-to person in a crisis. It wasn't supposed to be like this. He wasn't supposed to be the *cause* of the crisis. As the ringing tone assaulted my ears I pleaded internally, and then externally and very loudly, for him to answer. He had to know how much I needed him – how much none of this made sense. He had to know that I had been happy and that I had believed in us. There were many things I doubted in this life but 'Us' was not one of them. Us was my constant.

"Answer! Answer! Please answer!" I pleaded before feeling Rose sit down beside me and gently take the phone from my hands. I watched as she switched it off, unable to argue with her, and I watched as she took my hand and held my cheek in her palm and told me it would be okay.

"He's not worth it, darling. He's really not worth it."

And I fell in to her, allowing her to hug me until I caught my breath again in large heaving motions and until the urge to throw up had passed.

"Tell me it's not real," I muttered.

"Sssh," she offered because, in fairness, there was nothing else she could say. "Sssh, my darling."

Rose was not only exceptionally calm in a crisis – which was a good thing, given my father's uncanny ability to cause chaos everywhere he went – but she was also exceptionally efficient. Within half an hour of the return of my ability to breathe properly she had me wrapped in a blanket on the sofa with my second cup of hot sweet tea on the go. The first sweet tea I'd had since I was a child – I embraced it, feeling slightly sick at the overly sweet taste but comforted all the same. She had called Mark's parents and indeed they did not know where he was and seemed to be as shocked as I was – if a little less hysterical over the whole thing, which served only to put me into even worse form.

"They never liked me!" I wailed as I gagged on the super-sweet tea.

"Tush and nonsense," she tutted as she whipped together a casserole so that I would have something to eat when the notion took me – which, given how I was feeling, was likely to be in around three years' time. Amid a flurry of tears I could see her hide a couple of particularly sharp objects – you know, just in case – and then I heard her on the phone to Cara, my cousin and former bridesmaid, inviting her over.

"I could call Ivy," she offered and I gagged, but this time not at the sweet tea but at the notion of Ivy my sister, other former bridesmaid and smuggest creature on the planet.

"Oh Jesus, don't call Ivy. Ivy will enjoy this far too much."

Rose looked at me with the flicker of a glare which told me she was mildly disappointed in me but I pushed it aside.

"Of course she won't enjoy it, Kitty. Don't be silly. She could help."

"Rose, I love you very, very much but Ivy never has been and never will be the person I go to in a crisis. You know that. If Cara is coming, that's enough. Honestly."

Rose shook her head. "I don't understand you girls sometimes," she said before giggling, like this was a teenage spat about who gets the poster space on the back of the bedroom door, not like this was about how my sister wouldn't be at all supportive as my life crashed around my ears.

I stood up, strode to the kitchen and poured the super-sweet tea down the sink before reaching into the fridge and hauling out the emergency bottle of wine I always kept in the vegetable rack.

"You've had a shock," Rose twittered "Alcohol might not be the best thing."

"Rose," I said, stabbing the corkscrew into the top of the bottle with a viciousness it didn't quite deserve. "Once again, I say this with love, but of course this is not the best thing for me. The best thing for me would be for all this not to have happened or for me to be able to do like Superman does in whatever Superman film he does it in, and fly around the world really really fast and turn back time so that I could talk to Mark because he won't bloody answer his phone and he's not here." I stabbed the corkscrew again, pushing the cork deeper into the bottle. "And I didn't do anything wrong and I don't understand it and my brain hurts so much from trying to understand it." I stabbed the bottle again and the cork plopped squarely into the cool liquid below, small particles dispersing around it. I would drink it anyway. If anyone had offered me turps at that stage I would have been tempted to knock it back.

Tipping the bottle and watching my glass fill, I continued: "And I would go and look for him but I don't know where to start because no one seems to know where he is!" Then, "*James!*" I shouted and Rose looked at me, her look of mild concern now replaced with a look of mild fear. "I'll phone James. Where's my phone?"

Rose shrugged her shoulders but the slight twitch of her eye towards the top of the fridge gave it away. Pushing past her like a demented woman – and with the corkscrew still in my hand – I reached up and pulled my phone down, switching it on and cursing the damn thing for not being faster.

"James will know. Sure Mark could barely fart without having to fill James in on all the finer details. He'll know and he'll have to tell me."

When the address book finally came online I scrolled down, found my husband's best friend's name and hit the call button.

"His loyalty will probably lie with Mark, you know," Rose warned.

I glared at her and instantly felt cross with myself. She was only trying to help – and she was only speaking the truth.

He answered on the third ring – a cheery hello as if nothing at all had gone cataclysmically wrong with anyone's life at all that afternoon. "Kitty, how are you?"

"Do you know where Mark is?" I kept my voice calm.

"Haven't seen him since last week. Sorry, I don't know where he is. Is he in trouble then? If he calls round should I warn him he's in the doghouse?" He sounded chirpy, as if he enjoyed the notion of Mark being in trouble. Something told me James didn't know that things were actually pretty serious.

"When you saw him last week did he tell you he'd left his work?"

"Left his work?"

"Yes. Walked out. Quit. Packed it in."

"Jesus, no. What happened?"

"I don't know," I said, feeling strangely comforted that James at least sounded half as shocked as I did. "I only just found out. And he hasn't come home. He's left me, James!" I wailed and the very sound of the words leaving my mouth crumpled what very little was left of my reserve.

Rose walked calmly over and took the phone from me, answering the questions James thrust at her as best she could before hanging up and steering me back to the sofa where she removed the glass of wine from the vice-like grip of my hand and replaced it with another cup of hot, sweet tea.

"It's good for the shock," she soothed and I lay back praying that even one hint of the numbness which had enveloped me earlier would return.

None of this made sense. None of it.

I sat bolt upright. "I need to try and find him, Rose. I think maybe I'll just drive around."

"Darling," she said softly. "He's not a dog who has wandered off – chances are he won't be prowling the streets hiding in the shadows."

"I can't just do *nothing*," I proclaimed. "I can't just sit here."

"I don't see you have much choice."

3

Rose left, somewhat reluctantly, when Cara arrived. She was worried, I know, that Cara and I would go all Cagney and Lacey, or Thelma and Louise and set about tracking Mark down and making him pay for his actions.

The truth was, by the time Cara arrived, any strength I had to do anything more than lie on the sofa trying to quell the increasing waves of nausea sweeping over me had gone. I cried, in five-minute bursts, before swearing and trying his phone again. Rose had urged me to just switch my phone off – to stop torturing myself – but I couldn't do that. What if he phoned? What if he was having a breakdown of sorts and was sitting in a lonely hotel room realising just there and then how much he needed me? No, I couldn't and wouldn't switch my phone off. All I could do was glare at it, and lift it, and check it was working with an almost obsessive compulsion.

Cara walked in and sat beside me. She didn't say anything. She just looked at me, her brown eyes filled with concern, and I allowed her to hug me even though Cara and I didn't really ever hug.

"I'm sorry," she said, shaking her curly blonde head. "I'm sorry. He's a bastard and I'm sorry."

I nodded but a little part of me bristled. I wasn't ready to have anyone call him a bastard. I didn't know if he even was a bastard. He had kissed me, softly and tenderly, that morning when we woke. A bastard wouldn't do that, would he?

"Tell me, what happened anyway?" she said, settling beside me.

Rose, who had put on her coat and was heading for the door, handed Cara the letter before kissing me goodbye and telling me she would call later. I nodded to her but one eye was on Cara. I wanted to see her reaction as she saw the words. I wanted to know if she thought this was as completely nuts as I did.

Her eyes widened and her head shook gently from side to side and then she looked at me. "And his mum and dad? Do they know where he is?"

"Nope."

"James?" she said hopefully.

"No, he's pretty much shell-shocked too."

"And he's not been at work in a week?"

"Nope."

"And you didn't know?"

"Nope. As far as I was aware he was coming and going as normal. It was all normal, Cara. All normal. There has to be something wrong with him. This isn't how he behaves. This isn't who he is. Mark doesn't walk away from things – not that there was even anything to walk away from. We were fine, weren't we, Cara? I mean you saw us together all the time. Did we look like we hated each other? Was there some simmering tension there that I was too stupid to pick up on?"

"No!" she said. "Absolutely no way. No way at all."

"Then I just don't get it. Oh God, Cara. I don't get it."

"Jeez," she said, staring ahead of her and, while it would have been nice if she had said something comforting and wise, I knew myself there wasn't much she could say.

"I'm sorry," she added as I lifted my phone and tried his

number again, listening to the tinny voice telling me I was being forwarded to an answering service.

"Mark, we can work this out. I don't know what is going on with you. I'm worried. I love you. Please, call me."

I went to bed with my phone on his pillow, just in case he would come to his senses and call me in the wee small hours. Cara slept in the spare room to make sure I was okay. I tried to sleep but found myself playing over the minutiae of our last few days together – trying to find some sign that something was about to go completely and utterly tits up. But I couldn't – everything had been just as it always was. There was no awkwardness, no signs that he was depressed. He hadn't even been distant.

I played over several scenarios in my head as the clock ticked through the hours. The first was, of course, that he had indeed had some sort of breakdown. I didn't like that scenario – even though it pointed no blame in my direction. I didn't like it because he was out there, alone, and could be doing something reckless and dangerous, and every part of me wanted to protect him.

The second scenario was that this was all an elaborate hoax – perhaps part of a new reality-TV show, a twisted sicker version of *Candid Camera* or *Beadle's About*. He would show up the following day with some grinning eejit of a TV presenter in tow and tell me it was all a big laugh. I would call him a big rotten eejit and everyone would laugh and it would be only after the camera crews went home that I would cry and tell him never, ever to do that to me again because the thought of him just walking away was the most painful thing I had ever had to go through. Things would be a little strained for a while but we would get over it. That particular scenario was probably the one I liked most and around three thirty, when I was mildly delirious through lack of sleep, I managed to convince myself that was entirely plausible and totally likely and I even managed to drift off to sleep for a while.

The third scenario, which I filed under *Very Least Favourite* was the one which pervaded my dreams and which caused me to jolt awake just as the sun hit the windows. That scenario was that this was actually happening, and he actually meant it, and something had been broken in our relationship, and I had been walking around with my head in the sand or in the clouds or up my arse where I hadn't been at all aware that it was always going to go spectacularly wrong.

I glanced at the clock – it had just gone six – and then I looked at my phone which had no new messages, no secret missed calls, no big 'I'm sorrys' and 'I'm coming homes' about it. I threw it across the room and got up. There was no point in trying to sleep – not when a whole new dose of adrenalin was coursing through my bloodstream. I'd take a shower. I'd take a shower and leave my phone lying in the corner of the bedroom, thereby giving it the chance to ring without me hovering over it. A watched phone never rings and all that. Maybe if I left it, if I stopped cocking one ear and checking endlessly, it would finally spring to life.

Letting the hot stream of water wash over me, I tried to stop myself from shaking and had to bite my lip to stop myself from wailing. It was midway through my second rinse of shampoo that a whole new emotion washed over me. "The bastard," I said, softly at first before repeating it loudly. "The bastard!" We promised we would always talk to each other and we would always be honest. We would tell each other if one of us was annoying the living daylights out of the other. We promised that. In a chapel. In front of everyone we knew and in front of God. But most of all we had promised it to each other. We hadn't promised to just clear off one day. He couldn't do this. "Bastard!" I said a third time, stepping out of the shower, hauling a towel round me roughly and stomping back to the bedroom where I lifted my phone, dialled his number and shouted to the silence of his answer machine. "You call me. *Now.* You pick up your damn phone and you call me. I'm your wife. And you owe me that. So you please call me *right now!*"

And then I threw the phone down again and dressed in jogging bottoms and a T-shirt, hauling my wet hair back into a ponytail and pulling on slipper socks, and went downstairs where I poured a long, cool glass of Diet Coke even though it wasn't even seven o'clock yet and I reached for the biscuit tin and mainlined some Kit Kats. Then I put on trainers and went for a jog – ostensibly because I figured moving about would ease the anxiety flooding through me but also because I hoped being out and about would give me some sort of a sign – a sign that this was a blip in the road. Sure all good relationships had them – even Dad and Rose who had been together since I was fourteen had the occasional row. There was that mid-life crisis episode of course when Rose had stormed out for three whole days. She came to stay with me at my university digs and insisted on going to the Student Union every night and drinking pints even though she didn't even like beer. "I never had the chance to be a student myself," she'd said, as she sidled up beside me at the back of a design and marketing lecture. She took brilliant notes, as it happened, and it had been nice if a little weird to have her there as a study buddy. The memory made me smile and then I remembered everything that was happening in my life there and then and I frowned and ran on, faster and harder until my legs hurt almost as much as my heart.

Cara was happy to see me when I got home. When I say happy, I do of course mean a strange mixture of absolutely fuming and relieved. "Where the hell were you? You left. You didn't tell me where you were going. You didn't even take your phone. You didn't even leave shagging note. I didn't know where you had gone. For all I knew, you could be swinging from a big, tall tree around now."

"If I was going to top myself," I said, "I would have left a note. Just so you know." I knew it wasn't the right thing to say and that I should have apologised for being a feckless bitch but part of me wanted to scream that she couldn't really expect me to act rationally, could she? Which, I suppose, was kind of the point she was making. I then felt like a whole new level of shit, which was impressive given how shit I had been feeling in the first place. "I'm sorry," I stuttered. "I didn't think. I just needed to run."

She shrugged. "Just don't do it again, okay?"

I nodded and poured myself a glass of water. "Did it ring at all?"

"What?"

"My phone. Did it ring at all?"

"No – sorry," she said, sipping from a cup of tea.

"Oh," I said, sinking onto the chair and putting my glass of water on the table. I didn't even have the stomach for water this morning.

"I'll take the day off work so I'm here for you," Cara said softly. "You don't have to do this alone."

"But I'll be at work myself," I said.

Her expression was as shocked as if I had said I would be running buck-naked round the city walls singing the score from *The Sound of Music*.

"Really? I mean, do you think it's best?"

"It's my business," I said, holding on to whatever constants I had in my life for dear life.

"It's a wedding-dress shop," she said as if she was telling me something I didn't know.

"I have customers who have appointments."

"Who maybe don't need to be seeing a broken-hearted woman selling them their big dream?"

"I'm not a broken-hearted woman. I don't know what I am. I don't know what is going on – where he is or what he is doing – so for now I'm confused and scared maybe but I can still sell dresses." I was surprised by how determined I sounded because I'm not sure I actually felt it. Cara clearly wasn't convinced so I took a deep breath. "Look, Cara. I have to do this because I can't sit here, waiting and not knowing. I have to do something and, since I happen to own a lovely bridal shop which has customers waiting to be served, then I might as well do that."

She chewed on a nail and sipped from her cup again. "Then I'm coming with you."

4

Erin

Two glasses of wine had relaxed me. The nerves were easing even though my category was up next. I slipped my feet back into my very high shoes just in case they called my name – not that I really expected them to call my name. But, if they did, I didn't want to walk up to the front of the function room in my bare feet or be caught fumbling for my shoes by the photographers. I did not want a place on the 'Wall of Shame' in the office – that place where embarrassing photos of *Northern People* staff in compromising positions were posted in the name of a bit of office banter. Me with my head under a table at the Northern Media Awards would not be a good look – no, best to be prepared.

Locating my shoes, I slipped my tired feet into them. It had been a long day – a hair appointment, a make-up appointment, picking up my dress from the dry cleaner's and driving Paddy home from chemo.

"I don't have to go if you don't want me to," I had said, tucking him in bed with a cup of tea, full use of the Sky remote and his laptop.

Snuggling down under the covers, he had sighed. "Erin, you

are going. You are going because you are great and you will win."

"We don't know that I will win."

"It will be a dirty big fix if you don't," he said, his eyes drooping – his need for sleep etched on his eyelids.

"I can stay and look after you – sure Grace can accept it for me if I win – which is a big 'if'."

"It's a wee 'if'. Now go, woman. Get ready. I'm only going to sleep anyway. You'll be back before I wake up."

I had kissed him on the top of his head, reluctant to go but kind of excited too. I didn't often get a night out – and I never got a night out where there was a possibility I might just scoop an award at the end of it all. Grace, my editor at *Northern People*, had said I was in with a chance. "Your work has been outstanding this year," she'd told me, while I grinned like a five-year-old who had just been sent to the top of the class. "The feature on childhood obesity really got people talking. Your campaign to save the cityside playpark had great support and your opinion pieces have a great following. You've really come into your own this year."

I smiled and blushed furiously. It had been nice to hear and I had worked hard, but I didn't take compliments well.

So, when Paddy told me I looked gorgeous, as I stood in my little black dress, my sky-high heels and my auburn hair tamed by a very talented hairdresser and piled on top of my head, I had snorted. "Aye right . . . a pig in a dress is still a pig!"

"Erin Brannigan. You look gorgeous. You do not look at all pig-like, and if I was in a fit state I would show you just how gorgeous you look. Don't put yourself down. Now clear out and bring me back your award – and a doggy bag, for when I don't feel like I want to throw up."

"Really," I said again, "I don't have to go." Though by this stage I really, really wanted to go.

"Get out," he said, using what little strength he had left to throw a cushion at my head.

So there I was, beside Grace, slipping my feet back into my shoes and waiting for the MC to announce the award for Feature Writer of the Year. I looked at Grace, who winked at me and then I tried to plaster an 'I don't really mind who wins' face on. Okay, so there were no TV cameras – just a few photographers, mostly hoping for their Wall of Shame moment – but, still, it would be no good to be seen pouting.

I had worked hard for this. I had thrown myself into work – which was a welcome distraction from Paddy and from the wedding planning. Jeez, don't pout. Smile. Listen. Grace nodded in my direction and it was clear I had won. And I hadn't even heard my name being called out.

"You should make the most of it," Grace said, ordering two more Cosmopolitans from a waiter with impossibly tight trousers and an even tighter smile. "This is your big night."

"I should tell you something," I said, sidling into her as if we were best friends and not boss and lowly employee. "I can't really get too wasted. I'm going wedding-dress shopping in the morning."

I swear her face lit up, the way women's faces tend to light up when you mention wedding dresses, and as the light beamed from her she took on an almost soft and dreamy look.

"Oh, how exciting! God, I remember when I shopped for my dress. It was such a brilliant day. Oh where are you going? Are you going to The Dressing Room? You *so* should go to The Dressing Room."

I nodded and gulped. Yes, I was going to The Dressing Room and I felt kind of nauseated at the thought. What I really wanted to do was stay and drink at least three more Cosmopolitans and revel in the glory of my big win and enjoy my boss looking at me with admiration. Much as I loved the very bones of Paddy, wedding-dress shopping was not something I looked forward to one bit.

Some people are allergic to penicillin. Some are allergic to peanuts. I knew a girl once who was allergic to salt and vinegar crisps and her lips would swell up in an exaggerated pout if she so much as sniffed a bag of them. Me? I was allergic to weddings – and all things wedding-related.

So there was no one more surprised than me to find myself with an 11 a.m. appointment at The Dressing Room on a Friday morning where I would be on a mission to buy one of those big white frocks I had mocked for years. I ordered another Cosmo and tried to focus on the award and my night and not on the following morning.

The glossy purple door of The Dressing Room taunted me. The stark white walls and sash windows looked very inviting – pretty, even – but I wasn't fooled. If I had my way I would never even contemplate crossing the doorstep but, as I had learned very quickly, once you get a ring on your finger you become the plaything of a horde of female family members who love nothing more than a good wedding.

I didn't want a good wedding, I had told my mother in an ill-judged move which almost had her reaching for the smelling salts – I wanted a good marriage. And I knew that I would have that. Paddy was a good man and he wanted to marry me. His actual words were "I need to marry you" and he had a look of urgency about him which melted my resolve.

He had first asked me when we had been together four months. I had said no and he knew my reasons and he accepted that – even if he had adopted a look on his face as if I had kicked him square in the testicles, with steel-toe-capped boots on. He hadn't asked again for another seven months, until Christmas rolled about and he'd had one too many Drambuies after his festive dinner. He had kissed me under the mistletoe and I had allowed him to. Paddy was a good kisser – the best kisser I had ever encountered – and dizzy with lust, a little part of me had wavered and I'd had to walk away in case I said yes, but I wasn't ready to say yes yet. I wasn't sure I would ever be ready. That didn't deter him from asking again and again and, eventually, when he said he *needed* me to say yes, I finally realised that this was about more than me. You can't say no to a man with one testicle, can you?

But no, today would be tricky enough – what with all that taffeta, chiffon, silk and wedding-dress-trying-on – without thinking about the C word.

I took a deep breath, pushed my hair back from my face and walked towards the shop door. I would plaster on a smile and play along with the whole wedding-dress/wedding-planning frenzy which my life had become.

My mother would meet me there. As would Paddy's mother. They were both just about ready to go into orbit with the excitement of it all. My mother was relieved I was finally going to get married. Paddy's mother was delighted he was finally getting married. They both did an absolutely top-notch job of pretending this was a perfectly normal wedding not foisted upon anyone by possible life-threatening illnesses. We didn't talk about that. We just talked about garters (yes, I would definitely have one), doves (no way, I was terrified of birds), champagne (the best stuff for the top table, the cheaper variety for everyone else) and dresses (my mother was holding out hope I would wear a meringue which would make Katie Price's dresses look tame).

What I wanted was to nip down to the Guildhall with a couple of witnesses and sure we would still be married. But I realised I was now a mere pawn in a very big game of chess and I had to go where I was moved – and really, it didn't really bloody matter, did it? As long as I had Paddy.

I had never been in The Dressing Room before, but I had been reliably informed it was the best damned little wedding-dress shop in town. The staff, I was told, were friendly and welcoming and didn't laugh at your stretch-marks or sniff at you snootily if you asked for a dress in anything above a Size 12. The advertising girls at *Northern People* had said they loved to work with Kitty, the owner, and that she would be extra nice to me. I could do with a little friendliness if the truth be told, so hopefully this wouldn't be too awful.

Walking into the reception I saw a young woman, with blonde curly hair and an impossibly trim waist, sitting at the counter examining her nails and looking as if this was exactly the very last place on the planet she wanted to be. She looked up at me and offered a smile which didn't quite stretch to her eyes and asked if she could help.

"I'm Erin Brannigan. I have an appointment?"

She looked down at the book in front of her and traced her finger down the page until she tapped what I can only imagine was my name against the time I was due in. She looked up and smiled again. "Ah, Erin, welcome to The Dressing Room. I'm Cara. I don't actually work here." She glanced behind her at two large doors. "I'll let Kitty know you're here." She wandered off rather distractedly through the doors, leaving me standing like a bit of a lemon in a very calm room where headless bridal mannequins stood on guard around me.

I shouted after Cara with the curly hair that it was fine, I was waiting for someone anyway. And then I looked at the headless brides, bedecked in their finery and muttered: "Yes, honestly, I'm okay."

They didn't answer.

So I sat down on a very lovely purple-covered chaise longue and flicked through a magazine filled with stark-looking models, all right angles and collarbones, wearing wedding dresses that cost more than I earned in a month. "How much?" I stuttered, looking at one particularly blingy tiara which looked heavy enough to crack my skull if I wore it for more than ten minutes. I put the magazine down, a little bit scared of it if truth be told, and sat back and looked around again. Yes, this place was actually quite calming – headless brides aside. It was bright and airy, which helped any gathering claustrophobic feelings. The solid wood floors were pretty. I'd always wanted real wood floors – but we had laminates instead. There were flowers of varying hues in vases around the room and fair smattering of twinkling lights here and there draped over distressed white display cases which screamed vintage glamour.

There was still no sign of Cara and her curly hair or the person who actually did work there, Kitty. There was also no sign of my mother or my future mother-in-law which surprised me. I glanced at my watch. It was five past eleven. I hadn't expected them to be late. Both had sent me cheery text messages throughout the morning to check, double-check and triple-check the arrangements and both had expressed levels of excitement which, frankly, scared me senseless. I glared at the scary magazine and back to my watch and to the door through which Cara had disappeared.

It was then I heard the clatter of two women clearly hell-bent on making this a morning to remember. My mother and his mother stumbled through the door, arms linked together and laughing like naughty schoolgirls. If it wasn't eleven in the morning I would have wondered whether or not they were on the drink, but it seemed they were just giddy like two little girls delving into their mother's dressing-up box.

Mum pulled me into a huge, lung-squeezing hug and whispered, "My baby, getting married!" as if it were news to me.

While Sue, his mum, blinked back tears as she looked at the headless brides. "Oh, these dresses! Oh Erin! You will be beautiful. Paddy will be blown away."

I was worried, it had to be said. If they could react like this now, what the frig would they be like when they actually saw an actual dress?

Their *ooh*-ing and *aah*-ing was interrupted by the arrival of a short pale-looking woman with eyes as sad, if not sadder, than Cara's. She smiled too and I almost wanted to hug her and tell her it would be okay even though I didn't know anything about her.

"I take it you are the bride-to-be?" she said cheerfully (almost too cheerfully), extending her hand to mine.

I smiled back. "Yes, Erin Brannigan."

"Ah Erin," she smiled. "From the magazine? I've been told to treat you well. If you want, you and your friends can come through to the dressing room and we will talk about what you might like and what kind of dresses and styles you favour. I'm Kitty, by the way."

"I'm her mother," my mum said, extending her hand and speaking in a posher than normal voice. "Anne Brannigan."

"Nice to meet you," Kitty responded with a genuine warmth which kind of made the sadness in her eyes seem even sadder.

I knew that sadness. I'd seen it a fair few times in recent weeks.

"And I'm the mother of the very handsome groom," Sue chimed in. "Sue."

"Well, Sue and Anne, and Erin of course, let's go and look at some very pretty dresses indeed."

I followed her, walking in front of the two grinning mammies. Inside what could only be described as the inner sanctum of the shop there were more dresses than I could ever have imagined in every shade of white, cream, ivory and oyster. There was even a rather extravagant and delicious deep-purple satin number – with a corset which would have made me look absolutely amazing. Like a sexy purple Quality Street. I actually gasped when I saw it and had to fight the urge to reach out and stroke it.

"Oh, I take it that one is just for show," my mother said haughtily, cutting through my thoughts.

I glanced at her, hoping to see some hint that she didn't really hate it as much as it sounded like she did. There was no such hint.

"Well, we have sold that design before but I know it's not to everyone's taste," said Kitty.

"Quite," my mother said and I had to fight the urge to remind her it was far from a snooty voice she was reared and that Kitty was actually on our side.

"So how about we sit down and see what is *your* taste?" Kitty looked at me.

I was grateful she did, but decided it would be best not to tell her that the purple gown was absolutely and totally my taste, at least not in front of my mother.

With deep, rich fabric and the forgiving boning not being an option acceptable to the woman who had given me life, and keen to steer her away from the flouncy numbers she so loved, I answered as best I could. "I'd love something relatively simple – but flattering. Actually, flattering is what really matters. My hips are not my friends." I tried to smile but was suddenly conscious of my Size 14 jeans and the extra padding on my rear end.

"You have a lovely figure," Kitty said gently.

I disregarded that attempt at flattery. "I don't really fancy loads of bling. No crystals or sequins. And I'm not overly worried about white." I made the final comment with a wink.

Kitty laughed. "Let me pull out a few dresses and you can try something on."

I wasn't entirely sure what I should do. I saw the dressing room to the left and a lovely podium with tasteful mirrors positioned around it in the middle of the room. Was I to follow and hold the dresses for her? Was I to start stripping off there and then? Was I to sit where I was? I started, I have to say, to feel a bit panicky and had to fight the urge to just get up and run out.

This was not what I wanted – a wedding because we felt we had to. A dress to make my mother and his mother happy.

Kitty turned to me, a gown in ivory draped over her arm, and she tilted her head just slightly. Suddenly I felt as if every single emotion running through my head was now written in huge bold writing across my face.

"How about we just get a little glass of water, or cup of tea, or a wee sip of Prosecco first? Sure we're in no rush," Kitty said, looking directly at me.

"Tea," I muttered.

"Prosecco!" my mother clapped and squealed in a slightly less than snooty voice while Sue clapped along. "Yes, some fizzy stuff!"

Kitty put the dress back on the rack and I noticed her run her

29

hand along the soft silk then take a deep breath as if to try and steady herself – or as if she needed a cup of tea or a glass of alcoholic beverage herself. "I'll just get Cara to organise it for us. Can you excuse me for a minute?"

"Take your time," I nodded and she smiled softly.

"I just need a moment. Cara will be with you just now."

5

Kitty

My hands were shaking as if I was going through a killer dose of DTs. I had to steady myself against the worktop, close my eyes and count to ten while I breathed in and out as slowly as I could.

I had, probably completely stupidly, thought it would be okay. I thought I would have been able to come into work and put it out of my mind for a little bit.

Which was a bit stupid of me, wasn't it? How I'd ever thought standing surrounded by beautiful dresses, pictures of smiling brides and promises of happy-ever-afters was going to provide a welcome distraction was beyond me.

It hadn't helped that Rose had arrived looking very solemn and insisted on asking Cara how I was before meeting my eye. I had reacted perhaps a little too angrily, sticking my face in front of hers and telling her very loudly that I was fine.

"Your dad is worried about you," she said, still in a whisper.

"I. Am. Fine," I repeated again, "And we have a job to do and customers to serve and dresses to get ready for pick-up, so can we please stop acting as if we are at a wake and just get on with things? It's unsettling me, Rose, to have you looking so

31

serious. You never look serious. Even when you were burgled you laughed and said you would enjoy buying new stuff with the insurance money. I need you to be smiley, Rose, now, if that's okay?"

She'd nodded and plastered on a wide smile which made her look slightly demented. "You're the boss. I'll do whatever you say."

"Well, how about making sure the two dresses which are due out today are steamed and ready to go?"

"As you wish," she said in a fake sing-song voice as she curtseyed before me and scurried off.

I turned to see Cara looking straight at me with the same sorrowful expression Rose had had.

"What?" I barked at her.

She shrugged her shoulders. "Nothing. But, Kitty, you should know. You're kind of scaring me."

"I'm just trying to do my job."

"I know that," she said slowly and carefully, "but you're also being a little bit of a scary bitch and I love you very, very much so I don't think you should be here."

"He'll expect me to be here. If he wants me this is the first place he would look on a Friday. He knows Fridays are busy. And, added to all that, I told you I need to be busy."

"Okay," she said, backing off. "So I'll help. Just tell me what to do."

"I have some ordering to do. Can you mind the front desk? Call me if any of my appointments come in and I'll get on with this."

"Okay," she said. "If you're sure."

"I'm sure," I said.

I'd watched her clatter down the iron stairs in her impossibly high heels. She looked very glam – not at all haunted and scraggy like I did. Glancing in the mirror, I tried to flatten my hair a little and slicked on some lip gloss, and then I absolutely promised myself I would do some work. I had a few orders to chase and a couple of new orders to place. I had to book a stall at a bridal fair and arrange to see a rep about a new collection. It should have been a busy day. It should have been the kind of day I absolutely loved and it should have been the case that, before I knew it, it would be six o'clock and I'd be locking up and smiling at the thought of sharing a pizza and a bottle of wine with Mark.

It hadn't been like that though. It had been crap. I'd sat down and flicked on the computer screen in front of me. I'd opened the right files, so the thought was there, but instead of doing the work I was meant to do I'd sat staring into space and occasionally at my phone and then checking my email in case he'd opted for that approach instead.

He hadn't.

When Erin Brannigan arrived it had at least forced me away from torturing myself in front of the screen.

She seemed nice. A little more serious perhaps than some of the brides who walked through our doors, but nice. Some brides would be so excited to be buying their big dress for their Big Day that I'd almost want to sedate them. Erin didn't have that joyous exuberance about her. There was something about her which screamed that she didn't really want to be there. I'd noticed it as soon as I saw her and part of me wanted to give her a hug.

It was a shame her mother didn't seem interested in the purple dress (our Purple Quality Street as Rose called it). Erin's eyes had lit up just that little bit more when she saw it, but I could see – as was so frequently the case – the mother of the bride was very much in the driving seat when it came to the wedding preparations. Still, I would do what I always did and say nothing and try and make the bride as comfortable as possible and find a dress which suited her and made her look fabulous but which her mother would also approve of.

There was just that moment though – when I touched the dresses, when I felt all the love and hope and trust that went with them – that I thought I'd start to cry or throw up. Neither of those reactions would be conducive to selling a wedding dress so it was then I excused myself on the pretext of making tea or pouring a glass of fizz and I found myself taking as many deep breaths as I could without hyperventilating.

I was aware of Cara walking into the room behind me and, summoning up the strength to speak, I implored her not to ask me if I was okay. "Please, just pretend this is a normal day and everything is fine and I'm just here taking a breather," I muttered.

"Okay. Well, ignoring the fact that if this was an ordinary day I wouldn't be here and would be at my own work, is there anything I can do?"

"Can you bring tea and Prosecco down to the dressing room? Rose will help."

"Will you be down soon?" I could tell that she really was asking if I was okay without actually asking if I was okay in case I went all scary-psycho-friend on her.

"Soon," I said, "I just need a bit of time. Two minutes. Honest."

She gave a half-smile and left me to wander through the workroom where I could sit and try to gather my thoughts before returning to the dressing room and putting on my best 'I love weddings' smile.

I couldn't bring myself to look at my phone, which was mocking me at this stage, or my emails. So I just stood and looked out the window at a group of tourists (probably American – the baseball caps and 'fanny packs' gave it away) meandering along the city walls. The sun was shining and their faces were beaming. I wondered, as I always did, what brought them to Derry – what their story was? Were any of them harbouring a horrible heartbreak? I sighed and turned away and took a deep breath. I needed to get a hold of my emotions and settle myself. I closed my eyes and took a series of deep breaths.

When I opened my eyes again I found Rose standing perilously close to me, her head tilted to one side.

"*Sweet living Jesus!*" I screeched, stepping back to try and gain some sense of personal space.

"Sorry," she sing-songed. "I just wanted to see if you were okay. You were standing very still and to be honest I just wanted to make sure you were still alive."

"Dead people don't tend to be standing up, Rose."

She shrugged her shoulders. "It happens."

She said it with such authority that I didn't dare question her but made a secret vow to Google it later.

Breathing in again – but with my eyes open so as to avoid any confusion – I forced a smile on my face.

"Rose, you are very good to me," I said and gave her a hug while resisting the urge to collapse in a heap and allow her to hold me up. I had to do this on my own. I had to get through this all on my own. "Right, we have customers and I'm a professional. I can do this."

"Of course you can, pet. You do know that, don't you? You can get through anything."

"Yes," I nodded. "But sometimes I really, really don't want to. I just want it to be back the way it was. I can't believe it isn't the way it was."

"Things have a way of working out, pet," she said, smoothing my hair. "Just give it time."

I sniffed and nodded again.

"Cara has the tea sorted," she said. "I was just coming through for a couple of wineglasses for the fizz. Will we bring them down together?"

I nodded again and followed her like an obedient child, fully aware that everything in life felt a little bit easier when I had my step-mum with me.

Anne and Sue were sitting misty-eyed and a little tipsy when Erin emerged from the changing cubicle looking uncomfortable and overdressed in swathes of tulle. This had been very much *not* the dress she wanted nor the dress I would have chosen for her, but her mother had been quite insistent.

"Just one meringue, love," she had said, all hint of her earlier

35

airs and graces gone. "Just one big dress for me? Just to see? You never know, you might like it!"

"Might like it . . ." Sue had echoed, staring into the bottom of her wineglass.

The pair had only had two small glasses each but, from their demeanour, I was beginning to think they might have started their very own pre-wedding celebrations before turning up at the shop. This was not uncommon – but, in fairness, usually the bride-to-be was as tipsy as her bridal party and not wearing a face like she'd sucked a lemon, while drowning in tulle.

"You look bewdiful, darling," Anne slurred. "Like a princess."

"A princess," Sue echoed and the pair looked at each other and dissolved into tears.

I looked at Erin and she shrugged her shoulders.

"Oh Erin! What a day we will have," Anne slurred.

"Paddy will just love you," said Sue.

"Paddy loves me already," Erin said softly. "And much as I can see you love this dress and as much as I love you both, this is not the dress I will be wearing when we get married."

"But," her mother intoned, "it's lovely!"

And it was lovely – a full skirt, a boned corset, a lot of sparkle – it was the perfect dress for a certain kind of person. Some girls simply came alive when they put it on, but Erin looked completely uncomfortable and not one inch the radiant bride.

When I watched a bride trying on dresses I always knew, instinctively, when we got the right one. Something would change in her demeanour. She would stand a little taller, thrust her chest out a little further, and smile a little wider. Something in her would change. It sounded a little clichéd and a lot cheesy – but she would become a bride right before my eyes.

Looking at Erin again, blowing her hair from her face and standing with her hands on her hips, she didn't look like a bride at all. She looked kind of scary.

"Tell her," Anne said to me. "Tell her she looks lovely."

"She looks lovely," I said with a smile. "But maybe we want her to look more than lovely. We want her to look the best she ever has done and I think I might have just the dress for her. This one is indeed very nice – but it's a big seller. Don't you want something that really stands out?"

Anne looked at Erin and then at Sue, who was in danger of falling asleep, and then at me. "I suppose."

"So how about we get Erin out of this dress and into something everyone is happy with?"

Anne smiled and Erin smiled and I even felt myself smile and just for a second everything that was going so horribly wrong in my life at that moment slipped from consciousness.

"I have a few ideas in mind," I said, helping Erin back into the cubicle and helping to unzip the dress.

"I'm sorry my mother is a little loud," she whispered.

I shook my head as if to tell her not to worry herself about it one bit. We saw a lot worse in The Dressing Room. All manner of people walked in through our doors.

"Don't worry. She's fine. She's just excited."

"She's just a pain in the arse," Erin shrugged with a smile. "But she means well."

"Well," I said, "let's just get rid of her dream dress here and find the dress of *your* dreams."

"Can I let you in on a wee secret?" she said, tilting her head towards mine. "I never wanted to get married in the first place."

6

Erin

The last time I wore a big flouncy wedding dress it was scratchy and horrible and made my skin turn blotchy. When I say wedding dress, I mean First Communion dress. My mother had told me I was getting married and, being a child and an eejit, I kind of believed her. As I hauled my frock on – convinced I was destined to meet my groom in the chapel – I felt its starchy, lacy high-necked horribleness scratching at my skin. I started to feel a little faint. And panicky. As if I might actually wet my brand-new special-occasion knickers.

My mother smiled and hauled a brush through my hair – which had developed the look of a ginger Afro about it thanks to a nit infestation and a bad cut – before sliding some silk flowers on a comb on the crown of my big, orange head and arranging a veil around my face.

"Oh Erin, you look like a wee dream," she said, misty-eyed.

I looked back at her and felt a tear slide down my cheek and splash onto my brand-new shiny patent-leather shoes.

"I don't want to get married, Mammy!" I sobbed. "I want to stay here with you and Daddy."

She looked at me and smiled, a funny, lopsided kind of smile which made me feel as if I was being very silly. "Oh Erin. You don't really have to get married. I was only teasing." She pulled me into a big hug and kissed my frizzy hair.

I breathed in her Chanel No. 5 and felt myself relax. My brand-new special-occasion knickers would be safe today.

"Do I not have to get married ever ever, Mammy?" I asked, flashing a gapped-tooth smile in her direction.

"No, darling. You never have to get married ever. But we do have to get to the chapel and get this First Communion over and done with. So shall we go, my princess?"

Of course there had been another time – another dress. But it wasn't a wedding dress as such. It was a dress I wore to a wedding – my wedding, or my nearly wedding or whatever you might want to call it but that didn't count either. And I'd left that one terrified of marriage too and vowing that I'd never, ever do it again. But that, of course, was before I'd met Paddy. That was another lifetime ago entirely. Almost as distant in my mind as that day in the flouncy First Communion frock.

Kitty walked back into the cubicle with two dresses over her arm. Mercifully neither had an inch of tulle near them. "These might be more your thing," she said softly before hanging them up against the wall so I could see them in all their glory.

Sheer, slinky, figure-hugging. If I had been wearing brand-new special-occasional knickers there would have been a very good chance that I would have had a similar panic-induced pee in them.

"I can't wear something like that," I implored, feeling my pale skin blotch and scratch at the very thought.

"Of course you can," Kitty said brightly.

She had that air of confidence about her. She hadn't even paled, all that much, when I told her I didn't want to get married in the first place. Of course I didn't furnish her with the full sorry details of my marriage reluctance or the big old fat cancer-shaped reason for my change of heart. She hadn't even patronised me and said "Everyone gets nervous" or told me not to worry. She had just nodded and asked me if I wanted to continue with my search for the perfect dress.

"We can reschedule?" she had offered, calmly and softly.

"And have those women kill me? No! We must do this." I had laughed then, and patted her on the arm. "I didn't want to get married, but I love Paddy and this is the right thing for us, for him – so I suppose we just have to find the right dress for me to make this all as bearable as possible."

"These might help," Kitty said now, still softly, and she held a dress up in front of me.

I was acutely aware of the size of my arse, and the curve of my hips. I was aware that my stomach was far from flat and it never had been. I looked at the dresses in front of me – at their unforgiving, sleek, shiny, brilliance and I shook my head.

Kitty sat down beside me and took my hand. She was clearly used to dealing with hysterical brides – not that I was hysterical. I was just, well, kind of determined that those dresses and my body would never meet.

"I've been in this business a long time," she said softly, "and, believe me, I would never give you a dress to wear that would make you look horrendous."

I pointed in the direction of the tulle nightmare which I had been wearing just moments before.

"Your mother chose that one," she said with a wink. "And we have to humour our mammies, don't we?"

It was a fair cop.

"Look, try one on. How about that one there? I assure you it will be nice."

I looked at the duchesse satin number in front of me, gathered at the waist and pooling into a small puddle-train. An asymmetric number, I wondered would it show off my fat shoulders too much (well, one of them anyway). It did have a little bling and bling was something I was expressly against. But in this instance, well, it was kind of nice. Subtle even. A slight swirl of crystals curling upwards.

It was a beautiful dress and I had no doubt on the right person it would be outstanding. But I wasn't convinced I was the right person, or even in the vague vicinity of being the right person. I looked at Kitty as if she was just a little bit mad and she looked back at me as if I was just a little bit mad and then, to stop the bad looks if nothing else, I nodded and agreed to give it a whirl.

"Now this will be a little big," she said, "because we only keep sample gowns – so don't worry if it feels a little strange. I'll do my best to give you an idea of how it will look when made to your exact measurements. Dresses as figure-hugging at these always need a little tweaking – no two of us are the same."

I nodded. The dress was a little big? It looked tiny. I feared Kitty was in for a real shock.

She had to help me, of course, because wedding dresses have inbuilt scaffolding all of their own, even ones which look as though they would be fairly slinky and therefore easy to slip into. It was clear that no one ever slipped into a wedding dress. Stuffed would be more accurate. Folded perhaps. Tucked in, in places. But Kitty was an expert and within a minute or two she had me zipped in, and where the dress had been a little looser around my thighs she had gathered tighter with pins so that it clung to me in the right places. She pulled and straightened and tucked in and then she was standing back looking at me with a broad smile across her face.

"Oh, now that, Erin, is beautiful."

I felt myself blush. There was no mirror in the cubicle. To see myself I would have to walk out to where my mother and mother-in-law-to-be were waiting and look at myself, at all angles, in the mirrors around the dressing room. Part of me wanted to believe Kitty. The dress *felt* comfortable, which was something I absolutely wasn't expecting given the effort it took to put it on. Then again, part of me knew Kitty was a saleswoman and she wanted, above everything else, to sell me a dress.

"Really?" I asked, feeling like that six-year-old all over again, needing a bit of reassurance.

She took a step back and looked at me again before reaching for a clip from her pocket and asking me to twist my hair up into a makeshift French roll with it. I did it and waited for her reaction.

"Definitely beautiful. Perfect. Will we go out so you can get a proper look at it?"

"Yes," I said, suddenly very nervous.

It had been different trying on the tulle nightmare. There was never, ever a chance that it was going to be 'the one'. There was nothing about it which appealed to me and, even when I had put it on, Kitty had pulled a funny face and laughed before apologising. "It is nice on some people," she had said. "But, don't take this the wrong way, definitely not on you." She'd said it in such a way that I had been reassured that ultimately she was on my side in all of this so I tried to remind myself of that as I agreed to step out of the cubicle in the dress she really did think would suit me.

"Okay," I said, breathing in. "Let's go."

Kitty went on ahead of me and as I walked out the chatter from my two companions stopped immediately. I didn't want to look at them. I didn't want to see their reaction before I could gauge my own. *This is it*, I told myself and turned to face myself in the mirrors.

I let out a gasp. I couldn't quite believe it was me. If it weren't for the pasty skin looking back at me, I wouldn't have believed it *was* me. The dress gave me curves in all the right places as opposed to where they normally resided which was most definitely in all the wrong places. It sculpted my body. It gave me a shape to be proud of. It made me look beautiful. Jesus, it made *me* look beautiful. My heart started to thud. This was the dress. My dress. My wedding dress. And it made me look amazing. I'd even fancy me in it. Oh, God, I felt as if I could sing and laugh and cry all at the one time. It was beyond comprehension that I could look this good – but I did. I was suddenly aware of my mother and Sue sobbing into their hankies. Kitty was smiling but I noticed that misty look in her eyes. And I realised I was crying too. A big, fat tear plopped onto the gorgeous satin and I looked into the mirror again and saw the pained expression on my face that I had been fighting all this time. I never wanted to get married, but here I was in a dress that I loved. I would wear this dress, which I loved, to marry the man that I loved but I couldn't escape the fact that we were getting married because he had cancer and he might . . . No. I wouldn't think that way just now.

"He'll be blown away when he sees you," Sue said and all I could do was nod back, like the stupid, stupid nodding dog I had become because I absolutely couldn't speak for fear that one big fat tear which had slid onto my beautiful dress might turn into a big stupid flood that no one could stop.

"Well, well, how did you get on? Did our mothers kill each other? Did you kill them? Should I be expecting the police at any moment?"

Paddy was sitting, feet up, on the sofa reading the newspaper. He was grinning at me in his trademark infectious manner and I smiled back.

"We all survived. But there was a hairy moment with a big frock that we must never, ever speak of again." I put my bag on the floor and gestured to him to move his feet from the sofa to make room for me. God, I really wanted to curl up beside him just then – just the two of us in our own wee world that didn't involve weddings or cancer, or testicles. "Budge," I smiled and he put his paper down, shifted over and allowed me to cuddle up to him.

"Was it really, really awful and the worse thing ever?" He kissed the top of my head and I elbowed him gently. He knew how I was absolutely opposed to weddings and he liked to tease me at every opportunity. 'I knew I'd get you to agree to this someday,' he would say. 'Okay, so maybe I went a bit far in my attempts, but I got there in the end. I always win!' he'd grin and I would grin back like a big feckwit but secretly hope that he was right and that he always would win.

"It wasn't actually that bad, apart from the aforementioned

big-frock episode of which we must never speak. I actually chose a dress!"

"Really?" He sounded genuinely shocked.

"Yes, really. I've to go back in a few days when I'm absolutely and completely sure and then Kitty – who runs the shop – will get out her tape measure, feel me up, take all our money for the next three months and bob's your uncle. Your wish will come true and I will be transformed into the most gorgeous bride the world has ever known."

"You would look gorgeous in your pyjamas, Erin."

"Well, you could always agree to my plan to run away just the two of us to the Guildhall then? No fuss or formality and I could wear my pyjamas if I wanted . . ." Part of me, admittedly, would be really unhappy not to wear the dress which made me look like some kind of Greek goddess, but a bigger part of me would be just delighted not to have to go through with the 'Big Day'.

Paddy looked down at me and kissed me again. "Erin, if you really don't want to do this, we don't have to do this. But it would be the biggest honour of my life not only to marry you, but to walk down the aisle of St Eugene's Cathedral with you on my arm."

"No," I said, pushing away my own negative thoughts. "We'll do it. And I want to do it. And I want to do it with you. And – and I know you won't believe me when I say this, but I felt a little excited today. The dress really is lovely. You should see it – it's ivory and –"

"*La la la!*" Paddy sang, sticking his fingers in his ears. "You're not supposed to tell me. I'm the groom, remember? I'm not supposed to know anything about the big dress. It's bad luck."

"Fair enough," I said, kissing him and getting up to make a pot of tea. I didn't want to add that I was pretty sure we'd had our share of bad luck already.

"Did I tell you?" I called behind me as I walked. "I think both our mothers were scuttered before they even got there! The lady that runs the shop, she offered them a glass of champers and they weren't even one glass down before they were acting like a bunch of schoolgirls! Your mother had to be talked out of trying on a wedding dress herself."

I heard him laugh, a deep throaty laugh which made me feel funny – a strange mixture of wanting to keep him forever near me and never let anyone else near him ever, combined with the very real desire to shag him senseless. But of course we had to wait until he was brave enough to try that, so we would settle for some full-on cuddling instead – preferably in bed, while naked.

I switched the kettle off, walked back to the living room and told him as boldly as I could that, as I had just endured a mammoth wedding-dress trying-on session for him, the very least he could do was take me to bed and do bold things to me. Thankfully, he obliged, and I knew that one day we would even manage to go further than third base again.

Paddy had found the lump himself. He had been embarrassed telling me, but when I said I would have a good feel to double-check, he perked up a bit. I found the lump too but we managed, with the help of Google and a bottle of wine, to convince ourselves it was absolutely nothing to worry about at all. We had even had a post-lump-finding bonk and I had successfully pushed the scary thought that something might actually not be right to the back of my head. Paddy said he would make an appointment with his doctor the very next day, but when a week passed and no appointment was made I once again took things into my own hands (excuse the pun). The receptionist at the doctor's had been very matter of fact. She didn't scream "A lump! My God, a lump! Get a doctor stat!" so I had felt reassured. She was calm and so was I and when I told Paddy he appeared calm as well. We were just one big gang of calm people.

Two days later we went to the appointment. I had woken during the night and noticed that Paddy's breathing just wasn't as rhythmic as it normally was at three in the morning. He was not asleep. I turned, curled my body around his and kissed his neck and whispered that this time tomorrow it would all be over and we would be reassured. We would be able to put all of this behind us.

Paddy didn't want me to come into the doctor's with him. He left me with a well-thumbed copy of *Hello* in the reception trying to maintain my calmness and had walked towards the consulting room with his hands in his pockets and his shoulders hunched. I had, of course, wanted to go with him. I had wanted to hold his hand and explain to the doctor that we knew we were being silly but sure wasn't it better to get these things checked out? I knew he would be mortified at having to get his tackle out. He was, of course, absolutely fine getting it out in front of me – but a strange man, who would have a good grope and a feel was well beyond his comfort level, regardless of what medical credentials the man might have been in possession of. I sipped from the bottle of water I had brought with me and tried to fight the dizzy sensation which was clambering over me. This time tomorrow we'll be wondering what we were worrying about, I reminded myself before losing myself in a story about Katie Price's love life – which was at least two husbands and a boob-job out of date.

He walked out of the consulting room fifteen minutes later, clutching a leaflet. I didn't like leaflets. I was pretty sure they didn't make leaflets to say: "Congratulations! You are absolutely perfectly okay!"

I looked at him expectantly and he forced on a smile. "Well, next stop, the hospital. Someone else gets to have a play with my bad boys."

"Lucky buggers," I muttered, willing myself to stand up and walk to him and get out of the stuffy doctor's surgery before I passed out. Damn legs. They wouldn't move and my hands were shaking. He reached out to me, helped me up and I cursed myself for being the weak one.

"I think you broke Mum," Jules said, laughing down the phone that evening. "Dad said she came back from the big shopping trip, tried to dance with him around the kitchen and then fell asleep on the sofa. Her snores would have deafened you."

"Maybe I should call her and check she is okay?"

"Dad says she has gone to her bed proper now. She needed a dark room and a couple of paracetamol – and a box set of *Inspector Morse*. This is serious Mum-in-recovery mode."

I laughed, and sat down at the kitchen table where I sipped from the vodka and Coke I'd just poured myself. Paddy had been dispensed to pick up a Chinese for dinner and I'd taken this as my chance to catch up with my baby sister.

"She wasn't that bad," I said, "which of course means she was horrendous. But she seemed to enjoy herself. You should have seen the dress she chose for me!"

"Shove the dress she chose for you! I want to know about the dress you chose for yourself. Dad said a decision has been made."

"Almost," I said, smiling as I remembered how great I had looked in it. "Kitty said I was to go home, think about it, maybe even try on a few dresses elsewhere and if I still loved it I was to come back and get measured up."

"Does that mean more wedding-dress shops? Maybe I could make it down for the next trip?"

"No! No more shops. This is the dress, Jules, and while you are welcome to come all the way from Belfast to see it, I won't be trying on any other wedding dresses ever, ever again. This is the one."

"Ooh Erin, are you getting excited about a wedding? You, the wedding-phobe?"

"The dress did make my arse look really amazing!"

"Really?" she sounded surprised – too surprised for my liking.

"Bitch," I retorted.

She laughed. "Erin, you know I'm only teasing. Jeez, that is what big sisters are for. Tell me," she said, and I heard her sip from her wineglass, "what is it like?"

"It is exactly the very opposite of what you would expect me to wear."

"I'm intrigued."

We chatted on, amiably, for the twenty-four minutes it took for Paddy to pick up our chilli beef, rice and prawn crackers and serve them on the table – with our fancy cutlery and everything. We didn't once talk about the big C – but it didn't feel like we were avoiding it either. We were just chatting. Jules spoke easily about her work as a PA in a Belfast law firm where the lead partner was a bit of a Lothario and she spent her day trying to make sure his various women never found out about each other as well as trying to do her actual job. We spoke about what movies we had seen and what books we were planning to read and she told me about a new handbag she was lusting after.

As I hung up the phone and looked at the very gorgeous man sitting opposite me, his glasses a little lopsided and his stubble sprouting through, I realised I was actually incredibly lucky. So lucky, in fact, that I was even looking forward to going back to Kitty and handing over a large proportion of my salary for a dress I would wear only once.

7

Kitty

I still hadn't heard from him. Not a peep. It had been just over twenty-four hours since I'd opened the letter which blew my life apart but it felt like so much longer. I felt as if I hadn't spoken to him in weeks. I missed his voice. I missed just knowing he was in the next room, or on the end of a phone. I missed knowing where he was, full stop. Not that I was a crazy psycho wife or anything who tracked his every move. We just spoke – a lot. We told each other everything. At least I had thought we had told each other everything. Clearly I was delusional.

I sat on the sofa, afraid to move in case anything else changed in my life. I had survived work. I had even enjoyed part of it – seeing Erin in her dress had been a highlight. She seemed so transformed – so graceful.

It reminded me of my wedding dress – how I felt like a princess the moment I put it on. That sounds pathetic, I know. Me. A modern, career-orientated woman who enjoyed feeling like a princess. I was an eejit. I would walk up and down our kitchen, step, together, step, together, practising marching up the aisle. I would put my tiara on my head when no one else was in the

49

house and try on my wedding ring just to see what I would look like married. I felt amazing. I felt loved.

That was the thing with me and Mark. I'd always felt loved. Perhaps that was why feeling abandoned was so hard to take. I glanced towards the kitchen door. I was thirsty but it would be a bad move to drink any more tea. My head was spinning enough as it was without adding an extra dose of caffeine to the mix. I didn't dare drink alcohol, no matter how much I wished it was there to numb whatever was running through my head.

Maybe, I thought, I should phone Rose after all. She had offered to come and sit with me but I had shooed her away. She had been so good the night before, sitting with me while I had the mother of all tantrums and holding my hand until Cara arrived. I could have called Cara but she had promised her mother she would take her out to dinner and, while she had said she would cancel, I knew they didn't get that much time together.

So I decided to sit in on my own. I flicked the TV on and stared numbly at *Coronation Street* and *EastEnders*. At least someone was getting it worse than me, I thought, as the drums beat their ominous tune at the end of the Albert Square soap. And then, because it seemed like the only thing I had the energy for, I took to my bed and cried at the empty space beside me.

We had been together a long time – just short of eleven years. We'd lived together for ten of those years. That's a lot of time sleeping next to someone. While sometimes I'd craved the bed all to myself – to stretch out and luxuriate under the covers all on my own – I'd never wanted it like this. I'd wanted it to be when he went away for a stag weekend, or on business. I never wanted it to be when he just disappeared off the face of the planet leaving nothing but a note to let me know he was still living. I glanced at the clock. It was gone eleven. It would be a whole eight hours until my alarm clock would sound. Seven hours until we were in respectable-enough territory for me to get up and start my day. I was tired. I was bone-tired. I was couldn't-see-straight-tired. But there was no chance I was going to sleep. I hauled my duvet around my shoulders and wandered like a giant marshmallow downstairs where I did some Grade A staring into space on the sofa. I even poured myself a drink – a vodka on the rocks with not even so much as a hint of a mixer. It caught in my throat, the harsh fumes making my eyes water. But it seemed like the perfect thing to do – the kind of thing heroines in movies would do. If I wasn't careful I would find myself pulling out our wedding album and poring over the photos. I nodded, raising my glass in the direction of the oak sideboard which housed our very own book of dreams. No – that would send me over the edge and I needed to keep it together. My eye was drawn, once again, to my phone. There was no point in phoning him. I knew that.

But it was one of my very limited options. I didn't know where he was. I didn't know anyone who knew where he was. The only way I could conceivably get to him was through his phone. Maybe he wouldn't be expecting me to call at this time. He knew what I was like – I was normally sound out to the world at ten thirty. If I withheld my number . . . maybe, just maybe . . .

I picked it up and changed my settings and then I dialled his number and crossed my fingers at the same time, just longing to hear his voice. If he heard mine, properly – not just in a voice mail – I knew he would talk to me. He might be going through a lot just now – but he wasn't a bastard. I knew Mark and he wasn't a bastard.

My heart thumped – right there in the middle of my chest – as his phone rang. It rang three times, my heart sinking (and thudding) with each shrill tone. Then, midway through the fourth ring he answered. His voice came at me, muffled over the din of a bar, confused and definitely drunk. "Hello?" he sing-songed like he was out having the time of his life and I found myself unable to speak. I wanted to say so much. I wanted to ask him where the hell he was. I wanted to beg him to come home – but there he was, sounding like he was out on the razz, thumping bass beats behind him and I couldn't speak. I could barely breathe. I hung up, threw the phone away from me. Pouring another vodka shot from the bottle, I downed it as fast as I could, cuddled the bottle to me and pulled the duvet over my head.

My alarm didn't wake me. The ringing of my phone didn't wake me. The thumping on my front door didn't wake me. It was the hauling off of the duvet and the rattle of the vodka bottle on the floor which did it. Ivy stood over me, slightly horrified, and I blinked to acclimatise to the light before trying to stand up and falling backwards onto the sofa with an unceremonious thud.

"Rose is worried sick," Ivy started, shaking the duvet out and folding it. "And you know Rose, she never worries about anything. And yet you have her taking palpitations and needing a sit down."

"Where is she?" I muttered, looking around Ivy for a glimpse of our stepmother.

"She's at the shop," she said, as if that was the most obvious thing in the world.

It wasn't to me. In my mind it was still hitting midnight and I was still swigging from my vodka bottle running into my third chorus of 'Need You Now' by Lady Antebellum.

I looked at Ivy blankly.

"It's gone half ten," she said. "Rose opened up at nine. She was sure you'd be there soon. She's been trying to ring. She couldn't get an answer. Not on your landline or your mobile. She called me and asked me to come round and I've been standing for the last five minutes battering on your door to no avail until your next-door neighbour offered me your spare key."

Arse.

So Rose was hyperventilating. And my neighbour now knew there was scandal in the making. I was hung-over – or indeed possibly still drunk – and Ivy was standing over me with her trademark pious and superior look.

"My husband has left me," I said, as if it was news to Ivy and indeed to me.

She nodded. "I heard." She carried on folding the duvet and tidying up the living room, even though it was relatively tidy anyway.

I started to bristle. "You could have called," I said petulantly, standing up again and walking through to the kitchen for a Diet Coke.

Ivy followed me. "Kitty, you had Rose and Cara. You didn't need me." She didn't say that in a melodramatic fashion, or in a self-pitying fashion – more in a dismissive way. I wasn't on her radar most of the time. Not at all really, unless she got a distress call from Rose telling her I was missing in action. I pulled the ring-pull on the Diet Coke can and put it to my lips, only stopping drinking when I needed to breathe again.

"I'll call Rose now," I said. There was absolutely no point in entering into any kind of discussion with Ivy about our relationship. We just weren't that close. We both understood and accepted that.

"Might be an idea," she said, filling the kettle and switching it on. "I'll make some tea."

"I'm fine with the Diet Coke, thanks," I said, lifting the phone and dialling the number of the shop. As I dialled the memory came back to me, of calling Mark, of hearing his jovial tones, of hearing the music thumping in the background and I felt sick to my stomach.

I thrust the phone at Ivy, told her to tell Rose I was fine and then I ran to the bathroom and lay on the floor until the nausea subsided.

"You should take a shower," Ivy said, walking in and handing me a couple of towels.

I made a noise which in my mind was a statement of agreement but which I fully accept may have sounded like a death groan to anyone else's ears.

"Kitty, look, I know this is hard but you need to get up and get on with things. No point in lying down under what life throws at us."

I looked at her and wondered what exactly life had thrown at her that was so awful? She had her husband (who had not run away). She had children (two of them, one of each). She had a nice part-time job in an office where they loved her and offered her full pay through each of her maternity leaves. She was a Size 12 on a bad day. Yes, she had lost her mother at a young age but, you know, we kind of shared that one. And at least she had got to know Mum more than I did. My memories of the woman who gave me life were fragmented – a vague hint of a perfume I'd never been able to locate, the vague notion of a mop of curly permed hair. A soft jumper and a smile. No. I shook my head. I could not think of my mother today as well. One big desertion was enough for anyone to cope with.

"You're right," I said to Ivy, standing up and switching on the shower full pelt to signal the end of the conversation.

By lunch-time I was in a fit enough state to go to work. Ivy had made breakfast and I had found myself touched by the fact she even buttered my toast for me. She had opened a second can of Diet Coke and poured it into a glass with ice. She had even set two hangover-cure paracetamol out for me.

The duvet had been replaced on top of my bed, with the cushions arranged neatly and in formation on top of it. The windows had been opened and she had even loaded the washing machine.

"He took his clothes but left the dirty ones?" she asked, raising an eyebrow.

"I never thought about that . . ."

"I binned them," she said matter of factly. "After cutting them up a little first."

I looked at her and smiled, but found my eyes were watering.

"We might not always get along, sis," she said, "but he shouldn't have done this."

"Rose thinks he is having some sort of breakdown."

"Rose likes to see the good in people."

54

"But he's a good man," I offered, knowing how weak my words sounded, especially given how I'd heard him on the phone living it up the night before.

"Good men don't do things like this," she said, folding a tea towel and taking my glass from me and rinsing it under the tap. "Now, do you want to go to work? Or will I just tell Rose you're taking the day off?"

I contemplated it. I had thought about it while standing under the hot streams of the shower. No. I would go in. It was a Saturday. Saturdays were notoriously busy and the busyness would distract me, and exhaust me again. And I could just pretend the wedding dresses were ball gowns and not very special dresses which women would wear to get married, never really knowing if it would all work out or not.

Besides, it was my shop – my dream – I couldn't give up on it just because shit was happening in my home life and my belief in happy-ever-afters was on the wane. And Rose freaked when she had to deal with brides all by herself. She wasn't so much about the front of house stuff – she preferred to be sitting in the workroom upstairs, altering gowns, preparing them to be picked up and occasionally wandering downstairs to coo at a bride-to-be in her finery.

"I'll drive you in," Ivy said, lifting my car keys so they were out of my use. "You may have showered but there is still a faint whiff of vodka and I'd be happier to drive you than let you take any more risks."

Ordinarily I'd have jotted this down as one more example of Ivy being a bit of a sanctimonious bitch but, given that she had cut the crotch out of Mark's favourite jeans in an act of solidarity with me, I took it to be a gesture that showed maybe, just maybe, she cared.

"Thanks," I muttered.

Erin

An orchiectomy sounds so much nicer than it actually is. It sounds as if it involves orchids and petals and maybe angels gently stroking you. It does not sound as if someone is shelling one of your testicles from your scrotum like a pea from a pod.

The doctor spoke and I sat holding Paddy's hand, gripping as tightly as I could. Paddy's eyes were focused straight ahead and he was nodding – but his nodding was all off. There was no rhythm between the doctor finishing his sentences and Paddy's responses. I knew it was up to me to take it all in. Cancer. Well, most likely cancer. They couldn't be sure, you see, until they popped that bad boy out and looked at it under a microscope. The blood tests didn't look good though. Or the ultrasound.

Paddy had tried to make jokes through it. As he lay on the table, with his tackle on display, he had told me he never thought he would be the one in our relationship to have ultrasounds. I'd laughed and said my turn would come to worry about ultrasounds. Which was ironic, given that they were talking about taking half of his baby-making equipment away. I felt my head swim a little and nipped at my leg to bring myself back into focus. I had to be the strong one.

They wouldn't waste much time, the doctor said. They would book him in straight away. They would whip that bad boy out as soon as they could. And they would poke at it and dissect it like it was the main course in a Bushtucker Trial. I glanced at Paddy and he had gone quite pale. I didn't blame him.

"What are my chances?" he said and I wanted to block my ears.

I didn't want to hear about chances – I wanted certainties. I wanted 'It will be all rights'.

"Testicular cancer is one of the most treatable cancers," the doctor said solemnly. "If you're going to get cancer this is the kind that you'd want to get, in most cases. Hopefully we have caught this early but the only way to really know is to get in there and look at what we are facing."

"And you have to remove it?" Paddy asked. "You can't just do a biopsy or whatever?"

"I'm afraid not. The only way to be really sure is to look at it all. We can insert a prosthetic testicle into your scrotum during surgery if you want."

"And sperm. Should I freeze my, erm, sperm?"

"You may want to consider that, yes. As a precaution. If you need chemotherapy it will probably halt your sperm production – though in most cases the sperm count increases eventually and may even return to normal."

Paddy nodded – a nod that went on a little too long.

"Try not to worry too much," the doctor added as if cancer was something you could just shake off like the common cold. "Until we know what we are facing, try to remember the odds are in your favour."

I didn't want to hear about odds.

We walked out of the office holding hands but Paddy soon let go.

"Don't tell anyone about this," he said, facing straight ahead. "Not until we know. Not until we know everything."

I reached out to him but he shrugged away.

"Erin, this isn't personal. But I can't just now. I just can't."

"Erin!" Paddy called from the car as I glanced one last time in the mirror to check on my hair and whether or not it was behaving itself. It was mildly frizzy but maintaining a degree of restraint with the help of some heavy-duty clips. I smoothed it again and looked myself up and down. A crisp white V-neck figured T-shirt. Some nicely pressed cargo pants. A pair of new mules with toenails freshly painted. I looked nice and neat and tidy as if I wouldn't stand for anyone messing with me. I didn't know why but I was slightly nervous about meeting our wedding co-ordinator at the hotel. I knew that technically she was on my side but whenever she started talking about corkage charges, room hire and buffets I got uncomfortable. Mental maths was so not my thing. Weddings were not my thing – and even though she was perfectly lovely, I couldn't help but worry that she was trying to rip us off. Therefore, rule one of any meeting with the very bubbly and excitable Fiona was that we went looking our best, in nice clothes with an air of importance about us. This was easier for me admittedly than it was for Paddy who was looking a little frail these days but, still, the effort was worth making.

"Erin!" he called again, as I heard his key turn in the ignition. I grabbed my bag and my keys and clattered down the hallway at lightning speed.

"Are you okay to drive?" I asked him as I clambered in beside him.

"Erin, yes, I'm okay to drive. How many times?" He winked at me and smiled but there was a hint of irritation in his voice which didn't go unnoticed.

I tried to let it wash over me – and I tried to remind myself even more not to fuss.

"So," I said, "we are going for a choice of main course. Prosecco and strawberries on arrival for our guests – a fruit punch for the lightweights. A buffet at ten, just a small one, and chair covers and white linen tablecloths." I said all this with a feigned enthusiasm for his benefit.

"It will be a brilliant day," he said. "I'm really looking forward to it."

"Me too," I lied, as we headed in the direction of mad Fiona and the very expensive hotel where I would be handing over even more of my money for the sake of a great day out for our family and friends.

Jules had said I needed to start getting excited about it. Yes, she said, she knew I was a wedding-phobe and that, given what had happened with my one previous serious but ultimately doomed relationship, she could understand why. But this was different, she argued. This was Paddy. Paddy was a babe. He was the love of my life.

She was right. I had known, quite quickly, that I wanted to spend the rest of my life with him. I had known that entirely before the horrible cancer diagnosis. So this commitment thing – the worry and icky feeling that came with it – was nothing to do with feeling sorry for him. I did want to be with him. I did want to marry him. But the big wedding? The big standing in front of everyone and declaring our smugness at finding each other? Knowing that a great deal of them would be there – like mawkish peasants at the steps of the guillotine – wondering if we were going to do the whole "till death do us part" bit so they could sob into their hankies. The fuckers.

"Why don't you just see it as a big party?" Jules had offered.

"A big party isn't likely to set me back the best part of a year's salary. A big party in my book is a rake of dips from Tesco, some bags of tortilla chips and a strict bring-your-own-bottle etiquette code. I might even spring for some balloons or a few banners – but mirrors and tea lights? A cake that costs the same as a weekend away in Dublin? No, I wouldn't factor that in."

Jules laughed and I had found myself laughing too. "You're right, of course," I said. "This is just a big party. This is not about our marriage – not really. Our marriage will be between us and us alone and hopefully last a very long time indeed."

"And the party, and the marriage, mean a lot to Paddy. It's giving him a positive focus."

"I know, I know," I nodded. "I just have to get myself in the right celebratory mindset. It's hard, though, trying to stay measured and realistic about everything else but then trying to get all gung-ho and excited about this."

"Erin, I say this with love in my heart, but you need to lighten up. Celebrate it. Enjoy each other. Plan a Big Day like no other and start thinking you might actually enjoy it. You might surprise yourself, you know."

I took a deep breath and looked at Paddy. "You're good with figures. You listen and listen good. Write it all down, or get her to write it down. Do not be swayed into upgrading to the more expensive fizz. Prosecco is fine. Don't let her bat her eyelids at you either. You're marrying me, remember?"

He smiled and kissed me. "I promise to behave."

Fiona was a five-foot-two-inch powerhouse of a saleswoman with exceptionally blonde hair and exceptionally white teeth. She wore a power suit and high heels which made my feet hurt just to look at them. She also wore a headset, which she barked into frequently. I, at times, wondered if it was actually connected to anything or just to the voices in her own head. She seemed efficient – exceptionally, ball-breakingly efficient. I admired that, in my own way. I couldn't cope with a job which required that kind of organisation. Given Fiona's responsibility of making sure everything ran very smoothly on countless wedding days for countless hopeful couples, I would combust with worry over the whole thing.

"Right," she declared loudly, sitting down and clapping her hands. In front of her on the table sat a clipboard which was as much of an accessory for her as her headset and her killer heels. She opened it and smiled. "Let's get down to business." She handed us each a photocopy of the proposed schedule for the day and ran through it at a lightning pace without looking down to double-check the details or, it seemed, even taking a breath. She was like a robot. A very scary robot.

We nodded along, occasionally offering a "yes" or "hmmm" or maybe even an "okay". At one stage I looked at Paddy who seemed genuinely very interested in the notion of speeches before the meal and cutting the cake just before the buffet. I wondered if there was such a thing as a Groomzilla.

I just listened and tried to think 'big party, big party, big party' while visualising how amazing my arse looked in the dress.

As if she could read my mind – which was entirely possible given her determination to know every single little detail – Fiona turned to me and asked if I had my dress yet.

"Yes," I said, "I think so. Well, yes, I do. I've chosen one. I just need to order it."

She looked horrified. Absolutely as-if-a-zombie-had-just-walked-in terrified. "You haven't ordered it yet? But it's less than a hundred days until your wedding. Wedding dresses don't just appear," she said, nodding in Paddy's direction for support. "They take months to order in."

"I, erm, I didn't know. But sure we have months – it will be fine."

"Three months may not be enough," she said solemnly. "But all we can do is hope. Where are you ordering it from? Maybe I could put in a call?"

She poised her pen over her paper while reaching into her pocket for a phone. I wondered who she would phone. The wedding-dress mafia?

"The Dressing Room," I replied reluctantly because I really didn't want her to phone Kitty and tell her I was a slack bride who had left wedding-dress buying until the relatively last minute. And I didn't want Fiona with her super-sense of efficiency to know why this whole wedding was a little bit last-minute and rushed. "But I'm sure it will be fine."

She wrote the name of the shop down anyway. "I know Kitty, and she is very good. But I'll still make a few calls. We have to have you looking your best. And Paddy – have you arranged your suit yet?"

"All sorted," he said smugly and part of me wanted to elbow him right in the ribs just for being such a smarmy smuggy teacher's pet. "We got them last week. Best to be prepared." He winked at me. The pig, he was enjoying this a little too much. Maybe it was the time to elbow him after all.

"Good man," Fiona said, as if he were three years old and just told her he had managed not to pee his pants for one entire day. "That's what I like to see." She grinned at him, her sharp pearly whites glinting in the daylight and then looked at me – just a short glimpse but one which I couldn't ignore, and I knew that I had just crashed through the floor in her estimation and she would forever see me as a slack bride.

I, however, reminding myself of how much this meant to Paddy, bit my tongue and stopped myself telling her to stick her colour schemes and complimentary cake knife. I'd take my wedding elsewhere . . . although in fairness, with just three months to go, the chance of getting any kind of a venue outside of a chippy were slim to none. Although, I'd have been happy with the chippy. I glanced at Paddy who was smiling widely, wider than he had done in a while, and I reminded myself that this would all be worth it.

9

Kitty

The shop was busy when we arrived and an excited bride, who had come in to view her newly arrived dress, accosted me almost as soon as I walked through the door.

"Is it here? Is it gorgeous? Is it just perfect? We did get the underskirt, didn't we? I've lost half a stone. Do you think it will still fit? Can we get it taken in? And the bridesmaid dresses? Can we look at those too?"

I blinked at her, the brightness of her pre-wedding tooth-whitening temporarily blinding my hung-over eyes. I wondered if I still smelled vaguely of vodka. Normally I could rattle off answers like you wouldn't believe – appeasing even the most excitable of brides. Normally I'd have rattled back a very quick 'Yes. Yes, Perfect, yes. The underskirt is here. If it doesn't fit, alterations are no problem, and come at no extra cost. Yes, we can look at bridesmaid dresses, whenever you want.'

Today was different though. Today I was in a grief-stricken slump, Mark's cheery "Hello?" still playing in my head. He had been in a bar. Drinking things. Sounding carefree. The bastard.

I turned to Ivy and back to the toothy bride whose name was escaping me. Amy. Or Anna. Or Andie. Or something.

"Yes, yes," I muttered, waving my hand around, "all that yes. Can you just give me a few minutes?"

I turned to the reception desk where Rose was mouthing the name 'Angie' at me in an exaggerated fashion and I spun back on my heel.

"Angie," I said more confidently, "if you want to go through to the dressing room, I'll have your dress with you in just a few minutes."

She squealed with delight – as did her mother and her three bridesmaids and the sound actually made me wonder if my brain was going to explode and seep out of my ears – before she clacked her designer heels loudly across the wooden floors to where Rose was now holding open the doors to the dressing room.

Once they were ensconced inside, with Rose nodding and smiling and telling them she would bring them Prosecco, the door was closed and Rose looked me squarely up and down.

"She spoke to him, and he was having a good time," Ivy said.

Rose looked to me for confirmation of same.

"That's not entirely accurate. I phoned him. I hid my number and he answered. He sounded fine. He sounded more than fine . . . he was in a bar or somewhere like that . . . and I hung up. I just couldn't . . ." I felt my voice trail off, my head swim a little, whether through the realisation that Mark could be fine without me or through the crushing hangover.

"He won't be fine," Rose said. "Mark my words. He won't be fine at all."

"Well, I'm certainly not," I said, feeling myself shake.

"You should go home," Rose said.

"After madam here dragged me out of the house – no," I said, nodding at Ivy who was standing, arms crossed, looking at the pair of us. "And besides we have Angie and her dress. Jesus, we do have Angie's dress, don't we? It is ready?"

"Steamed and in the dressing room, behind the curtain, as always. Now, why don't you get yourself a glass of water? I'll get some of the fizz and we'll do what we do best."

"And I'll head on now," Ivy said gruffly. "But you're to behave yourself, Kitty. No more scenes like that. Not over a man. And certainly not over Mark."

All traces of her previous compassion were gone. She seemed snitty and grumpy and cold and I forgot it was she who had tidied my house and helped me brush my hair when all I wanted to do was sit on the bed and stare at the wedding picture on the wall.

She had turned and walked away before I could say feck off and, as the door slammed, the brass bell ringing above it, I heard Rose say, not too quietly, "That one will learn some day."

"You sent her to me," I said, accusingly, as we walked up the spiral stairs to the office.

"I couldn't leave here and Cara wasn't answering her phone. I'd have got your daddy to call round to you but I was afraid of what he might find and your dad has a weak heart."

She spoke with her usual upbeat intonation but the message was clear. I'd scared her – scared her so much she'd called in the big guns in the form of Ivy and her acerbic ways.

"I'm sorry," I said to her back as she continued on her way.

"Never mind. Let's just deal with Angie now."

Yes, no matter how crap things were I had to go in there now, to where my bride-to-be – the most important person in the shop – was waiting with bated breath to see the dress she had probably dreamed of since she was five years old and wandering up and down her mammy's bedroom wrapped in an old lace curtain and too-big high heels.

Get a grip, Kitty, I told myself and took a deep breath. Don't think about Mark, not for the next half hour anyway and then you can mope all you want. Happy face, Kitty, happy face.

Steadying myself further, I opened the door to the dressing room – to where Angie sat, tapping her feet on the floor and looking as if she might combust with excitement.

"Okay, Angie, the dress is here – behind that curtain. We can just bring it out, or you can go in and try it on and then come out to show your mum and your friends. It's your choice."

"Can I try it on?" she asked, her voice cracking with emotion.

It wasn't unusual for even the most seemingly confident woman in the world to crumble with emotion at the thought of her big frock. I had seen it time and time again and usually a little bit of me crumbled too. This time however I fought the urge to tell her to get a grip and sagged with relief when I heard Rose walk into the room with the Prosecco to whoops of delight from the assembled women.

Angie's gown was exquisite – in shot silk with delicate beading on the bodice, and a full skirt which screamed fairytale. We had already looked at accessories and decided that less was definitely more and a stunning crystal-encrusted headpiece would finish the look off perfectly. I could feel her shaking as I helped her step into the gown and zipped it up. I handed her a hanky and told her she looked stunning and felt utterly wretched because, for the first time ever, I was simply going through the motions and not really feeling what I was saying.

When she left, deliriously happy by all accounts, I felt I had cheated her and myself and the guilt hit me like a ton of bricks. It was three o'clock and I knew we had two brides-to-be coming in to look around our collection and all I wanted to do was close the shop and go upstairs, lie on the floor of the workshop and sob my heart out.

"It's always darkest before the dawn," Rose said, kissing me on the head. "I'll put the kettle on and make us a nice cup of tea. I even have some chocolate biscuits – fancy ones, with chocolate chips and everything. You can have two if you want."

The hangover which was hanging heavy in my stomach surfaced and demanded feeding.

"Okay," I said.

"Okay," Rose said. "Don't let this hurt you too much, pet."

"I won't," I lied and watched as she made the tea and allowed me to choose my biscuits from the tin before she chose hers.

I had just ushered out another bride – a very fussy one who had tried on twelve dresses in total and still wasn't convinced any of them were for her – and was at last able to turn the sign on the door, lock up, sit down on the purple chaise longue and survey the carnage of the dressing room. I was just willing myself to have the energy to get up and deal with it when I heard my phone beep – a message coming through.

It wasn't going to be Mark. I knew that. I just knew. But I wasn't expecting it to be James. **Kitty, can we meet? Need to talk to you? Dinner? On me? Custom House? Eight? Yes?**

My brain ached. Too many questions. And dinner? Out? With a man who wasn't my husband? These were questions I just couldn't cope with.

"Rose!" I called and she walked into the room and looked at me. "I have a text, from James. He wants to talk in a restaurant."

"Do you think you should?"

"He's his best friend," I offered. "If anyone has any idea of what's going on in Mark's life it will be James. Well, you know, it should have been me but, since I don't have a clue, James is the next best thing."

Rose sat down beside me and lifted the phone, scrolling through the message. "But did you not talk to him on Thursday? Did he not say he didn't know where Mark was?"

She had a point, but I was clutching at straws and I couldn't see why he would want to see me if he didn't know something that he hadn't perhaps known on Thursday night.

Sharing this theory with Rose, she shook her head – just a little – and sucked in her breath. "I'm not sure this is a good idea, Kitty. Why not come home with me? You have your old room. Your daddy would love to see you – you know how he worries. And if James really does have something to tell you, he doesn't need to take you to fancy restaurant to do it."

"But he just *might* know something . . ."

"He might," Rose said softly. "But last night you drank yourself into near oblivion and I had to send your sister round to rescue you. Consider the possibility you might be just a little vulnerable right now and going out, to a very public place, with your husband's best friend, who might know something about why your husband has cleared off, may not end well. Come home. Invite him round if you want. I'll make egg and chips, like you always liked, and I'll tell your dad we're watching *Casualty* and James can come and you can talk in the front room and then when he's gone I'll know you are okay."

The thought of Rose's egg and chips, and watching *Casualty* on the sofa with her just like I did when I was a teenager was appealing. Life was easier then. So much less complicated. There was no Mark or James or disappearing acts or strange invites to restaurants on a Saturday night but at the same time I had to know. I couldn't not go. If I did I would only spend the evening watching the clock, and my phone, and driving myself clear bonkers.

"I'd love to come home," I started, and Rose looked at me, knowing me well.

"But?"

"You know I have to go, Rose. If there is something to know, I can't go on not knowing. And even if there is no big bolt out of the blue, hopefully James can help me make sense of it." He knew Mark as well as I did, or at least as well as I thought I did. I don't want to bombard him with my entire family – I think we need to talk alone, well, kind of alone. A restaurant is perfect. Hopefully it will stop me making a complete eejit of myself. I want to keep my cool."

"You will call me after?"

"I promise."

"I know," she said, momentarily dropping her cool and calm exterior, "that I'm not your mum. Not your real mum. But I do worry."

"You're more of a mum to me than she ever was," I said, hugging her closely. "And I know you worry even if you don't show it much and I love the very bones of you for it. But Rose, you know me enough to know I can be a stubborn cow when I want to be – and I need to be now."

She nodded and smiled. "That's why I love you," she said, pulling away from our hug and brushing herself off. "Now, lady, let's get these frocks back on their hangers before we go home. It's almost six and your daddy will be getting weak from hunger. You might not want my egg and chips, but your dad loves them. And that's not a euphemism. Now, will I put on my Andrew Lloyd Webber CD while we tidy? Or are we in a Doris Day mood?"

I didn't have the heart to tell her neither appealed, so we settled for a rousing chorus of 'Don't Cry for Me, Argentina' while my stomach churned and I wondered what on earth James could have to say to me.

I went home, showered, stood in front of the mirror in my bedroom and wondered what to wear. What do you wear when you're going to meet your husband's best friend to discuss said husband's disappearance from the face of the earth? What I wanted to wear was pyjamas and bed socks. What I wanted to do was lie down, on the floor, and cry and not have to face any of it. I was tempted to phone Rose, to get her to drive on over in her wee yellow Smart car to pick me up. But no, I steadied myself. I would do this.

Picking out a pair of dark jeans and a pale lilac sweater, I dried my hair and pulled it back in a loose pony-tail. I applied the lightest layer of foundation and a dash of blusher and decided that was enough. This was not a social occasion. This was a not a fun occasion. This was not a nice meal out with a friend. This was business. Picking up my car keys, I decided I wouldn't drink. I would use driving as a perfectly reasonable excuse for keeping my wits about me. The last thing I wanted to do was make a show of myself in the restaurant. I would be calm. I would be collected. I would be just like Rose.

James was waiting for me when I arrived. He stood up as I walked into the room and, as he looked at me to acknowledge that he had seen me, I noticed it. It was almost imperceptible but it was there – a shake of his head. I felt my stomach lurch again and I gripped the car keys in my hand tighter so that I could feel them digging into my hand – anything to ground me a little in the moment.

"Kit," he said, awkwardly kissing me on the cheek.

"Just tell me what you know, James," I said, pulling back from him and steadying myself on the back of the chair.

He sat back down and then gestured to the chair opposite him. "Sit down."

"I don't want to sit down," I whispered. When someone tells you to sit down before imparting news to you, it is rarely because they are about to tell you something good. My mind flashed back to my daddy, his face serious, gesturing to me and Ivy to sit down and us giggling as we did, telling him he looked very serious indeed.

I had been thirteen, Ivy sixteen. We had been having a perfectly lovely day before then – before he asked us to sit down and told us mum was gone.

I didn't want to sit down, but I suddenly felt like I had no choice. My legs felt weak below me. I sat. Pushing all memories of my mother out of my head, I didn't take my eyes off James.

"We could do the niceties," I said, holding his gaze, "but you know why I'm here, James. You know something, don't you?"

He lifted his knife, put it down again and lifted his napkin, unfolding it nervously before putting it back on the table.

"I spoke to Mark today," he said.

"What did he say?"

"He told me you called him last night. Or he thinks it was you. He said you hung up."

I shrugged my shoulders. Why Mark, or James, would be surprised that I was calling my partner of eleven years after he walks out with nothing more than a sad, sorry little letter to explain himself was beyond me.

"He wanted me to tell you he is okay," James said sheepishly, looking down at the napkin he had discarded.

"I sensed that by the chipper tone in his voice and the thumping music in the background," I said, trying to keep calm. It would do no good to shoot the messenger, or poke him in the face with the fork I was currently tapping against the table.

"Shit, Kitty, look, I know this is awful –"

"Did he say why he left?"

James' gaze remained on the table in front of him and he sighed. "He said he needed some space. He just wanted to find himself. He said he knew that sounded wanky but he had to do it. He said he didn't know any more who he is or what he wants."

"Or if he still wants me?" The question stuck in my throat and I felt tears prick at the corners of my eyes. This was not what I wanted, to cry in a public place. I sniffed and tried to steady my breathing. I regretted bringing the car. I could really have done with a drink just about then.

"I couldn't get him to say much," James offered.

"Did he say where he was, even?" I needed James to tell me something that I didn't already know.

"He didn't. He wouldn't be drawn at all."

"Bollocks." I wiped the tears that were threatening to fall hastily from my face. I took a deep breath. "Did he say if he was with anyone?"

I looked at James, who had returned to staring at his napkin and I could see the flush of colour rise from his neck and up through his face. I felt my stomach twist and my heart sink.

"He . . . he said no, he isn't with someone. Not now. But, Kitty, there was someone. And he said it didn't mean anything but he needs to think about what he wants."

The words washed over me like waves, drowned out by a crashing sense of disbelief hitting me full force. I hadn't just heard those words, had I? I replayed them, let them echo through me. There was someone. It was over. It didn't mean anything – except it made him leave. He needs to think about what *he* wants. Where did what *I* wanted come into this?

"Who?"

"I don't know all the details."

"Well, tell me the details you do know and tell me now," I heard myself say – surprised at how calm I sounded.

He ran his fingers through his hair and sipped from the glass of beer he had in front of him before looking at me again. "Kitty, you have to realise I knew nothing at all about this. When I spoke to you the other night, I wasn't lying. This is as much out of the blue for me as it is for you and if it is any consolation to you at all I told him he was being a dickhead and in danger of throwing away the best thing that had ever happened to him."

"James. Just tell me."

"It was someone from work. A temp. She's not even there any more. He said it was just a couple of times. That it was over before it started."

James looked distraught – then again I imagine I wasn't looking my best either. I let the words sink in, glaring at a waitress who walked over to our table to let her know in no uncertain terms that now was not the time. Then I felt like shit because it wasn't her fault my husband was a cheating bastard. Oh Jesus. Mark had cheated on me.

"Kitty . . ." James started as I stood up, turned and walked away without saying another word. I had wanted to hear more, but now I wished I hadn't and that I could put the words back into the Pandora's Box they had jumped out of and close the lid. Mark had cheated on me. And he had left me. And it was down to his best friend to tell me the details. I didn't look up as I walked out of the restaurant and broke into a sprint as I headed towards the car park. In the distance I could hear James calling after me and I cursed as I couldn't get my car door open. The tears that had threatened to fall in the restaurant were now coursing down my cheeks and I roughly dried them on the sleeve of my jumper. This was just crap – just utter crap.

Managing to unlock the door, I climbed into the driver's seat just as James came level with me. It wasn't his fault, at all, that

Mark was a bastard but that didn't stop me from once again ignoring his calls for me to stay and talk. I drove off.

When I reached the house, I couldn't go in. I sat there for a while and looked at our home – the home that we had shared together, which we had bought together, which we thought we would bring children home to together. I sat there and wondered what I had done to make it go so wrong. What had I done to push him away? Why did he have to be so utterly clichéd about it – a temp, in work, 'it didn't mean anything'? I would have respected him more if she had been the love of his life. It would have hurt but, Jesus, I would have understood shitting all over your marriage if you thought you had found the love of your life. But just someone who worked with you for a bit, who you shagged because you could? I sat there and I couldn't bring myself to go in, so I turned and drove, without really thinking, to Dad and Rose's.

It was Daddy who answered the door, who pulled me into a hug and didn't ask any questions while I sobbed – just letting me rid myself of every tear in my body. We sat together on the sofa, him rocking me back and forth while Rose held my hand and made soothing sounds. I was grateful they didn't ask questions. I couldn't bring myself to say the words just yet. I felt humiliated to the very core of my being. Every molecule in my body hurt and when I was finished crying – when I simply could not cry any more – Rose guided me to my old bedroom and pulled down the covers, allowing me to climb in, still fully clothed bar my shoes, and she stroked my hair until I fell into a restless sleep. I let her because it felt nice, and I needed her to mother me. I needed to know she cared. I needed to know someone cared.

10

Erin

"It's not the best news, but it's not the worst news either," Dr Carr had said as I sat beside Paddy who was recovering from his op and had in fact spent the previous evening sitting with a bag of frozen peas nestled into his crotch. Paddy looked pale and tired. I looked pale and tired. Even Dr Carr looked pale and tired and for a moment I felt sorry for him. It must have been truly pants to spend your working career telling people they had cancer. No one would welcome that news. No one would thank you for it. No one, I would think, would even be able to take in all the nice things you may say afterwards about treatment options and positivity and getting the best care possible because the big old cancer word would be hanging there in the air.

Paddy and I hadn't really used the word. We had spoken very openly about the fact that he was having an operation. We had secretly enjoyed the look of uncomfortable queasiness spreading across the face of male friends when we described the procedure he would undergo. But we didn't really explain why. I'm sure people knew. One or two even asked if it was, you know, cancer. But we just parroted what Dr Carr had told us over his large moustache when we met him. No diagnosis had been made. This was just a test. One of a few tests Paddy would undergo. More blood tests. Paddy joked he was losing so much blood his Guinness intake would have to increase, purely for medicinal reasons of course. He couldn't be going into surgery with a low blood count, now could he? He had CT scans as well. Scanning every inch, inside and out of his body to see if there was cancer elsewhere. That scared me more than the operation if truth be told, even though Dr Carr had told us that this was standard practice.

"Stay away from Google," Jules had warned as she spoke to me one lunchtime.

I, of course, was sitting in front of my computer, Googling testicular cancer as if my life depended on it. Which it kind of did.

"There's a ninety-five per cent survival rate," I said.

"That's good," Jules said.

"Do you think so? Really? Because the way I see it, that's a one in twenty chance it won't be good. And that sounds pretty shite to me."

"Think of that as a nineteen out of twenty chance that he'll be okay," she said softly.

But I knew she was mentally counting the people around her and imagining one of them just dropping dead.

"You have to wait until you know the full facts. You have to wait until you find out exactly what you are facing before you start talking about odds and the like."

"Don't tell me you wouldn't be thinking about the odds if it were you?" I asked.

"Well, of bloody well course I would, and you would be telling me to calm myself and not to jump to conclusions before I knew the full facts."

She was right of course, but it didn't stop me worrying.

I knew that I was probably heading for hell when I walked in on Paddy watching *Bridal Boot Camp* on Wedding TV and had to stop myself asking him if he was sure they had only taken one testicle in the operating theatre and hadn't actually made off with every part of his masculinity. I did stop myself, however, and snuggled down beside him, handed him a cold beer and asked him could we watch *Match of the Day* instead?

"I'm a bit wedding-obsessed, aren't I?" he asked, smirking as he switched over. "Or maybe this was all an elaborate ruse all along while you were out of the room to get you to turn over to the footie without any fuss?" He winked at me and I kissed him.

I couldn't resist, even though his breath smelled vaguely of beer and garlic from the pasta we had eaten earlier. "You are a sneaky one."

"I'll try anything," he laughed. "I mean, look at the lengths I've gone to, to finally get you to marry me. There aren't many men who would lop their bits off."

"In fairness, it was the doctor who did the lopping."

"But it was me who supplied the faulty gonads!"

Once again I realised that I would be hell bound, because I wanted to shout: "Can we please not talk about your balls for just one night, thank you very much?"

It wasn't that I didn't care. It wasn't that I didn't admire the fact he could laugh about it – it was just that for six weeks, since the day when it became a reality and not just an operation and a maybe, it had been part of every decision-making process, every conversation and the first thing I thought of every morning. It was Saturday night. I was chilling with a beer. I wanted to *not* think about it – the big Cancer in our lives – and instead just enjoy my beer and football on the TV and kissing Paddy.

So, because it would be cruel to shout at the cancer patient while he talked about his faulty bits, I pushed all my negative thoughts to one side and tried to strike up a conversation about some player or other with over-gelled hair kicking a football off side, or something.

"I'm a bad person, aren't I?"

It was first thing on Tuesday morning and I was whispering down the phone to Jules while Paddy slept upstairs.

"What makes you say that?"

"For getting impatient and annoyed and not wanting to think about cancer for a while?"

"I think that makes you human," Jules soothed.

"But it's not like it's me that has cancer. It's him. If he wants to talk about it, if he wants to joke about it and all, surely it's my job to gee him on? It's not that I don't want to be supportive, it's just . . . well . . . it's not bloody funny, is it?"

And I realised, with a thump, it wasn't funny at all and it was scary. It wasn't that I had never realised I had been scared before but now, three hours away from when I was due to go and order my wedding dress, I realised just how scary it was.

The night before his surgery we had sat holding hands and chatting and Paddy had remained his usual positive self. "Once it's gone, it's gone," he had said. The thought that it could have spread, that it could require more treatment . . . we didn't want to go there. The doctors had tried to warn us, but Paddy remained resolute that we would be the lucky ones.

"We've done everything right," Paddy said, "and I'm young and fit and we will be fine."

"Of course you will be," I said.

"At the end of the day, if you're going get cancer, this is the kind of cancer you want to get," he said, mimicking Dr Carr.

But he looked pale and, even though he was smiling, I could see the fear in his eyes. It was a far cry from three nights before when he had decided to have a farewell party for his testicle. "I'm not ashamed to have this bad boy out," he had said, as he called his friends one by one and invited them round for drinks and shenanigans before the big op. He had been the life and soul of the party, which had started awkwardly as people didn't really know what to say, or even where to look. Not that he had his bits hanging out, or anything, but I just knew people had a morbid fascination about what he was about to go through.

Jules had travelled from Belfast for the party and afterwards had helped me put a blanket over Paddy and a pillow under his head when it was clear that there was no way we were going to get him moved from where he was sleeping. She had helped me clean up after the last guest had gone and, as we sat in the fug of stale smoke and the stink of warm wine, she had asked me how I was.

"I'm fine, sis, honest."

"Honest?"

"Well, as fine as I can be. I'm okay. It's not me having surgery, is it?"

"You are still allowed to be not okay. You don't have to be strong all the time, Erin."

I snorted. "Of course I do. He needs me."

"He is strong himself, you know. Sure wasn't this party his idea? Does that sound like a man struggling?" She smiled, but she also gently put her hand on my knee, which was her way of letting me know that it was okay to turn into a blubbering mess.

I was kind of surprised that she didn't know me well enough to know that I didn't do blubbering mess. Not any more anyway. No. I was to stay strong, which is exactly what I did as Paddy was wheeled away from me towards the operating theatre and I was left with a bitter coffee to keep me company while they sliced and diced him.

And I stayed strong when they told us the cancer was a Stage II and would require a dose of chemo to try to kill it off. That it had spread, just a little, thankfully, and that meant it was one of the more aggressive forms of testicular cancer. But it wasn't in his lungs or organs and that was a good thing. But the thought of it spreading – those sneaky wee poisonous cells sliding around inside his body, sneaking into his nooks and crannies, invading his healthy areas and making them black and manky and rotten made my skin crawl. The doctor repeated again that the chances were good but my brain focused on the words "try to kill it off" – I didn't like 'try', I liked definites. Still, I had promised to stay strong so I had patted Paddy's hand and tried not to throw up and said sure it wouldn't be a bother to him at all and what was a wee dose of chemotherapy among friends.

But that was then and this was now and, talking to Jules on the phone, I didn't want to be strong any more.

"I don't think I can do this . . . this wedding," I said. "I don't think I can keep smiling through it all. Standing there knowing everyone is watching us, knowing what is going on in our lives and knowing the battle he is fighting."

"Of course you can. Remember it's a 'big party'. You can do a big party. Sure it won't beat the big testicle farewell bash, but it will be good."

I laughed, limply, because it was expected of me.

"And you said the dress was stunning?"

"It is."

"And sure at this point you are only ordering it and you said the girl in shop was lovely, so you have nothing to fear about that at least."

I made a nondescript kind of a noise, neither a yes nor a no and certainly not a 'you know the funny thing is I never thought I would trust another man again to want to marry one and now that I do I'm well aware I could be a widow before our first anniversary' kind of a noise.

"I suppose," I added.

"Look, if this is all too much for you and if taking Mum with you is even more too much for you, then wait until Saturday. I'll come down for the day and go with you, and this is not being all altruistic by the way, this is me wanting glimpse of the frock."

"Okay," I said, "although scary Fiona at the hotel says we've left it much too late and I'll probably end up getting married in something off the peg because there is no way a wedding shop can deliver a couture gown in less than six months or something."

"You'll have a dress, and you'll be stunning. Put your mind at rest if you must and call The Dressing Room and talk to them about it. But, Erin, it will be okay. I'll be there. I'll hold your hand. You need your hand to be held sometimes, you know. Now, on you go to work and try not to freak out."

"Yes, Jules," I sing-songed, knowing that when Jules was in

protective sister mode there was no point at all in arguing with her.

"You know it makes sense."

"Yes, of course. It makes perfect sense. I'll make an appointment for the afternoon. I'm assuming you'll want to stay over here and not at Mum and Dad's?"

"Oh God, yes, of course, please."

"I shall prepare the guest chamber in honour of your arrival then."

"You do that. Now, take care, Erin. I love you loads, you know that."

"I love you too," I said, smiling and already looking forward to the weekend.

I hung up, feeling a little more positive and not quite so scared about the dress-buying, and the wedding and the whole cancer thing. I was smiling to myself when Paddy walked into the kitchen and wrapped his arms around me, kissing the back of my neck gently.

I turned to face him, kissing him gently, then slightly less gently. He kissed me back and for a split second I dared to hope it could become something more than just kissing. It wasn't long though before he pulled away.

"You don't mind, do you?" he said. "I'm just not ready."

And I sighed and told him of course I didn't mind because it would be wrong of me to say anything else and I did, after all, love the very bones of him and if that meant waiting until he felt comfortable enough to have sex with me again then I would. Even if it killed me. He went about making his breakfast, and I went about calling The Dressing Room and arranging an appointment for Saturday. It dawned on me that perhaps wearing white wouldn't be such a big faux pas after all – as I was pretty sure whatever virginity I once owned was in danger of growing back.

11

Kitty

I knew the smell wasn't good. Every time I turned over the whiff of three-day-old body odour hit me square in the nostrils. I just didn't have the energy to do anything about it. It took every ounce of energy I had to get up and go to the bathroom when nature called. Showering, grooming and general cleanliness were a step beyond me. Dad had tried several times to rouse me. He had come into my room, pulled open the curtains, sat on the edge of the bed and tried to encourage me to eat something. He had given me hugs and told me I was his best girl, which was remarkably brave of him given the smell of me. He had said things would get better and he should know and I had nodded and shook my head at the appropriate moments. I didn't want to hear that things would get better – not yet. I needed to feel how I was feeling.

I had tried to phone Mark a few times. When I say try to phone him, of course, I mean that I had lifted my mobile, scrolled to his number and looked at it, wondering should I press the call button and if so what would I say, before dropping back on the duvet and falling back to sleep.

What could I possibly say to a man I didn't even feel I knew any more? Who I wasn't sure I ever really knew in the first place? He wasn't the kind of man I ever would have thought would have lived a lie. Jesus, did people really do that? Have double lives? Put on one very convincing face at home and something completely different elsewhere? I wondered had he nuzzled her neck the way he did mine. Did he reach for her hand the way he did mine? The very thought made me want to vomit.

I hadn't realised I had been living the plot of a soap opera without my knowledge. I always thought my life was pretty straightforward. Not boring but, you know, not out of the ordinary either. Not worthy of the *EastEnders Omnibus* anyway. We did normal things – shared meals together, went for walks, talked about work and laughed at old re-runs of *Frasier* together. It wouldn't have set the page of a Mills & Boon novel alight, but I was happy. Genuinely happy. Not smug or anything. Well, maybe just a little bit smug. But why wouldn't I be? I was in love with a man who had chosen me. He had asked me to marry him and we were content in our little suburban existence.

Except that – we weren't. He certainly wasn't. That thought would wake me from my sleep at three in the morning. And again at four. And again at five. And a few times in between. It would wake me and it would take the very breath from my body as sure as if he was in the room and had physically punched me in the stomach himself. But at least the pain from a physical punch would ease after a while. This pain didn't ease. It just ebbed slightly until I fell into a dreamless sleep, only for the cycle to repeat itself.

Rose put her head around the door on Sunday night – or at least I think it was Sunday night – and in her usual calm and collected way asked me if I wanted clean socks and pants brought over from my house. I didn't respond.

She returned an hour later with a small suitcase from home and sat it by my bed before kissing me on the head and telling me Dad was worried about me. Had I the energy to respond I would have told her I was worried about me too. But I barely had the energy to fart, let alone speak. So I grunted. And she left again.

She put her head round the door on Monday as well –

bringing me some tea and toast which I didn't eat and some water which I did drink. She didn't ask me if I was going to work. I think she knew the bedraggled smelly hobo look was not going to sell any wedding dresses. Mondays weren't particularly busy for us anyway – we usually spent them checking stock, following up orders, with Rose doing some alterations in the work room. Not that I was in a state that I could ask her if she would be okay. I didn't care about The Dressing Room that day. I would have gladly burned it and its collection of sodding wedding dresses to the ground. If I'd had the energy.

Cara visited on Monday as well. She brought grapes and chocolates and some magazines as if I was in hospital. She stayed for an hour while I cried and left when I fell asleep having spoken hardly a word.

James sent about a million texts, which I just started to ignore. I didn't get why he was the one apologising when it was Mark who had been the one in the wrong. In fact it was still Mark who was in the wrong. It was barely fathomable. It was Monday – four whole days since he had ripped our world apart and he hadn't even tried to get in touch directly. I had never gone this long without speaking to him. From the moment we had met we had been inseparable. Surely he must have been feeling it too? You can't just stop caring about someone. You can't just switch off what you had.

If I had any talent at all for writing really bad poetry, I'd have written some corkers in those few days. I'd have made Sylvia Plath look like Dr Seuss. I was the lowest I had ever been and it was not a nice feeling.

On Tuesday, around noon, Ivy arrived. She took less of a pussy-footing approach than my dad, Rose or Cara. She marched into my room, opened the curtains and windows wide, hauled the duvet off my stench-ridden bed, ordered me to shower and dragged me into the bathroom.

"There are only so many times I'm going to do this," she said, as she switched the shower on and let the water run to scalding hot.

I watched the curls of steam rise and wished I could float

away on one of them – somewhere where Ivy was not forcibly removing my lilac jumper, hauling it over my head past my chip-pan greasy hair.

"There are only so many times I'm going to come over here and get you to pull yourself together."

"Technically, you've not come here before to tell me to pull myself together," I said, breaking my silence at last in a big way.

"Don't be smart," she said, hauling off one of my socks while I sat petulantly on the toilet and let her. "I know you're going through a nightmare but you can't lie down under it. You have to get up and get on with things. You have a business to run. You have a life to live."

I shrugged my shoulders. Ivy made to try and unzip my jeans and I pulled back. Enough was enough.

"I can do this myself."

"Well, why haven't you then? Now get on with it. I'll make some soup and see you downstairs in ten minutes. Don't be a minute longer or a minute less. I'll come and check. And you know me well enough, Kit, to know I will break down this door if I have to, should you not show your face. And don't even think about climbing back into that scratcher of yours. I'm taking the sheets and putting them in a boil wash. I'll be taking your phone downstairs with me too, so if you mess with me, so help me God, I will put it in the boil wash with your sheets."

I wanted to stick my tongue out at her but felt tears prick at my eyes instead. I was in the horrors and she was shouting at me so I felt myself start to snivel, and I didn't even have sleeves to wipe my nose on.

"Oh Kit, for goodness sake," she said, brusquely but a little softer than before, as she hauled some loo roll from the holder and handed it to me. "You can't lie down under this. He's not worth it."

"I loved him," I managed. "I love him."

"I know," she said, sinking to her knees beside me. "But lying here festering in your own filth isn't going to make things any better. It's certainly not going to win you any friends – or keep your business going."

"I don't care about my business!" I sobbed.

"Oh Kitty, for goodness sake, of course you care about your business. You built it up from nothing. Don't let him take that away from you too."

I looked and her face was serious and bordering on cross. And Cross Ivy was scary. Cross Ivy had been an almost constant companion to me after Mum had gone. She was the tough-as-old-boots teenager who kept me and Dad going when we wanted to collapse on the floor and cry. Or when we drank ourselves stupid, which was Dad and not me, in fairness. She had to grow up pretty quick and she never let us forget it.

"I'll get showered," I said. "I promise."

I couldn't quite find the words to say 'I'm sorry for being an emotional wreck and I'm sorry Mum walked out when we were younger and you had to pick up the pieces and that you feel like you've been picking up the pieces ever since.' So "I'll get showered" was a good compromise.

She nodded, stood up and left the room and I used what little strength I could find to stand under the shower and let the hot water wash over me. I even managed a quick wash of my hair.

I had dressed in fresh pyjamas and had brushed through my hair. I smelled more fragrant and the breeze blowing through my bedroom had cleared most of the sweaty fug away. Glancing out the window I could see it was a fine, bright day. It was the kind of day which normally put me in a pathetically chipper mood – where Rose and I would listen to the radio in work, loudly singing along with the latest tunes and doing the occasional impromptu dance routine. It was the kind of day where we could take our sandwiches out to the courtyard at lunchtime and speak in posh voices about "taking luncheon in the garden". It was the kind of day where I would phone Mark and ask him to meet me in the pub after work and we would have a couple of cold beers before wandering home, hand in hand. You see, it was the hand-in-hand bit that threw me. You didn't cheat on someone you walked hand in hand with. The word *cheat* jarred in my head and I forced myself to take a long, deep breath. No, I had to pull myself together or Scary Ivy would come and kick my arse.

Padding downstairs the smell of chicken soup assaulted my nostrils. She was such a traditionalist – chicken soup for the stomach and the soul.

"You need to eat something," she said, ladling some into a pink polka-dot bowl. Everything in Rose's kitchen was pastel and floral and floaty. Bright and cheerful, just like the woman herself.

I sat down at the table and muttered a thank-you.

"I don't mean to kick your ass. Well, actually I do mean to kick your ass. Your ass needs kicking."

"You wouldn't understand," I said, thinking of her and her happy marriage to Michael – a very sensible and reliable bank manager who wore corduroy trousers and checked shirts from Marks and Spencer and who always had a pen in his top pocket.

"I understand," she said. "Not that my husband has walked out on me, or anything. But she left me too. She walked out on us. She cheated on us. I know what it is like to feel betrayed and I didn't let you lie down under it then and I'm not going to let you lie down under this now."

"It's just . . ."

"Just unexpected? Oh Kit, we have dealt with unexpected before. Don't you remember?"

It started when Dad asked us to sit down. I turned off the television and sat beside Ivy, both us wondering why Dad's voice was trembling just that little bit.

My stomach started to feel funny, you know in the way your stomach feels funny when everything in your life has shifted. You don't even have to know there has been a change before it hits . . . the uneasy feeling.

"Girls," Dad said, his eyes darting around the room as if he was looking for divine inspiration on what to say, "there is no easy way to say this."

I looked at Ivy and she looked at me. Neither of us spoke. I think we were too terrified to even begin to imagine what would come next.

"I'm afraid Mum has gone . . ."

Daddy looked funny. And not good-funny. His face had a

kind of frozen, haunted, horrible look that, even though I was only thirteen and by dint of my age exceptionally self-absorbed, I knew I never wanted to see again.

"Gone?" Ivy said, in a high-pitched echo of what Daddy had said and it almost sounded funny. Almost.

I felt a strange mixture of a giggle and a cry catch in my throat. I knew he wasn't going to end his sentence with 'to the shops' or 'up the town'. I knew this was something serious and bad and I started to feel shaky.

"I'm sorry," Daddy said, as if it were his fault. As if he was gone. As if he had done the hurting. As if he had walked out on us. "I'm sorry, girls. I don't know . . ." his voice trailed off.

"What do you mean, gone?" Ivy asked, her voice still high-pitched and pained.

Daddy just shook his head and sat down in the battered brown armchair opposite and looked at the letter in his hands.

"Go and get her," Ivy said, louder.

"She doesn't want to be got," he said, folding the letter and putting it in his pocket. "She says she's sorry. Oh girls, I'm sorry."

I always wondered what that letter said. Whatever it was, it was clearly not for our eyes. Over the years I imagined in turn it said all sorts of horrible things about how we were awful daughters and she never wanted us anyway, to saying she just had to be a free spirit. Regardless, we didn't see her again for three months and even after that we only saw her sporadically and the bond was broken. We were broken. The trust was gone. And Daddy kept apologising, just as James had done that night in the restaurant, even though it wasn't him who had left and it wasn't him who had broken us.

"I know, Ivy. I know we have. I just feel lost and I know I should be up kicking arses and getting angry on it but I just . . . I just can't help it. All I have the strength to do is mope. Don't you just think I need to mope? Don't I deserve to mope?"

"Do you want him to win?"

"It's not about winning. It's about me not understanding what the hell has just happened to my life."

"Then ask him."

"But he won't take my calls. He'll only talk to me through James." There was a slight whine to my voice which annoyed even me.

"Then talk to James and tell James to tell his friend to stop being such a god-awful eejit and talk to you like a man. Is he four? Is he still at school? *Wanker*." She blew her fringe from her face and slammed closed the dishwasher so I could hear the pastel-coloured plates inside rattle loudly.

I bristled at her calling him names. Okay, so she was right and he was behaving like an arse but I wasn't ready to hear her say it. I wasn't ready to hear anyone say it – I was struggling enough to come to terms with his betrayal in my own head.

"Okay," I said. "Okay. I'll try. I promise I'll try. I'll go to work and be a good girl and do what is expected of me."

"And don't make me come over here and kick your arse again?"

"I won't make you come over here and kick my arse again."

"Good woman," Ivy said, in an only mildly patronising tone. "When Mum left we said we could get through anything. We can still get through anything."

I nodded and half smiled, thinking to myself that she didn't have to get through any of this. This was something I had to get through myself. I was in this on my own.

12

Erin

Jules was hyper. She was so excited she was practically bouncing from one foot to the other, like a child desperate for a pee but too excited to leave the sandpit she was playing in.

"It's so pretty. I want to buy it and work here and surround myself with pretty dresses," she said outside The Dressing Room, puffing on a cigarette to steady her nerves as if it were she who was about to hand over a huge wodge of money for a dress she would wear only once.

"Those things will kill you," I said, and she stuck her tongue out at me playfully before dropping the butt to the ground and grinding it with the heel of her impossibly pointy boots.

"Jesus, sis, don't be going all cancer-preachy on me just because Paddy's going through the mill," she said, with a wink and a smile so that I couldn't get mad at her.

Not that I ever got mad at Jules anyway – she didn't have a bad bone in her body and apart from her dirty smoking habit was almost faultless.

"I'm not going all cancer-preachy on you. I'm just kind of fond of you. And besides, I've had enough of chemo to last me a lifetime so if you don't mind . . . Besides, they stink." But as I spoke she was already liberally spraying herself with a bottle of Jo Malone which she kept in her handbag for such occasions.

"Sure don't I smell lovely now?" she said, grinning and slipping a Polo mint in her mouth before offering me the packet.

I shook my head and linked arms with her. "Are you ready to go in now?"

"Yes, ma'am," she saluted.

"And you will behave yourself?"

"Yup."

"Because I don't want this Kitty woman thinking our family is entirely populated with eccentrics and loony bins."

"But we *are* entirely populated with eccentrics and loony bins," Jules smiled.

"Speak for yourself," I answered. I was pretty sure I had left all eccentric and loony qualities behind me. If I'd ever really had them. I suppose there was my moment of madness with Ian – which was actually about six months of madness with Ian – which ended very, very badly anyway. Christ, I shook myself, the last thing I wanted to think about on the day I bought my wedding dress was Ian – the man I nearly eloped with – or did elope with, but who chickened out at the last minute and left me sobbing into my last-minute makeshift bouquet, bought for a few pounds that morning. I should have known really – getting married in civvies with supermarket flowers – it wasn't going to end well. Paddy sometimes referred to Ian as the one who got away. I would laugh and say "not so much got away as ran screaming for the hills" and we would laugh because there was no doubt in my mind that Paddy was the big love of my life. But for a while, for a year or two, Ian had made me feel completely unlovable, unworthy and unmarriageable. And I had vowed, no matter how much I might love anyone ever again, I would never, ever put myself in a position where I could be hurt and humiliated again. Yet, here I was, about to get married – admittedly with a proper bouquet this time – to a man who might still leave me, but in an even more horrendous way. I stopped, pulling back from Jules as she opened the door to walk through. I didn't speak but she turned to look at me and I'm pretty sure the fear and mild nausea was written all over my face.

"Look," she said, "it's a big party, remember? For you and Paddy. Paddy who loves you. Paddy who isn't going to run away and who will do everything in his power to make sure he never leaves you. You put a big smile on your face now and I will be on my best non-eccentric behaviour, even when I see you in the very beautiful dress and feel the urge to squeal like an over-excited teenager."

I looked at her and knew she understood exactly how I was feeling and I knew I would walk into the shop, try on my dress, get measured and hand over my money and do my very damndest to feel happy and look happy and maybe I would allow myself to *be* happy if only for a little bit.

Breathing out, I looked in the mirror. Okay, so the dress even withstood me breathing out. This was good. There would be a minimal need for sucking my belly in. Kitty was standing back, looking at me and smiling. She was smiling so damn hard that I was pretty sure there were tears in her eyes. I glanced at the mirror again. My hair was scraped onto the top of my head, the frizz curled into a loose bun, while a tiara glinted back at me – adorned with crystals, twisted to reflect the light for optimum sparkliness. Kitty had pinned a floor-length veil to my head – one which hung softly, delicately, gently grazing my shoulders. She had even given me a pair of not-too-high heels to wear to get the full effect.

If I had thought I was in love with this dress the week before, I was now insanely, madly in love with it. Kitty's eyes were not the only eyes with tears in them. I thought back to the cool cotton summer dress I had worn for my aborted wedding day before – how the straps had dug into my shoulders, how I was aware of it straining that little bit over my stomach, how I had clipped a slightly wilting flower into my hair which was set on frizz level 99 and had worn a pair of shoes which nipped at my toes. I couldn't have felt less bridal if I had tried. But now, now I felt like the queen of the all the brides. Dragging my gaze away from the mirror I looked at Jules, who had stuffed her fist in her mouth and was jiggling her knees up and down in an overly excited manner. I tilted my head, my tears turning to laughter and she removed her hand from her mouth.

"I told you I wouldn't scream like a teenager," she laughed. "But I didn't promise I wouldn't do the excited jiggle," she said, jiggling her knees up and down again. "You look stunning, sis, absolutely Paddy-will-faint-with-the-sheer-joy-of-it stunning."

"Better than the legendary cotton wedding dress?"

She nodded vigorously, which of course I fully expected her to do because in fairness I'd look better in sackcloth and ashes than in the wedding attire I'd turned up in to marry Ian.

"Better dress. Better groom. Better chance of it lasting more than five minutes."

"I hope you're right," I said, switching my gaze back to the mirror, eager to get just one glimpse of myself again. I know that sounds kind of vain, but when you are like me – who could easily fit in the not-a-natural-beauty category – and you see yourself looking amazing, you like to get a good gander. My eyes were drawn to my own reflection in a way they never were before.

"I think this is definitely the dress for you," Kitty interjected. "I mean, I was pretty sure last week but I hate to try the hard sell. Seeing you now, I have to say you should go for it."

"I should, shouldn't I?" I said, smiling at her, knowing that the hard sell would be the last thing she was capable of. She looked, well, too soft. Too vulnerable. Too much of a romantic.

Remembering Fiona the over-zealous-wedding-planner's words in my head, I jolted back to reality. Would we get it in time? Were wedding dresses that hard to come by? Cotton summer dresses hadn't been an issue, you see. I had simply gone to M&S and picked one up on a Tuesday morning when it was fairly quiet and then I had gone and eaten a dirty big scone and drank a pot of tea all to myself before going home and cleaning the flat Ian and I shared.

"The wedding is in three months – well, technically two months and three weeks. Will that be a problem?"

Kitty shook her head. "I took a call from your wedding planner during the week, which allowed me to call the supplier and, while time is a little tight for sure, we should have it here in two months."

"Brilliant," Jules said loudly and brightly while I, without warning, felt a big bubble of emotion rise up in me and I made an horrendous "*Bleurgh*" sound as my eyes started to water and my stomach constricted.

"It's okay to feel emotional," Kitty said, suddenly at my side with a tissue poised to stop me shedding hot salty tears on the fine satin gown I was wearing.

"I'm getting married," I stuttered, which was very much in the stating-the-obvious category.

"You sure are," Jules said, suddenly also at my side dabbing at my eyes with tissue.

I stood, half-stooped, a big rack of sobbing yuckiness just screaming to be released from my body. And suddenly, even though it was gorgeous and even though it made me look gorgeous, all I wanted was to have this dress off. And to not be here. And to be with Paddy and for him not to be sick. I wanted it to be like it had been in the beginning – well, maybe not the beginning when we were unsure of each other and I was still aching from Ian's betrayal, but what it was like about six months in when I knew I loved him and more than that knew that he loved me. Christ, he loved me. And we were happy. Even when I said no, that I wouldn't marry him because I didn't ever want to put myself in a position where I'd be left like a cold snotter at the altar, we were still happy. We still never doubted each other. Paddy, God love him, he understood. He would tell me softly that he wasn't Ian. That he was sure as sure could be that he never wanted to be with anyone else. He would tell me Ian was an arse and I would laugh and snort and look a little wounded and sometimes he would ask me if I still loved Ian. I didn't. I did for a while, before Paddy came along. For a while I would have given anything for Ian to love me again – or what I knew of love, which was frig-all. Romantic, overblown notions of what it should be like. I knew with Paddy, undeniably, exactly what it should be like. And then he got cancer. And he had his testicle removed. And that wasn't enough. And he was having chemo, and we didn't know if that was enough. We had to wait. Was there anything more frustrating – so utterly soul-destroying – as waiting? For test results. For it to come back. For it to feck off for evermore. There was a giant big question mark hanging over our relationship and it was likely to stay there for a long time. I hauled at the zip, twisting and turning to try and take the dress off while Kitty stepped forward, exuding an air of calm, and took my two hands in her own.

"It's okay," she said. "It's okay. Take a deep breath. Here, Jules, it's okay, isn't it? Come and stand here and talk to your sister and we'll get her out of this dress and we'll make a cup of tea and settle ourselves. It's a big moment. I know."

I felt her unzip the dress and, while Jules breathed along with me, I let an almost-stranger undress me in the middle of a shop in the city centre.

Jules handed me a bottle of beer which I looked at, pausing before bringing it to my lips and sipping. It was cold, delicious – numbing even.

"You make a beautiful bride," she said.

"When I'm not having a panic attack and making a feckwit of myself," I replied, trying to smile but grimacing instead.

"Don't worry," she laughed pulling a face. "I don't think anyone noticed." I thought back to Kitty's slightly horrified face and found myself starting to giggle.

"The first time I go to her shop I bring Mammy, acting the

eejit high on the very whiff of taffeta, and then the second time I'm the one who starts wailing like a frigging banshee."

Jules stifled a giggle herself and clinked her beer bottle against mine. "You never do things by half, Erin. That's for sure. Always a drama."

A little bit tipsy, I climbed into bed later that afternoon. Drinking during the day never had agreed with me and, even though we had only two bottles of beer each over a long, chatty lunch, I could feel my head swimming and my eyes drooping. I had a lovely dream where everything was just peachy and was just how I wanted it to be – work going great, Paddy and I still bonking every second night, and nothing to worry about except my frizzy hair and the economic woes of the country I lived in. And I didn't even worry about the economy too much.

I woke up to a series of text messages, most of which were from my mother asking if I had actually ordered the dress and then wondering if I had chosen a veil, a tiara and shoes. One message was from Paddy, who was spending the day with his own family, telling me he loved me. Another was from Grace reminding me I had arranged to do a phone interview with a local entrepreneur that evening, and asking how the dress-ordering went, and one was from Jules with the words Just a big party. See you later. I smiled and put my phone back on the bedside table before padding down the stairs, switching on the kettle and trying to rattle my brain into a fit enough state to conduct my interview.

Of course some people would have been disgusted to work at the weekends when they had spent the whole week at the coalface, but I loved my work. And that was not just something I said around my boss to make her think I was a great worker. I genuinely meant it – and when I had a good interview in my sights I would get a little buzzing sensation in the pit of my stomach. Sometimes when a story was really good, when all the pieces of the puzzle slipped into place and the deadline was looming, I felt almost invincible. Does that sound stupid? I mean, I know it's not heart surgery or international politics, but talking to heart surgeons and international politicians felt good. And writing pieces about people overcoming adversity was pretty cool too. It reminded me that people could, and did, overcome terrible odds. Stirring my coffee and adding just a splash of milk, I switched off my nervous bride-to-be persona and switched on my award-winning journalist head. It was then I felt in control again.

13

Kitty

Rose was singing 'Secret Love' at the top of her lungs as I woke and acclimatised myself once again to my old bedroom. It had been ten days since Mark had gone. Ten days since I had spoken with him. Ten days since anything made any sense. Ten days since I had shaved my legs or paid any attention whatsoever to my bikini line. It was already looking unkempt – and yet I couldn't quite find the energy to do anything about it. I rubbed my legs together and felt the stubble, which was actually turning into fairly soft hair at this stage. Rose was singing about highest hills and daffodils. She could actually hold a note. It was only when Daddy joined in that I woke up enough to get out of bed and wander down the stairs to tell them to keep it down.

Of course, seeing them in Rose's pastel-coloured kitchen singing to each other almost took my breath away and I didn't have the heart to tell them to keep it down. Instead I stood and watched, wondering how, after seventeen years, they still seemed to be as in love, or more in love, than they ever had been.

I listened as the song reached its crescendo and then I clapped, biting back tears. Rose turned and curtsied to me while Daddy bowed and smiled.

"I thank you," he said, oblivious to his own tunelessness, while Rose winked behind his back.

"Morning, pet," she said, opening the fridge and taking out a bottle of Diet Coke from the shelf. "I'm only letting you have it for breakfast because you're having a hard time," she said, as if I was still sixteen and needing permission. "And I'll even make you a bacon sandwich."

I had to admit that for the first time in ten days I actually felt hungry.

"How are you feeling today, love?" Daddy asked, sipping from the slightly chipped *Best Daddy in the World* mug I had bought him when I was twelve.

"Not quite awake yet," I said, relishing the numbness which came when I wasn't quite awake. That said, I didn't feel quite so fragile. It had been a week since I had spoken with James – therefore it had been a week since the last bomb had dropped. My brain, while not happy about the situation, had at least processed it. It still made me want to boke with horror from time to time, but the desire to lie down and die had passed. Or at least had started to come and go. This had to be an improvement.

James had of course texted me every day, just to ask if I was okay. I hadn't replied but what was I really supposed to say? "Yes, just hunky dory, thank you" or "I feel as if my insides have been torn out and trampled on"? He ended every text saying he was sorry, as if it was him who'd had an affair and walked out.

I sipped from my Diet Coke and listened to the sizzle of the bacon in the griddle pan. Maybe today I would text James back. Maybe today I would even go home. God knows there had been a pint of milk in my fridge which would probably be close to walking itself to the bin all on its own by now. Cara had tactfully told me the night before that perhaps hiding in my childhood bedroom was not really dealing with what was going on. I had said that there was probably some truth in what she was saying but the thought of being there in my house, alone, was too scary. She would come and stay for a few days, she said, if I wanted. But I wouldn't have the same freedom to wander around in my dressing gown and eat ice cream straight from the tub and cry at the ads on TV if Cara was around all the time. Rose was letting me away with it at home. As long as I washed my face before I went to work and didn't tell the brides to run for the hills, it was pretty much a free run as soon as we got back to base. Diet Coke for breakfast. Ben and Jerry's for dinner and free rein with the remote control so that, should as much as a hint of an emotional advertisement come on the TV, I could sob to my heart's content or turn it over if I so desired.

Daddy handed me my sandwich, on thick white bread, the butter oozing over the plate. Yes, I was definitely hungry and for more than ice cream, which had to be progress. Yes, today I would go home. Even if I didn't stay there, I would at least make it through the door.

It was just before noon when I pulled up at home. I had showered and tied my hair back and put on my freshly washed and ironed clothes – courtesy of Rose who had an ironing fetish. She had offered to come with me but I had declined. Daddy had offered to come with me too, his brow crinkled with concern, but I had smiled and hugged him and told him I would be just fine. Honest. A part of me really hoped I would be too.

I can't deny it. I felt a little shaky walking up the path. I was struck by the thought that he might actually be there. He might actually have come home. That ten days would have been enough for him to realise all that he was throwing away. Yes, we would have work to do, I thought, crunching on the gravel driveway, but we could talk and if we could talk it might still be okay. The fact that he had cheated on me, well, I pushed that to the back of my head because I could only deal with one crushing reality at a time and him being gone was today's issue.

I put my key in the door, half-hoping to open the door to find the heating on and the television blaring from the kitchen. I half-expected the fug of his Sunday-morning cooked breakfast to assault my nostrils and for him to wander out to greet me in his saggy tracksuit bottoms – the ones I absolutely hated. But the house was empty and cold and felt not at all like home. It was just a shell. Everything was just how I had left it the week before. The laundry hamper was still overflowing. The now musty towel from my shower was still lying on our bed. It all felt so wrong. How could nothing have changed?

Taking a deep breath, I lifted the towel, bundled it with the rest of the washing into the machine and switched it on, relishing the comforting swishing sound as the drum filled with water. A bit of noise about the place made it feel better. I don't think I realised how quiet our house could be without even a hint of him there.

I knocked the heating on to take the chill out of the air, while opening the windows at the same time to allow some fresh air in. I knew it was wasteful but I didn't particularly give a flying damn. I figured I was allowed to be a little wasteful just around now. I switched on my iPod and plugged it into the docking station – flicking through the playlists to find some choice Motown, which was normally my cleaning and tidying music of choice. And then I set about cleaning. Bleaching the bathroom to a loud chorus of 'Rescue Me', stripping the bed to 'Signed, Sealed, Delivered', dusting the living room to a mellow 'Sitting on the Dock of the Bay' and lying on the floor almost defeated to 'What Becomes of the Broken Hearted' – it was only when 'Try a Little Tenderness' hit its crescendo that I found the strength to stand up again and blast it out of me, not giving a damn that the windows were open and I wasn't by any stretch a natural-born soul singer. I wasn't even a fit-for-the-back-row-of-a-choir singer.

By the time my house was gleaming, my washing was out on the line and my iPod had exhausted all my favourite cleaning classics I was tired and ready to relax and not feeling quite so scared by my own home. First I would have a shower, and tackle my undergrowth, and then I promised myself I would sit down and watch TV or something equally meaningless in what used to be my comfort zone.

This had to be an improvement. I was actually quite proud of myself and even jotted off a quick text to Cara to tell her I was just fine and then I forwarded that very same text to Rose and Daddy just so that they would stop worrying. Because, I knew they were worrying. I glanced at my phone, wondering if now was the time to text James. It probably was. I was feeling stronger and really it had been unfair of me to ignore him for the past week when it had been clearly accepted that he had not done anything wrong.

I'm sorry for not being in touch. Please don't worry. I'm fine. Or at least I will be fine.

I sent the message and stood under the shower and tried to remind myself that I had made a great deal of progress and tried to ignore the sinking feeling in the pit of my stomach that there was something missing from my house.

Showered and revived, I switched on the TV, pulled the throw from the sofa over my knees, cuddled into the cushions and tried to lose myself in an old black and white movie. When my phone beeped to life, instinctively I lifted it. The hope that it would be a message from Mark hadn't quite left me but I knew deep down that it wouldn't be from him. I should have known it would be from James, given the frequency with which he had texted me that week, and sure enough it was from him.

I hate how we left things. Can we talk?

I pulled my knees up to my chin. I didn't know if I wanted to talk. I couldn't say that James and I had ever been particularly close in the past. Sure we'd had a laugh or two over the years and he had helped me deal with a drunken Mark on a few occasions when we were all younger and much less sensible. The three of us had spent a weekend together in a caravan in the Gaeltacht which would forever go down as the worst weekend of our lives. But we didn't really do deep and meaningful. That said, he was the nearest thing I had to Mark in my life at the moment and the best chance I had of getting any answers.

I'm at home. Call over after 6.

I pressed send, threw the blanket off my knees and wandered into the garden for some fresh air, my throat suddenly feeling all constricted and scratchy. I wondered if I should phone Cara or even Rose and ask them to come over for moral support but I didn't want James to feel like he was walking into an interrogation. No, I would face it alone. Even if the thought of it made me want to boke.

Unlike Mark, who was never on time for anything in his entire life, not even our wedding, James was always punctual and arrived at six on the very button. We stood, awkwardly, not quite sure how to greet each other. It wasn't a quick-peck-on-the-cheek type of scenario. He held a bottle of white wine in his hand which he gestured with awkwardly in my direction. I took it, muttered a thanks and allowed him to follow me into the kitchen. It was a little strange to have him here without Mark around, but those were the breaks.

Lifting two glasses from the cupboard, I turned to ask, "You want some?"

"I think we need some," he said with a smile.

"I certainly feel as though a drink would help," I said, unscrewing the lid of the bottle and pouring us both drinks before gesturing towards the living room where we sat opposite each other on my matching chocolate-brown leather sofas without saying a word.

"This isn't the slightest bit awkward, is it?" James smiled, sipping from his glass and casting a glance downwards.

"Not at all," I smiled back – in more of a nervous way than anything else because it was bloody awkward. Each of us waiting for the other to speak without having a notion of what either of us might say. I didn't even know if there was anything to say –

apart from the obvious 'Well this has all gone royally tits up, hasn't it?'

James had been best man at our wedding and he had become misty-eyed during his speech, wishing us many, many happy years. He had even taken me around the floor for a dance later and whispered that Mark was a lucky man and we made a wonderful couple. "One of those Hollywood couples – you know, happy endings and riding off into the sunset."

Yep, we were a Hollywood couple all right – just more of a Brad Pitt and Jennifer Aniston kind of a couple than a happy-ever-after kind of a couple.

"Look, I know I've said it a hundred times, but I'm sorry it was me who told you," he offered. "I'm sorry he did it in the first place if the truth be told and that he didn't have the manners or guts to tell you to your face."

"Did he tell you? Before now, that is? Did you know?" I had to ask and I felt strong enough to deal with it if he said yes, that he had been complicit in the whole sorry affair all along, but James just shook his head.

"I swear to you, I didn't know."

He looked genuine enough. But then Mark had looked genuine enough when he told me he loved me just hours before he cleared off.

"I would have told him he was a prick," James offered, sitting back in his chair a little more and sipping from his wine, a little more deeply this time. "I would have punched him," he added and I smiled because I couldn't imagine James ever punching anyone in his life.

"He was your friend. He is your friend. You must have talked?" I curled my feet under me and stared at my wineglass, the smell enticing me to lose myself in the drink.

"We talked," James nodded. "But in the way men talk. It's not a myth, you know. We don't often do feelings. We talked work and beer and *Top Gear* and football. If I asked how you were he would tell me you were fine – busy but fine. There was no hint."

"But he told you last week?" I had to know every detail.

He sighed, sipped from his wine, even deeper this time, and looked back at me. "When you phoned me and told me he was gone . . . I just . . . just couldn't believe it. So I called him and he answered."

I bristled. I thought of all the times I had called. All the times I had shouted at my phone to try and get him to answer. I thought of how I'd slept with the damn thing on my pillow and had rung it almost on the hour every hour to make sure it was working. I thought of how I had cried really quite hysterically . . . and then I thought of how Mark had answered the first time James had called. I was trying to process all this information when I realised he was still talking.

". . . needed to get away. He needed to clear his head. He sounded, I don't know, strange."

I thought of the cheery tone in his voice that time I had called – *strange* wouldn't exactly have been the word I would have used.

"He said he had wanted to tell me, wanted to tell us both, but he got caught up in everything and didn't know where to go or who to turn to." James shrugged his shoulders.

I just drank from my glass again, already starting to feel a little tipsy. It was, of course, entirely possible my head was swimming for another reason – a reason related to the general feckwittery of my husband and not to anything alcoholic.

I forced myself to breathe, realising I had been holding my breath and that I was in serious danger of turning blue and passing out.

"I know this is shit," James said.

"More than you realise," I stuttered, unsure if I wanted him to keep talking at all.

"He told me about her then. He said he just felt flattered and he said he had been an asshole."

I nodded my head. "Was it my fault?" I asked. "Did he say it was my fault? Did he say I was awful?" I was aware there was a whine in my voice and I sounded pathetic and needy. I watched as James shifted uncomfortably in his seat, the slide of his arse against the leather sofa giving me all the answer I needed. Clearly it was my fault. Or Mark thought it was my fault, which meant I could now legitimately crucify myself into believing it was indeed all my fault. Despite my deep breaths and the fact that I had stopped gulping at my wine, I felt a little nauseous.

"He didn't really go into it," James offered limply and I plastered on a fake smile and got up to open a window and let some air in.

"Yes, he did, James, but I won't ask you to go over it. Not now anyway. Part of me wants to know, but I'm not stupid enough to think I'm ready to hear it. Did he say why he couldn't tell me himself? Why he didn't talk to me?"

James shook his head. "Not really. He said he didn't really know how to explain it."

"Like hell he didn't," I spat, my smile fading and my anger rising.

"He's a dick. He's my best friend but he's still a dick and I'm so sorry. I shouldn't have come over. This was a bad idea." James made to stand up but I gestured – some weird international-sign-language type thing – for him to sit down.

"No. It was kind of you. To tell me. To let me know. I know this must be hard for you too."

"You've no idea how hard," James said, running his hands through his dark hair and sitting back into the chair and sighing. "You really have no idea."

James had left when the bottle of wine was finished and when we had simply said "This is hard" too many times for it to be socially acceptable to continue saying it. He had told me to call him if I needed anything – anything at all but especially man things – like leaving the bin out, unblocking drains, that kind of thing. Of course I was more than capable of all of this but it was nice that he offered. I had crawled into bed – for my first night back in my marital bed after knowing my husband had cheated on me – and mercifully I slept. I wasn't haunted by weird dreams. I didn't wake up in the night, turn to put my arm around Mark and start sobbing. I just slept and when I woke up I got up, made a proper non-Diet-Coke-related breakfast, dressed in my black trousers and purple satin blouse and went to work.

I didn't cry in the car – not even when Snow Patrol sang about 'Chasing Cars' on the radio. I did not even get the mad rage when a car which looked like Mark's but wasn't cut me up at the traffic lights. I didn't slump in despair when I opened the doors to the shop and saw our mannequins dressed in their white lace and shot satin. I just switched on the radio and ran upstairs to the workshop to put on the kettle in preparation for Rose's arrival. There was a calmness on me that day – one step further from the day before. Maybe each day would see me move a step on. Of course that new-found inner strength didn't stop me checking my email to see if he had sent me a message or checking his Facebook for any updates (there was none – which was a blessed relief for now – I lived in fear of him telling the world he had gone from married to 'it's complicated' or even worse, married to single). There were no messages on the office answer phone – no form of communication at all from him or anyone else. I opened the sash windows, watched as a lone tourist walked along the city walls as the traffic sounds grew louder. It was a lovely day – not overly warm, with bright shards of blue sky and the promise of a day that would stay dry. I was standing at the window, breathing in and smiling, when I saw Rose walking down the street, dressed in bright pink with a purple scarf around her neck. There was no missing her – she exuded the calmness and happiness I could only dream of and which I hoped would be contagious. She was launching into a chorus of 'Oh What a Beautiful Morning' as she walked through the door and I walked down the stairs. Seeing me, she stopped singing and gave me that same look she had been giving me every day since Mark had left – that slight-tilt-of-the-head-are-you-okay look.

"Morning, Rose," I said, giving her a quick hug. "I'm fine, honest. And yes, I survived the night back in the house. And nothing bad happened. James came over and we talked, but I didn't get all over-emotional or make a show of myself and today I am determined not to mope around but instead to get on with things – because even though wedding dresses are the least of my notions at the moment, this is my business and what I need to do."

She hugged me back and I breathed in her perfume and allowed myself to lean into the softness of her embrace.

"Good woman yourself," she said. "I'll just go put the kettle on. We have a ten thirty appointment, a fitting at one and a few orders to put through. That rep wants to know what samples we want in too, when you get the chance, and I've a couple of alterations to be getting on with. Wee buns to us."

"I have the kettle on already for you," I smiled, relishing the thought of a busy and distracting day. "And I even brought a couple of muffins from the bakery so help yourself. And then let's get this day started."

"Okay, boss," she smiled, heading for the stairs and stopping to look back at me. "Are you sure you're okay?"

"You don't need to ask," I smiled. "I'm getting there. Now go get your tea – I know you are good for nothing without it and I'll go and make sure the dressing room is ready. Bit early for Prosecco this morning perhaps – so can you make sure there's some fizzy water and the like in the fridge, just in case?"

"Will do," Rose said and disappeared from my view.

I walked into the dressing room and set about opening the French doors to let in some air and switching on the various spotlights which would show off the dresses and the bride-to-be in the best way possible. I tidied the magazines on the table and made sure the flowers in the vases still looked acceptable and didn't need to be replaced. Then I made sure the changing room was tidy and that there were a couple of boxes of tissues sitting around for when the bride and whoever was accompanying her became emotional. It was all looking good. I still got a thrill from seeing our dressing room ready for an appointment – it still gave me butterflies in my stomach and I smiled as I stood for a second on the podium and tried to remind myself to believe in happy endings.

My ten-thirty appointment was a second-time bride who was as nervous as any young bride we had in the door.

"I had the full works first time," Nuala Lochlainn said. "Big rock. Big do. Big hair. Honeymoon in Mauritius. All that was missing was the big romance. But this time – I have that."

She smiled, a gorgeous full-faced smile which accentuated the gentle crow's feet at her eyes and her dazzling white teeth. She flashed a simple engagement ring at me – yellow gold with a modest solitaire diamond set in it. "We're doing it a little less flashy this time, but I want to knock his socks off. My friends said this was the place to come . . . so here I am." She smiled at me and then at her two friends who were sipping from their Prosecco glasses despite the early hour. Gesturing to her almost flat tummy, she smiled. "Two kids. I definitely want a dress which hides the evidence. Something elegant. Not too fussy. Something which makes me look about ten years younger if possible." She laughed and I mentally ticked off another number on my wedding-dress bingo. If I had a fiver for every time a bride told me she wished a dress could make her look younger or thinner, I would be a very rich woman. Still, who didn't want to look amazing on her wedding day? My entire business was built on that very notion.

"Nuala, let's have a little look and see what we can come up with," I said while mentally working through the dresses in our stock until my brain focused on two or three dresses which screamed youthful, flattering, non-fussy elegance.

And then I smiled as I watched Nuala transform into a bride

before my eyes even though she had not so much as a scrape of make-up on and was crying tears of joy.

"You look lovely," her friends wept as I stood back, admired my work and heard the ding of the bell on the door announcing the arrival of another customer. I knew Rose wouldn't hear it – by this stage of the morning she would be hunched over her sewing machine singing along to the *Grease* soundtrack – *Grease* being a definite Monday-morning favourite. So I excused myself, walked through to the reception area of the shop and came face to face with a woman who I had not seen in five years and who I had not wanted to see ever again, if I could have helped it.

"Mother," I said, the words sticking in my throat.

"Katherine," she replied. "I wondered could we talk?"

14

Erin

My desk was my sanctuary – nestled in the corner of the office, close to one of the few windows we had. I didn't go for the Zen workspace of some of my colleagues – I went for the this-is-my-space approach. I had a handmade clay desk-tidy which Jules had made for me at one of her night classes. I had a picture of Paddy and me, grinning like eejits at each other, in my direct eyeline. I had coloured Post-It notes with inspirational quotes scrawled on them. In my top drawer I had an emergency supply of make-up for touching my face up before any big interview and a spray bottle of Frizz-Be-Gone for particularly humid days. I kept a flat pair of shoes and a heeled pair of shoes in my drawer. My motto, I would joke, was 'Be Prepared'. Of course Paddy would joke that my motto should actually have been 'Obsessive Compulsive' – but I liked to be in control. I liked to know what I was doing and when I was doing it. I liked things black and white. And most of all I liked things the way I liked things. I made no apologies for that. I just wanted a nice life in perfect keeping with my inner control-freak tendencies. So my workspace was my workspace and when I walked in every

Monday morning I liked to know that my pens would all be pointing downwards in the pen jar just as I had left them and that my notebooks would be sitting pointing in the same direction that they had been the previous Friday and that, of course, my drawers would contain the same in-case-of-emergency supplies.

I smiled at my colleagues as I walked in – nodding towards Grace's office which was to my right and seeing that she was deep in conversation with our editor in chief, Sinéad. When those two conspired, one of two things happened – something magnificent or something really, really bad. I could cope with the magnificence but not the something really bad. I sat down at my desk, looked at all my personal possessions surrounding me and switched on my computer. I decided it might just be a very good idea to throw myself into my work and not worry about whatever they were up to.

Paddy had still been sleeping when I'd left. He was tired these days – and that worried me as it was only a week till his next cycle of chemo and by this stage he was normally at the bouncing-back stage. Still, I reminded myself, we'd had a busy couple of weeks – the wedding planning was reaching fever pitch. Just the day before we had written out the invitations and, as I sat at my desk, I was aware of them resting in my bag, all stamped and ready to be sent out into the world. I was sure that if he just got a good few days, a bit of calm and quiet, he would feel better. Sure wasn't I feeling a little bit tired myself?

I keyed in my password, listened to the computer whizz and whirr into life and opened the window beside me to let in some fresh air. I lifted the yoghurt and granola from my bag and tucked in, all the while dreaming of a sausage bap from the shop next door. But, you know, I had a figure-hugging dress to fit into and skin which needed to be glowing and not spot-ridden. I ate my granola while checking my emails and making a few appointments for interviews and then I downed the first of my requisite four bottles of water a day – and all the while Grace and Sinéad were still chatting.

My emails were not yielding a lot to get excited about – but then again it was a Monday morning and things tended to take a little while to get going on Mondays. As usual, everyone seemed to be in a haze of post-weekend lethargy until at least eleven and, had it not been for Sinéad and Grace and their council of war, I might have been inclined to ease myself into the day in the same way.

We were two weeks into the new magazine cycle – about now things should be coming together and the pages of *Northern People* should be filling nicely. I had a few things underway – our usual fixtures and fittings were done and I had a few features lined up – but I had a feeling I would have to pull something even more remarkable out of the bag now. After all, I was now an award-winning features writer. There was no room for a slack month. Now was not the time to rest back on my laurels. Feeling a headache building, I swallowed two paracetamol from my stash in my top drawer, smiled politely at colleagues who passed by, got my head down and went on with things.

The creak of the door alerted me to the fact that the big meeting was done – followed by Sinéad stalking out of Grace's office. It wasn't that Sinéad was scary – it was just that she was, and how can I put this without fear of losing my job . . . uber-efficient. To a point where she did not tolerate gladly anyone who was not as uber-efficient as she was. She smiled in my direction – a brief flash of white – as she passed on her way back to her office where she would shut the door indicating an absolute 'Do Not Disturb Unless Absolutely Necessary' policy.

She hadn't closed Grace's door, this much I had noticed. And I glanced up to see Grace standing in the doorway, peering out at me, a sneaky half-smile on her face.

"You two have been scheming, haven't you?" I asked, forcing a smile on my face but feeling my heart sink to the bottom of my shoes.

"Can you come in a wee minute?" Grace said. "It's nothing bad, I swear."

Somehow I didn't believe her. I lifted a notebook and pen – prerequisites for any meeting with your editor – and followed her into her office, feeling a little like a lamb being led to the slaughter.

"Sit down," she said, smiling as she sat behind her desk and looked at the notes she had obviously taken from her meeting with Sinéad. She glanced up at me. "You look shit-scared," she said.

"I am shit-scared," I laughed back. The thing with Grace was that you could say it like it was – to a point of course. She was still my boss and for that reason if nothing else she made me feel nervous.

"Look, we just want to run something past you and this is something you can absolutely say no to – but I think it would be good for you and for the magazine. We all know how tough things are in the magazine world these days and we can't deny our circulation is taking a hit – so we are looking at spicing things up a bit."

Images of me, dressed in lingerie, pouting from Page 3, sprang into my mind and I felt my face redden. I blinked several times, trying to regain my composure. Surely they wouldn't ask me to go that far? Or anywhere near that far? Or even anywhere in the vague direction of that far?

"You're more of a name now. We want to capitalise on your recent success in the media awards. We get a good response to your stuff, Erin. When we put you on a story we know we can trust you to do a good job."

This was starting to feel like a buttering-up exercise and I wondered where exactly it was going.

"We think we should make more use of you – make you even more of a name. Your opinion pieces get a good response and people are clearly interested in what you have to say."

I nodded, wishing she would get to the point, but secretly enjoying a little bit of the flattery while she tried to get there.

"One thing that people always want to read about is, well, weddings. And people like you. So combining weddings and you – well, it could be good."

"I'm already combining weddings and me, in real life," I said, still not sure where she was going.

"But would you write about it? Would you share the details with your readers?"

"And tell them about the dress and the flowers and all the girly things?"

Grace nodded.

"And this will make me appear to be a more serious journalist how?" I was happy enough to do the human-interest stories. I was happy enough to write my opinions on a wide variety of subjects. I was happy to do almost everything Grace asked me to do in the name of the magazine and my profile, but did I want to show all my Bridezilla colours all over the pages of the magazine? Did I really want people to be reading about my meltdowns? It was embarrassing enough that I actually had them without publicising the fact.

"You could tell them it all," she said, her face a little more serious now.

I saw her sit back in her chair and cross her arms. I saw a glimpse of uncertainty on her face.

"It all?" I asked.

"Look, I know this seems hard . . . to ask you to do this . . . but if you told the readers your story, if we brought them in . . . if we shared your strength of character . . ."

"If we told the world my fiancé has one testicle and cancer and that we are marrying in case he croaks it?" I felt the tears sting in my eyes. "Don't take this the wrong way, Grace, but this makes me less of a serious journalist and more like a guest on the *Jeremy Kyle Show* – spilling the very intimate details of my life for all and sundry to read!"

She ran her hands through her hair and took a deep breath. "Shit, Erin. Look, I know this sounds scary."

"With respect, Grace, you have no idea just how scary 'it all' is – and I'm not just talking about work. I'm talking about 'it all'. And to put it out there? Jesus . . . I don't think so . . . not to

Paddy and not to me." My voice was shaking as I spoke. I don't think I had ever spoken so firmly to Grace in my life.

"I want you to think about it," she said. "Just think about it. You might find it helpful. For you. It might help you come to terms with it all. It might raise awareness of what Paddy is going through – you know how men are. You know how lax they can be looking after themselves. You could make a difference."

"There are other ways to make a difference – ways that don't put every detail of my life out there for everyone to read."

She nodded slowly. "Of course there are. But think about it. Talk to Paddy. Come back to me when you have considered it fully. I've done it, Erin. I'm not picking this out of the sky. I did the whole baring my soul in this magazine a few years back. It worked. It helped me. Christ knows it just about saved my marriage . . . Look, I won't pressure you but I don't want you to go with a gut reaction either."

She stopped speaking and I couldn't find the words to say what I wanted. Not without risking my job anyway. I nodded and turned to leave.

"Erin, I mean it when I say no pressure. Please believe me," she said.

I returned to my desk and stared blankly at my computer screen. No, of course there was no pressure. My boss really wanted it. She believed telling our story could boost our ailing circulation. Telling Paddy's story could help other men. Telling my story could boost my profile. No, there was clearly no pressure at all.

I picked up a bottle of wine on the way home from work. Paddy was unlikely to want to share it with me – he hadn't been one for drinking much since he had started chemo but I certainly felt the need for a tall glass. Grace and I had managed to avoid each other perfectly throughout the rest of the day. Sinéad had walked past at one stage and whispered "Just think about it." I didn't think I needed to – but that didn't stop me phoning Jules.

"So," she had said, "supposing Paddy didn't run for the hills at the very thought of sharing his very intimate bits for everyone to read about . . . do you think it might actually be a good idea?"

I breathed out. "But it's not what I want to do."

"You want to write. This is writing and more than that it is writing your story."

"Putting my neurosis out there for everyone to see? I mean how much would I tell them? Where would it end? Would I mention Ian and the wedding which never was? Would I tell them how I sat in the hospital chapel when Paddy had his operation and prayed like I had never prayed before? Do I tell them I cried all over my wedding dress and took a panic attack?"

"You tell them what you want to tell them," she said simply.

"I don't know," I said – and I didn't know. I was very good at telling other people's stories – their tales of woe, their tales of triumph over adversity. I wasn't sure I wanted to tell my own.

"Well, they don't need an answer just now, do they? Did they not say to think about it? Take your time."

I sighed, rubbing my temples and craving something more than the water I was drinking.

"I suppose. Thanks, sis. Love you."

"Erin," she said, "It will be okay, whatever you decide. But come to think of it . . . if you decide to go for it, if you decide to tell your story, make sure you write in a really gorgeous and totally irresistible sister."

Smiling, I put the phone down and tried my very best to get on with my work.

"I've made some dinner," Paddy called from the kitchen and I walked through, the smell of one his world-renowned chillies catching me square in the nose.

"I've brought wine," I called back, sitting the blue plastic bag from the off-licence on the table and reaching into the cupboard to pull out a wineglass, kissing Paddy on the side of the cheek as I went. Opening the bottle, I poured a grand big healthy glass of red and sank a good quarter of the glass without stopping for breath.

"Tough day at the office," Paddy asked, eying me suspiciously. I nodded and drank again.

"Would you like some?" I asked and he shook his head.

"I might try a beer later – last of the party animals, that's me," he smiled, bringing the wooden spoon laden with chilli to my mouth for me to taste.

Blowing on it, I tasted, made the appropriate yummy noises and went back to my wine.

"Are you going to tell me about it?" he asked, tilting his head to one side.

"About what? The chilli? It's lovely. Best one you've ever done," I said with a wink.

"About work – or whatever it is that is bothering you? Did Jules call you a Bridezilla again? Did someone eat the last Bounty bar out of the chocolate machine?"

He was smiling, which made me smile too – even though my bad day was about nothing as frivolous as a bar of chocolate or my sister being up to her usual shenanigans.

"You're mad funny," I smirked. "And as it happens – not one bite of chocolate has passed my lips this entire day. I've been very good. I've had my two litres of water and everything."

"And you are now going for your two litres of wine?" He nodded towards my glass, which was down to the dregs.

"Pet, if you don't mind. I don't really want to talk about it. Not now anyway. I'll just have my wine – eat my dinner and maybe I'll have calmed down by the time that's done."

He looked at me quizzically again, shrugged his shoulders and turned back to serving the dinner.

I felt a stab of guilt. We didn't keep things from each other. We told each other every little detail of our lives and when I had a bad day at work I usually came in and gave him all the details, both guns blazing, until he brought me round with a silly joke or a funny story – or the offer to go and see whoever had annoyed me and punch them square on the nose. Which was funny, of course, because I don't think Paddy had ever punched anyone in his life.

I watched him busy himself draining the rice and sighed, but didn't feel strong enough to broach the topic of how Grace and Sinéad wanted the very details of our life to be printed for all to see across a few glossy pages.

"How've you been today?" I asked as he turned to set the two plates down on the table.

"Not too bad – tired, I suppose. But sure I'm always tired these days. I'm hungry though, that's a good sign, isn't it? A strong appetite and a desire for beer? Could be worse."

"Could indeed," I said, tucking into the dinner in front of me.

"Sorry I've nothing more exciting to report – but basically it has been a day of lying on my arse and watching trashy TV. Jesus, there is a lot of rubbish on the TV during the day. And it's strangely addictive. I think I might need a 12-step programme for my growing *Judge Judy* addiction. If I'm not careful I'll be talking like trailer trash and wanting to sue anyone who so much as looks at me sideways. Actually," he said, putting his fork down, "I'm so bored I'm thinking of going back to work. Part time maybe, or from home. Just something."

Paddy had not gone back to work since his operation, allowing himself time to recover. We had thought it would be only for a couple of weeks, but then we were told he would need more treatment and the more treatment left him exhausted and sick and not fit to spend his days in a busy graphic-design business working into the wee small hours on pitches. Some days, on the days after his chemo, he could barely lift his head from the pillow, never mind set about designing a masterpiece. But he was bored – it was part of the reason he had thrown himself so full-on into the wedding plans: it gave him something to do. That was fine, he could take that at his pace. Work would be tougher – and he needed all his strength if he was to beat this once and for all.

"Are you sure you would be able for it?"

"I'm willing to give it a go. I spoke to Dave. He said they would try and work something around me – around the chemo, which is nearly done anyway. They would build me up slowly and then, hopefully, after the wedding I'll be back in full health and ready to get back to it full time."

I allowed his positivity to wash over me for a bit. He was talking about being back in full health and God knows I wanted him back in full health more than anything.

"I won't let this beat me," he said. "I won't let it beat us and I'm tired of my life being on hold because of it. I want to get on with things, not lie about watching Judge poisonous Judy and playing the Xbox. Life is for living."

As he said this he shovelled a huge mouthful of chilli into his mouth and smiled back at me brightly. I smiled back. He was seizing life by the balls – if you'll excuse the metaphor – and maybe it was time I did too.

"I think that sounds brilliant," I said. "Really brilliant. You should go for it. And since you are going for it . . . can I run something by you about my work?"

15

Kitty

It wasn't that my mother and I had some big cataclysmic falling out. We just, at some stage, ceased to feel that we really had any place in each other's lives. It was fair to say that probably started just about the time she walked out on us – and had been sealed around the time she apologised for not being able to make it to my wedding as she had booked a cruise and it was too good an offer to miss. And sure, wouldn't I have Rose anyway, she had said with a sniff. I didn't know if she had wanted me to beg her not to spend a fortnight in the Caribbean and instead walk me down the aisle with Daddy, or if she genuinely was the selfish person I had always pegged her as. Regardless of the reason, I had told her, brusquely, that was fine and that I hoped she would have fun. Then I had gone back home and cried all over Mark for three hours until it looked as if my face would be permanently blotchy and swollen and I would look like a very tragic bride indeed.

Mark had reacted angrily – telling me my mother didn't deserve me. When it came to telling Dad, I had painted on the biggest smile I could and told him that seriously it was fine, I didn't mind at all and that it wouldn't at all put a damper on my day. It was strange, but no matter how bad I felt about it I felt a hundred times worse when I saw my father's face – just that flicker in his eyes that he in turn tried to hide.

Rose stepped up to the mark beautifully. She did everything a mother of the bride should have done. She took me dress-shopping. She insisted on paying for my shoes and my veil, just as her special treat. She took me for lunch after we had done our shopping and she joked that she would buy the biggest hat she could find and then clatter it with flowers to make it even bigger.

Rose made sure Daddy went to his suit fittings – and wore clean underwear and socks for the occasion.

She helped me choose the flowers and loved every second of poring over the tiny details of the wedding until I was happy they were just right. "We should do this for a living," she had laughed – and I had laughed, too, originally. Mark had laughed and Daddy had laughed and then Rose and I had looked at each other – both with that wicked glint in our eyes – and the idea for The Dressing Room was born. I would oversee operations – Rose would do as much as she felt able and we would work together.

We had already sourced our premises, plotted our colour scheme and started working on the renovation of the old building – thanks in part to a heritage grant and also to a whacking great business loan from the bank – by the time I walked down the aisle and saw Rose in her not-too-big hat, smiling at me and waiting to take Daddy's hand as I took Mark's.

I'm not saying I didn't miss my mother that day – but it was more because I was hurt she didn't see fit to be there than any sense that her presence would make the day feel more complete.

We didn't speak much after that. We sent cards, the occasional text. There were a few awkward lunches and one pretty disastrous Christmas dinner, that being the last time we had broken bread together. Shortly after, she had relocated to London and hadn't seen fit to come back until now.

She may well have been my mother but that woman, who now stood before me in the shop Rose and I had built from scratch, was not my mammy.

"I'm busy," I told her.

She looked around at the empty reception and back at me and I felt as if I was ten years old and having to justify my very existence.

"I have a client in the dressing room. I've just nipped out to check on something."

"It won't take long," she said, walking towards me as my inner deflector shield shot up around me. I was feeling vulnerable enough at the moment – rejected enough – without having my mother come back into my life and trample all over my stomped-on heart.

"Mother," I started, stopping as I heard Rose's footsteps on the stairs behind me. This for some reason made me feel nervous – as if I was about to be caught cheating on my stepmother – even though Rose had never, ever in my presence said one negative thing about the woman who had actually given birth to me. I glanced behind me and back at my mother, like a startled rabbit stuck in the headlights of a very fast oncoming car. I made to speak but realised that I had completely lost the ability to form any kind of coherent sentence.

"Violet," Rose spoke first, looking at me with a serene smile on her face and then back at my mother whose lip had curled in a most unattractive manner.

"What a surprise," Rose continued. "Sure isn't it lovely to see you. This is the first time you've been here – in Kitty's shop, isn't it? Isn't it gorgeous? Hasn't she done well?"

My mother nodded and offered another cursory glance around the reception. "I've heard it's very popular," she said.

"It is," I said, almost boastfully, at once annoyed with myself for feeling the need to impress her. "Rose and I have done a good job, even if I say so myself."

I was surprise to see the slight hurt in my mother's eyes but, as soon as it had passed she plastered a smile on her face and was agreeing, reaching her hand out to Rose's to shake it. She hadn't offered her hand to me. Or a hug. You would have thought after five years she might have wanted a hug. I looked at her. She hadn't changed much over the last five years. Her hair was a little longer, and a little more blonde perhaps. She wore the same kind of eclectic floaty expensive clothes she always wore – the kind of clothes which Rose wore – only Rose would go for pastel colours while Mum would opt for sludgy beiges and grey. I should really tell her those colours did her no favours.

"I wasn't expecting to see you," I said.

"I should have called," my mother replied, sitting down and leaving me under no illusion whatsoever that she was not about to leave any time soon. "But I didn't know if I would be welcome, if the truth be told, so I figured that surprising you would be the best course of action." She smiled that same strange, half-forced smile at the end of her sentence and I almost felt sorry for her. Of course I felt more sorry for me, who had experienced enough surprises in the last few weeks to last me a lifetime. A month or two, or a year or two, or even a decade or two of no surprises whatsoever would go down just nicely.

"Well, Violet, how about I make us a cup of tea while Kitty deals with our clients and then, sure, we can take it from there?" Rose offered as I stood with not a notion of what else to say.

"Okay," my mother replied, slowly standing and following Rose up the stairs while I stood in the reception and resisted the urge to throw myself on the floor and have a full-on temper tantrum.

Stay calm, I urged myself, as I walked, my hands shaking, back into my second-time-lucky bride and tried to make her experience memorable for the right reasons.

The conversation between my mother and Rose was flowing when I eventually joined them in the workshop. Rose was showing my mother the wall where we had pinned pictures of our beautiful brides alongside the various thank-you cards and notes we had received over the last few years. Beside the pin-board were a couple of framed pictures, images of us at the local business awards, grinning at our achievements.

"You really have done very well," my mother offered, turning to look at me.

She still made no effort to hug me. Then again I made no effort to hug her either. I was all done with hugging.

"I don't understand why you are here," I said, perhaps a little too brusquely. I saw Rose give me that 'calm down, dear' look she did so well.

"I wanted to see you. Is that so hard to believe?" my mother sniffed.

"Actually, it is – given our history. You must know that." She hadn't asked how I was. She hadn't asked after Mark. She hadn't told me she missed me. I crossed the room and sat down behind my desk and lifted a paper clip, nervously uncurling it.

"Touché," she said, that awkward smile on her face again. "But look, Kitty. The thing is . . . well . . . I know, I've been awful . . ." I snorted and she didn't even blink, just carried on talking, "I'm only realising now how awful I was."

As she spoke I was aware of Rose leaving the room. My place in hell was probably assured by the fact I was more concerned about where Rose was going than what my mother was telling me.

"But I've been getting things together. I know I've been selfish. I'm trying to make amends. And I'm making big changes in my life. Kitty, I've met someone. We're very happy and we want to get married. And I'd love you to be there. In fact, I'd love for you to help me choose my dress – here, of course, in The Dressing Room. I've come home to tell you that I want things to be different between us. I want my wedding to be a new beginning – for me and you, and Ivy too of course."

I thought of Ivy, how my anger towards our mother paled into insignificance against Ivy's, and I felt my face redden. "Have you seen Ivy?" I asked, thinking that she couldn't have. She would most likely have a black eye or at least a harrowed look on her face if she had.

My mother shook her head, the nervous smile gone. "No. No . . . I was thinking . . . if it wasn't too much to ask . . . you could help me with that as well."

I flicked the paperclip across the desk. Sweet Jesus. I had enough going on in my life without helping my mother build her bridges – bridges she hadn't just burned in her wake but incinerated.

"I . . . don't know."

My mother pulled a chair over and sat down opposite me, across the table. The physical barrier between us was nothing compared to the emotional one. I rubbed at my eyes. Christ, it never rained but it poured.

"I'm not sure I have the energy for this right now," I said, trying to stop my voice from breaking. It was around that point that I realised, even though this woman opposite me had become a virtual stranger, there was still a part of me that wanted so much for her to take me back in her arms and tell me it would be okay, that she loved me and that, indeed, I was worthy of being loved. But I looked at her – sitting there, thinking she could just walk in and we could pick up where we had left off – and I felt like screaming.

"In fact I *know* I don't have the energy for this right now," I said. "Mum . . . please. Just not now. Can you go?"

"Can we talk later?" she asked, her voice breaking, a pleading look in her eyes which made me want to scream.

"I don't know. I just don't know."

"Think about it," she said, pushing a business card in my direction with her mobile number on it. "I'm staying with your granny. You can get me there if you need me."

I nodded but couldn't think of anything else to say, so I watched her leave, sat back in my chair, poured a glass of pilfered-from-the-fridge Prosecco and downed it quick enough to make the bubbles catch in my throat and make me gag.

16

Erin

I wasn't used to wearing much make-up. I generally wore only a quick slick of foundation and maybe some loose powder to stop the foundation sliding off my face by 4 p.m. If I was going out for a very special occasion I might have added some eye shadow, mascara and lip gloss into the mix. I wore full make-up so infrequently I was pretty sure the Clarins eye palette in my make-up bag had been there for longer than the length of my entire relationship with Paddy . . . and maybe even a good deal longer than that. I did not own an eye pencil. And lip liners had no place in my world, never mind bronzers and the like. So I felt as if I had gained an extra two pounds in weight as Katie, our in-house stylist, transformed me from mild-mannered journalist to cover girl. Or at least picture-in-the-magazine girl. I looked in the mirror and thought my face looked strange – good-strange. Not really like me, or at least not like the me I was used to looking at every day. My hair had been tamed as well – sleeked with a slight wave, very 1950s glamour girl. Katie had poured me into a very figure-hugging outfit as well which I was worried wouldn't pass the sitting-down-not-bulging-out test. Paddy had been primped and preened too although, with nothing more than a mild fuzz thanks to chemo and common-or-garden male-pattern baldness, his hair didn't need much work. He had a bit of make-up put on him, which I knew I would tease him about later, and he had been dressed in a very fancy suit. Even though he was frail from his battle with illness, he looked edible, and I found myself distracted from the nerves of what we were about to do by thinking very much about what I would like to do later. He looked at me and smiled, a twinkle in his dark eyes, and I felt myself blush.

I would never have thought for one second he would have wanted to do these articles. But he had shocked me to my very core by reacting with enthusiasm while I had cringed and stuttered my way through recalling the conversation I'd had with Grace earlier that day.

"Why not?" he had said, sitting back across the table from me and grinning.

"Because, you know, it would get personal. I wouldn't be in control of it. Not really. Grace and Sinéad, well, they know what they want and they want us to bare our souls."

"I wouldn't be opposed to a bit of soul-baring," he said, sincerely.

"Really?" It was hard to hide the shock in my voice. Of course I knew Paddy was the kind of man who wore his heart on his sleeve. He didn't shy away from talking about his illness. He had even talked about it quite eloquently at his pre-op party – but that was in front of friends and family. People who knew. People who cared. People who were unlikely to laugh about it all behind our backs. People who were close enough to the situation to really care about what was happening to us and not just see what we were saying as some form of entertainment they read while waiting to see the dentist or while getting their hair cut. I know, by thinking that way, I was largely disregarding my own profession but this was personal. This was not telling someone else's story. This was not being objective. Much as I wanted to be, I could not be objective about my boyfriend's testicles and his battle with cancer.

"Erin, we both have to be on board with this. And we have to do it for the right reason. I'm not saying yes because I think it would do your profile good and put you in Grace and Sinéad's good books. I'm not doing it because I think you would make a brilliant job of it because you don't even realise what a good writer you are. I'm not doing it for any reason other than the fact I'm one of the lucky ones."

I looked at him as if he was slightly mentally disturbed. The lucky ones don't get cancer, surely. The lucky ones leave this world with all their bits intact.

He must have noticed the look of disbelief on my face as he reached his hand across the table and took mine. "I am lucky, Erin," he said as I shook my head. "I have you, and I'm getting through this and we're getting married. Jesus – I couldn't be luckier. We caught this cancer in time."

I had to resist the urge to shrug my shoulders or shake my head or give any indication whatsoever that perhaps things weren't brilliant. And that we wouldn't beat it. Chemo wasn't just handed out willy-nilly, excusing the genitalia-related pun.

"Not all are lucky. Not all men have girlfriends who march them to the doctors, or stick by them, or agree to marry them not knowing what they might be facing –" His voice had started to break and I could feel his strong, big, heavy, manly hands tremble just that little bit.

"So we tell our story. You tell our story. You get men to look after themselves. You show them that it doesn't have to be the end. Tell them that we are going to have the biggest, best wedding we could hope for. Most of all, Erin Brannigan, tell the world I love you and you love me. What more could I want?"

Of course, even though I'm not a typical hyper-emotional woman, I had cried and told him I loved him too and then, when he had gone to bed exhausted, I had texted Grace to let her know that we would do it. This was followed by a call to Jules during which she veered back and forth from telling me it was a far, far better thing we were doing and telling me that we were clearly off our heads. "Your whole life, in a magazine!" she said incredulously before jumping almost seamlessly to a squeal of excitement that I would be getting a make-over and free new clothes for a photo shoot.

"I always wanted to get a proper photo shoot done," she said, "but the only way I think it will ever happen is if I take to glamour-modelling or the like."

I thought of my poor, flat-chested sister and laughed and she laughed too and then, because I really didn't want to over-think things too much, I changed the subject and we spent a good half-hour debating the merits of McSteamy versus McDreamy and wondering why no doctor we had ever come within twenty miles of had ever, ever looked even half as sexy as either.

When I eventually went to bed I had one those strange pre-wedding dreams where I imagined things took a strange and disastrous turn. This time, I was sitting at the altar – my dress hitched up, peeling potatoes in preparation for the wedding breakfast. I woke at four, still delirious, shook Paddy and told him that we should ring the hotel and make sure they ordered in extra spuds just in case. He laughed, kissed me on the forehead and told me that particular dream would definitely need to make it into one of the articles.

And thus we found ourselves, dolled up and trying to take the whole photo-shoot thing very seriously while Grace looked on from behind the photographer urging us to channel our inner Posh and Becks.

"There's no need to look so terrified of each other!" she called as I looked at Paddy who was trying not to laugh. "You both look fantastic. Sure, aren't you madly in love?"

"Of course we are." I grinned nervously at her. "It's just that we're used to being madly in love with each other in the privacy of our own home."

"It's not a porno shoot," Grace laughed.

I heard Paddy lose the will to hold in his laughter beside me. I almost, almost elbowed him in the ribs but I was sure doing that to someone with cancer would be considered very bad form indeed.

"Your giggles aren't helping," I smiled at him, a bubble of laughter rising up in me. Christ, he looked handsome. So handsome that I kind of wished it *was* a porno shoot. Not that, you know, I'd do a porno shoot. I'm not that kind of girl, honest . . . but still, how amazing, how healthy he looked . . . with that smart suit and that touch of make-up . . . I realised how I wanted him. As my urge to laugh turned into a nervous giggle, Paddy reached across and kissed me lightly and suddenly there was no one else in the room – or so it seemed – and if there was a clicking of a camera, or more encouraging pep talks from Grace, I didn't really notice. It was okay then. I was relaxed and I knew that the pictures would be stunning. To me, they would be perfect.

I felt a little overdressed and definitely over-made-up as Paddy took me for dinner when the photo shoot was done. "Sure, looking as good as this, we might as well make the most of it and hit the town," he'd said.

Of course I knew by 'hitting the town', he meant dinner and then home to rest, but dinner and home to rest sounded good to me. We had become quite reclusive these last few months, which was understandable, and in recent weeks we had definitely noticed that people had stopped asking us to go out. It was as if we had put a *"Please do not ask as refusal may offend"* sticker in our social calendar and everyone was staying well clear.

The thought of dinner anywhere other than our kitchen table or living room had me almost dizzy with excitement.

"Champagne?" he said, with a smile. "It feels like some sort of celebration."

I smiled. "Champagne sounds good. Champagne sounds absolutely perfect in fact."

It would simply be the proverbial icing on the cake to what had been a pretty wonderful day. "Great," he replied. "And you can have a dessert after and all – let's push the boat out."

I laughed. He knew better than anyone that there was never any question that I would not have left that restaurant without a dessert. A dessert was a must – an essential. A necessity. In fact, the first thing I did when I got the menu at any restaurant was check out the desserts. Even if I was on a diet. Even if I had vowed that nothing that did not contain at least two of my requisite five-a-day would pass my lips, there was always, always room for dessert. In fact, as we waited for the waiter to bring us our drinks I was already salivating at the prospect of a slice of Baileys Cheesecake.

Thankfully the cheesecake didn't disappoint nor did the champagne. Although given Paddy's general reluctance to drink very much I ended up drinking more than my fair share and tottering precariously out of the restaurant, fighting off a pretty serious dose of sugar-and-alcohol-induced giggles.

They didn't ease up in the taxi on the way home and thankfully Paddy was such a lightweight these days he caught a dose of giddiness himself and we laughed all the way home until we walked to our front door and I fumbled for my keys. Even though I was carrying the smallest clutch bag imaginable I still struggled to find them and, as Paddy bent his head to look into the bag and help me, our heads collided and pulling apart we both stopped laughing and started staring.

I recognised that look on his face – even though it had been a while since I had seen it. I didn't dare hope and then he leant towards me, taking my face in his hands and kissing me gently but fully on the lips. I barely wanted to move, apart from allowing my body to respond, kissing him back – holding back – allowing him to set the pace. This was not my move to make any more. This was where it got hazy. This is where I was unsure of myself. There was a time it wouldn't have been an issue. I'd have been in like Flynn. He'd have kissed me in that way only he could kiss me and I wouldn't need asking twice. We worked together. We fitted. We had good sex and we weren't one of those couples who had to make an effort to make it happen. We wanted each other and it was really, truly wonderful. (Not to boast or anything.) But then, of course, there was the cancer. And the surgery and bits were taken away. And he was sore. And while we didn't really discuss it that much, because I believed it was worth giving him as much time as he needed to come to terms with an altered body and what it meant, or didn't mean for him, I kind of thought that of course he must feel self-conscious. I was a little scared too, if the truth be told. He hadn't had his prosthesis fitted. I was afraid, I suppose, of how it would look down there. Would I hurt him? Would he be able to do things the way he had done things? Would we do more damage? He was broken enough and I didn't really want to break him any more. So I never pushed him. I didn't show my frustration. I settled for cuddles and kisses and kept my hands to myself where appropriate. All the while I missed him – I missed the intimacy. Here we were planning our wedding, sending out invitations and choosing vows and living like brother and sister afraid to look at each other the wrong way.

So when he kissed me on the doorstep, when I felt the difference in how his lips touched mine, how his hand moved from my face, down my neck, down my arms until he was holding my hands and pulling me closer to him – I knew. When he took the keys from my hand and opened the door, pushing it aside before taking my hand again and leading me through the door, I knew. When he closed the door and kissed me again, deeper this time, with that urgency I had needed so much, I knew. When he pressed me against the door, pressing his body close to mine, I felt my heart soar.

It had been a long time – a time where I had been patient but desperate. Where I had understood but where I missed the physical intimacy which had been such a big part of our relationship. Where I had felt him want me. Where I had felt loved on a whole other, amazing level. And that night, after we had our photo shoot and a drink or two and a lovely day in each other's company, I felt loved on that level.

We fell into bed, moving gently, carefully, taking our time and taking care of each other. I cried. I'm not afraid to admit that and after, although everything was brilliant, we lay in silence. I could hear Paddy breathing, I could feel that his hand was shaking a little as I threaded my fingers into his. I was scared to talk, scared to ask him if he was okay. Scared to break the moment. I'd let him take the lead.

We lay for a while, in silence – until he kissed me on the top of the head.

"Erin Brannigan," he said, "I cannot wait to marry you. I will love you every day of my life. I promise you this."

It was then that I cried again – and when he was sleeping I got up, crept to the sofa, opened my laptop and started writing my first article for *Northern People* – about the man who had taught me to love again.

17

Kitty

Rose was cleaning even though the kitchen didn't need to be cleaned. She was doing a great job of smiling brightly – perhaps too brightly – as she rubbed the same circular patch of worktop over and over again. I lost count at the thirtieth circular motion. Daddy was sipping from a mug of tea which had to be cold by then. He had been nursing it for half an hour and I had counted him ladling four spoonfuls of sugar into it when two was his usual limit. He had a fixed grimace on his face which occasionally morphed into a vaguely twisted smile when Rose looked in his direction. My daddy didn't still love my mother. He didn't feel anything much for her any more, bar some strange feelings tied in with the fact she was the mother of his children. I know he had taken time to trust again and even when he had met Rose and they had fallen in love and married, it had been a good while before he could feel secure that she wasn't going to suddenly announce she was bored, needed space and disappear leaving him on his own with little or no warning.

Even though a long time had passed, even though we had all moved on, to have my mother walk back into our lives, to walk into my shop as if things were just fine and dandy and announce she was getting married and she wanted to buy a wedding dress from me – well, that was always going to put the cat among the pigeons. And we knew, as we sat in uncomfortable silence in Rose's floral kitchen, that there was one pigeon in particular who was due to arrive at any minute and whose feathers were completely ruffled.

Rose had called her. After I had a small session of hyperventilation in the shop wondering how on earth I would break this news to Ivy, Rose had said there was no point in working myself into a state about how I was going to tell my sister and sure wouldn't it be better just to get it over and done with so that I wouldn't make myself sick with the worry of it.

"You've had enough to be worrying about these days. Ivy is a big girl. She's a grown-up. How bad could it be?"

Rose generally knew what she was talking about. She generally didn't get things wrong but on this occasion she was spectacularly wrong. Ivy swore, slammed the phone down, and we went home where we waited for her to arrive. With Rose's over-exuberant cleaning of the worktops and Dad's sipping of his cold tea, I felt as if we were on the edge of an Ivy-shaped earthquake.

The door opened with a thud and Ivy, her cheeks flushed, walked into the kitchen. She looked at all three of us and said, loudly and not so calmly: "What. The. Feck?"

"Language," Rose said absently, without thinking.

"English," Ivy said petulantly.

"Watch how you speak to Rose," Daddy said.

If I had closed my eyes I would have been back in my teenage years and this would have been a typical evening in our house.

"I can't believe she's back," Ivy said. "And she's getting married. And we're supposed to be happy about it? Or *you're* supposed to be happy about it? Because I wasn't even important enough to be told in person."

"It's not like that," I started, wanting to tell her that Mum had wanted in some ways to protect her feelings (not caring too much about mine, it seemed).

But she wasn't for listening.

"No, it's not like that, is it?" Ivy asked. "I don't own a bridal shop. I can't offer a discount on a meringue of her choosing!"

"Ivy!" Daddy said as I felt her words hit me square in the face.

"It's not like that," I said again, trying to find the words which would say exactly how I felt. Words that would make it sound like I was neither covering for my mother nor sticking up for her. I felt a knot in my stomach. I didn't know what to say, or how to react. It was like this every time Violet reared her ugly head. I would feel torn between the fact she was my mother and despite my best judgement there would always be a bond between us that I couldn't deny, and the fact that she was perhaps the most selfish person in the entire universe and I actually disliked her greatly.

Ivy sat down – well, to be more precise, she threw herself down on a chair – and snarled in our direction: "Well, if she thinks I'm having anything to do with her and with this wedding, she is sorely mistaken."

"I think she wants to make amends," Rose said, trying to keep her voice bright and measured.

"She can want what she wants, but she sure as heck isn't going to get it," said Ivy. "Not from me. She can't just sail back in and expect to play happy families – not after what she has done."

"It was a long time ago," Daddy said.

"No," Ivy said, matter of factly. "It wasn't. That first thing – that big old leave-your-family-and-clear-off thing – *that* was a long time ago. I could get over that." Her voice was firm and quieter. "But not everything since. The lies. The disappointment. The not going to weddings. The excuses. The not caring. The refusing to acknowledge us beyond the odd card or reluctant phone call. The not wanting to be a part of our lives. The way everything she has ever done in relation to us has always, and every time, been on her say-so, when it suits her, never mind when it suits us, or we need her."

"I haven't needed my mother for a long time," I offered and I saw Daddy flinch a little and Rose rub the worktop a little harder. I'd thought what I was saying would make them happy. I'd thought I was getting it right. I felt a migraine building and I couldn't see how spending any more time in that kitchen, where everyone was glaring at someone who wasn't even there and who was off planning her wedding and wondering just what kind of a discount I would give her on a designer dress, was going to resolve anything.

"I need to go home," I said, standing up. "In case you aren't aware, I have enough shit going on in my life right now without sitting here and rehearsing the whole 'mother is a bad person' argument again and I just can't face it at this very moment, so if you'll excuse me . . ."

"Kitty," Rose started, "look, stay. Don't leave like this."

"Let her leave," Ivy barked, crossing her arms firmly in front of her chest.

Daddy didn't speak.

"I'm not leaving 'like this'," I said, in his general direction. "I'm just leaving because I don't want to think about it any more and my head hurts."

"I'll get Cara to call over to you," Rose said.

"I don't need Cara. I don't need anyone," I said, as softly as I could. "I just need a couple of paracetamol, a dark room and some oblivion for a while."

"Just run off then," Ivy said.

I couldn't help but bite back with a "Grow up, Ivy!"

Rose sighed and Daddy looked at the floor and my headache threatened to make the small vein in my temple actually erupt.

I got into my car, swore as I crunched the gears and put the car in reverse and pulled out of driveway, only narrowly missing ramming right into the car parked opposite. Clutching the steering wheel while trying not to think too much about just how close I had been to a mighty big insurance claim, I took a deep breath and realised how my mother had done what she always did best – yet again. She dropped bombs into our lives and waltzed off – on this occasion to plan a wedding which she somehow expected us to happily be a part of. I needed a lie-down, and quickly, and I needed to keep it all together until I could get that lie-down because things were tough enough without a car crash adding to my woes.

I surprised myself by making it home in one piece, in spite of another near-miss at the newly installed traffic lights on the roundabout. I was never so glad to see my own front door and to open it to that lovely familiar scent of home and the sound of silence. Kicking my shoes off I walked up the hall and into the kitchen where I poured myself a tall glass of water and rifled in the corner cupboard of my shiny white kitchen for a packet of paracetamol. Holding the cool glass to my forehead I took several deep breaths before taking the two tablets and assuring myself I had every right, if I so wished, to take to my bed and not get out of there until the following morning at the very earliest.

And that is what I should have done. I should have ignored the blinking of my answer machine, knowing that nothing good could come of it. I should have known, given how things had gone up to that point, that it was one of those days which would have been better to write off as a non-starter. The thumping in my head should have been one of those kinds of karmic warning-signs that I should go to bed, directly to bed, and not interact with another human being until the fug of the day and its ill winds had passed. But I was nosy. It was unheard of for me to leave an email or text unread, a call unanswered or a message unlistened to. As it happened, there were two messages. The first was from James which sort of warned me about the second message. Which was from Mark.

He could have phoned the shop. He would have got me there, until five anyway. But he didn't do that. He didn't do it because that would have been the one way he would have had to say what he had to say to my face. He could have texted me, even, but again the response time would have been fairly immediate as Mark knew my phone was an integral part of my being. No, true to form, Mark left a message where he knew I wouldn't get it immediately, where I couldn't confront him immediately, where he wouldn't have to take my raw anger and hurt without giving me time to digest all that he said.

It was his way. Any time we had any kind of disagreement he would do something similar, leave a message or a note and disappear off the scene for an hour or two to allow me to process where he was coming from. He knew I was a soft touch, a romantic at heart. He knew I didn't like to argue – that I didn't like tension. It was in a strange way kind of comforting that he returned to that same form, leaving the message on our machine. Our old habits hadn't been completely annihilated. But it was strange – and uncomfortable – to hear his voice. The cheeriness was gone – that "I'm out on my own in a bar without the missus" joviality which I got from him that time he had answered the phone not knowing it was me on the other end. He sounded, well, kind of lost and my heart thumped. Every part of me – every part of me that loved him – every part of me that had felt he was the most important person in my life for the best part of the last decade – the part of me which knew our secrets, those things that were just ours and no one else's, just wanted to reach through the phone and pull him close to me. Without hearing the words he was speaking, the tone of his voice – the neediness from him – just made me want to let him know it was all okay. It would be okay. I thought of him – the him I knew and loved – the man who showed me his vulnerability – his loss and his weakness – and I wanted to bolster him up. I wanted to do all those things I had promised for him on our wedding day and in the years since. I felt my head throb, along with my heart, as my mind raced so loudly there was no way I could take in what he was saying. Beyond that one word – the one word which I needed to hear – I could not have told you a single word uttered from his mouth. "Sorry," he started and a part of me started,

139

rightly or wrongly, and probably very wrongly, to consider letting him back into my life again without even knowing if he wanted back in. He had the upper hand – I realised – and that scared me.

My head was now spinning as well as throbbing and my breathing was rushed. I wished Cara was with me. Or Rose. Or even Ivy, though I hated her at that very moment. I just wanted someone there to hold me up because without them I felt myself sliding to the floor and looking at the phone accusingly as if it had just opened some big Pandora's Box of emotions I couldn't deal with. Not on the day the woman who claimed to be my mother had shown up at my shop looking for a dress fitting, and not after I had spent a week in a stinking festering depressive coma in my father's house.

My mind tried to piece it together. I thought of the message James had left me. He had been almost apologetic that he was calling me. It was strange, I supposed, given that he was Mark's best friend and the pair of them had been thick as thieves since the age of twelve, but I didn't question it too much.

"I promised if I heard anything I would call you," he said. "Well, I did hear something. He's back. He called me earlier and he said he would be calling you too. I told him he was an arsehole. Just so you know. That he didn't deserve you . . ." His voice had trailed off briefly at that point. I could almost hear the cogs in his mind turning. "He doesn't deserve you, you know," he said and then he had hung up and I had looked at the message indicator on the machine – the blinking light which let me know there was a second message.

Sitting on the floor, listening again, I smiled at James' voice – at his concern. But I bristled at him calling Mark an arsehole even though the world and his mother could tell you that – Mark had indeed been a major arsehole. I pressed the button to listen to Mark's message again – determined that this time I would actually listen to what he had to say. I would try and adopt my sensible head – and leave the reaction of my heart aside. I would force myself to listen to it rationally – to not think about how we had met, how we shared that first kiss on a moonlit beach in front of a fire he had built without the help of a lighter or a box of matches. I would not think about how he cried when he saw me walk towards him on our wedding day or how his smile would cause the corners of his eyes to crinkle. I wouldn't think about the fact that even though he was eleven years older than he had been on the day I had met him, he looked as young and as handsome to me as he ever had done. More than that, though, to listen to him without my heart breaking entirely, I wouldn't think about the fact he had left me, that he had walked away and that there had been someone else. I would just think about the man – the voice on the other end of the phone – and see if my gut told me what way to think and more importantly what way to feel.

"Sorry," he started. "I'm so sorry. I messed it all up, Kitty. I don't really know why or even really how. I didn't really think about it – I was caught up in it. But I'm sorry. I realise I've no right to ask you or expect you to talk to me and I understand, really I do, if you don't want to just now – but I want to talk to you. To tell you face to face that I messed things up and I'm sorry that I did. It's true what they say, that you don't know what you've got till it's gone. I'm on the same mobile and I'm staying with Mum and Dad. You can get me there. I won't torture you. I won't keep asking. But please, just give me a chance to explain."

He didn't mention the other woman. He didn't explain anything really but listening for a second time, the urge to call him, to ask him to come over was strong. Almost too strong. I thought of Ivy cutting his clothes up. I thought of Cara telling me that I didn't deserve to be treated that way. I thought of James telling me he was an arsehole. I thought of my daddy holding me while I cried and of Rose's pursed lips whenever I mentioned Mark's name.

I couldn't cope with this. I didn't want to think about it. I didn't want to be weak, but I didn't want to let him go. And my head still hurt, which made me cry. So I left my mobile on the kitchen table, unplugged the phone and scrambled up to the bedroom where I hauled the curtains closed – thick, cosy black-out curtains we had bought at Mark's insistence because he needed it to be like a coalhole to get a good sleep. I lay there in the pitch dark in the early evening and cried myself to sleep, thinking that just a few weeks before, my life had all been going along in a perfectly lovely and controlled way and now I was curled in a bed crying and not knowing what the hell I was going to do about the mess my life had become.

18

Erin

I had a silly smile on my face the following day when I went to work. I couldn't help it. It had been a while. And I felt deliciously satisfied. I had had sex. If it had not been a very personal thing indeed, I would have shouted it from the rooftop of the *Northern People* building. That would probably not be terribly professional, so I settled for sending Jules a quick text with just two words in it: **Mission accomplished**. Then I sent Paddy a text to tell him I loved him. I may have written something vaguely flirty and innuendo-laden as well but it wasn't over the top. It felt a little strange, to even talk about it. Sex had been such a taboo since the operation that it felt strange to think that it was back on the agenda.

I switched on my computer, poured myself a cup of black coffee and opened the email I had sent the previous night, recounting how Paddy and I had met and fallen in love. It was a nice piece – it was honest but, I hoped, not overly soppy. I didn't want the readers to think they were buying into a full-on boke fest.

I'd show it to Grace just as soon as she got in and hope that she liked it. And then she would show it to Sinéad, who hopefully would also like it and then we could look at sending it to print. I'll admit I was nervous. There was something very different about writing your own story from writing about other people's lives. I didn't want to over-egg the melodrama with this. I didn't want to make our story nothing more than a source of entertainment to our readers. But then, we did have quite a remarkable story to tell. And I suppose it looked as if we were finally coming out the other end.

Everything felt a little brighter that day. I had a message on my work answer-phone from Rose at The Dressing Room confirming my appointment that weekend for Jules to look at bridesmaid dresses. Fiona, the super-organised and mildly terrifying wedding planner from the hotel had sent both Paddy and me a detailed email outlining our requirements and how they would be met which, rather than making me want to vomit with nerves, as emails from Fiona normally did, made me feel as if everything was moving on just as it should. I even decided that I would make sure to talk, that very day, with the band and the DJ we had booked for the reception after Fiona had taken weak at the mention of their names and said their language could sometimes be "colourful".

"I don't think 'Smack My Bitch Up' is appropriate wedding music," she said with as much tact as she could muster, which was not a lot.

I had made a mental note on that occasion to smack my sister up, she being the one who had recommended the band and told us, in fact, that no other band in the entire world would be as cool for our wedding. Jules had sworn she hadn't known that certain less-than-desirable songs were on their set list and then had paused and laughed and pondered whether or not she had actually known but had been too drunk the last time she had seen them to really take it on board. The whole thing had made Paddy laugh uproariously and had made me drop my head to my hands and wonder if the whole Big Day was doomed. That morning, however, as I sipped my coffee, edited my story once more and planned my day – all these little pre-wedding wobbles seemed surmountable. The band would be told, simply and firmly, that they would not be swearing at any stage during the festivities.

"The pictures are lovely," Grace said, smiling as she walked past my desk. "You scrub up well."

"Are you trying to say I'm not a stunner every day, boss?" I laughed – aware that my hair was particularly frizzy and my face particularly pale. Although there was still a while to go until the wedding, Jules had persuaded me to go make-up free as much as possible to try and give my skin a rest. As I had no plans to leave the office that day I thought it was safe to go bare. I hadn't factored in the harsh lights making me look a little more like Ronald McDonald than a pale and interesting Irish beauty.

"Well, of course you're a stunner," Grace said with a wink. "But in the pictures you are extra stunning!"

I smiled and then because I was in a just-got-laid kind of a giddy mood I pulled the ugliest face I possibly could just as Liam, the grumpy photographer who had taken our pictures the day before, walked past and muttered, "Sweet Baby Jesus," under his breath before adding: "I'm glad I'm not taking your wedding photos."

Grace laughed and I laughed and it felt like one of those lovely days where you can see the bad in no one and where you think that just maybe there is hope for the human race after all. I guess I had really, really needed to have sex the night before and, having made that lovely leap, everything seemed a little brighter.

"Have you the first article done?" Grace asked, heading towards her office.

"Just emailing it to you now, boss," I smiled and watched as she retreated into her domain. I saluted in her general direction and went back about my business, while hearing Liam mutter again – this time about being a lick-arse.

"You'd just love me to lick your arse!" I called, in a

completely inappropriate move clearly buoyed by my reawakened sexuality.

We both blushed, which at least took the pallor from my face.

I was trying to recover from that, sip my coffee and get through to the dodgy wedding band who clearly didn't do phone-answering in the morning, when a message popped up in my email from Grace, asking me to drop into her office when I had five or ten minutes. She'd had enough time to read the article and I imagined she was going to give me feedback and suddenly I felt a little nervous. Again, this was different from my usual pieces. This was my life. If she hated it, she wouldn't just be judging my writing, she would be judging me too.

Nervously I lifted my notebook and pen and walked into her office, perching myself opposite her and trying to read her face for any hint of reaction.

"I like it," she said slowly, sitting back, looking at her computer screen and then looking back at me again. I could hear the 'but' forming in her head and I wasn't wrong.

"I like it, but . . ." she said, looking at me. "I feel you've held back in this piece, Erin."

Held back? I'd described the discovery of a tumour in the man-I-love's testicle – for anyone to read about.

My eyebrow must have risen to a whole new level because Grace looked at me and sighed. "Don't get annoyed. Listen to me."

I nodded. I would not get annoyed – not on a day which had been going so well – and I would listen to her. That was not to say I would agree with her, but I would definitely listen.

"The piece is well written. It's even funny in places," she said. "The strength of your feelings for Paddy really comes through, as does your trepidation about the wedding, your fears about the future and how you are coping together with what you are going through."

"Yes, I thought so too," I said, wondering where exactly in any of that I had held anything back. Jesus, I'd even written a section about my concerns about over-underwear-buying when going to try on big frocks. I'd had a whole big-knickers-will-hide-my-tummy-but-make-me-look-like-a-ninety-year-old internal dialogue as I dressed that morning – deciding in the end to stop off at M&S for some new sensible midi-briefs before the fitting.

"I know . . . but the thing is this. The intro, it intrigued me. You know the bit where you say you were one of the cynical people who had given up on love? Like a heroine in a chick-lit novel who had been hurt before and had built up huge walls around her heart?"

I cringed. It sounded cheesier when read back. "Yeah, I'm sorry about that. I was in a bit of a romantic mood when I wrote that."

"Don't apologise. I'm a romantic at heart myself. Just because Aidan and I have been married for ever doesn't mean I don't still remember those first few months and years of falling in love –"

"But?" I pre-empted.

"Well, I know this is a magazine article. But I'd love to know more, you know. I'd love to know about why you lost your faith in love. Why it was so important that Paddy brought down those walls."

I swear to God, I thought I could almost see a tear form in her eye – but it wasn't as big as the lump that was forming in my throat at the very thought of revisiting the whole Ian/abandoned wedding/great depression of 1999 scenario.

"I'd like to know more," she repeated, shrugging her shoulders.

"As my friend or my editor or as a very nosy person?"

"A combination of all three. This piece is good, but it could be better. There is more to tell and our readers would like to know. Hell, I'd like to know. I've worked with you for four years now. I've driven to Dublin with you – that's three and a half hours in the car, five if you take my driving into consideration. I've been drunk with you. I've handed you a tissue to mop your tears after Paddy's diagnosis and handed you tampons over the cubicle door. I consider us fairly close, and yet I've never even had an inkling there was a life before Paddy – not a romantic one anyway. I'd like to know more."

I looked at her. She had a strange, animated expression on her face – a mixture of intrigue and annoyance. I wasn't sure if she wanted me to spill my guts right there and then.

"There's not a lot to tell."

"Except that you were once hurt so badly you built up a big wall around your heart that only Paddy could ever knock down?"

Jesus, she was getting soft in her old age and she was obsessed with walls and knocking them down.

Thinking on it, Grace had always been on the soft side. She was definitely good cop to Sinéad's bad cop. But still, it surprised me to see her go so gooey.

"It was a long time ago. I was twenty-two. His name was Ian. We ran away to Gretna to get married, which is much less exciting than it sounds. He left me at the altar and I haven't heard from him since."

"Left you at the altar? Jesus – how?"

"Well . . . basically . . . he left me at the altar. I imagined he walked away. He may have got a taxi. I don't know."

"You are being facetious."

"You are invading my personal emotional space," I said, and instantly cringed because that was truly the most wanky sentence I had ever uttered in my entire life.

"If you ask me, you have unresolved issues."

Grace was all about the unresolved issues. She had undergone counselling a few years back after the birth of her first child and now she believed wholeheartedly in the power of counselling, dealing with your past and if necessary telling the whole world about it. Because as much as she was my friend, she was also a damn fine journalist with a killer instinct for a story. If the truth be told, if the shoe was on the other foot or the pen in the other hand, I would be asking an interviewee the same awkward questions and wee-ing myself with excitement if I was able to break beneath the surface and reveal a little bit of juicy back story. Much as Ian was my personal emotional space, he was also my juicy back story.

"I don't know," I said. "It was a long time ago and I'm over it and surely revealing the deep secrets of our battle with cancer is good enough? I mean, I know how to write a tear-jerker. And I've cried writing this. I think it's good."

Grace looked at me sympathetically, but not sympathetically enough that I still couldn't see the story-mad twinkle in her eye.

"It is good," she said. "It's one of the strongest things you have written. But it could be even better. We expect a lot of you now, Erin. The readers expect a lot of you. You're the Feature Writer of the Year. This could solidify that position. This could get you noticed."

She wasn't going to let up. When Grace got a notion stuck in her head, she was like a dog with a bone.

"I'm going to have to think about it," I said. "And I'm going to have to talk to Paddy. This involves him too. But seriously, Grace, I don't really think about Ian any more. I don't necessarily want everyone to know I was left at the altar or that I made a complete eejit of myself in my early twenties. I don't class anything about the entire Ian situation as positive."

"Just think about it. That's all I ask," Grace said.

I nodded before standing up, walking back to my desk and sitting back down, feeling slightly less of a shiny happy person than I had been before.

Paddy looked tired when I got home – and told me he hadn't done too much that day.

"You tired me out yesterday," he said with a smile as I kissed his forehead.

Seeing him looking a little pathetic – tired and weak – I felt a wave of guilt wash over me. Had the photo shoot and the evening out taken too much out of him? Had I pushed him too much the previous night?

I sat down beside him and took his hand.

"What's wrong?" he asked.

"How do you know anything is wrong?" I asked, turning to look at him.

"I'm not stupid, my lovely lady," he said with a smile. "You didn't call me this afternoon. You walked in here like the Mother of Sorrows and before you sat down you went straight to the fridge and opened a bottle of beer. And, to top it all off, you have sat down beside me and not immediately told me to turn *Deal or No Deal* off and I know you reserve a special kind of hatred for Noel Edmunds – so something is obviously wrong."

I looked at him again, tired, with a blanket over his knees and looking pale, and I felt a lump form in my throat. And I didn't want in that moment to talk to him about Ian and whether we should tell the world, or talk about the article and work.

I cuddled into him, fighting back my emotions and simply whispered. "I can't wait to marry you, Paddy. I love you with all my heart."

He kissed my head and we sat there for a while and I watched the entire episode of *Deal or No Deal* without saying a single word or calling Noel Edmunds a pain in the hole.

Every couple has the talk. Everyone has that "Well, tell me all about your past" chat – and we were no exception. We had been together around two months and it was about five in the morning. We had been up all night, chatting, laughing, drinking wine and getting completely lost in each other. We had talked about everything from favourite films to our first memories of school. We had told each other about our families. I had told him about Jules – and how we were best friends as well as sisters but how we used to murder each other when we were teenagers. He had told me how his mother could be a bit stuffy, but that she was a lovely woman at heart (not that he was a mammy's boy, he stressed). He had told me about a three-year relationship he'd had with a woman called Caroline which had ended fairly painlessly after they just drifted apart. He had told me how he loved her once – genuinely – but that it was just one of those relationships that was never going to work long-term because ultimately they wanted different things. That was when I told him about Ian and about how, ultimately, we wanted different things as well (me wanting to be married to him, him wanting to be a million miles away from me).

Of course I had been full of bravado when I told him – hindsight being wonderful and me having realised we would never have worked anyway. But at that stage – when we were in the process of falling in love with each other – I didn't dare tell him how I fell apart. How I almost became a modern Miss Havisham. How I wore my inexpensive cotton dress for four solid days and how the flowers wilted in my hair as I lay in my hotel room and tried to make sense of what had happened. How I cried all the way home on the plane like a big eejit, still with my flowers in my hair which by that stage was greased off me. I drank three small bottles of wine on the forty-five-minute flight, and given that I hadn't eaten for four days I got off the plane at Belfast pissed as a fart and ran into my mother's arms sobbing while she tried to tell me it was okay. She didn't tell me until a week later – when I was coherent again and not quite so suicidal – that she had been apoplectic with rage and disappointment that I had run off and not told her about my plans. She decided then to tell me how she had never liked Ian anyway – and even though at that stage I didn't like him much myself I still told her to frig off. I will never forget the shame of it. I had never sworn at my mother before and have not sworn at her since and yet that day in our living room I told her in as strong a voice as I could muster to frig off. In fact, I believe what I may actually have said was "Frig away off". Even now I could still see the expression on her face if I thought about it.

So no, none of that was something that I wanted to share with Paddy, especially not a few months into a relationship when I wasn't quite sure where we were headed.

I saved those revelations until after proposal number two, when I decided to tell him how I was allergic to weddings. I told him how I had always detested the idea of a big wedding but how Ian had convinced me there was something wild and very romantic about eloping to Gretna Green. We were just out of college – feeling like we were standing on the edge of our futures. It was a strange time – there was so much we wanted to do and that we felt we could do. But I suppose I was a little scared of all the change. I had come into my own at university – it had been a time free of any real responsibility besides making it to lectures and getting my assignments in on time. The rest of the responsibilities centred around making it to the Union bar on time and spending time with Ian. We had become inseparable and obsessed with each other in the way you can only when you are nineteen and think you know everything. So, when he slipped the ring-pull off a can of Harp on my little finger (it wouldn't fit on my ring finger) and said, on graduation night, that we should do something wild, I agreed.

And I found myself, scared of changing and scared of staying the same, buying a cotton dress in M&S and sneaking away to get married without telling a soul.

19

Kitty

The part of me that wanted to phone Mark was overrun by the part of me that hated him and wanted to make him feel even a tenth of what I was feeling. I came to that conclusion at around 3.45 a.m. when I couldn't sleep and had wandered out to the garden to sit on the decking. It was a cool night and I wrapped my dressing-gown tight around me.

Just a few weeks before, Mark and I had sat out here until the wee small hours, drinking and talking. We'd had The Baby Conversation (which we always referred to in a deep, serious voice before laughing at each other).

We would consider it in the following year, we decided. But I'd start taking folic acid there and then, just in case. If we decided to leave the condoms in the drawer now and again that would be okay. We felt, we decided, secure enough to take the next step in our relationship.

My business was well established and had survived the worst of the recession so far. I'd brought in a few less exclusive lines which met pinched budgets, but I still gave every bride the star treatment. Mark had said work was going well – he was pretty sure he would survive any cull which might or might not come. I didn't realise as he talked that I was the one who was going to be a victim of a cull in the very near future.

Having kids had been one of those things we'd just kept putting off. Whenever we had The Baby Conversation we would both inevitably say we didn't feel ready just yet. I didn't feel old enough. I enjoyed my life. I suppose I kept waiting for that one morning when I would wake up and just know it was the right time. That time hadn't come – but I was starting to become increasingly aware that I wasn't getting any younger. The day I found a stray grey eyebrow-hair was the day I finally freaked out and the day we had the big conversation. It was hard to think it was just a few weeks ago.

I had called Mark at work and, because he is a man, he didn't seem to get why one stray eyebrow-hair would have turned me into a screaming harpy, but there I was, my normally cool and calm exterior all but gone, telling him that we absolutely and completely had to talk that evening.

I had stormed about that day in very bad form, if I remember correctly. Rose had bought me an emergency Flake and a hot chocolate from Starbucks and I had glared at them. A stray grey hair was one thing. Middle-aged spread was another step further.

"I think I want a baby," I had said to Rose, as calmly as I would have said 'I think I'll have a tuna sandwich for lunch'.

She didn't miss a beat but carried on working at the sewing machine, just glancing up. "That's nice," she said. "A baby would be nice."

"How do you know you're ready though?" I asked, thinking of the grey eyebrow-hair and the wrinkles which were starting to appear around my eyes. When I looked at myself in the mirror these days I was often shocked to see a proper grown-up staring back.

"Oh, I don't know, darling," she said. "I only knew I was ready when your daddy asked me to marry him and I knew I was inheriting you and Ivy. And you were mostly reared. It's a different set of circumstances. I've never had one of my own – never really felt the need. Do you feel the need?"

"I don't know. Maybe. Maybe I'm just afraid that if I don't I'll miss out on something?"

"Have you and Mark talked about it?"

I nodded and told her about The Baby Conversation – how we had it first time after we were married and seemed to have it every six months or so – always granting a stay of execution to the stock of condoms in the drawer beside our bed. There was always a reason. The business was taking off. We had a holiday planned. We wanted to buy a bigger house. We were too tired. We had stuff we wanted to do. It was just so heart-stoppingly scary.

"But we can't keep putting it off forever," I mused.

"But don't just do it because you think it is something you should be doing. That's no reason to become a parent. I love you and your sister very much and I'm glad I had my parenting experience with the pair of you – but it wasn't just something else I ticked off a list. When I first met your daddy, I had to think long and hard about whether or not I wanted to take on two teenagers who, from what he told me, were prone to teenage tantrums."

I grimaced and stuck my tongue out at her, remembering the first time we had met and how I had refused to acknowledge her presence in any way.

"But you are glad you did, though, aren't you?"

She smiled. "Of course I am – but there was a time when I wondered if I was wise . . . Look, pet, all I'm saying is, being a parent changes your life forever. So be sure your life is ready for a change – both you and Mark."

"You're right," I had said and that was how the conversation followed that evening.

I had felt calmer when I got home. I had stopped and bought our favourite bottle of wine and cooked steak and garlic potatoes for tea, which we ate on the decking in not too uncomfortable silence. Mark hadn't asked how I was when he walked through the door. I think perhaps he was afraid to, considering the fact I had screamed at him down the phone earlier and ominously demanded a talk. He had simply commented on the delicious cooking smells and thanked me for the wine while offering to pour me a glass. I nodded and smiled and for some reason I hadn't launched right into the big talk either.

In fact we had talked about home improvements and a holiday (Italy, we decided) first before the silence kicked in properly and we looked at each other, each waiting for the other to start.

"I'm not getting any younger," I started.

"None of us are," he said, sipping from his glass and topping mine up.

"But remember that scene in *When Harry Met Sally*, when Sally tells Harry how Charlie Chaplin had babies in his seventies or something? It's different for men."

"I don't want to be changing nappies when I'm in my seventies," Mark had smiled.

"Do you have any feelings about doing it in your thirties?" I asked.

He paused, a small smile creeping across his face as he looked at me: "I think I would like that."

So we had talked on – and planned that once we got the Italy trip over and done with – which we were dubbing our final fling – we would start on the baby-making proper.

We never even booked the holiday. And we sure as hell didn't get as far as the baby-making.

Sitting on the decking now, in the very early morning, listening to the very rare car pass by and watching the first streaks of light start to rise in the sky, I wondered was that what broke us?

When he had smiled as we talked about having a baby was he really thinking about his other woman? Was he already planning his escape route? Did he really forget those holiday brochures in work, or had he never really picked them up to begin with because he knew he would be leaving. When he was quiet – those few times I had noticed him staring into space and reckoned he was probably thinking of something very mundane like how Jeremy Clarkson is a twat – was he thinking of her? Was he thinking of leaving me? Was he wondering what clothes he would take with him? What he would write in his note? Where he would go and who he would go with?

I wanted to know the answers, but at the same time I didn't want to know. And that sympathy I felt when I had listened to his phone message – that sympathy which had made me want to run straight to him and tell him I loved him and no matter what we would be okay – well, that sympathy just disappeared into the shadows.

When the sun rose, and I woke on the sofa in the living room looking out at the garden, things seemed a little clearer. I picked up the phone and first of all called Rose to tell her I would be a little late. I lied, which made me feel guilty, saying I was still feeling the after-effects of my migraine and needed a little space to myself and she didn't question it.

"Of course, pet," she said. "You know, you shouldn't take it all to heart. Your mother can be insensitive at times. And Ivy always was one to fly off the handle."

I hung up, feeling guilty that in the hours since Mark's message had registered on my family-crisis radar – I hadn't given a flying fig or even thought about my mother or Ivy.

Then I took a deep breath and lifted the phone again and dialled another number, impatiently waiting for the man on the other end to answer. His voice sounded sleepy, but not so sleepy that he didn't immediately wake up on hearing my voice.

"I was hoping you'd call," he said.

"I'm sorry I didn't call last night. My head was turned. I just didn't know what to think."

"You've called now," he said pausing, waiting for me to make the next move.

"Can we meet up?"

"Of course we can. Starbucks in an hour?"

"Please," I said, hanging up and feeling myself shake. I'd grab something to eat. That would bring me round. Then I would go and have a shower.

And then I would go and meet my husband's best friend and ask him what the hell I should do about the husband who wanted to 'explain'.

James got it, I suppose. He knew what it was like to feel abandoned. Not that he had been in love with Mark. Not even slightly. But he had been his friend and he had been left without proper explanation too and he was just as confused about the whole situation as I was – albeit in a more dignified manner.

I'm pretty sure he had never lay about the floor sobbing to sad songs and that he didn't look at old photos of them together and wonder where it all went wrong.

Then again, things would be different for James and Mark, wouldn't they? I was pretty sure, now that Mark was back, that he and James would pick up exactly where they had left off, maybe after a cross word or two. James would probably call Mark the "c" word (you know, the bad one) and Mark would offer to buy him a pint and they would be back to their usual selves by last orders.

But even though that thought made me feel quite jealous, and if the truth be told a wee bit sick at times, at that precise moment James was the only person who could truly empathise with what I was going through.

I showered and dressed, grabbed my bag and keys and left.

James was sitting at the back of the coffee shop, stirring his coffee with one of those little wooden sticks they give you. A second coffee, which I assumed was mine, sat opposite him. I sighed. I wouldn't have the heart to tell him that coffee was not my thing and really I only ever went to Starbucks for the chocolate coin.

He looked nervous. It was a warm morning but he was wearing a jumper and a heavy jacket and was hunched over the table. He looked tired as I watched him sit back and sip from his drink. Sitting down opposite him I noted the look in his eyes and realised I must be looking equally tired and nervous.

"So has he been in touch then?" he said, pushing the second coffee towards me.

He looked so nervous I decided to fake it and drink the coffee like it was my favourite thing ever – taking a short sip and putting it back down, lifting my own little wooden stick and stirring it.

"I've not spoken with him, but he left a message."

"And you didn't call him back?" James sounded surprised.

"I didn't – don't – know what to say to him. I don't know what I want to do at all. I don't know whether to kill him or just beg him to come home."

James shrugged his shoulders.

"Have you seen him?" I asked, thinking of the pint-and-bad-word-and-best-friends-by-closing scenario.

"No. I did speak to him though. He is sorry."

"Sorry mightn't be enough – not for me." I felt the tears spring to my eyes and I was mortified. Glancing down I almost jumped out of my skin when I felt James' hand on mine. Was it wrong to feel it comforting? Was it wrong for it to send a shiver of . . . something . . . through me? It could be that it was just the warmth and weight of his hand – a man's hand – on mine, but I felt myself inhale sharply and look back at him.

"I can't imagine what you are going through," he said. "To trust someone, to be in love with someone . . ."

I allowed his words to wash over me – to soothe me. It wasn't as if he was doing a Cara and telling me that Mark was a shithead. He wasn't doing an Ivy and telling me I had to pull myself together. He wasn't doing a Daddy and looking personally wounded and haunted – as if all this was bringing back horrible memories for him. He wasn't doing a Rose and telling me that if you love someone you should let them go, or that everything happens for a reason or that God never closes a door without opening a window. He was just holding my hand and sympathising and not trying to push me one way or another.

"I don't know what to do," I said.

"Go with your gut. Kitty, you know that I love Mark as a brother, but go with your gut. Don't let him hurt you again. Make sure you can trust him. You're worth more than that."

I looked at him again and back to my hand where I realised his hand still rested – and it still felt okay. I looked at him and saw the words forming in his mouth. A tiny voice in my head screamed '*Don't!*' but the bigger part of me – the part that liked the warmth of his hand on mine willed him to say it.

"If you were mine," he said, "I would never have hurt you like this. I wouldn't even look at another woman, never mind sleep with her. I'd never leave – never run away. I'd be proud to come home every night. I told Mark as much. I told him that he was a lucky bastard. I told him that before you were married, when the pre-wedding jitters kicked in. I told him you were amazing and I told him he was lucky to have you. Kitty, you know that, don't you?"

I looked at him, his eyes wide and sincere. As the words washed over me, as the compliments sank in, my heart sank with them.

When he told Mark.

When Mark had pre-wedding jitters.

When James had to tell him to marry me.

When Mark wasn't sure.

When he didn't talk to me.

When he didn't let me know how he was feeling.

Maybe it had all been a lie all along. I looked into James' eyes again – and I realised that nothing made sense any more except for that one moment with him, there, and his hand over mine and him telling me I was amazing. I didn't know what to believe about anything else in my life any more – but I knew I could believe that James thought I was amazing.

And nothing else mattered.

20

Erin

"Don't be a Dramatic Drawers," Paddy teased as I hit print and closed down my laptop.

"Why not?" I huffed, pulling my hair back from my face and sighing.

"Because it's not that big of a deal."

"So walking in, sitting this article on Grace's desk and declaring: 'Here's your pound of flesh,' would be OTT then?"

He laughed, ruffled my hair and said that yes, it probably would be a bit of an overreaction. Paddy hadn't been a bit bothered if I told the story of Ian and my missed marriage. He had laughed it off as no big deal.

Seeing him react in such a light-hearted way made me wonder if I was completely mental – that the fact dredging up memories made me uneasy meant that I was faulty in some way.

"It's the past," he said simply. "We are all about the future. So what if they want the story of the wedding that never was?"

"But, well, it's embarrassing, isn't it?" I had said, thinking of our readership discovering how I was jilted at the altar – finding out I wasn't getting married via a message from a rather flustered registrar who couldn't quite look me in the eye.

"Depends on how you write it," he said, holding me close. "It could be the most humiliating moment of your life or it could be your luckiest escape. After all, if he hadn't dumped you, you would never have allowed yourself to fall madly in love with me and we wouldn't be getting married and spending all this lovely quality time together planning our own Big Day and our own future."

He was right, of course. But I felt like an extra layer of shame and privacy was being stripped away as I battered the keyboard on the laptop and wrote about Ian and how he broke my heart and made me vow never to trust anyone ever, ever, ever again.

In fact I had stood, on a Scottish heath, the wind tossing my Bosco-like hair and had vowed, in a dramatic style that would have made Scarlett O'Hara proud, never to fall in love again. What's more, in a Scottish pub I had sung 'I'll Never Fall in Love Again' – or at least my own unique version of it loudly after eight Peach Schnapps and pineapple juices – which I have never had the stomach for since, funnily enough. Peach-flavoured boke will do that to a girl.

Paddy could see right through me, so hair-ruffling done and printer churning out 1500 words on the wedding that never was in the opening throw at a series of articles on weddings, cancer and happy-ever-afters was his way of grounding me. He was good at that.

After the big diagnosis of cancer – after he had walked away in a bit of a mood (which I could hardly blame him for) – he had spent precisely thirty-six hours moping before crawling into bed beside me.

"Frig it," he said. "Sure I'm balding a wee bit anyway. The chemo will save me having to buy one of those hair-clipper sets for a while at least. And I've kind of regretted I've not lived a wilder life – so, you know, getting some quality hardcore drugs on the NHS could be pretty trippy. And it could be worse. I've not got the worst-case scenario. You know, it's not the best-case scenario either – but what's a bit of chemo among friends? And we have the wedding to look forward to."

"The wedding?" I asked, raising an eyebrow.

"Yes, the wedding. My darling, lovely Erin. I love you. I love you more than anything and I would be so happy if you would, finally, agree to marry me." His expression changed and he looked at me intently. "You see, I *need* to marry you."

In that moment, as we were together digesting what lay ahead, what had been and where we were just then, I knew I would agree to anything. And I wanted to make him happy – to make this better. I nodded my yes and he pulled me to him, kissing me softly.

"I'm not him. I won't hurt you," he whispered after a while.

"As long as you don't jilt me at the altar," I had whispered back, trying to keep my tone light.

"I solemnly promise I won't," he said.

"Then I'm a happy woman."

"As long as you don't mind marrying a bald man with one testicle."

"Even with half a pair you have more balls than Ian ever had."

"And I'm better in bed, obviously," he had said.

"Goes without saying."

"And you love me more?" he asked and that was the first time I had noticed any sort of hesitation in Paddy's voice.

"You never, ever need to ask me that question," I said, looking into his eyes in the dark of our bedroom.

"Don't I? It's one thing when we were having fun together – when it was all rosy in the garden and the *craic* was flying. When we didn't have to worry about surgery and fertility and our future and whether or not I'll be here in five to ten years."

I put my fingers to his lips, as much to try and stop my hands from shaking as anything. "The *craic* will still be flying. We will still have fun together. I mean, Jesus – wig-shopping will be a hoot. And as for your fertility – sure we have Paddy Popsicles in the big freezer in the hospital. And as for your being here in five or ten years – you will be. You said it yourself. This is not the worst news we could have received. This is shit news – but not the worst news. But anyway, as for being here – if you manage five minutes after we say our wedding vows sure you will have already beaten Ian the feckwit hands down. So everyone is a winner."

And though we both plastered smiles on our faces and kissed each other gently, we didn't quite feel like winners that night.

Grace looked up expectantly as I walked into her office. Sinéad was there and she spun around with that look in her eye that we knew all too well in the newsroom. When Sinéad was on the hunt for a good story – when she could smell that something could be that little bit different – she was like a woman possessed.

"Well?" she said, not giving either myself or Grace the chance to speak.

I handed her the printed article, adding that I had emailed copies of it to her and Grace just then but that I still had some reservations. Sinéad brushed those away with a simple hand gesture, as if she was brushing crumbs off her shoulder, and sat down, her back to me, and started reading.

Grace raised an eyebrow at me before shrugging her shoulders. "I know this has been tough," she offered, "but I have a feeling it will be worth it. We've just been talking and we were wondering, could we make this a real human-interest series? Would you have pictures of you and Ian? You know, back in the day, that you could share?"

Even though I'm usually quite an impulsive person by nature, I knew it would probably be a very bad idea to tell my bosses to frig off. I don't think, in that situation, I could even have got away with a 'feck off'. Instead I sat down, beside Sinéad and opposite Grace.

"Look, here is the deal. I've changed Ian's name and any identifying details in the piece. He is to be known from here on in as 'Tim'. Because of that I really don't think I can be plastering his picture in full gloss across our pages."

"We can Photoshop his face," Sinéad offered, glancing up over her glasses at me before going back to reading.

"What? And make him George Clooney or something?" I said, my voice dripping sarcasm.

"We could pixelate him?" Grace offered.

"I'd like to do more than pixelate him," I muttered before immediately getting annoyed with myself. The fact that I was thinking about Ian/Tim/George Clooney in such a way unsettled me. My rage towards him had dissipated years before – and now for some reason it was bubbling under the surface again. Which, of course, made me worry that I was feeling something for him again. And I didn't want to feel anything for him any more except maybe apathy.

"It's a great piece," Sinéad said, handing it over the desk to Grace. "And I don't care if we do put George Clooney's face on him – as long as we use it. It's great stuff – open and honest and from the heart and the perfect scene-setter for next month when we run the great love story, and that wonderful piece about your relationship and the cancer battle and then we can follow it up with the wedding. Loads of pictures – full glossy. It will be perfect."

Perfect was not the word which sprang to mind, but I resigned myself to the fact that this article would appear in print in precisely eight days and my disastrous relationship history would be there for everyone to see.

"Remember that time I almost married George Clooney, but he jilted me at the altar?"

"Yeh wha'?" Jules asked, and over the phone I could hear her choking on whatever it was she had been drinking.

"It's a long story, but let me tell you, this month's *Northern People* is going to be a real hoot."

"You do realise," she said, "that you are making very little sense at all right now. Are you feeling all right? Have you been drinking? Do you need a wee lie-down?"

"I've not been drinking – but I might need a wee lie-down," I said, brushing my hair back from my face with my free hand and sitting back in my chair. "Grace has persuaded me to tell the Great Ian Saga in the magazine."

"I thought you were doing the whole wedding/cancer/happy-ever-after story?" she asked, sounding as confused as I felt.

"I'm doing that as well, but we're doing a whole Erin's-life-in-shameful-memories thing first."

"And George Clooney comes into it where?"

"Photoshop," I offered, lifting a pencil, tapping it against the desk, but losing my grip on it. As I watched it fly across the room, I heard Jules sigh.

"I think I preferred it when you were simply freaking out about your wedding dress and the big party."

"I like to vary my routine from time to time," I smiled, having given up on trying to retrieve the pencil without appearing to any onlookers as if I was doing some strange and slightly frightening aerobic workout. "But if you must know, I may well do the dress-freaking-out thing again when we go to The Dressing Room later this week to choose a bridesmaid dress."

"No, no, you won't," Jules said. "Just hang on a minute there, Bridezilla – that will be *my* day to shine! After all, I will be the wearer of the dress on that occasion. There will be no freaking out allowed from you, Missy! I want my moment in the gorgeous-dress sun!"

"Well, if I'm not allowed to freak out then, surely I'm allowed a double-freak-out now?" I dropped my voice to an almost-whisper. "Jules, all this thinking about Ian. I never thought I would think of him again. Not this way – not dragging over everything that happened. I thought that was very soundly locked in my past and filed under Tough Lessons – but thinking about him now . . . I'm worried." I felt myself blush, almost afraid to speak in case voicing my feelings made them even more real. "It's dangerous to revisit the past. What if I find I'm not as over him as I thought I was?"

"Bullshit," she said. "You no more have affectionate feelings for Ian than I have feelings for Jimmy Carr. And you know how Jimmy Carr gives me the rage."

That was a fact. She could never watch the TV when he came on – she would start to hyperventilate with resentment.

"Why is it getting to me then?" I asked.

"Because you are human and it's only natural to look back at past relationships when you are about to make a big commitment."

"I'm sure about the commitment I'm making," I said loudly – perhaps too loudly – which in itself made me feel strange, because I was sure. I loved Paddy. I wanted to be with him.

"You can't Photoshop Ian out of your life, not really," Jules said. "So just acknowledge it was something that happened. Jesus. It was a lifetime ago. It was the late nineties for god's sake. Everyone did something a bit stupid in the late nineties."

"You were in your early teens," I chided. "What did you ever do that was stupid?"

"Oh, sister of mine," she said with a laugh, "if I ever told you I would have to kill you. I had my wild days."

I thought back to the geeky younger sister who had welcomed me back from university at holidays as if I was bringing the plague back in with me and I doubted she ever put a foot wrong. She never seemed to leave the house in those days – preferring to lose herself in internet chat-rooms and alternative music. Those were the days before she found her inner fashionista and party animal.

"Aye, right," I said.

"You better believe it. Look, sis, stop freaking. Let the article run. And then next month write the big 'I love you' about Paddy. Then get married – and then can we all just get on with our lives, cancer and other such matters permitting?"

She was right of course – it was time to acknowledge the past and move on to the future. Even if none of us were particularly sure what that future would hold.

"I know, I know," I agreed.

"Now," she said, "speaking of bridesmaid dresses, which are

infinitely more important than your crisis of the day – no pink, no peach, no frills, no flounces. No netting. No puffballs. No powder blue. No yellow – not with our hair colour. No shiny polyester. No bows. Definitely no bows. And none of that wrap/shawl shit – I would probably end up throttling myself on it. And while we are at it, the shoes must also be fabulous – but vaguely comfortable. Oh, and back to the dresses – whatever we get must be compatible with Spanx – the full-length down-to-your-knees, up-to-your-boobs ones."

"Is that all?" I asked.

She paused. "I think so."

"Grand then," I said, realising I was still at work and this conversation was stretching beyond the acceptable time-limit for a private call during office hours. "Look, I'd better go and start trying to find alternatives to the yellow-and-blue puffball with the bows on each shoulder that I had picked out for you then?"

"Ha! You're fecking hilarious, Erin. Hi-lar-ee-ous."

"I know. I do try."

"Look, sis," she said. "It will all work out. I love you."

"I love you too," I said and hung up.

Then I dialled home.

"Paddy," I started, "how do you feel about the fact that I once nearly married George Clooney?"

21

Kitty

I'm not sure there is an accurate way to describe how I felt when I arrived at the shop ready for work. My head was whirling – and not just from the after-effects of the migraine. It's a wonder I made it to the shop in one piece. There had been a few near-misses on the drive into town as my mind wandered from my mother's unexpected return, my mother's impending marriage, Mark's pleading phone calls and James' admission. Not that James had said much – not in that way where you know for certain what he was thinking. But it was clear. The touch of his hand left no room for debate. The look in his eyes left even less.

And my heart was thumping. I'm not sure if it was anxiety, worry, stress or lust. I'm not sure that it wasn't simply gratitude that someone had looked at me with genuine affection when I had seemed to have got everyone else's back up.

We had held hands for probably less than a minute after he stopped talking – a little bit too long for 'just friends' and I had been the first to move away. The moment, while nice and comforting in a way, was wrong and the warmth of his hand while initially welcome soon felt claustrophobic. This was just too much to deal with. Mark's jitters. Mum's wedding. James' warm hand.

I picked up the coffee cup which I had been fake-drinking for the last ten minutes and took it with me – sipping from it without thinking as I sat in the car, wishing it was something stronger. I didn't know whether to laugh or cry – so I did a bit of both before fixing my make-up in the car mirror, tossing the coffee cup in the nearest bin and heading into work where I vowed I would keep a very tight lid on my emotions and go about selling wedding gowns and ordering stock as efficiently as possible. No hint of hysteria would show on my face. No squeak of emotion. No sly tears or deep sighs – nothing at all which would alert Rose to the fact that yet more drama had played itself out in my life.

Taking a deep breath, I pushed open my beloved purple door and walked in to find Rose packaging up a tiara in our special lilac-crepe paper for a grinning bride. I smiled as I watched the exchange, Rose sprinkling silver stars into our sturdy white paper bags, emblazoned with the shops' name in delicate cursive writing, before tying the handle with purple ribbon and handing the package over. Although I was only looking at the back of our bride's head, I listened to her chat excitedly about her plans for hair extensions and natural-looking make-up while Rose told her to make sure to bring in a picture after her Big Day so we could see it.

Grinning, her eyes filled with hope, love and excitement, the bride turned and bustled past me. And I grinned at her too and wished her well.

"A happy customer?" I said to Rose as the door swung shut and the bell above it tinkled.

"Exceptionally. Said she had been looking everywhere for just the right thing and sure didn't we have it all along?" Rose smiled warmly.

I nodded and asked which tiara she had chosen.

"Are you okay?" Rose asked, as I made a note to reorder stock of that particular model.

"Fine," I said. "Headache mostly all gone."

"You don't look okay," she offered. "You know Ivy was only acting in a typical Ivy way. She feels it differently to you."

I just nodded again. "Rose, I love you very much but can we keep it strictly business today? Business is the least complicated thing in my life right now and I'd very much love to just lose myself in pretty dresses and sparkly jewellery. I might even rearrange the dressing room a bit."

"You only rearrange the dressing room when you're stressed . . ."

"That's not true. I also do it when I'm premenstrual and feeling a little OCD, or sexually frustrated, or in a cleaning mood. Sometimes I just do it when I want to play with the pretty dresses."

"Well, then, you go right ahead, my darling."

"And you know what – the purple dress?"

"Our dream dress?"

"I think I'll put it away for a while."

Rose looked at me as if I was losing my mind, and I glanced at myself in the silver gilded mirror behind her and wondered myself if I was losing my mind just a little bit.

I'm aware this next bit may make me look like a complete nutter, but when the last customer of the day had left and Rose had, somewhat reluctantly it has to be said, gone home, I set about taking down the purple dress to put it into storage. Mark and I had chosen that dress together – when I was in the first flush of excitement at opening the business and now I couldn't look at it without thinking of him.

But as I took it off the mannequin the notion struck me that I'd never actually tried it on. It had come from the supplier and Rose and I had *ooh*ed and *aah*ed at it an appropriate amount before dressing the mannequin in the centre of the dressing room and toasting it with a glass of something cool and sparkly. And there it had sat ever since – dazzling every bride who walked through our doors. Many fell in love with it – few ordered it. Few were so bold. Some ordered it in white – but the purple was

171

something else. As I felt the weight of it in my hands, the softness of the material, the urge became too strong.

Stripping to my underwear in the middle of the deserted shop felt a little strange, as did stepping into the dress and wrestling to try and zip it up by myself. But it wasn't long before it was on – an almost perfect fit – and I was looking in the mirror at myself as I swished around in it. Sure, my hair was a bit frizzy, and my make-up had most definitely migrated from where it was meant to be to somewhere halfway down my face. I didn't look my best but, seeing myself in the mirror, swathed in purple satin, trussed into a bodice which pointed my boobs in the right direction, I looked better than I had done in days. I even slipped my feet into a pair of our sample shoes – high ones with lots of bling which made my feet scream for mercy but which elevated me in the dress to a whole new level. I figured as I was only going to pack the dress up and put it in storage anyway I might as well enjoy my moment, so I swirled and twirled and may even have sung a little as I went. The rest of my life was getting so surreal that I might as well act out a little Disney-princess magic as well.

What I wasn't really expecting, though – all things considered – was the rap on the door which came at about 8 p.m. – when I was lying on the chaise longue in my purple dress, admiring the rearranging I had been doing for the last few hours.

No one called to the shop at this time – this part of town, hidden behind the walls and away from the main streets, didn't have many people in it after normal closing hours. So it is fair to say I jumped at the noise and looked around me, terrified that the shop was about to be broken into. And there was me, on my own, in a big flouncy wedding dress not even half able to run for my life. The knock came again – louder and more insistent this time – and I could hear the door being rattled as if someone was trying to force their way in. Glancing around the dressing room, I was disgusted to see it didn't really hold any weapons which would scare off a would-be attacker. And my phone was in reception. *Arse.*

I was just about to go into a complete panic attack when I heard a familiar voice call my name and my heart started beating faster than it would have if a burglar had actually battered the door down.

Forgetting what I was wearing, even the tiara I had pinned to the top of my head, I walked straight to the front door of the shop and flung it wide open to see Mark standing there, looking miserable, and my head and my heart hurt again. The blessed relief I had experienced while dancing around the dressing room was gone.

He looked at me strangely, his gaze moving from my face to the rest of my body and, while I was covered in yards and yards of very expensive and shiny material, I suddenly felt more than a little exposed.

"Nice dress," he said with an awkward smile.

Much as I tried, there was no amount of waving my hands in front of my body which would cut it when it came to trying to cover up just how ridiculous I must have looked to him.

"What do you want?" I said, embarrassed and scared, my heart thumping loudly in my chest.

"You didn't return my call," he said and, though his tone wasn't accusing, this opening gambit put me squarely and one hundred per cent on the defensive.

"You cleared off," I said, crossing my arms, trying to hide myself and how ridiculous I looked.

"It wasn't like that," he said.

"Yes, Mark. Yes, it was. It was like that. You left. You told me it wasn't working. You walked out on me, on us, on everything we were planning for and hoping for. You walked away. So if I didn't call back, don't lay the big guilt trip on me. How dare you even try?" My anger was building and I looked at him as if he was a complete stranger before my eyes. This was the man I thought I knew . . .

"If you let me explain . . ."

"I tried to let you explain. I tried calling you. How many

missed calls did you have, Mark? Twenty? Thirty? Forty? How many times did you see my name and think that I wasn't even worth talking to?"

"I wasn't in a place where I could," he said, trying to put his foot in through the doorway.

I stopped him. I was frigged if there was any way I was letting him into the shop just then.

"Well, maybe *I'm* not in a place where *I* can right now!" I shouted.

"You owe me the chance . . ." he said, his voice trailing off, his eyes darting again to my ridiculous get-up.

"Mark," I said, my voice catching at saying his name, "I don't owe you anything. I know what you did. I know how you left. I know how you ignored my pleas for you to talk to me. I know how I have questioned everything about myself and about us for the last few weeks. The only thing I don't know right now is who you are and I'm really not in the humour to find out. Please," I said, feeling myself start to well up, "just go. Just please go."

He didn't fight for me. He didn't push his way into the shop. He didn't – and this killed me – even say sorry. He just nodded and turned and I closed the door and watched from the window as he walked away, head bent low, hands in his pockets.

It was then I walked upstairs, took off the dress I was wearing and, instead of packaging it away neatly as I had planned, I bundled it into a bin bag and kicked it around the room until I was too tired to allow the tears which had been threatening to fall all day to cascade.

When I picked myself up, I dressed myself and the mannequin in something altogether more suitable and left the shop, locking up just as the sun was beginning to set. Feeling vulnerable – and not just because I was in a deserted street all by myself – I texted James and told him I needed to see him.

He arrived within the hour, with a bottle of wine in his hand. "I figured you might need a drink," he said and I nodded, thinking that I probably needed to drink something stronger than wine but then again, since the vodka incident, wine was probably strong enough.

"I didn't know who to call," I said, sniffing as he poured us each a glass. "He just showed up and James, I don't know what is going on his head. Do you know? Do you understand this even one bit? He said he wanted to explain but I just couldn't listen to it. I just couldn't."

James handed me my wineglass and I sat it on the worktop and looked at him. "I don't know what to think about anything any more," I said as the tears which had been pooling in my eyes started to fall.

"Hush," he said softly, pulling me into a hug. "It will be okay, Kitty. It will all work out."

I let him hug me without resistance and in that one moment we were just two people, betrayed by the person we trusted most in the whole world.

"It will all work out," he whispered as he handed me a hanky and he didn't pull a face when I blew my nose and downed my wine in record time. And I felt slightly better. Just slightly.

22

Erin

"You're very welcome back." The smiley older lady grinned at us as we walked through the doors of The Dressing Room. "Kitty will be down shortly. She's just checking on the progress of your dress, Erin, and then she will be down."

My heart fluttered a little at the mention of my dress and Jules did a little excited dance, grabbing my arm.

"It's a beautiful dress," the lady continued. "It will be stunning on you."

I blushed and nudged Jules back. "I hope so," I said, having made an executive decision to focus entirely on the future from now on and not at all on the past.

"Kitty wouldn't have sold it to you otherwise," she continued. "She can be brutally honest if a dress looks rotten. Don't be fooled by her smiley exterior."

"Are you talking about *my* smiley exterior, Rose?" a voice from the top of the stairs called and Kitty came down.

She smiled at us warmly in a slightly exaggerated manner which made me wonder if she was trying to prove a point to Rose or look happier than she really was. Still, I had to push those thoughts to the back of my head because it was no business of mine to ask this virtual stranger if she was okay.

"Right," she said, leading the way into the dressing room while we followed. "Let's get down to business. First of all, I have good news. I've just spoken with the designers of your dress and it will be with us in about three weeks' time. That's super-quick for them – but they owe me a favour anyway so have no fear, Cinders, you will go to the ball. And we'll even have plenty of time for alterations if we need them."

It shocked me, to the very core of my being, that this news actually brought tears of relief to my eyes. Maybe I was turning into the Bridezilla Jules had dubbed me after all. I looked at my sister, my eyes watering, and she pulled a funny face.

"Enough of the waterworks, Bridezilla," she said, taking my hand and giving it a little rub. "Today is all about *me*. Bring on the frocks!"

Kitty laughed and I couldn't help but laugh too as we sat down and Kitty asked us what colours we were thinking of.

"I've not really thought about it," I said, chewing on my lip, and Jules took over.

"She might not have but let me tell you about dos and don'ts. I want this wedding to be classy – I'd like to look very elegant and not at all like some extra from *My Big Fat Gypsy Wedding* – sequins to a bare minimum and all midriffs covered if you don't mind." She then started to list off all the colours she had already ruled out.

Thankfully Kitty laughed along. "I don't tend to stock those more colourful items," she said tactfully, "but let me show you what I do have."

She led us into a smaller dressing room where the white dresses on the walls were replaced by an array of gowns in subtle tones and glossy colours. She began to take dresses from the rails and hold them up against us, considering each one intently.

"This green is nice," she said. "It would suit your colouring."

Of course green was the natural choice for redheads such as

us and as such I tended to want to avoid it like the plague, but this was a rich colour – a delicate dress, strapless with a delicate belt, fastened with a diamante buckle.

"Try it on," I urged my sister and she smiled at me. "I promise there's not even a hint of cheap and tacky about it."

"I know," she said, grinning back. "I love it."

Shooing Kitty away when she offered to help her, Jules disappeared behind the sumptuous purple curtain and started changing while Kitty took out a few other dresses just in case. I watched her work and marvelled that she knew instinctively what would and wouldn't look good on Jules. She selected some tasteful accessories to try out as well.

"I think I enjoy picking her dress more than my own," I said to Kitty's back as she arranged her various bits and pieces. "Less stressful. Even if she is a little high maintenance."

"It's not often we get a bridesmaid who is more high maintenance than the bride," Kitty said, turning to face me. "You are remarkably calm."

"Apart from the crying-all-over-the-dress the last time?"

"It's the bride's prerogative to have at least one meltdown. Believe me, in comparison to some, you have positively cucumber-like qualities. You told me before that you never really wanted to get married, but it seems to me you must be very sure of what you are doing."

I spluttered a response and then felt guilty for spluttering my answer. I was sure of what I was doing – perhaps just not of how we were doing it. For some reason, although I did not know Kitty Shanahan at all and owed her no form of explanation, I felt obliged to say more – to explain. Feck it, sure wasn't it going to be all over the magazine soon anyway?

"It's not the way I planned," I said. Then I explained that I hadn't really planned it at all but Paddy's illness had made us re-evaluate how we felt about each other. I surprised myself by remaining calm while I told her – even when her face dropped and she looked at me with genuine empathy and emotion at the mention of the big 'C'.

"You're very brave," Kitty said.

"Funny thing is, I don't consider myself brave at all. Sure what's the alternative? Paddy has cancer and we have to deal with it. We can't just say 'No thanks, we'd rather not.' We can't hide under the duvet and pretend that it's not happening. So we have to get on with it and we have to make the most of it. And sure, didn't I get a big old diamond ring out of it?" I flashed her the sparkling trilogy ring on my finger. Paddy had been very specific about getting three stones set in the ring – one for the past, he said, one for the present and one for the future he was determined we would have.

"It's no wonder you got emotional here the last day, all the same," Kitty said. "It's unimaginable."

"You would do the same," I said, looking at her hand, noting the wedding band and engagement ring she was wearing. "If it was your husband, you would do the same. You would get on with it. It would be hard but you would. That's just the way it goes."

Kitty smiled and shook her head. "Well . . . it's a bit more complicated than that, but I get where you're coming from."

I noticed her glance down at her rings and fumble with them awkwardly, twisting them on her finger. I was about to ask her if she was okay when the curtains swished open and Jules sashayed out.

Swinging her hips and smiling broadly, she walked the length of the dressing room and twirled, shaking her bum in our direction before walking on. Although she was barefoot and bereft of make-up, and merely holding her hair up away from her neck – she still looked stunning.

"I'm not sure," I smiled. "I don't want you to upstage the bride. Kitty, are you sure you have nothing a little more, you know, frumpy? Maybe in peach, or bright orange? Something clashy and gaudy?"

Kitty laughed and Jules pulled a face.

"Listen to me, sister," said Jules, "don't rain on my Gorgeous

Parade. This is gorgeous – it makes me look fabulous. Don't be a hater!" She laughed, before smiling gently. "Besides, there isn't a hope in hell that I will look better than you. I've seen your dress, remember. I know you look amazing, so we will just be two stunners together."

"You will indeed," Kitty said, offering Jules the accessories to try on.

And of course they simply accentuated her natural beauty. I would have hated her if I didn't love her so much. She had such a lovely glow about her that there was no doubt in my mind at all that we would be buying that dress and any of the accessories Jules wanted to go with it.

And a thought crossed my mind about the articles for the magazine and our way forward.

"Kitty," I said, as Jules disappeared behind the curtain to get changed again, "can I talk to you about something?"

Kitty raised an eyebrow but answered immediately: "Of course."

"Well, you know how I work for *Northern People*?"

She nodded.

"Well, for some mad reason I've agreed to write a series of articles on planning to get married. They are to be more than a simple 'how to' series – more about the emotions and the planning and, well, about Paddy and me."

"That sounds lovely," Kitty said.

"Well, emotions and all aside, we do, because we are a glossy mag after all, want to do some fashion stuff as well – and here in The Dressing Room would be perfect for us." The shop just seemed like the perfect setting for a photo shoot – it was stunning, its location perfect and, well, if the truth was told I'd just kind of warmed to Kitty. She seemed nice – like she genuinely cared above and beyond the basic business arrangement. And I liked Rose too – she seemed quirky and full of character – full of life, even, and full of life appealed to me at the moment.

Kitty seemed delighted – a broad smile, a genuine one, spread

across her face and she said she would very much like part of our story. "I would be honoured," she grinned.

The other positive thing, of course, was that she ga\ discount on the dress which I felt a little guilty about but turn down all the same.

We arranged an appointment for three weeks from when the dress would be in and we could get our photo t̶

As I went to leave the shop she hugged me very tigh whispered: "Even if you don't feel it, and even if you feel you don't have a choice and it's something you have t̶ anyway, I still think you are brave. And I hope you get the h̶ ending you deserve – I have a feeling you will."

I let her hug me, and I even hugged her back a little becz it felt to me that she needed it, before Jules and I stepped b out into the real world and away from the calm and comfor̶ The Dressing Room.

With the dress bought and our spirits high, we decided to st for a quick drink in the pub before picking up a takeaway bring home.

Standing in the Chinese, Jules pondered over the men "Can't completely pig out," she said. "I want that dress to loc great on me on the Big Day."

My stomach rumbled as I pored over the menu myself. decided to push all thoughts of my dress to the back of my hea and order some crispy beef with loads of noodles and a chil sauce. Resolving to starve myself the next day I placed my orde adding on an extra portion for Paddy. I'd arrive home wit dinner, a four-pack of beer, a bottle of wine and a smile on n face and I imagined all three of us would have quite the relax̶ evening – Jules was staying with us, bedding down in the spa room, as a night at home with our mother would be enough send her over the edge.

"Frig the diet," Jules declared, ordering her dinner and a c̶ of full-fat Coke, "Sure I can always eat fruit and Special K week to make up for it."

Arm in arm, warm plastic bag swaying between us, we made our way to the taxi stand and on home.

I was surprised to find the living room empty, the house quiet. The car was still outside so I surmised Paddy must still be in. Calling up the stairs, I expected him to shout that he was in the bathroom or having a snooze or that he would be down in a minute, but silence greeted me.

At first I didn't consider it strange at all. I figured he had probably taken a stroll up to the corner shop.

We sauntered through to the kitchen and I started pulling plates from the cupboards and hauling wineglasses from the press.

"I am sooooo hungry," Jules said, spooning a mouthful of chicken fried rice into her mouth before she even served it onto a plate. "You should have let me have another packet of bacon fries in the pub."

"You had two already," I gently reminded her.

"And lovely they were too," she said with a smile. "Should I put Paddy's out too, do you think?"

I glanced at the clock, as if that would give me the magical answer as to when he would be back.

Realising the futility of my actions, I shrugged my shoulders then told her to go ahead. The shop was a mere two minutes away. Even if he stopped to talk to someone, or spent a while choosing his treat of choice, he should be back within five minutes. Or we could always heat up his dinner in the microwave.

So three plates filled, and his left sitting on the worktop, we went into the living room, sat on the floor and tucked in.

My plate was empty and my wineglass half done when I looked at the clock and realised ten minutes had passed and he still wasn't back. Of course, Jules being Jules, she assured me he was a big boy and was just fine and that I needed to calm down.

And I did calm down, for all of about another ten minutes and then, when he still wasn't home, I started to feel a little twitchy. It's not that I needed to know his whereabouts every

second of every day, or that it bothered me that he might be out somewhere – it was just unusual for him not to tell me if he was going out for anything more than five minutes. Unlike a lot of men, Paddy was a text addict – and messaged me frequently throughout the day. I was used to getting a running commentary of what he was doing. I tried to think back to the last time I had heard from him that day. I had texted him when we left The Dressing Room to tell him we were going to the pub and had invited him to join us if he had felt up to it. He had texted back to say he was feeling a bit tired and was just going to take it easy. That had been maybe three hours before and I hadn't heard anything since.

"This really isn't like him," I said to Jules.

"Ooooh," she giggled drunkenly. "Maybe he has cold feet and has run off!"

Which was precisely the very worst thing she could say to a woman who had previous experience of a man getting cold feet and running off. She realised almost as soon as the words were out of her mouth that she had said the wrong thing. It was probably the expression of sheer horror on my face which gave it away.

"Oh Jesus, Erin. I didn't mean that. I was joking. I wasn't even thinking. It was stupid of me to say . . ."

But while she talked my mind ran through the scenario that after all my worrying, all we had been through, Paddy could and might still walk away. That cancer was not the only thing I had no real control over. My mind raced – with thoughts of calling off the wedding, of people laughing. To lose a husband once was unlucky, to lose one a second time – well, that was nothing short of humiliating. And, Jesus, the article would be in the magazine about the great big jilting and how this time was different.

"You're not a bit funny," I said to Jules which was pretty calm considering inside my head was screaming. "He wouldn't do that," I said, my brain internally finishing that sentence with a 'would he?'

"No. No, he wouldn't," Jules said as I rifled in my bag for my mobile just in case there was a message I had missed. No, there was nothing. So I hit the call button to dial his number, hoping that this was just one of those things and the drink and wedding paranoia was sending me over the edge.

For a moment I breathed a weird, stilted, sigh of relief when I heard his phone ring in the house. He never went anywhere without his phone. He certainly wouldn't run off without his phone. *Phew!* But the phew was replaced with a strange uneasy feeling – if he wasn't here but his phone was and he was gone too long to only have nipped out to the shop, then where on earth was he?

I followed the sound of his ringing phone upstairs. It was coming from our bedroom. Maybe Paddy was here after all. He was probably asleep and just hadn't heard us when we came in. That man could sleep through anything. Well, almost anything. The persistent ringing of his phone would normally wake him. He hated to think he would miss out on any *craic* at all.

I walked into the room and sure enough he was in bed. "Paddy!" I called. "Wake up! You've missed your dinner!" My entire being was flooded with relief that he was here and hadn't run off – so flooded with relief that I climbed into bed and cuddled up beside him. "C'mon, sleepy head! Wake up."

But Paddy didn't wake up.

Jules called the ambulance. I stayed with Paddy, trying to rouse him. He looked so pale – sheet-white like a mannequin of himself. But he was breathing. It was shallow and rasping in places but it was breathing and I sat beside him, rubbing his hand, asking him to wake up – pleading with him to jump awake and shout 'surprise' and all the while pleading with every deity I could think of to make sure he kept breathing. Just keep breathing – just one more. Just stay with me.

"You're not getting away that easy," I said. "You're not leaving me." I wept, my head on his chest, feeling for that gentle rise and fall, listening to the thudding of his heart, pleading with it to keep going. This was not in the plan. He was getting better. Chemo was nearly done. He'd had the damn cancer cut out. This was not what we had bargained for.

Jules walked into the room, her face almost as sheet-white as Paddy's.

"Is he . . . ?"

"No," I said, not lifting my head from his chest. "No. He's here. You're here, aren't you?" I stroked his arm, feeling his warm skin against mine and praying with every fibre of my body that this would not be the last time I felt his warm skin against mine.

"They'll be here soon. What's wrong with him, Erin?"

I didn't shake my head. I didn't shrug my shoulders. I was afraid to move, even for a moment. "I don't know," I said, "I just don't know."

23

Kitty

When I left work I had a smile on my face. That's not to say my life had become any less complicated. My mother was still looming large, having left a message on my phone to say she would call in to the shop for a look around at the start of the following week. The manner in which she spoke was as if she was making an appointment with the dentist – not trying to build any bridges of any sort. Mark had been texting, infrequently. His message was less staid – he wanted to meet. We needed to talk, he said, but I didn't know what to say. And I wasn't ready to have him trample all over my heart again – not face to face anyway.

"Honestly? I don't think you are strong enough," James had said softly as we talked about it the night before. He had taken to calling over every evening and he had listened to me try and make sense of it all. I knew he was right. I wasn't ready to hear the gory details. I didn't want to hear how some other woman made him happy – how he was bored with me and us and what we stood for and had to look elsewhere.

I hadn't told Rose about James' visits. Nor had I told Ivy. I imagined neither of them would take the news well. And I didn't know how I felt about it, if I was honest with myself. He was a good shoulder to cry on – a nice solid set of shoulders and it was nice to have him hug me – for him to tell me that I was special, that Mark didn't know what he was missing. I suppose that small part of my self-confidence which had not been left bruised and battered suspected he might have had feelings for me. As the nights had gone on, I could see a certain look in his eye. But I was so confused and until I wasn't confused any more I didn't want to talk to anyone about it. Did *I* have feelings for James? It was a hard one to answer. I had known him for so long. I had been in love with Mark for so long. There was a chance I was still in love with Mark – more than a chance really – you don't just switch that off. You can't just switch that off – no matter how much you may want to.

But I had started to look forward to his visits. He listened to me talk about whatever I wished and smiled and nodded in all the right places. He had even cooked me dinner the previous night, while I sat on the sofa chatting to him over the kitchen island. I made a mental note to tell him about Erin – how she had asked me to be a part of her feature for *Northern People* – and I would tell him how she and Paddy had overcome so much to get where they were.

If it was me, I would have fallen apart. Sure hadn't I fallen to pieces over the last few weeks and wasn't I just about starting to pull myself together, slowly and not so steadily now? But Erin and Paddy, they had grabbed the world by the balls (excuse the pun) and were just getting on with things.

That in itself made me just as determined to get on with things – to put a smile on my face despite what the world was throwing at me – returning mothers, errant husbands and all.

I had never noticed James' smile before. That's not to say I hadn't seen him smile, but I'd never had much cause to pay attention to the gentle way in which it transformed his face. I noticed it that night, sat on the decking, sipping wine. He was smiling as I told him about Erin and her sister and their infectious laughter. I had told him how Erin's love for Paddy showed through brightly and he had grinned.

"That's what I dream of," he said.

"What?"

"You know, that happy-ever-after where you know that the person you are with will always be there and really will be that for-better-for-worse person you always wanted to be with."

I knew exactly what he meant. It was exactly the kind of relationship I had thought I'd had with my husband – you know, the man who had actually promised to love me for better for worse.

Before we had married we had actually had that discussion one day while painting the living room of this very house.

"If all my teeth fell out and I could only eat soup and kissed like an old man?" he had asked.

"I'll still love you," I said, slapping magnolia paint onto the walls.

"Your turn," he said.

"Okay . . . what about if I put on seven stone and my boobs touched my knees when I sat down?"

"Oh baby!" he laughed. "I'd still love you. Now, how about if I was one of those people who had a horrible accident, fell into a coma and when I woke up spoke with a funny accent, like Jamaican or something?"

"I'd still love you, man," I said in the worst Jamaican accent possible. "What about if I went on the X Factor and made a total eejit of myself, you know, like one of those eejits that only goes on it for the *craic* – like Wagner or Jedward – and the whole world was laughing at me?"

"I'd still love you. If I developed terrible flatulence and it always smelled like cabbage?"

Laughing, I stopped what I was doing. "Mark, my darling, you already *have* that condition and, yes, I still love you. I'll always love you."

"For better for worse?"

"Yep."

"For richer for poorer?"

"Well, I'd prefer the richer part," I said, "but if we have to do poorer we'll manage."

"In sickness and in health?"

"Again, let's hope for the health bit more, but you betcha."

"And all that other stuff that I've not learned yet but will absolutely learn in time for the big ceremony so that you don't divorce me before we are even married?"

"Absolutely," I said and we abandoned the painting for about twenty-four minutes while we were otherwise engaged.

Looking at James now, how he wanted that, I veered between wanting to tell him that I wanted it too, that I still believed in it, and wanting to tell him that it was all bullshit and no one – not even Paddy and Erin – could make those promises to each other knowing that those feelings wouldn't ever change. Things do change.

I took a long drink from my wineglass. "We all want a happy ending," I said sadly. "It just doesn't always work out that way."

"It's not over till it's over," he said. "Everything happens for a reason."

"You sound like Rose. Ever the optimist."

"I do feel bright about the future," he said, drinking from his bottle of beer. "And I feel bright about yours too."

James and I didn't really talk about Mark. They hadn't been in touch, he said. He said he didn't really know Mark any more.

That did shock me, when I thought about it. Those two had been thick as thieves for as long as I had known them. I had always, always assumed that should things go tits up between Mark and me, James would no longer be a fixture in my life. It wouldn't have bothered me. It's not like we were particularly close. We were polite to each other. We had a great laugh every now and again – usually under the influence of a few drinks.

At one stage Mark and I had tried to set him up with Cara –

but it simply hadn't worked. It's not that they didn't get along – they did, but simply as friends. Cara had told me James just hadn't seemed interested in her in that way and that had been the end of that.

Cara had asked me earlier that day if I didn't find it a little strange? That he was calling round, and that he was supporting me so. I told her that of course it was surprising but that it was nice all the same.

"He makes me feel, I don't know, like it wasn't my fault."

"But you know it wasn't your fault. You don't need James to tell you that. We are all telling you that. Me, Ivy, Rose, your dad."

I shook my head and reminded her that no, actually, people weren't telling me it wasn't my fault. In fact, Ivy wasn't telling me anything at all because she was still so enraged that I hadn't told our mother to frig off to the back of beyond. My dad had just gone into quiet contemplative mode. I figured once he had told me that he knew what I was going through, he was all out of things to say. So when he saw me, he just gave me sad looks and lots of hugs and then went back to sitting and staring into space. Rose had gone a little quiet too – which was probably piggybacking off the fact that Daddy had gone quiet.

So James and his reassurance that none of this big old mess was my fault, not even a little bit – well, I was more than happy to listen to him. And I was more than happy to watch him smile.

It was nice how we talked – and it wasn't all about Mark, or relationships, or failed relationships. We talked in that way you talk to someone when you are just really getting to know them. He admitted that he had cried watching *Forrest Gump* and I admitted I'd taken against ever watching that film again as it made me such a crying wreck by the time the wee boy at the end writes the letter. We had laughed as we shared memories of our separate misspent youths – the drunken nights in Waterloo Street, the walks home because it was quicker than waiting for a taxi, the cheap but so very tasty fast-food to line your stomach after a skinful. We talked about the places we had visited and the places we hoped to go. We discussed the merits of *Deal or No Deal* and *Come Dine with Me* and planned our menus for the latter. And then, when the grief hit me about what had happened, he would listen and soothe me and hold me in his arms until it felt better.

He didn't try to kiss me. I didn't try to kiss him. But there was a part of me that wanted to – a part of me that was confused and lonely and needed to feel better about myself. And I knew he wanted to kiss me too. He told me so. "If it were in any way appropriate I would lean across and kiss you right now," he had said, which left no room for misinterpretation.

I had blushed, felt flustered, a mixture of flattered and scared, and I had offered to top up his drink. When I returned he had pretended everything was normal and I was happy at that stage to play along. But when he left, and I went to bed and tried to sleep there was a big part of me that just couldn't stop thinking about exactly what it would feel like to have him kiss me.

Rose arrived at work with an extra-large bouquet of ivory roses, tied together with a purple satin ribbon. She had picked up a box of chocolates and had baked some shortbread to offer alongside the Prosecco which she carried in from the car.

"The Jo Malone candles I ordered arrived. I thought we should light a few around the shop, give it a nice glow and a lovely smell," she said, taking out the Blue Agava and Cacao candles and dotting them around the room. She was on top form – in a super-organised, mega-efficient way which made me feel a little nervous. She was a great worker, but she didn't normally get right to it. Normally she put the kettle on, made some toast in the kitchen and listened to a wee bit of Ray Darcy before she got started for the day.

"You okay, Rose?" I asked as she breathed in the soft scent of the candles and arranged the flowers.

"Perfectly tickety-boo," she said. "How are you?" She smiled at me but I wasn't convinced.

"You want a cup of tea?" I asked, making for the stairs to head to our tiny kitchen.

"You know, I'm grand, love," she said. "I'd rather get organised down here and have everything looking its very best, if that's okay."

"But tea? You always have tea."

"There will be time for tea later," she said, turning to smile at me again.

I noticed she was wearing a little more make-up than usual – there was a definite shading across her eyelids and if I wasn't mistaken a sweep of lip gloss across her lips. Come to mention it, her hair looked a little more teased and she had accessorised her uniform with a little more bling than normal.

It was then the penny dropped. Clearly I had been blocking it out as something which I absolutely was not looking forward to at all – but this was the day my mother was coming to look at wedding gowns. Realising this, I wished *I* had put on an extra slick of lip gloss and had teased my hair a bit more. At that moment, part of me wanted to hug Rose for being thoughtful enough to make sure the shop was looking and smelling its very best. That was, of course, until I realised that she probably wasn't doing it for my benefit. Even though Mum had left Dad. Even though it had been a very long time ago indeed, there was a part of her that somehow felt she was in competition with the woman who was about to walk back into our lives.

"Mum's coming today, isn't she?" I said.

"Oh, is she?" Rose asked, blushing. "I'd forgotten," she said slowly and not at all convincingly.

"Rose, I know you, you know. All this effort, for my mother. Ivy would go mad at the very notion but thank you. Thank you because she will be taking in every detail."

"That's what I'm worried about," Rose said, and she sat down and put her head in her hands.

"Oh Rose," I said, going to her and taking her hand. "We have a fab shop here. It's beautiful and popular and a very nice place to visit indeed. And we work very well together – and that makes for a lovely atmosphere."

She nodded. And I nodded. And we sat there lost in our own thoughts for a while. I was hoping that, compared to the break-up of my marriage and all the confusion that my growing friendship with James was causing, choosing a wedding dress for my mother would be a walk in the park. But I didn't really believe that.

My mother arrived with a smile on her face and a spring in her step at her allotted time – not a minute before and not a minute after. She breezed through the door and air-kissed me, acting as if everything was just perfectly okay and as if there wasn't an ounce of tension between us. Then again, I suppose there wasn't really any tension – there was just a vague nothingness – a little bit of awkwardness perhaps as we both tried to think of something appropriate to say in the circumstances. Of course it was Rose who came to the rescue, jumping in with a cheerful "Hello, Violet," and offering her a cup of tea or a glass of something sparkly. My mother's face lit up at the mention of a little something sparkly and Rose said she would go and get a glass and a bottle and offered me one just in case I might need it too. I admit I was tempted, but also very afraid of the possibility of a wine-in, wit-out scenario so I decided to stick with some fresh orange juice. Sipping it, I tried to calm the uneasy feeling in my stomach and remind myself that emotional baggage (of which there was a lot) aside, she was a customer and I wanted to do the best job I could. And the fact that she was a customer aside, she was my mother and I wanted to make her proud of me and let her know that I was good at my job – that I could do this well.

"Right," I said, leading her into the dressing room. "Are we good to go or are you waiting for anyone else to join you?"

"No," she, said, shaking her head. "I thought it would be nice, just us. You know, Mum and daughter. And Charles, well, he doesn't have any family as such . . . so, you know . . . It would be nice if Ivy was here – but she didn't get in touch so I'm assuming she still has a few issues."

I blushed, shrugging my shoulders – not wanting to let down my guard and let her know that Ivy wasn't the only one with issues or that her arrival had heralded an almighty row and set everyone just that little bit off kilter.

Forcing a smile on my face, I asked her about Charles – inwardly praying she'd never expect me to call him daddy, or that he wasn't some twenty-seven-year-old gigolo after her for her money and nothing else.

"He's a good man," she said coyly. "You'd like him. Or at least I think you'd like him. I suppose it's a bit crazy of me to assume I know what you'd like. But he's a good, solid, dependable man. And he loves me. And I love him too."

She spoke quietly, blushing slightly as she did, glancing at me every now and again, her head bowed, her eyelashes fluttering just that little bit. It was as if she was embarrassed – as if she was afraid I wouldn't like him on principle. But it wasn't as if he had taken my mother away – she had done that herself before anyone had even heard of Charles.

Still, I felt a little sorry for her – shopping for wedding dresses with no family but me for company – a complete and utter basket-case of a daughter with ambiguous feelings for the blushing bride.

"That's good, Mum," I said. "I'm glad you're happy."

"I am, love," she said, and a part of me bristled.

She didn't call me 'love' – it sounded strange. It sounded too familiar and I know that is a strange thing to say, given that she is my mother, but when she had left a part of us had broken that had never been fixed. 'Love' – that's what Daddy called me, what Rose called me – what Mark had called me.

"I waited a long time to find him – to find someone who makes me feel like this. I know I sound really soppy, but I imagine you are used to hearing all manner of soppy declarations working here. And of course from the lovely husband of yours – how is he anyway?"

She was my mother. She was standing beside me confiding in me about the man she was going to marry and asking me about the man I had married and I couldn't bring myself to tell her it was all completely messed up – that he had left, he had cheated – he wanted back, but I didn't know what I wanted, except that I wanted to kiss James. And perhaps do more with James. But I didn't want to tell anyone that – and certainly not the smiley, shy woman in front of me who was trying so hard to bond with me.

"He's fine, just fine," I said, brightly, grateful that Rose wasn't in the room because she wouldn't have been able to keep quiet.

And I turned my back on my mother and told her I had a few things which I thought might suit.

"I hope you don't mind me picking a few things out," I said. "I'm not sure what you are going for but I have a few ideas. Now, not all these are traditional wedding dresses but bear with me. I think they could be really special."

She smiled and sipped, perhaps a little too quickly, from her glass which let me know she was nervous too. I was grateful at that point for Rose coming in, smiling at us and sitting down beside my mother while I went to collect the dresses I had set aside.

I had a few traditional numbers – classic lines which would flatter her neat figure. Dresses cut on the bias, with soft lace boleros, soft floral corsages – shapes and patterns which flattered the more mature figure but which would make her still feel very much the bride. Not quite knowing what her style was any more, I picked out a trouser suit in a soft ivory which I thought would look lovely on her – and a few styles in a pale oyster colour which would offer an alternative to the traditional bridal look. I hung them in front of her – biting my lip and watching her face for any sign of a reaction. I felt every inch as if I was an eight-year-old handing over a school report hoping that it would make her proud.

Slowly she looked from dress to dress before standing up and walking over to touch them, to examine the detail more closely. Every one of them would look stunning on her, I thought, watching a smile start to creep over her face. It was strange how familiar her features were – the little curl in her hair which I knew would be impossible to tame, the slight dimple in her right cheek which wasn't matched on the other side. I felt as if I was looking at a part of me – and it was strange because suddenly the part of me which had hated her for leaving us was happy for her that she had found her own happy ending. If she could – then I could. Just because life hadn't worked out the way she planned, didn't mean it had worked out wrong.

She turned to me, with tears in her eyes, and smiled. "Can I try them on?" she asked. "Will you help me try them on?"

24

Erin

I had fallen into a strange twilight zone. Faces came and faces went. People spoke to me – some of which I took in, some of which I didn't. I spent as much time as I could just staring at Paddy, taking in his face, his features, drinking them in.

"You need to go home and get some sleep," the nurses urged, as I curled up in a chair in his room and stuffed a pillow under my head to try and sleep.

"I'm okay here."

"You're no good to him sick and tired. You'll be unwell yourself."

"I can't go home. I need to be with him."

"He's getting the best care."

I looked at him, deathly pale, bruising on his arms, on his face. He looked as if he was already gone. As if he had given up on me and had left. He had spoken to me a few times – mostly incoherent ramblings.

This was not how it was supposed to be. This was not what we had bargained for. The chemo we knew about. We knew it would make him throw up. We knew it would make his hair thin and maybe fall out. We knew that he might get ulcers. That he would be tired. But all those consequences were wrapped up in a nice big bow of 'this will make you all better'. No one mentioned it could make you worse, that it could damage your blood cells – that it could make you anaemic, weak beyond words, needing more treatment, seeing your skin bruise for no good reason. No one mentioned it could for all intents and purposes leave you lying in a semi-comatose state, unable to be roused by your girlfriend who would be utterly and completely convinced that you were dead.

It had taken a while for the message to get through to me that he was still alive. I know I became mildly hysterical – which surprised me. I'm usually calm in a crisis, but it was Jules who stayed calm and me who had flipped out. I have vague memories of it – memories of screaming at her that we had been eating calorie-laden Chinese food and having a giggle while he had been dying up the stairs. And I had screamed about everyone leaving me – and of how the wedding was a bad idea and oh Jesus, the magazine, and then begging him to be alive even though the paramedics had told me he was still breathing and had a pulse.

Even when I had calmed down – when I finally believed them that he was still with us, I didn't want to leave him, so I curled up on a chair and held his hand – afraid that I might bruise it – and watched him sleep, exhausted by the lack of decent God-fearing blood cells in his body while they talked of treatments and transfusions and stopping the chemo and whether or not that was a good thing. And a part of me – a big angry, tired, irrational part of me wanted to shout at the top of my lungs: "It was only a bloody lump in his testicle. It wasn't supposed to be like this!"

Instead, I sat like a good little non-hysterical fiancée at the side of his bed and tried to listen and make sense of it all. Every now and again, when the nurses left his beside, I would whisper in his ear that it would be really very nice if he were to wake up.

And then I would whisper that I loved him and I would tell him I would kill him for scaring me when he woke up. And regardless of who came to see him, who sat in that room with us and told me I needed to get some rest, I would just shake my head and say I was absolutely and completely not going anywhere.

So I sat there, except for pee breaks and occasionally brushing my teeth with toothpaste bought from the hospital shop, for two whole days. He wasn't unconscious the whole time – he would wake and we would talk, briefly. He was confused and every conversation followed the same pattern – where I tried to explain what happened. He would nod, say he understood, then ask if it was his day for chemo, ramble a bit about something surreal and obviously from his dreams and then drift back off again.

That was natural, they said. The chemo would have weakened him, they said. But I kept thinking of how he hadn't really seemed any different recently. Yes, he was tired – but chemo left you tired. And weak. And I'd never heard of this old carry-on before – this lying there with your blood all frigged. Sure chemo was supposed to help. This didn't seem awfully helpful to me.

"You do need to sleep," Jules said when she called round. "You're starting to look as bad as he does." She glanced at the bed where Paddy was sleeping.

"Thanks, sis," I said, but I knew she was talking the truth. My hair was about ready to walk off my head. My skin had broken out and I looked beyond pale – and with a rich auburn hair-hue that was not a good look to sport. My clothes felt sticky on my body – but I felt as if my place were right there, right then.

"His mum is here, his dad too. They will sit with him. He won't be alone."

"But he's sick, Jules."

"And you'll make yourself sick too and two sick people would be too much to handle. Seriously. You'll be no good to him if you're out of it yourself."

I shook my head but found myself dreaming of my bed – of

laying out straight, and of standing under a hot shower. "Okay," I muttered, defeated, and she smiled.

"Okay, honey. You'll be back here soon and he should be in much better form then. And you'll be in better form yourself – onwards and upwards!"

I nodded and followed her out of the room, looking back at Paddy and drinking in every inch of him.

"Good girl," Jules said, taking my hand and suddenly every muscle in my body felt heavy and tired. The wave of exhaustion that hit me made me dizzy and sick.

"Yes, I need to go home," I said.

After I had a few painful words with his parents, Jules led me away into the sunlight where the brightness and noise of the outside world made me crave the quietness of my bed even more.

Too tired to cry and too tired to think any more about what had happened over the last few days, I dozed off in the car as my sister drove me home and when she led me upstairs and tucked me into bed, the bed where Paddy had being lying when I thought he was dead, I did my absolute very best not to think about what had happened in the room. As I drifted off into unconsciousness, I was grateful to block it all out.

I woke to see my boss peering at me, which was exceptionally surreal and made me jump about six feet off the bed. Looking at her through blurred eyes, trying to figure out where the hell I was and what the hell was happening, I tried to form a cohesive sentence. Strange little images of hospital rooms and concerned faces flashed through my mind and I wondered for a second, as I tried to focus, if I was indeed in hospital again – as a patient this time – and my boss was coming to visit me.

"Sorry – sorry – I didn't mean to wake you!" Grace said softly. "Your sister said you had been sleeping a while and to check if you were awake – I was just going to leave when you stirred."

I wondered there for a second about how exactly I had stirred. Had I snorted awake, wiped the drool from my mouth and looked at her with a slightly gormless expression on my face? Had my eyes sprung open and had I looked alarmed? There were certain things I could cope with, that I expected, but having my boss wake me in my own bedroom – that was certainly not one of them.

"Are you okay?" I asked her, which sounded strange as it came out of my mouth, but seemed more likely to allow me to keep my job than asking 'What the hell are you doing in my bedroom?'

"Of course, I just wanted to see you were okay. We've been worried about you, and Paddy of course. Sinéad wanted me to ask if there was anything at all we could do to help."

Straightening myself up and rubbing my eyes, I tried to focus.

"I'm fine. We're fine. He's getting the treatment and slowly coming round and we're told he will get there, please God . . ."

I heard myself talk but it sounded so robotic – as if I was trying to reassure myself as much as anyone else. I didn't actually know if I believed a word I was saying. After all, they had said it was 'just' testicular cancer – that is, was the Holy Grail of cancers and that he would most likely be fine. And that the chemo, well, it wouldn't be too harsh and that he was responding well and would be fine. And every week when his bloods were done, they were doing okay and he was doing okay and we were all in a big happy okay bubble. And then he collapsed. While I wouldn't go so far as to say he nearly died, I was definitely reeling from a curve-ball kind of a situation and wondering what on earth they had got wrong or couldn't predict.

"That's good," Grace said, "that all sounds positive. What a fright you must have had."

I nodded. "Yes, it was terrible."

"Well, take as much time as you need from work. Sinéad said please not to worry. We'll be fine."

"Thanks, Grace, I appreciate it," I said. "Why don't you go down, get that sister of mine to make you a cup of tea and I'll just freshen up and be down."

"Okay," she said.

I sat in my room as I came to full consciousness and realised that my breath smelt really bad and my hair was like a bird's nest.

Standing under the hot water in the shower, after a quick teeth-brush and while on my third shampoo and rinse, it dawned on me that in precisely two days' time a magazine was going to hit the shelves in which I talked about a past love and talked about the wedding we were planning. In that moment, as the suds ran down my back, the whole thing just felt so completely inappropriate. How cocky had I been to think it would be plain sailing – that our story would, without a doubt – have a happy ending? Jesus . . . it could all go wrong. The last few days had shown me that and there we would be like two big mad eejits grinning from a magazine cover about our hopes for the future and our determination to beat what was thrown at us when the simple truth was we didn't have any say in it. Being positive wasn't going to beat this. Putting our faith in things working out wouldn't guarantee they would – in fact, it was almost as if we had tempted fate. Look at us all smiley and happy and thinking we'll be grand! Would there be time, I wondered, to pull the article? The mag would be heading to the printers, but we might just be able to catch it.

After rinsing frantically, I grabbed a towel and quickly dried off. I threw on a T-shirt and some jogging pants and padded downstairs to where Grace was sitting in my living room, drinking coffee and eating biscuits while Jules grilled her on the finer points of magazine-writing – as if she didn't quite believe all the stories I had told her about the profession over the years. I sat on the sofa and waited for Jules to shut up.

"But really," Jules was asking, "are there many freebies? The freebies must be cool."

Grace laughed. "There aren't as many as there used to be – but they can be good. I can't remember the last time I actually bought any make-up."

"I am jealous – beyond jealous. Erin, do you get free make-up? You never said! Would you want to share it with me any time soon?"

I nodded. "Raid my drawers – take what you want."

"Oooh er, missus!" Jules fake-laughed before pounding up the stairs, leaving me with Grace – with whom I was going to have an awkward conversation.

"Can we pull the article?" I asked, deciding that jumping right in was the best possible course of action.

Grace looked confused, her eyebrow raised slightly. "Pull the article?" she asked as if checking she had heard me right.

"Yes, pull the article," I said, glancing at my watch wondering if the presses were rolling yet.

"The mag has gone," she said.

"But it won't be printed yet. They will still be plating it up. There should be time."

"But why?" she said, paling slightly. Last-minute changes never went down well – ever.

"It doesn't feel right. It doesn't feel a little tiny bit right. It feels in bad taste – it's all too uncertain."

"You said he would be okay."

"I'm not a doctor and I'm not a psychic and I don't want to tempt fate – to become some sort of *cause celebre* for bleeding hearts everywhere. This, this is too much. It's more than I was prepared for."

I felt a thousand and one thoughts scramble through my head, trying to come out. I felt tears prick in my eyes. Oh holy hell, I knew it then that I was going to cry in front of my boss and there was nothing I could do to stop it.

"I only wanted to be with him," I spluttered. "I was happy. We were happy. I didn't want this. I didn't want a big wedding, and a crazy wedding-planner from hell, and a magazine article and my life laid bare – and shagging, stupid, bastarding, shitting cancer and anaemia and whatever other shit life is throwing at us. I don't want big things – I don't want the world on a plate. I don't want to be a superstar millionaire Pulitzer-prize-winning writer with a string of bestsellers under my belt. I don't want a fancy car and loads of free fancy make-up and a hundred and one pairs of designer shoes or anything like that. All I want is a quiet, uneventful life and that's too much. You know all that cosmic-ordering bullshit? All that ask and you shall receive crap? I've ordered and I've asked for it – and prayed for it. And did I get it? That quiet life? Just us and our life, and our Saturday afternoons in the pub and our weekends away and just being able to be there for each other? Did we get it? No, Grace. We didn't. I didn't. And it's as if the Universe – the big stinking fecker – is mocking me. So if I put my life out there again – if that article rang all happy ending and the triumph of love and hope then the bleeding Universe would see this as the perfect opportunity to turn things up another notch. Grace, the thing is, there aren't very many notches left. I'm all notched out."

I'm aware that Grace probably heard the first two sentences of what I said. The rest was a kind of breathy, ranty, tirade of overtired emotional tears and snotters. To give her her due, she didn't look horrified. In fact, about six sentences in she had put her cup of tea down and stood up and walked towards me to sit beside me on the sofa and hug me – and she kept hugging me while I finished my rant and then again while I cried and sobbed and snorted a little bit every now and again.

We were still hugging when I finally quietened down and even though I was aware that with every moment the magazine was more and more likely to be on the presses, I just didn't care any more. I was not in control. Paddy was not in control. Nothing we would do, or not do, would make us be in control. That alone scared me more than I had ever been scared in my life.

"I know this seems impossible," Grace said eventually. "I know it is horrid and I know it must be so very scary and that you are doing everything you can to try and make sense of it but, you know, sometimes life just doesn't make sense. No matter how much we want it to. I don't mean to be glib but Forrest

Gump was right when he said that shit happens sometimes. It just does. There's nothing wrong with getting upset about it – and letting it out. It's much better than holding it all in until you have a complete meltdown one day."

"I think I might have had that meltdown today," I said through watery eyes as I tried to steady my breathing again.

"We've all had them, pet," Grace said. "Sure isn't the day I walked out on my family and ran away to a hotel now a thing of legend in *Northern People*? Didn't it act as a catalyst for a big change in my life? My one-day breakdown – sure it brought me and Aidan closer together in the end and it did my career no harm."

I smiled, thinking of the articles I had been shown which my boss had written a few years before when she had decided to go public with her woes in the magazine. She had spoken openly about her battle with depression, her low self-esteem and her battle with her weight. I had read the articles and admired her honesty – thinking they must have helped so many women who felt the same.

"A meltdown does you good, every now and then – but it's always best to try and catch them a little earlier. You know, before you leave your partner and your child – that kind of thing?"

Her smile was warm and the squeeze of her hand reassuring. "All I'm saying, Erin, is that there is only so much that any of us can control. But we can't spend our lives fearing the worst or expecting the worse – even when it feels like we can't get a break. Trust me – I was that person. It didn't make me happy."

"I'm scared," I said, just as Jules walked back into the room grinning from ear to ear at her haul of my make-up. The grin fled pretty quickly when she saw me.

"Of course you are," Grace said softly. "It's scary. It's really scary – I can't even begin to imagine."

"But it's not going away, is it?" I asked.

"I'm afraid not. Not now anyway."

I felt my sister sit down at the other side of me. I put my head in my hands and ran my fingers through my still wet hair.

"This," Grace said. "All this . . . all this shit. All these hard times. All that you are going through that you never bargained for and never wanted – it doesn't make what you have any less of a love story. It doesn't make it broken or wrong or too hard. It makes it better in a lot of ways. I'm not just saying this from the point of view of an editor who is kind of scared of Sinéad and doesn't want to haul a magazine back – I'm just saying, don't give up. Don't get too scared. Just roll with the punches."

"Okay," I sniffed. "Do you think there is any chance of getting a few less punches every now and again?"

"Let's hope so," Grace said.

I dried my eyes and took a deep breath and noticed Grace glance at her watch before looking at Jules and me.

"It's okay," I said, "The magazine can go. Just let it happen."

"Just roll with the punches," Jules said.

25

Kitty

"She looked amazing," I said, topping up my wineglass and offering James a top-up of his.

"Must have been strange, seeing your mother dressed as a bride," he said.

"In the grand scheme of things I was not expecting to happen in the last month, it was right up there."

"And do you think your sister will come round to the whole idea?"

I shrugged my shoulders and sank into my chair, putting my feet up and allowing James to give them a rub. It was strange how quickly and easily we had fallen into a little routine together.

"I don't know. I'm stubborn but Ivy takes it to a whole new level."

"And did you tell her about Mark?"

I shook my head – a little embarrassed if the truth be told. I was embarrassed to admit to James I wasn't sure what to tell my mother, never mind how to tell her. "I couldn't find the words," I said.

"You should just be honest," he said strongly. "Tell her he doesn't deserve you. He never did."

I bit my lip, thinking of the text message I had received earlier from Mark asking for one last chance to talk. I hadn't replied.

"He texted again," I said.

James frowned, stopped rubbing my feet and sat forward. "And you told him where to go?"

"I didn't tell him anything," I said. "I haven't replied."

"Because you have nothing more to say?"

"Because I don't know what to say."

James looked perplexed, as if my answer in some way annoyed him. Again it crossed my mind that his complete hatred now for Mark – who he had been inseparable from – was a little strange. Buoyed by drink I sat forward and looked into his eyes.

"Why do you hate him so much now? I mean, I know why I'm confused. Why I'm angry – but you, it's strange. I appreciate your loyalty, I do – but I never thought that loyalty would be to me. I don't get it . . ."

He looked back at me, his eyes round and honest, and he shook his head. "I know it must seem strange to you . . . I can't . . . I would tell . . . no . . ."

He stuttered and mumbled and looked away and I knew there was more he wanted to say and more that I needed to hear.

"If there is something I should know then, James, you should tell me."

He looked at me in the eyes again, and took my hand. "I just don't understand him. I don't understand how he could doubt you – how he could for one second think that there was anyone better than you."

I closed my eyes as he spoke – grateful to listen to his words of comfort, grateful just to know that someone thought there was no one better than me. With my eyes still closed I tilted my head towards James. I could feel his breath on my face – it smelled of wine. It felt different to Mark – even with my eyes closed. I felt his hand hold mine even tighter and felt his lips search to find mine. He kissed differently to Mark – more urgently but yet still tender, still with feeling. Mark used to kiss me with feeling. The last time he kissed me it had been with real, true feeling. It was only a small kiss – a goodbye kiss as he went to work. It wouldn't have lasted more than a few seconds, but I knew he meant it. My head swam, dizzy with wine and the image of my mother in a wedding dress, and all the weird experiences of the last few weeks and the pleading of Mark that we should meet and talk. I felt James' hand move up my arm, tenderly with the touch of someone who did think I was better than anyone else, and that was nice. That was good. That was, in that moment, uncomplicated and pure and I allowed myself to kiss him back, to give in to being wanted and needed. I allowed myself to kiss him, and allowed him to kiss me. I allowed him to caress my face, to push my hair back gently and curl it around my ear. I allowed him to kiss my neck, to stroke my back – delicious tickling soft touches that made my whole body ache to be held tighter and kissed longer.

When we broke apart, I looked at him, his eyes heavy and dark, his lips full – almost bruised-looking – and I knew mine felt and looked the same and I stood up, took his hand, and without words led him upstairs to the bed I had shared with Mark and we had sex. Passionate, angry, amazing sex which allowed me to completely block out everything that was going through my mind except what was happening right there and then in that hot and sweaty moment. Nothing mattered but the feeling of my skin against his – the curves of this unfamiliar body lying against mine, moving against mine, making me feel as if every single nerve-ending in my body was on fire. It was new, it was different. It was filled with longing and every part of me responded to this feeling that he wanted me.

It was only after he was asleep, when I crept downstairs for a drink of water and noticed the unfamiliar jacket on the sofa where he had left it, the empty bottle of wine where with Mark it would have been an empty bottle of beer, the smell of his aftershave on my skin, that the reality of what I had done came crashing in. There it was in all its stubble-rash, aching-thighs, slightly sweaty glory. I had slept with someone else – well, I hadn't slept. I had had sex, calling a spade a spade. I had humped someone else and not just any 'someone else'. I had humped, shagged, slept with Mark's former best friend.

Standing, shivering in a T-shirt and nothing else in my kitchen, I wished to all that was holy that I still smoked. A cigarette would go down really well right now – and not just in a post-coital way. Oh Christ. An hour before it had seemed like it was all uncomplicated and could just make the world more simple – to just feel without thinking. But once the feeling was done, the thinking was back with a vengeance. I looked at the clock on the wall, it was gone twelve – late for sure – but surely not too late to call someone in a crisis.

I lifted my phone from the worktop and scrolled through my address book. Ivy – well, no, I didn't think she would appreciate a call just now. Calling after midnight with an existential what-the-frig-have-I-just-done crisis would not be a way to mend our broken bridges. Rose – she would be there for me, I knew she would – but she was also exhausted. The effort of making sure the shop was looking its very best for my mother, followed by the effort of maintaining polite conversation with her for the hour and a half she was in the shop, had left her worn out and she had been vowing to go home and fall head first into a bottle of Malibu when I last saw her. Cara – well, she would be in a club around now, or with a new boyfriend, or asleep and not really in the mood to listen to me have yet another crisis of confidence.

One number stood out to me – and it was the one person I couldn't call. The person who had put me in this position in the first place and made me horribly vulnerable and open to making a mistake. And this was a mistake. I never understood that before – how people could sleep with someone 'by accident' – but, caught in that moment and just feeling loved, I had found myself in someone else's arms – lost in them, lost completely but not as lost as I felt after, standing in the kitchen. I looked at Mark's name again and slammed my phone down. It was broken now, all of it – and it wasn't just his fault any more.

Wrapping a fleece jacket around me I went out to sit on the decking and stare at my phone again. I needed to talk to someone – and an hour before that would have been James because I believed he understood. But he didn't – things had changed there too. I scrolled through my address book again, through my log of calls and saw where my mother had asked me to input her new mobile number that very afternoon.

"Call me if you need me," she'd said and inwardly I had pulled a funny face while I fought to the urge to petulantly say 'As if' like the teenager I was when she left me. My finger hovered over the screen. Would it be too much to call her? Would it be weird? Shove it, I knew it would be weird. We hadn't had a heart to heart in years. The last one we had was probably in around 1989 when she counselled me on how exactly I would survive if Matt Goss from Bros never returned my affections. I remembered, though, how she had held me as I cried. She hadn't laughed. She hadn't mocked me or told me to wise up and pull myself together – she'd just said that it would be okay. That life sometimes works out differently to how we would have hoped but that wasn't necessarily a bad thing. I hadn't understood what she was saying then, not really. But I allowed myself to let her words soothe me. I remember cuddling into her, the smell of her Max Factor powder puff and her Charlie perfume making me feel safe and secure. We sat there for what seemed like ages, on my single bed with Matt and his brother Luke looking down at us from the walls, and then she offered to make me my favourite ever dinner of chips with a fried egg and I had followed her down the stairs and watched her set about preparing my meal. I loved her – my mum. I loved her and trusted her, just as I loved and trusted Mark. She had hurt me – and he had hurt me too. I felt tears prick my eyes as I sat there, in my T-shirt and fleece, my legs getting cold, and I realised I couldn't talk to either of them – not now. But that I needed to talk to them. I tapped out a text message and sent it to both Mark and Mum.

I don't know what happened with us. It doesn't make sense. Please can we talk?

I pressed send and then typed another message which I sent to Ivy, Rose and Dad.

I know I don't make much sense at the moment. But I love you.

Then I climbed back upstairs and looked at James fast asleep in my marital bed. Thankfully he didn't stir as I lay down, as close to the edge of the bed as possible and hoped that he would stay asleep and that I would be able to get out of the house and out to work with as little physical contact with him as possible. It was done, it couldn't be undone – so I just had to try and get on with it the best I could.

The following morning was played out like that famous scene from *Morecambe and Wise* as we prepared breakfast. He moved close to me, smiling, helping me make toast and eggs while I dodged him in what would have looked to onlookers like a perfectly choreographed dance of awkwardness. I had got up before him – not having slept much, which at least managed the whole morning-kiss, morning-glory, him-having-notions-there-would-be-a-repeat-performance weirdness.

I had been showered and fully dressed when he walked into the kitchen, his hair a little messy, his smile wide.

"Last night . . ." he started and I turned my back to him on the pretext of getting some bread from the cupboard.

I turned to face him before he could continue, waving the loaf at him in a slightly manic fashion. "One slice or two?"

"Two," he replied absently. "I'm hungry. Must have worked up an appetite."

"Eggs?" I interjected, trying to keep my voice light.

He nodded. "Kitty –" he began.

"James, I hate to rush you but I've a delivery arriving at the shop soon and I need to be out of here pretty quick," I lied. "I tried to get them to let Rose sign for the stock but they're quite fussy, apparently. It's the couture stuff – I have to check it as it comes in. Any flaws at all and it all goes back. Nothing short of perfection is good enough so, you know, I have to be there."

I knew I was rambling and I hoped that if I just kept rambling for long enough he would get the hint and leave. But it would seem he took my rambling for nervousness as he walked towards me, took the butter knife from my hand and put it on the worktop. He must have taken the slight tremble in my hand as some sort of emotional, physical, perhaps sexual reaction and he kissed me on the lips. I didn't want to kiss him back. It felt wrong. The attraction, the need, which came with the night-before's talk and the glasses of wine was gone but I couldn't bring myself to just push him away so I kissed him for as short a time as I figured I could get away with and reiterated that I had to go. I knew I was being a coward – a horrible, horrible coward and the look in his eyes – confused and wounded – let me know he may have suspected my feelings too. Still I didn't explain to him. I said it was later than I thought it was and that traffic would be heavy and getting parked in the city centre was never easy.

"Help yourself to whatever you want to eat and let yourself out," I said, grabbing my phone and my bag and heading to my car.

I threw all my belonging onto the passenger seat and pulled out of the driveway, feeling more than a little panicked. How I didn't hit anyone I will never know as I drove like the clappers to work and opened up the shop a good half hour before Rose was due to arrive, or any dress delivery was due to come in.

I opened the door to the courtyard, wandered through and sat down, glancing at my phone. There was a message from my dad – the same reassuring words that he had been offering me for the last three weeks and I smiled and in my mind I hugged him. Rose replied with a cheery message that she would bring the buns in for morning break and that I would be okay and she loved me. Ivy was fairly typical Ivy. She told me she loved me but I was a dick sometimes. I at least admired her honesty and even though I was feeling quite emotional, it made me smile. There was no response from either Mark or Mum. I took a deep breath and decided that for that day I would focus on the things that I did have control over and that was the shop, my customers and my clients.

"Feck it," I swore softly before going to the office and switching on my computer. There were a number of emails from suppliers, including one from the company making Erin Brannigan's wedding dress. They would be able to complete the order even quicker than anticipated, they said, and as soon as I gave them the final few measurements they would put the finishing touches to the dress.

I smiled widely. I would phone Erin later and tell her the good news and perhaps speak to her about the photo shoot she wanted to do in the shop. She would make a stunning bride – but I knew she didn't believe that for one second. She was one of those women who had no understanding at all of how beautiful they really were. Erin was one of my favourite kinds of brides – the kind that came in without fuss, who listened to my suggestions, who transformed into a radiant bride as soon as the gown was on. She had looked stunning in the sample dress – she would look even more remarkable in the dress tailored to her own curves. I looked up her number and wrote it on my hand. I'd call her as soon as I could be sure she would be at work.

I could do that well. I could do that without messing it up or making it all more complicated. Just the thought I would make her feel better made me feel better. I was just congratulating myself on turning my morning around already when my phone started to ring. Looking at the display my heart thumped to see that my mother was calling me. I had asked her for help. I had told her we needed to talk – and I was about to get my wish.

26

Erin

Paddy was brighter when I returned to the hospital. He was sitting up and reading a newspaper and there was a half-eaten sandwich in front of him. His saline drip had come down and he had no wires or tubes anywhere on his body. He still looked pale and his lips looked dry and I had to fight the urge just to reach out and touch them – just to feel his breath on my hand.

"You look brighter," I said softly.

"You look brighter yourself," he said. "Washing your hair definitely improves your appearance."

I laughed and winked. "I thought you liked the finger-in-a-light-socket look?"

"I like all your looks, but some of them are definitely preferable to others." He put his newspaper down and patted the bed.

I tottered over, sat down and held his hand. It felt warmer than it had done in days.

"You're a dirty bastard," I said, smiling at him.

He shrugged his shoulders.

"You really scared me. I think I've lost about ten years off my life."

"I'm sorry," he said.

I know the good fiancée in me should have soothed and reassured that it was all okay and that as long as he was okay now I didn't mind that I had narrowly avoided a heart attack with the worry of the last few days. And I did, of course, deep down feel that way, but still there was a part of me which wanted to let him know just how much he had frightened me – intentionally or otherwise.

"So you should be. Are you planning on having any more near-death experiences any time in the near future? Because a bit of warning would be good."

"I didn't exactly plan this," he said, stroking my hand. "I'm sorry. I had been feeling pretty worn out but I thought it was just the chemo – you know, a cumulative effect. I didn't think . . ."

"But your bloods hadn't shown anything up?" I was asking him questions like he was the doctor – like he should have been able to self-diagnose – which was ridiculous, really. I bit my lip and looked at him, apologised for all the questions and held his hand tighter, leaning my head towards his chest. "Just don't do it again, babe. Please."

"I'll do my very best," he said.

"Good man."

We sat there in companionable silence – me listening to the rise and fall of his chest and his breathing as he rattled his newspaper and slurped from a coffee cup. Ordinarily such sounds would have set my teeth on edge and would have made me want to tear my ears off but it is amazing how your tolerance for annoying noises increases after someone nearly dies. He could have sat there and farted and burped, whistled and whined and I would have revelled in every glorious second of it.

The doctors arrived in shortly after – said they would do a blood transfusion to boost his blood cells the following day and continue to monitor his condition. Chemo – well, they'd have to call it a day with the chemo for now – but they were fairly confident that he'd probably had enough to see him right anyway. The doctor said it all quite glibly. She stood there, her hair curled up in a bun, her perfect patent court shoes glistening against her American-tan tights. She was probably not much over the age of twenty-six and I wanted to ask her did she really think that them being "fairly confident" was good enough – but I would have felt like her older teacher telling her off. I looked at Paddy, hoping that he would ask the right questions but he was nodding.

"Well that's good, isn't it?" he said. "A blood transfusion won't be so bad. And when can I get out of here?"

"We'll get the transfusion done tomorrow, check your bloods again and hopefully let you home soon after."

Paddy was grinning at me. "Home soon, Erin, did you hear that? And we can get on with the wedding plans."

The doctor's face lit up at the mention of a wedding. She was clearly too young to have been jaded by romance just yet. "Oh, you're getting married? When?"

"Two months," Paddy said. "We can't wait."

"Well, that's something to look forward to," the doctor said brightly. "What more motivation do you need to get better than a lovely big wedding?"

"It will be a great day," he said proudly. "In fact, if you want you can read all about it in this month's *Northern People*. Erin here is a features writer with the magazine. She's telling the story, testicular cancer and all, in the next edition or two."

The doctor looked at me strangely. I could guess what she was thinking. Sleazy journo sells her soul to tell her story for the sake of selling a few extra copies. She gave me that look – that beady-eyed look of someone whose entire perception of journalists came from soap operas where the raincoat-wearing, fast-talking hack would sell anyone down the river for a scoop.

"I must get a copy," she said slowly. "I'm sure it will be an interesting read."

I wanted to tell her to clear off. I couldn't help it and I wasn't proud of it I but had taken a complete dislike to this woman –

mostly down to her age, her old-woman tights and the fact she had been so glib about Paddy's treatment. Her looking down her nose at me didn't help either. I bit my tongue. Paddy wouldn't have been a bit happy at me telling her to clear off even if I could fully justify my reaction, given the rubbish few days we'd had.

"Yes," Paddy said. "Erin is a very talented writer. She's won awards."

Doctor Patronising smiled and nodded. I had *only* won awards for writing stupid little stories. She was curing people's cancers – or at least being "fairly confident" she had. I couldn't bring myself to talk to her so I stood up and walked to the window and let her get on with whatever else she wanted to say to Paddy before she left.

"Are you okay?" he asked after she went, as I stood, my back still to him.

"I'm fine, Paddy," I said through gritted teeth. I turned back to face him, plastering a smile on my face. "I'm fine. Just fine. Let's just get you home. Let's get on with planning this wedding and let's just pretend that everything is hunky-dory."

He looked hurt – and I felt hurt. This was not what I'd intended – not how I'd hoped this day would pan out. It was perfectly clear I was starting to lose my grip on reality – which is why it was the absolute perfect moment for Kitty from The Dressing Room to call and tell me cheerfully that my dress would be in sooner than anticipated and that at least that was one last thing I could put out of my mind. I thanked her for calling me, said I would call her when I was back in the office and arrange to come in again. Then I hung up, turned to Paddy and told him the dress was on its way.

"See," he said, with an optimism which made me want to scream. "Things are working out after all."

It was an almost joyous relief to get back to work. There was a strange comfort in parking at the office car park in my usual spot, lifting my coffee and bag and walking back in through the doors of the *Northern People* offices. There was a comfort in seeing the familiar faces of my colleagues even if some of them gave me that hugely sympathy-half-smile and asked in hushed voices how everything was. I had answered the question about seven times when I finally reached my desk and my comfort zone. I switched on my computer, delighted to hear it whizz into life. I listened to my voicemails – comforted that even when things had been beyond crazy in my life for the last few days the rest of the world had been carrying on as normal. The plethora of emails in my inbox made me smile even though most of them were generic press releases sent to hordes of people and not exclusively to me. When Liam walked past singing the *Match of the Day* theme tune and smiling at me, giving me a cheeky wink which said more than all the soft hushed tones and concerned half-smiles did, I felt myself relax.

Paddy had got out of hospital the day before. He had come home smiling, pretending that he wasn't even a bit tired or a bit sore and had set about making himself a cup of tea and some toast even though I had offered to do it.

"I'm fine to do it myself," he said. "I could do with getting up and about a bit. I was going a bit stir crazy in that hospital."

"You need to rest," I said to his back as he walked away from me into the kitchen.

When Paddy was in a mood like this – a 'feck cancer and everything about it and sure I don't need to take it easy' kind of a mood – there was little point in arguing with him. And we had been sniping more over the last few days. I had been unhappy with the doctors. He had wondered why I couldn't just trust that they knew what they were doing. I had told him I would take some time off when he came out of hospital. He had told me not to be so stupid. I had said we needed to take things easy. Maybe think about toning down the wedding. He had reacted angrily. Said that toning down the wedding was the absolute last thing we should do and that he wasn't dying and I was to stop treating him as if he was. I had barked back that I hadn't been treating him that way but that he hadn't seen himself lying sheet-white on a bed looking like a pathetic corpse. I had cried. He had cried. I had said we would carry on with our plans as normal, while fielding calls from his mother and my mother asking if we should maybe slow things down – each of them stressing they really wanted us to get married but maybe not when he was unwell. I had them in one ear, him in another and in my head there was a small voice screaming that I didn't know what I wanted.

I wasn't used to things being tense with Paddy. I wasn't used to these uneasy feelings. It sounds a bit 'look at us we're perfect', but we had never been a couple to bicker. Even when he was diagnosed and we were stressed and he got very, very drunk one night and threw up on the bedroom carpet – we still never bickered.

So when he insisted on making his own tea and toast, I took that as not only a sign that he was trying to be fiercely independent but a sign that he didn't want me to be there – that he was annoyed with me in some way.

I sat on the sofa and listened to the sounds of him pottering around the kitchen – the fizz of the kettle, the scraping of the butter knife against the toast, and felt an uneasiness in the pit of my stomach which was only made worse when his mother arrived shortly after and looked at me as if I was the antichrist incarnate when I told her he was in the kitchen making himself something to eat. She didn't say it but the look on her face screamed 'But he has cancer! People who have cancer can't make themselves toast! What kind of a slack wife are you going to be? Is it any wonder he ended up in hospital?'

"He insisted," I offered and it sounded pathetic even though it wasn't a lie.

She sniffed, walked past me and finished making the toast for her son while he took his seat on the sofa and let her fuss around him. I have never wanted to aim a cushion directly at my fiancé's head before but, in that moment, his head was in serious jeopardy.

So work had been a welcome relief when it had come and I swore that apart from those initial niceties I would not talk about cancer or weddings, if I could help it, until home-time rolled around again.

I sat back, set about answering my emails, returning my voice mails, setting up features for the coming week and enjoying a few quiet hours of blissful busy work which required very little forethought. I even indulged in a sausage bap at break-time and didn't feel even a little bit guilty. I was on a little work high and it felt great.

I was smiling to myself when Sinéad walked in and smiled at me. It wasn't one of those weird half-smiles – it was a full-on, non-sympathetic, no bullshit smile.

"You're back," she stated.

I nodded.

"Good to have you here. We'll have the first run of the magazine in later – come in and see it. The designers did a great job – you look amazing. This will be a big seller. Don't forget now to follow it up with something equally great next month. Have you the wedding-dress shoot organised yet? Or a column on trying to fit in the pre-wedding pampering while being exceptionally busy? And all that lovey dovey stuff too?"

So it would seem that I wouldn't be able to escape wedding talk after all. I smiled and put on my best very professional-journalist voice. "Of course, Sinéad. The copy is already on the way and I've arranged some pampering and a mini-makeover, and I'm in the process of arranging a photo shoot at The Dressing Room. Obviously I won't be trying on the actual dress that I will be wearing on the actual day and I'll probably get a few models in to do justice to the pretty dresses. It will be great."

"Brilliant," she said. "We'll discuss it more in my office. Two o'clock? We'll get the rest of the team in to plan for the next edition too – but I want your focus to be on all things wedding. Liaise with advertising, why don't you?"

I nodded because that's what you did when Sinéad asked you

to do something. She wasn't a bad boss, or particularly hard-nosed, but she was focused and very determined about what she wanted for the magazine. I guess it was that determination which had kept our circulation figures healthy in a time when the magazine industry was in freefall. She was always open to ideas but she definitely believed in her own above all else and, when she asked, you didn't ever say no. I knew it would have been career suicide to say that if she didn't mind I'd really love to escape the wedding talk at work. If I had told her what I was really thinking – that things were a little fraught at home and for the first time in the history of our relationship I wanted to tell him he was an annoying fecker – she might have shown me my marching orders right then and there. So nodding had to do and I did it with a smile.

"No bother," I added in a voice which I hoped didn't sound sarcastic.

"Great," she said. "It will be brilliant. I love it when we get a good beefy feature like this – ah, the readers will be in tears and snotters. Everyone loves a wedding story. Everyone loves a love over adversity story. Everyone loves nice dresses and lovely make-up and The Dressing Room will be a fabulous location. Maybe we could take some pictures out on the city walls too – if the weather is good. Check the weather would you, Erin? And pick the best day. Chat with Liam and talk to Grace about getting hair and make-up on board. Oh, I just love it!"

She smiled and walked away, her heels clicking rhythmically as she went. As far as moods went, this was Sinéad on absolute tip-top form. The excitement emanating from her was palpable which meant there was absolutely no way, no how I was going to be able to tone any of this down. I contemplated a second sausage bap, a king-size Galaxy bar and a can of full-fat Coke, and perhaps a foot-stomping tantrum of toddler proportions.

The article, spread over three glorious glossy pages, did look very well. I read it without cringing which was always a good sign and I noted that Grace had not changed the copy. Mentally I patted myself on the back for doing a good job. The pictures, one of me taken at the recent shoot and the others hauled from the Ian and me archives (with his face pixelated as requested). There was one of us standing on a beach, my arm around his waist, his arm around my shoulders. In his hand he was holding a beer can. Even though his face was blurred I knew he was smiling in the picture and there was me – my hair wild and frizzy, my face creased with laughter, my eyes bright, waving at the camera. I remembered the day well – it was about three weeks before the wedding that never was. Ian and I, along with four friends from university, had packed a picnic (largely liquid, it has to be said) and had driven in two old and probably slightly dangerous cars to the coast at Donegal where we had spent the day listening to Atlantic 252 on the radio – the tinny sound echoing off the rocks around us – drinking, dipping in and out of the sea and snogging with a complete lack of self-consciousness – the kind you only had when you were twenty-two and only starting out in the adult world. We had talked about the wedding, described this day – which lasted into the next day – as our unofficial stag and hen do combined. My smile for the camera had been genuine. So had Ian's. I remembered that day and night so well. We had laughed and swum until the stars had shone brightly in the sky and then we had pitched our tents. The others had headed off to their tents, but we sat there, me in front of him, lying back in his arms, our hands intertwined, listening to the gentle lapping of the waves against the shore, trying to count the myriad of stars above our heads.

"You all set for Gretna?" he asked, kissing my head and I snuggled closer to him.

"Yes. More or less. Sure we don't need much," I said sleepily.

"No doubts?" he asked, his hands still intertwined with mine, my back still lying against his chest so that I could feel his heart beating close to mine.

Yes, I know that sounds terribly cheesy and I was more than

likely romanticising the memory as I sat at my desk looking at the picture but that was how I remembered it. There were so many of the memories of Ian which I had re-coloured over the years – but that one, that moment? That day and that night? Still perfect. Well, almost perfect.

"No doubts?" he had asked and I had turned to kiss him, to show him with the deepness of my kiss and the urgency of my hands that I didn't have a single doubt in my head. What was to doubt? We worked in every way. The passion was there – God, it was there – he had only to look at me for me to want to have sex with him, no matter where we were or who was with us. We were one of those sickening couples who groped in the supermarket, who fondled in the fresh-fruit aisle, blissfully unaware of who was near and who may have been watching. We were the kind of couple who spent hours, days, entire weekends in bed only getting up to go to the bathroom or to answer the door to the pizza-delivery man. We used to joke about it, how we were inseparable, literally. How even when we were together we weren't physically or emotionally close enough unless we were at it.

We talked – God, we talked, morning noon and night, phone calls and emails and conversations about everything and nothing. We had the same goals – the same ambitions – the same silly early-twenties' ideals. We had the world at our feet and that world was going to start with our unconventional Big Day in Gretna Green.

"Doubts? Not a one," I whispered as my hand moved lower and he groaned with pleasure. "No doubts at all."

Blushing at the memory, I closed the magazine and sat back in my chair. I must not allow myself to think about Ian in that way. I must not allow myself to romanticise what we had in any way, shape or form because ultimately Ian was a pig. And, I reminded myself, even though he was doing my head in at that moment, Paddy was a better man than he was. I tried not to allow myself any time to think about things that had been so much less complicated back when that photograph had been taken. When I had been young, thinner, naïve. When I had never learned how life could be rubbish, or cruel or have a tendency to throw you curve balls when you least expected them and least wanted them.

I needed some air, I needed some space to just breathe and try to stop these confusing thoughts flying through my head.

27

Kitty

We agreed to meet in a public place. A neutral venue, a small voice in my head had said. A place where there couldn't be a scene. Not that I was looking for a scene. I was just looking for my mum. I had spent the rest of the day in work feeling marginally guilty about it all. I didn't tell Rose I was going to meet my mother. I didn't tell Rose I had slept with James, nor did I tell her that it was James who had sent me at least five text messages that day. It felt strange to keep a secret from her, but thankfully the shop was busy and we were kept on the go. That made it easier for me to keep my nerves under wraps as well. It was strange that I felt nervous about going to meet my own mother, but it wasn't often we talked, let alone shared secrets. I was grateful when the time came to shut up shop, kiss Rose goodbye and tell her that I was fine and would be right as rain the following morning after a good night's sleep – and no, I wasn't doing anything more exciting than just going home for an early night with a good book and a glass of wine.

She smiled and reminded me, once again, that both she and my dad were there for me if I needed them. I smiled, lied through my teeth and said again that I was fine and sure I would absolutely and definitely call them if I needed them. Rose had looked at me – her eyebrow slightly raised as if she knew I was lying – and paused for a second before moving on again and climbing into her Smart car and driving off, the trails of Andrew Lloyd Webber's greatest hits hanging in the air along with her exhaust fumes. I glanced back at the shop, pulling at the door to double-check it was locked, and set off down the street towards the café bar where I had arranged to meet my mother.

Pushing the door open, the smells of spices mingled with fine wines assaulted my nose. Although the day was bright outside, the restaurant was dimly lit with rich colours on the walls and music playing softly. My mother was sitting towards the back of the room, a bottle of wine in front of her with two glasses. She was sipping gingerly from her glass, readjusting the soft woollen shrug cardigan she was wearing. Her hair was perfectly set, pulled back from her forehead by a pair of sunglasses sat on top of her head. She looked young enough to be my sister. I suppose she had become a mother young – at just gone eighteen. Rose, in an uncharacteristic jealous moment, had commented that it was no wonder my mother had few wrinkles as she hadn't been raising Ivy and me in our teenage years. Rose had pointed to the crow's feet around her eyes. Pointing to her right eye she had said, "That was the night Ivy stayed out until 4 a.m. and your daddy was on the verge of calling the police" and, pointing to her left eye, "That was the time you smoked five cigarettes in a row trying to teach yourself not to choke on them, but instead you ended up violently ill all over your bedroom – and I mean *all over* your bedroom." I had laughed, shamefaced, remembering the projectile incident. Rose and my father had been relatively calm about it all – considering the mess of the new carpet and the fact I had been smoking in the first place. I wondered would my mother look different if she had stayed around? Would she look older or wiser? Would she not play with her coaster in the same uneasy way? Would she and I have

227

walked into the restaurant together, arms linked, weighed down with shopping bags, laughing about the day we had just had? Would it all seem less awkward? Would she have been the one to help me make sense of it all? Would I have had sex with James? I stood at the door, gently nudged forward by someone else coming in behind me, and wondered if I was doing the right thing. I looked again, at her holding the stem of her wineglass and sipping again, a little deeper this time, and I matched that deep sip with a deep breath and crossed the room. She looked up and smiled and I smiled back, a nervous smile, and waved limply. I watched my mother stand up to greet me, patting down her dress and reaching her arms out to me. I allowed myself to step into her hug and put my arms around her. It struck me, as we stood there, that I could not remember the last time my mother had hugged me or I had returned her hug. Perhaps it had been that time when I had realised Matt Goss was never going to love me back. Her perfume was different now, but the softness felt the same and even though I was angry with her, even though a part of me would never understand why she had left, I felt tears spring to my eyes.

"Mum," I said into her hair and she pulled me a little closer, "I need you."

"I'm here," she whispered – and, even though we were in a very public place and this was probably entirely inappropriate, I let her hug me a little tighter and a little longer and when we eventually pulled apart and sat down she kept a hold of my hand, even as she poured me a glass of wine and we chinked our glasses together.

With half a glass of wine in me, my tears dried, and our reassurances made that we would try our best to move on together, we started to talk.

"Was it really insensitive of me to come to the shop for a wedding dress?" she asked, blushing. "But, you see, I didn't know how else to get through to you. Charles said it might be a bit full-on – to just swan in and ask you to help me get our wedding organised but I kind of thought 'in for a penny' and all.

I thought it better to jump in at the deep end and I convinced myself it was a good idea – so much so that I was almost giddy when I first showed up. I know now it was stupid and Charles was right. I knew it was stupid the minute I saw your face but then it was started . . ." She giggled nervously and drank from her glass again before looking up at me from under her eyelashes – a coy Princess Diana style pose which allowed me to see that she hardly had any crow's feet at all.

I felt sorry for her that she was so unsure of herself in front of her own daughter and then again there was a voice in my head – which actually sounded remarkably like Ivy's voice – which was saying that of course she would be nervous. She had severed our relationship. I shook my head, trying in some way to dislodge that voice and let the part of me which felt for her, which wished things had been different, to surface again while she rambled on nervously. She was asking me if I thought it was all too much but she was not letting me answer.

"At that stage I wondered whether to just disappear again but Charles said, you know, I had started so I might as well finish. You know, like the TV show . . . oh, what is it?"

"*Mastermind*," I offered and she nodded.

"Yes, *Mastermind*. So I had started so I thought I might as well finish and, well, the dress was lovely . . ."

"It is," I said. "You will be beautiful."

"You'll be there on the day? Won't you? I know it is a big ask and I know that Ivy is probably a lost cause. But you will be there – you and Mark of course?"

At the mention of Mark's name, I felt what little resolve I had waver further and I bit my lip to avoid yet another over-emotional display. But it must have shown. My face must have fallen – my crow's feet must have multiplied or something – because my mother stopped talking and looked at me.

"Kitty," she said, "are you okay?"

"I'm fine . . . I'm okay . . . I'm, well . . . Mark . . . Mark and I . . . we split up."

"Oh Jesus," she said, holding my hand tighter and swivelling in her chair so that she was closer to me. "When did this happen?"

"A few weeks ago."

"And why? What happened?" She sounded genuinely shocked and in a weird way that comforted me. The whole how-the-feck-did-this-happen response of people who knew us, even a little bit, made me feel like the last few years hadn't just been one big lie even if it seemed that, on his part anyway, they had been.

"He left. He's off to find himself. It just wasn't working." I half-laughed and half-cried and waited for the reassuring hugs and requisite referral to my husband as a useless fecker.

My mother, however, just shook her head and looked downwards.

"Out of nowhere," I continued. "He just decided that I wasn't enough any more. And he went."

She looked back at me, her face flushed.

"I thought we were happy, all this time. I thought we had it all together. We were even talking about starting a family – and please don't tell me that at least it is a blessing that we didn't get that far because I don't want to hear that. So, I thought I was putting my whole life back together again. But he's back – and he wants to talk. And I don't want to talk because what is there to say?"

"Maybe he needs a chance to explain himself?" she offered.

"He did that, in a note. He left it for me and then left me, without warning. He just went. Walked out on our lives. How could he do that? How could anyone do that? Just walk out on their life? Walk out on the people who care about them?"

I felt my mother let go of my hand as I talked, saw her lift her glass and sink what was left in it before lifting the bottle and topping it up again. Her hand didn't come back to rest on mine as I chattered on about my feelings of betrayal and it was only when I saw her sniff and wipe a tear from her eye that it dawned on me that, as much as I was talking about Mark and what had happened between us, I was also ripping apart old wounds.

"Jesus," I said, stopping and not quite knowing where to go from there. I didn't want to simply say that it was okay and of course I didn't mean her and of course I understood how her circumstances were completely different, because I didn't believe that. Oh Christ, we were both making an absolute arse of what was already a pretty arsey situation.

"I didn't want to do it that way," she said softly, her body language changing, her demeanour suddenly bristly. "I didn't know what I wanted. I know I messed up. There hasn't been a single day since then that I don't wish that I'd done things differently. Your dad is a good man. You and your sister were good kids. I wish I had something deeper to say than it just wasn't enough . . . but it wasn't enough. I tried for a long time to pretend that it was – to settle down to motherhood and being a wife. I tried but I couldn't. I didn't want to hurt any of you but I couldn't go on hurting myself. I know that sounds selfish."

I let her words sink in. It sounded selfish because it was selfish. We weren't enough? We were her children. She had committed to having us, she should have gone on and committed to raising us. Just like Mark had committed to me, to us and to our future. Just as he had sat and talked through his dreams and hopes and everything else with me and then just walked away. I shook my head and realised this had probably been a bad idea to begin with.

"I'm sorry," I said. "This was too soon. Too much."

I lifted my bag and stood up and she reached out to my arm.

"Kitty, please. Sit down."

"Mum," I said, vaguely remembering when I used to call her mammy and she was my be-all and end-all, "you don't get to ask me to stay. Not now. I asked you to stay. I wrote to you and asked you to come back. To please come back but you didn't."

She looked wounded and, while I didn't like to see her that way, I thought about how wounded I was. I was then and I was now and I didn't have the emotional energy to try and make her feel better.

"I had to get out. I needed to get away."

"Why?" I said, my anger building. "Why? Were we bad people? Did we do something wrong? Did we treat you badly or make you miserable? For years I blamed myself. I thought, if only I hadn't been so grumpy. If only I had helped more around the house. If only I hadn't sneaked the last of your favourite biscuits or if only I hadn't told you that one time that you were the very worst mother in the world . . . Do you know what that is like, Mum? To be abandoned by the one person who should be there for you? And what about what you did to Dad? How you left him?"

"It's not as simple as you make it out, Kitty," she said, her eyes fixed on me, her voice a gruff whisper, clearly shocked that I was making a scene, that I was telling people in a public place that she was a horrible mother.

"Yes, I've heard the whole needing-to-know-who-you-were speech. I've heard it from you and I've heard it from my husband. And you know what? It's a cop-out. A big fat selfish cop-out. You found yourself – you made your life. You made your choices. You can't just walk away when it doesn't feel perfect. Jesus, you stay and you work at it because it deserves to be worked at. I deserved to be worked at – and here you are, smiling and choosing a flipping wedding dress in my shop, and expecting me to be some sort of big fat ageing fecking flower girl watching you get your happy ending. Well," I said, my voice filled with vitriol, "shove your happy ending! Shove finding yourself. Shove putting yourself first for once. What about us? What about me?"

Her mouth opened and closed and I didn't care because at that moment I was just sick, sore and tired of people using excuses as to why it was okay, why I should feel sorry for them, for abandoning me. Was I really just supposed to smile and comfort them and say that it was okay, as long as they didn't feel trapped any more? What was it about me that made people feel suffocated? In my adult life I had rationalised all those feelings

I'd had as a child – those strange feelings that I had pushed my mother away and that it had been my fault. I had told myself that was daft. Mark had helped me believe I was daft – he had held me as I cried about her ongoing selfish behaviour and made me realise this was about her and not me. And yet, he was the one who had walked out as well – who had abandoned me. To be abandoned once was bad luck – but to be abandoned twice? Well, that was no mere coincidence. Clearly I was very much faulty goods. This, all of it, had been a terribly bad idea. Suddenly I had the urge to be back in the small, humid bedroom where I had spent the long weekend after Mark's departure. I felt safe there. I would be okay there.

"Kitty, please," she offered again and I just held my hand up, turned and walked away and vowed that I was not going to look back. She hadn't.

Ivy and Michael were watching *Coronation Street* when I battered on their door. Both were in their pyjamas – which of course were ironed. Thankfully, they weren't matching.

It was Michael who answered the door and looked mildly alarmed to see me standing on his doorstep looking more than a little dishevelled, the make-up streaked down my face from the tears I had shed in the car on the way over. I sniffed – a loud, snottery sniff which made even me wince. The sound was not pleasant and I fully understood why Michael might look a little green around the gills as I dragged the sleeve of my cardigan across my face and asked if Ivy was in.

"She's in the living room," he said, stepping backwards out of way and letting me in. I nodded my thanks and walked past him, straight to the living room where Ivy was looking at the door.

Michael walked in behind me. "It's your sister," he said, as if she couldn't see me. "She seems a little upset."

I wondered for a second if I had stepped into some alternate dimension where I was wearing some sort of weird and wonderful invisibility-cloak. Ivy looked from Michael to me and back to Michael again. I sniffed again – thankfully not so loudly or in such a snotter-laden manner – and this was enough to bring my sister's eyes back to me.

"It's me," I said. "And yes, I'm a little upset. You were right. You were so right. She's just the same. She's just putting herself first. And Mark's putting himself first and it is all finally making sense now and it's just crap and I know right now you probably think all of this serves me one hundred per cent right because I think I know it all and I'm a big stupid eejit but I need you. Because you won't abandon me, sure you won't?"

Ivy glanced at Michael again who turned and left the room and then she got up, walked towards me and hugged me tightly, telling me it would all be all right – in the exact same way she had done when our mother had walked out on us all those years before.

An hour later and I was sitting in a pair of perfectly ironed pyjamas on Ivy's sofa, drinking hot chocolate from Emma Bridgewater mugs and eating toast, which Michael had made and presented to us before leaving again. Ivy had listened – uncharacteristically she hadn't offered her usual strong opinions. She had just nodded. She knew, I suppose, that she didn't need to offer those strong opinions because I was increasingly becoming aware of where I went wrong.

The only time she blinked – the only time there was a flicker of what-the-feck across her face was when I told her I had slept with James.

"I know," I said, as soon as I said it and saw her reaction. "It was a mistake. He has feelings for me – I see that now– but it was nice to feel needed. But I knew as soon as we were done that it had been a mistake. Sure, it made me no better than Mark. I'm a cheater too. I've been raging all this time about giving up on our marriage, but is that not what I did?"

"No," she said, shaking her head. "That's not what you did at all. It was different." She paused, sipped from her tea and smiled.

"What are you grinning at?"

She giggled and whispered. "James? Really? I mean, I don't mean to make light of things, well, not that much anyway . . . but James? Don't tell Michael but I always thought James was hot. Was he hot? Was it good sex?"

I blushed and smiled, relieved she hadn't castigated me there and then as a harlot. "It was . . . different."

"As in sexual-deviant different, or just not the same as Mark?"

I looked at her, sitting there in her stripy pyjamas with fluffy slippers on her feet and her hands wrapped around a cup of milky tea and I realised I hadn't really ever heard my sister talk about sex before and it kind of unnerved me. Even though it was me who'd started it.

"Not deviant, no," I smiled. "But different to Mark. Clumsy maybe, you know when you don't know each other very well and you aren't quite sure what to do . . . but yes, it was good, you know, physically. But emotionally . . ."

"I'm being inappropriate, aren't I?"

"Yes, a little. After all, your pyjama-wearing husband is not that far away, I'm a bit of an emotional wreck and, *eugh*, I don't need to hear my sister talk about S.E.X.!"

We laughed as we talked and I cried a little – but less than I had done and she made it all feel a little better and I was grateful to have spent some time in her company. She kissed me on the top of the head before I went up to bed in her spare room and, as I lay in the comfortable double bed in her perfectly designed guest room, I vowed that the day after would be a better day. As I was drifting off I heard the door creak open and my eyes jolted awake, really hoping I wasn't about to see Michael in his poly-cotton-mix pyjamas looming towards me. But it was my sister, who climbed into the bed beside me and hugged me close, just as she had done when I was smaller.

"It will be okay, Kitty cat," she whispered. "Everything will be entirely okay. We'll get through it and I'll be with you every step of the way. Me, you, Rose and Dad. And the rest of the world can go hang. We are family."

"I've got my big sister with me," I sang back, remembering how we used to sing that together when we were little. We squeezed hands and chatted a while longer until we both fell asleep.

28

Erin

Ian phoned two days after the magazine hit the shelves. There I was, having a sneaky look at the *Daily Mail* website at the celebrity-gossip section, when the phone rang. I answered absentmindedly – "Erin Brannigan, hello?" – and when I heard his voice my heart jumped to my throat before plummeting at the speed of light right to the very bottom of my boots. I'm not entirely sure if I said it out loud, but I think that I probably did. I'm pretty sure he heard me say "Shit" at least three times in quick succession.

"I didn't know you still cared," he said, his voice nervous in tone. He was trying to make a joke but it wasn't working.

Neither of us was finding this very funny.

"I didn't think you'd see it . . ."

"Well, normally *Northern People* wouldn't be my magazine of choice but I happened to have a doctor's appointment and my doctor is one of those rare breeds who keeps his magazines up to date and I saw your name on the front: 'Erin Brannigan talks love, marriage and broken hearts.' And of course I was going to read that, wasn't I?"

My face flushed – I could feel the crimson tide rising and I contemplated simply putting the phone down and pretending that I hadn't been having this conversation at all.

"I mean, when I read the blurb I figured I might have featured. I didn't really expect to see a picture of me in my swimming shorts staring back out at me."

"Your face was blurred. I – I didn't use your name," I stuttered.

He laughed that laugh that used to make me weak at the knees – before he turned out to be a complete bastard of course. "I'd recognise those shorts anywhere. And that beach. And that day, I remember it well."

"It was a long time ago. A lifetime ago."

"It was nice to remember it," he said.

"Even the bit where you left me at the altar?" My voice was light but inside I was wondering how on earth he could answer this one without digging himself deeper.

Of course I'd had my explanation at the time – he didn't want to settle down just yet, it had all got out of hand, he was sorry etc. I had tried so hard to talk to him after that, thinking that if we had just talked through all those concerns and all those worries we could have been fine and we could have gone ahead with our wedding and this whole jilting-at-the-altar carry-on would have been a blip in an otherwise blissful relationship.

That didn't happen though – he ignored me and I cried, and I shouted in his letterbox at four in the morning and he still ignored me and I cried some more and then I had gone a bit wild – drank too much, slept with two men I barely knew (not at the same time) and smoked cigarettes even though they made me vomit. When I had got all the screaming and crying, smoking and drinking and dodgy dalliances with dodgy men out of the way, I had woken up one Wednesday morning realising I could pretty much do whatever I wanted with the rest of my life and I wasn't tied to anyone or anything and I breathed a sigh of relief.

In fairness that had been more than a year after he had left me and in that time I had been to hell and back, but it had ultimately been a good thing. I told myself that and had continued to tell myself that until any shadow of doubt had been removed. Ian and what we had been through had, to a large extent, been consigned to my memory. Hearing his voice, discussing what happened with him, was unsettling. I felt as if everyone in the office was looking at me, listening in, aware of who I was talking to. I glanced up while I waited for his response but everyone was going about their business, oblivious to my beaming red face and my increasingly hushed tones.

"Yeah, well . . ." he answered at last, "maybe not that bit. I really was a bit of a dick, wasn't I?"

Although I was over him, my heart leapt to hear him say those words.

"Yes," I said, still doing my very best to keep my voice measured. "Yes, you were. But it was the nineties. We were all a bit stupid and simple then. Sure we all thought we were brilliant and witty and knew it all then. Eejits, the lot of us!"

He laughed again, that deep, delicious throaty laugh and I kicked myself under the table, a way of trying to remind myself that a) he was my ex for a reason, b) he broke my heart and I hated him, and c) I was in love with Paddy (who I was still annoyed with) and I was marrying him in two months' time.

"The folly of youth," he said. "And look at you now, all grown up and getting married. For real this time. With a big dress and everything."

"Yes," I said. "Yep, the Big Day. The real thing. A big dress and a bouquet from a proper florist's and all."

"Is he a good man?"

I paused while I tried to find the words. "A really good man," I said, because he was. Paddy was a good man. And this whole conversation felt wrong. "But look, Ian, I really must go, so unless there is anything else you need?"

"Coffee?" he asked.

"You want coffee?"

"With you."

"With me?"

"You can keep repeating or you can say yes. I just thought, you know, after all these years, just to meet. Lay some ghosts to rest. Catch up and move on."

The thought of laying some ghosts to rest appealed to me. There were so many uncertainties – so many things which felt unresolved that even though I knew that this was probably a bad idea I found myself agreeing to his request and we made plans to meet that weekend in the local Starbucks for a chat.

I hung up the phone, looked at the grinning picture of Paddy on my desk and felt wretched with guilt. I could just not show up, of course, but this was something that I needed to do. So I pushed the photo just that little bit out of sight and decided to go on with my day as if nothing at all unusual had happened.

Coffee is never just coffee. Not when a man asks you. Not when a man who nearly married you once asks you anyway. I knew that. That's why I bought something new to wear – why I skipped out in my lunch break and had a quick run around the city centre, stopping to pick up a taupe shift dress, nipped in nicely at the waist with a thin belt, in a small boutique close to The Diamond. It screamed professionalism – something that Lois Lane would most definitely wear waiting for her Superman to sweep her off her feet.

We had that chat once, Ian and I, in the cafeteria at university, just a few weeks after we had met, when we were still getting to know each other.

"What do you want to be when you are done here?" he asked over a bitter-tasting instant coffee.

"A journalist. I'm going to be a journalist."

"Like Lois Lane?" he said with a cheeky wink.

"Something like that."

"Well, Lois Lane needs a Superman," he had said and had winked at me again and that had been the start of a beautiful, if ultimately completely disastrous relationship.

I wanted him to see that glamorous Lois Lane type creature walk towards him in the coffee shop. I wanted him to see me wearing something glam and figure-hugging. The slightly washed-out trousers and wrinkled M&S blouse I had on wouldn't cut it. Looking at the dress in the mirror in the changing rooms, I decided I would need new shoes as well. The pair I was wearing were comfortable and at one stage had been vaguely sexy in a librarian kind of a way – but now they were wrinkled, worn, the patent scuffed at the heels from driving. They would not do. Lois Lane would not have scuffed shoes. I picked up a new pair of neutral court shoes, with a platform sole and killer heels, not looking at the cost, and handed them over followed by my credit card – but not before adding in a chiffon scarf, a new pair of stud earrings and a mother of pearl hair-clip. I would have to tame the frizz, I thought, adding a pair of oversized sunglasses to the pile before me. I could justify the extravagance, I told myself – after all, the wedding-planning had taken every penny, every ounce of our fun-spends. This was just a little blip. A little blip that would have paid for a good few dinners at our reception but nevertheless . . .

When I got home that evening, Paddy had smiled at me – after I had run upstairs and hidden the new items in the back of the wardrobe and wandered into the living room with a calm expression on my face.

"Good day at work?" he asked, from the sofa where he sat, counting out RSVPs for the wedding and sorting them into yes and no piles.

"Hmmm," I muttered. "Not too bad. Busy, you know." I didn't trust myself to speak to him. I didn't even really trust myself to look at him in case he saw my plans – and, well, let's face it, my deception across my face. "In fact, I'm beat," I told him. "I was thinking I'd just head up for a soak in the bath and then on to bed if that is okay?"

He glanced up, asked if I was sure I was okay. I nodded and repeated that I was just worn out and I left, making my way upstairs and pouring the deepest bath I could. Sinking down into the bubbles I wondered if I was mad – if all of this was just absolutely mad – if I should just phone Ian and tell him some things were best left in the past. No. I reminded myself – I needed some closure. I needed to show him I was okay – that I was good actually. That I was Erin Brannigan, award-winning journalist, and hadn't needed his help to do his Superman impression to help me get there. I had been a success in spite of him breaking my heart so violently that day. I tried to ignore the little part of me which fluttered at the very thought of seeing him again, after all these years.

I had brought my new outfit to work with me. I didn't want to draw attention to myself by wearing it leaving the house. I'd told Paddy I would be working late, helping plan the next edition – it wasn't unheard of. I purposely avoided calling Jules, knowing that I would be unable to keep what I was about to do from her. I had spent the day watching the clock, and looking back at the picture of us together on the beach. When most of my colleagues had gone home I slipped into the staff toilets, changed, applied fresh make-up and tidied my hair before slipping my feet into the very uncomfortable shoes I had bought and spraying myself with some Jo Malone which I kept for special occasions. Slicking on a little lip gloss, I climbed into the car and tried my damndest not to feel like a Very Bad Person.

Ian looked much the same as before – greyer around the temples. A little more wrinkled. A little more weather-beaten. He was dressed in a suit and was lost in a conversation with a person unknown on his iPhone. He looked very serious – the kind of serious he looked when he was discussing things which were very important indeed. Although I very much doubted he was discussing world politics or who was the sexiest Spice Girl on this occasion. I watched him for a few moments, noticing how animated he was, which made him spill the sugar that he was trying to add to his coffee; he tried to sweep it up without pausing in his rant to whoever was on the other end of that call.

I stood and watched him until he hung up. Lord only knows who he was talking to. I imagined it was probably some high-flying business partner but there was every chance it was a girlfriend or a wife and perhaps they were having some big domestic because she had found out that he was in Derry about to have coffee with his ex-fiancée. I felt a shiver of unease sweep through me and I was just about to turn to leave when he hit the end call button and waved to me, smiling broadly.

I wasn't sure how I was to greet him. Were we meant to hug? Were we meant to kiss? In a French way? Not with tongues or anything, just on each cheek? Were we meant to shake hands or just nod in each other's direction, vaguely acknowledging the other's existence before maintaining a respectable distance from each other across a wooden table with a couple of coffee cups and a white ceramic milk jug and sugar jar on it?

He stood up. I had forgotten how tall he was – how he made me feel small, dainty. I had forgotten the bulk in his body, the width of his shoulders. As I walked towards him I took a deep breath and reminded myself this was just about laying ghosts to rest – nothing less and nothing more. His smile widened further and we went for a strange, slightly awkward combination of a variety of greetings. He tried to hold my hand as I tried to shake his, and I leant towards him for a hug and felt his lips graze against my cheek, his stubble scratching me slightly. He was wearing Armani aftershave – the same one he used to wear when we were together. I was under no illusion he wore it for that reason.

"Erin, you look amazing," he said, standing back and looking me up and down. There was a longing in his eyes. His gaze took that little bit too long, his smile was a little bit too wide – too forced. "You really do," he said, and I tried to find words to respond.

I wanted to tell him he looked great too but I was struck dumb at the sight of him and I wanted to kick myself for regressing thirteen years to that person I was back then when I followed him around like a lost dog looking for his approval. I nodded. I really hated nodding – it made me look like one of those stupid dogs from the back of cheap cars. I only nodded when I was nervous – when I was freaking out just a little inside. Sit down, I told myself, pulling my hand from his and sitting down, thankful for the table and the milk jug and the very oxygen between us.

"I never thought I would see you again," I said, finding it hard to meet his gaze. I didn't tell him that in the past I had searched for him on Facebook only to find he was one of those rare beings who didn't have a profile. I had Googled his name and found out that he was working in Belfast, in PR of all things – the industry he had slammed as 'the dark side' when he was filled with ideals. But despite working in similar fields we had never met and, after a couple of years of panicking that one day we would come face to face in a work situation, I had just stopped thinking about him. There was the occasional time, of course, when a song played that was out at the time we had been together or when I got a whiff of Armani aftershave or gin – he loved his gin – that I thought of him. But mostly he was nothing to me – not until recently. Until things had become so difficult. Until I started planning a wedding and all those memories had come flooding back in full Technicolor.

"No, I got quite the surprise when I saw that picture in the magazine. It was a blast from the past. Christ, we were so young."

"We were so stupid," I said, pouring one sugar into the black coffee he had ordered for me. He still remembered, I noted, how I drank my coffee. He had even ordered me a cinnamon swirl.

He laughed at the word stupid. "We really did think we knew it all. God – we were going to get married? Shit! Could you imagine it?"

I laughed too, but I bristled and fought the urge to kick him very hard in the shins with my nice new shiny patent shoes. It wouldn't have been that bad, would it? It wouldn't have been that shit?

"It wouldn't have ended well," I said, and I knew that was true but part of me wanted to say he should have at least given it the chance to start. "In fact, it didn't end well, did it?"

He coloured. "It wasn't my finest moment. But in the long run . . . God, Erin. I think, well, I don't know . . . I could have handled it better. I just freaked out and yes, I'll admit I was a total coward and I took the easy way out."

"You left me to tell our friends. You left me to come home and face my mother and tell her, despite the note I had left being all dramatic and declaring I was off to get married, and the heartache I had put her through." I didn't tell him that I had seen the hidden 'I told you so' behind her eyes for years afterwards.

"That must have been shit," he said, looking at the table, stirring his coffee which was already very well stirred.

"It was," I said, not feeling the need to elaborate further. Shit is as shit was – there was no need to explain to him exactly how shit it had been.

"But things happen for a reason," he said. "Sure look at you now – fantastic-looking, ready to get married for real this time. Big dress and all. You seem to be doing very well for yourself and this man of yours, from what you wrote in the magazine, he seems like one to keep."

"He is," I said, because what else would I say? That lately, for reasons I couldn't quite fathom, I wanted to run screaming. Could I tell him that a week ago I had kept vigil by Paddy's bed begging for him to be okay and now that he was, now that Dr Glib had declared they had probably done as much as was needed, I wanted to throttle him? The irony was certainly not lost on me. I decided, wisely, not to go there with that. Instead I just repeated that he was certainly one to keep and then asked him about himself – was he married? It annoyed me that I cared.

"No, I'm single," he said. "Haven't found the right woman yet."

If, of course, this was a Hollywood movie he would have followed that with a simple 'Or should I say, I did find the right woman but then I let her go'. But this was not a Hollywood movie. This was a coffee shop in the middle of Derry two months before my wedding. And he didn't add anything. He just let it hang there.

"I bet you aren't short of attention," I said, cringing at myself, aware that it sounded very much like I was flirting with him. I sipped from my coffee in an attempt to cover up my embarrassment and reached for the cinnamon twirl, unwinding it and licking the icing from my fingers.

"You haven't changed a bit," he said, laughing. "You haven't learned to eat that like a proper grown-up yet!"

"I'll have you know, many proper grown-ups eat these just like this. It's the 'in' thing. Don't pretend you don't have your foibles. Don't pretend you don't eat all the chocolate off the side of your Kit Kats first before eating the wafer – because I've seen you, Ian, and those aren't the kind of habits you grow out of."

"Guilty as charged," he laughed again and I found myself relax. "Do you still eat all the chocolate off Peanut M & Ms before you eat the nuts?"

"Do you still always have to have two fried eggs side by side on your cooked breakfast so that they look like a pair of boobs?"

"Do you still wear mismatched socks under your boots just because you think it makes you a bit quirky?"

"Do you still secretly want to shag Fern Britton?"

He laughed and I laughed and I offered him some of my cinnamon swirl and he managed not to induce my wrath by continuing to unroll it instead of biting into it.

"This is probably the cheesy bit where I say it wasn't all bad?" he said, gazing at me.

"And this would probably be the part where I agree with you and say no, of course, it wasn't too bad," I said. "It was good a lot of the time. Immature maybe and misguided but good. We had fun."

"If I could go back and live just one of those days on the

beach again, sitting by the campfire, not worrying about anything or anyone and not caring about the future, I would do it in a heartbeat."

I smiled and nodded. "It would be nice, wouldn't it, for one day? But it's not real life. It wasn't then really, when you think about it. It was like our very own 'Summer of 69' – Bryan Adams could have written a song about it for sure. Drinking and lazing about and having no responsibilities other than whose turn it was to go to the bar next or who was going to nip to the pizza place."

"Hmmm, pizza," he said, smiling. "I would love some pizza."

"Still the same," I said. "Still want everything on it?"

"Except anchovies?" he smiled and I grinned back.

"Who the holy feck . . ."

". . . would eat anchovies?" he said, finishing my sentence and mimicking me.

We sat back for a moment, both lost in our memories. Or at least, I was. My rose-tinted glasses were most firmly perched at the end of my nose and everything had taken on a nice hazy, nostalgic glow.

"Would it be mad to actually go for some pizza? You know, coffee is grand and all but pizza tastes so much better. And maybe get a bottle of wine?"

It was tempting, very tempting . . . so I found myself agreeing. Worse than that, I found myself excusing myself, nipping to the toilets, texting Paddy and telling him I was going for a drink with the girls from work and then putting my phone on silent and stuffing it to the bottom recesses of my bag. I looked at myself in the mirror, tried to see a hint of the twenty-year-old I had once been and pulled my skin taut, smoothing out the fine smattering of wrinkles. I pursed my lips, reapplied my lip gloss, smoothed my hair down, spritzed some more perfume on my wrists and walked out of the bathroom and off on what was, for all intents and purposes, a date with the man who had once broken my heart into a million pieces.

No, a coffee was never really just a coffee.

29

Kitty

Rose and Ivy were both present at what became the official wedding-ring-removal ceremony.

It was at the end of a busy day in the shop and Ivy had arrived with a very big box of Thornton's chocolates and a bag of fun-size Curly Wurlies. Rose had chilled one of our final bottles of Rosé Prosecco and we had sat on the floor of the dressing room, having a little picnic to ourselves.

After my night at Ivy's, things had improved dramatically between us. She had vowed that she would be there for me, and she had said she would hold my hand every step of the way so that the person I was relying on for support was not my ex-husband's ex-best-friend – who had morphed into some kind of bunny-boiler stalker in the two days since we had slept together.

In fairness to James, even though I had been vulnerable and things had been terribly, terribly mixed up, I had probably led him on. I had kissed him back when he kissed me and ultimately it had been me who had led him to the bedroom and let him undress me and have his wicked way with me . . . twice. After the awkward morning after – which by the tone of his emails he seemed to think wasn't at all awkward and was in fact lovely and relaxing – I had texted him to say I needed a bit of space.

I don't know who I am at the moment and I need some room to find out I had written and had, in fact, sent that text to James, my mother and Mark.

My mother had replied with a brief message – self-pitying in tone – about how much her Big Day meant to her and how it would make it just perfect if I was there. Of course she had skipped over the whole assuring me that she loved me and that she was there for me in the wake of the soul-destroying, heart-wrenching, nightmarish end of my own marriage but that was Mum all over.

Mark had replied, almost instantaneously. **We need to talk, Kitty. You take the space you need but please let me talk to you at some stage.** He finished his text with **LYF** – our code for Love You Forever (which yes, I know is pretty vomit-inducing). Seeing those three letters ran a whole myriad of emotions straight through my body in very quick succession. Sadness, hope, anger, annoyance, love – they were all there and I had to stop, put the phone down and catch my breath for a second.

James had texted and emailed and called. And sent flowers. Two bouquets in two days. His messages varied between **Please call me** to asking if I had any regrets, to telling me to stay strong and that he was there for me. Ivy had threatened to call him and scream in her most menacing voice that he needed to back the feck off but I persuaded her against it. But I knew it was down to me. I needed to talk to him and put this right. Awkward as it would be, I needed to tell him it was a mistake. That it had been my mistake.

Sitting on the floor for our Bridal Nook picnic, I told Ivy and Rose what I had been thinking all day.

"I'm not saying I'm fine," I said. "I'm not saying I know exactly where I'm going or what I'm doing but I do know that it is time for me to pick myself up. I would love it if you were both there to keep me upright from time to time – you know, when

I've had a bit too much to drink and feel a little overwhelmed? – but I want to do this on my own. I have to start doing it on my own."

They had looked at each other and then across at me and then back at each other.

"Am I supposed to just crumple from now until eternity? Am I supposed to turn into some sort of demented divorcee selling wedding dresses and being sour the whole time? My husband cheated on me . . ." The words hurt, they cut through me, but them hurting wouldn't make them any less real. "I always said if he cheated then that would be it. Maybe it wouldn't have been if he had told me – if he had come home and cried that he was sorry and it meant nothing and he would never do it again – but he didn't do that. He cheated and he walked out on our relationship without even giving me the chance to try and stop him. His mind, despite his texts begging to talk, was clearly made up. If I took him back now, there are no guarantees that he wouldn't do it again. I'd rather live through the shit of piecing all this back together than live wondering every night if he was going to be home when I walked through the door. That's no way to live."

Ivy shook her head and Rose rubbed my hand.

"You're a brave girl," Rose said. "You will get through this."

"Oh, I know," I said, trying to convince myself as much as anything. "Sure didn't Daddy get through it? And we thought his heart would be broken forever? But he got through and he found you. He was lucky."

"I was the lucky one," Rose said coyly, sipping from her Prosecco.

I realised then that she might be just a little drunk. She always became very soppy about my father when she had a drink. As a teenager and in my early twenties it used to make me want to claw my own eyes out with embarrassment but now, well, when I realised how precious love was (and when I was a little bit tipsy myself) it made me feel warm inside. I squeezed her hand and thought of how I was the lucky one.

"So," I said, trying not to lose myself too much in the emotion of the moment, "it is definitely time to move on."

"I'll drink to that," Ivy said, raising her glass and tipping it against mine. "Whatever you need, sis, just ask. I know a great solicitor you can talk to. We can get an appointment with one of the advice agencies if you prefer – you know, about dividing your assets. I'm sure the business is in just your name? Whatever you need . . ."

Ivy was like that – practical, pragmatic, fatalist. She made up her mind and she never wavered from her chosen course of action. She kept going until she reached her goal and emotions rarely came into it. In some ways I envied her.

"I'm not sure I'm ready for that just yet," I said softly. "But I know you're the very woman to come to when I am."

"Small steps," Rose said, gently. "Small steps all the way and you will get there."

"Whatever you need," Ivy repeated, topping up our glasses.

"Well, first of all, I need to pee," I said, getting to my feet, wobbling a little. "Then I need to eat a few more of those Curly Wurly yokes. Then I need to put myself firmly first for a change. Rose, could you deal with Mum's order from now on? Whatever it takes? Ivy, as packing is very much your thing, can you help me sort out a few things at home at the weekend?" They both nodded and I clapped my hands together before darting to the loo. Sitting there, slightly hazy on two glasses of fizz consumed on a stomach empty of anything else but chocolate-toffee goodness, it glinted back at me – the platinum band studded with diamonds we had bought together on the Valentine's Day before our wedding.

It was beautiful – but that was all it was now. It didn't mean the same. It might not have been literally tarnished but everything that it stood for was. I had to move on and there was one way to start that process.

Walking back to the dressing room, I stood in front of my stepmother and my sister and I took it off. The indent in my finger remained. I wondered how long it would take to go – how long it would take for any trace of my wedding-ring-wearing to disappear altogether. I looked at the indentation and back at the ring and I thrust the ring towards Ivy, her being the more practically minded of the pair, and told her to put it away somewhere I would never look for it – like Michael's pants drawer or the like. Then I lifted my glass, necked it and decided it was most definitely time to go home before the notion took me to try on a wedding dress and perform a rousing rendition of 'I Will Survive'.

When I got home, I stumbled straight to the bedroom. Sitting on the edge of the bed, I thought the house didn't feel quite so empty. I lay back, rolling into the centre of the bed and stretching out. I glanced at the carpet – still clean, still fresh, not strewn with discarded sweaty socks and boxers. The room itself still smelled vaguely of the perfume I had sprayed that morning and not a mixture of Lynx aftershave and body odour. The laundry hamper in the corner of the room was not overflowing. There were not three mugs on his bedside table and the sheets were crisp and fresh. My finger still felt a little naked but I luxuriated in wearing soft, definitely unsexy pyjamas, and I lifted my book and read with no one grumbling at me to turn the light off or snoring beside me, or stealing the covers.

I woke up feeling light-hearted, well-rested and just a little bit hung-over – but it was nothing that a can of Diet Coke and a bacon sandwich wouldn't cure. Padding down to the kitchen, feeling the warmth of the sun stream through the windows this felt like every cliché in the book. It was the first step on my journey, the first day of the rest of my life, the first . . . erm . . . thing that I did that was different to the day before.

It was only when I reached into the cupboard for some bread that I realised just how different things actually were. There was a scattering of crumbs on the worktop, and the smallest splash of milk. Looking around, I saw that there was a mug with a drain of coffee in it and a teaspoon in the sink. I didn't drink coffee. I had a pathological hatred for spilling crumbs and not wiping them straight up without any form of hesitation whatsoever and I never dumped anything in the sink. Someone had been in the house. Jesus, maybe someone was still in the house! I glanced around, looking for clues but frozen to the spot at the same time, afraid that I might wake a biscuit-loving, coffee-drinking burglar.

I reached for my phone and called Ivy, praying that she would pick up quickly. When she did I spluttered down the phone that someone had been in the house.

"Jesus!" she exclaimed. "Are you okay? Have you called the police? Have they taken anything?"

I looked around again from my vantage point, pinned with fear against the Formica. The TV was still in the corner. My laptop was still on the kitchen table. The small ceramic bowl in which I threw my costume jewellery and bits and pieces when I was cooking was still filled with costume jewellery and bits and pieces. There was no obvious ransacking evidence. No broken glass. I had walked through the hall to get to the kitchen and the front door had been firmly shut.

"No. I don't think there is anything gone. It's just – it's just someone has come in and drunk some coffee and eaten some biscuits."

"Coffee?" Ivy sounded incredulous. "Kitty . . . it must have been Mark."

"Mark? No. He'd never do that surely!" But of course she was right. There was no other explanation.

"Look, I'll be over in ten minutes."

I hung up and stood there, listening. The house was absolutely silent. I should check upstairs . . . if it was Mark he might be asleep. Feeling braver, I walked out to the hall but as I passed the living room I saw that not everything was as it should be.

A jacket was lying over the sofa – a jacket that most definitely was not Mark's. And on the mantelpiece something was missing.

I tried to picture what had been there before and it dawned on me with a sinking feeling that what was gone was our wedding photograph – one in a glass frame of Mark and me staring at each other as we made our vows. I looked at the jacket, I thought of the coffee cup. I thought of who would have a spare key and thought of the conversation I had been avoiding because I was acutely embarrassed about what had happened and horrified at myself for letting it happen. Suddenly I felt very uneasy indeed.

I was moving towards the jacket to check its pockets and maybe verify my suspicions when my phone pinged to life.

I hope you don't mind that I let myself in yesterday. I know you wanted space but I needed to see you. I want to be there for you, Kitty, to help you move on.

I felt my heart sink further still – oh God, this was a mess. A big, horrible mess.

30

Erin

I woke acutely aware that my neck hurt and that I was cold. I was not immediately aware of where I was but a quick fumble at least allowed me to ascertain that I was fully clothed. I sat up and stretched, rolling my head from side to side to loosen the tension in my neck. My hair was still a little touch-damp. Opening my eyes, slowly, visions of the night before came back to me in pieces.

We had indeed gone for pizza, Ian and I, walking along the waterfront, not talking about anything really serious at all – just reminiscing. Trying to remember details of a time long ago. He had held the door open for me and we had entered the restaurant and sat in a small booth away from the window. This was not a conscious decision but I suppose to the casual observer it could have looked as if we were skulking around – hiding in the shadows. We had nothing to hide, but outsiders would not necessarily have known that. Ian had ordered a bottle of red – not the cheapest on the menu and we had laughed at that. There had been more than one occasion when we had scraped together the last of our money for a bottle of the cheapest, vilest plonk the supermarket had to offer and joked that sure it all tasted the same when you were three sheets to the wind anyway. This offering was rich, full-bodied and expensive – not to mention delicious. It may have been the nerves of the situation but I downed the first glass a little too quickly, before our garlic bread (which we both pushed around the plate nervously) arrived. I noticed his glass was emptied as quickly as mine and it wasn't long before a second bottle was on the table and we were laughing heartily about the wedding that never was.

"I got my suit in the Oxfam shop," he said. "I thought I was being so totally righteous and that I was going to save the world. All I could think on the day I put it on, though, was that some old codger had probably died wearing it. Christ, it was hideous!"

"Well," I said, laughing, "if you had stuck around you would have seen the Marks & Spencer finest summer dress I wore. I considered walking in barefoot but it was raining the morning of the wedding so I slipped on a pair of flip-flops."

He laughed loudly – probably too loudly – the kind of laugh that only comes after the best part of a bottle of wine has been sunk and every bloody thing feels hilarious.

When we had settled down, eaten and paid our bill and established once again ad nauseam that we were very foolish when we young, we set out strolling again along the riverfront – a little more uneasy this time. I'm not sure at what point he took my hand but after a while I noticed I was holding his. We were still talking but perhaps not laughing quite so much any more.

"Tell me about him," he said as we strolled.

"Paddy?"

"Yes, Paddy. Is he good to you?"

I paused, bit my lip and nodded. "He is. He always has been."

"So he's the one?"

"Would I marry him if he wasn't?"

"You almost married me . . ." he said and the words hung there.

I dropped my hand from his.

"What's different?" he asked.

My head was fuzzy from the wine – all the emotions, the fear, the worry, the stupid little niggly annoying obsessions with wedding favours and cars and the invitations bubbled up. In the cold light of day it would have been, almost, clear for me to see the difference but, a bottle of wine down and in the company of someone who reminded me of carefree, cancer-free times, it all felt a little hazy.

"He has cancer," I said, the tears springing to my eyes. "And you don't say no to someone with cancer, even if you aren't entirely sure they aren't going to hurt and leave you."

He looked at me, cupped my face in his hands and kissed me gently on the forehead. "Not everyone is me," he said. "Not everyone gets it wrong."

It started to rain then and he grabbed my hand crossing the road to his hotel while the rain battered down on us. Again if this had been a Hollywood movie this is where we would have kissed and I'd have followed him into his room and we would have had mad passionate sex. "I can't go in with you," I said, pushing my hair back off my face.

"We need to clear the air some more," he replied.

"The air's clear. Between us anyway. We made a mistake then and if we aren't very careful we will make one now. The mistake we made back then is one I learned to live with – I don't want to live with this one."

I thought of his words – that not everyone gets it wrong and I thought of Paddy who had only ever really loved me. Yes, he would give the most rampant Bridezilla a run for her money but he did love me. He'd never left me. And if he faced a battle where he might – sure wouldn't he fight it to the very end? Or isn't that what I had thought? It dawned on me that was why I was so angry at him. For just smiling and agreeing with Dr Glib and her "he probably had enough chemo to see him right". 'Probably' wasn't good enough – not when we were talking about the rest of our lives.

"I have to go," I said to Ian, letting go of his hand.

"Are you sure?"

"Yes," I said loudly over the hum of the traffic.

"He's a lucky man," he shouted to my back as I ran, breaking the heel on my new sexy patent shoes, towards a taxi stand and back home to where the man I loved would be waiting for me.

The house was in darkness when I got home. Glancing at my watch, it had gone eleven thirty. Ian and I had spent five hours chatting, reminiscing and flirting. The time had gone quickly but it had gone – and I was in no rush any more to get it back. I wanted to stumble upstairs, climb into bed beside Paddy and tell him that I loved him. I wanted him. I wanted him to fight for us and for himself. I wanted him to fight for the Us that used to be fun – that used to be even more fun than the fun I'd had with Ian when none of it was really real.

I closed the door, probably a little too loudly and, stumbling into the living room, switched on the light and flopped down on the sofa to take off the uncomfortable broken shoes. There was a bottle of Jack Daniel's on the coffee table. We hadn't had Jack Daniel's in the house before that night I was sure, and yet there wasn't much left in the bottle. Just one glass sat beside it, resting on a pile of RSVPs, leaving a condensation ring on them. Paddy wouldn't like that I thought, moving the glass onto the table, sitting it beside a wedding magazine. It was unusual for Paddy to drink, especially since he had been sick – and especially to drink so much but still, I thought, things had been stressful lately he had every right to want a bit of a blow-out. Sure hadn't I just blown out myself, spectacularly. I smiled and vowed to bring him up a pint glass of water when I went up and to tell him it was okay and, even though I would probably be horribly hung-over myself the following day, I would make him a bacon sandwich or fetch him a hangover cure of choice. Whatever he wanted – McDonald's, Wotsits, Lucozade, ice cream – whatever the heck he wanted because I loved him so very much.

Feeling a wave of relief that my meeting with Ian was over and that I hadn't been a stupid eejit and done something I would most definitely regret, I decided to send Jules a text – just to tell her I loved her and that I hadn't messed up, or something equally drunk and cryptic that she would phone me about the following day to ask quiz me on. Lifting my phone from the bottom of my bag where I had hidden it I noticed a series of missed calls and a few text messages.

The first was from Paddy: Who are you with?

The second was also from Paddy: Erin, please call me.

The third was from Grace – something boring and work-related. My eyes were struggling to focus on the words in front of me as they filled with tears. This was not good.

The next message was from Jules: Sis, WTF is going on? Paddy has been on to me asking if I know where you are or who you are with. Said his friend saw you with another man.

Oh shit. The bottle of Jack Daniel's on the table didn't seem so much a blow-out any more. His disregard for the RSVPs (his Bridezilla persona would never have let them get wet) made sense. Oh Jesus . . . we had been spotted. Ian and I. Frig knows what we were doing at the time. Was it as we drank coffee? Was it as we drank wine and laughed madly together? Was it as we walked hand in hand along the waterfront or when he kissed me on the forehead – when that kiss almost turned into something more outside the hotel?

I felt sick to the very pit of my stomach. I grabbed my phone and looked at the messages, looking at the time at which they were sent. We would have been in the restaurant. I breathed a very small sigh of relief – as if I had done something wrong but not been caught out. "I didn't do anything wrong," I said aloud, to myself, to Jules, to Paddy who was more than likely passed out in an alcoholic coma in our bed – convinced I had been cheating on him.

How could I explain this and how on earth would he believe me that nothing had happened at all when I told him the man I was with was Ian? I was dishevelled and still dressed in a new dress and killer heels and looking very much as if it wasn't just a night out with an old friend in a completely platonic way. You don't dress like this for nothing. I felt ashamed and sick as I thought of how this would look to him. He would ask me, I knew he would, that if nothing was happening then why had I lied and told him I was going out with the girls? Why was I dressed to the nines? Oh shit. I couldn't face this. Not now, not when I was drunk. Not when everything was hazy and I wasn't sure how to explain anything. Pouring a stiff glass of Jack Daniel's and swigging it back, I sat back on the sofa and tried to figure out exactly what I was going to say.

I woke up, still on the sofa and still not sure about what the hell I was going to say. The waves of worry swept through me in perfect time with the waves of nausea from the hangover.

The evening started to come back to me, slowly and painfully. Sitting forward with my head in my hands, to try and stop the room, and my world, from spinning, I heard Paddy on the stairs. I didn't really want to look at him – nor did I want him to look at me. I imagined I looked properly shocking – like something that had been dragged through a bush and perhaps thrown up on.

"You came home then?" he asked.

His voice was soft but that wasn't to say I didn't recognise the tone from it. It was as accusing as if he had shouted at me.

"I was home at eleven thirty," I offered. "I sat here. I had a drink. I must have fallen asleep."

"Tired, were you?" he asked accusingly.

"A little drunk," I said, nodding towards the Jack Daniel's bottle on the table. Was it appropriate for me to make a joke about him getting off his trolley too? Probably not. I stayed quiet, trying to word what I was about to say next in a way that wouldn't imply guilt when there was none to imply in the first place.

"It's not at all what you think," I offered, turning to look at him. He looked wretched, standing there skinny in baggy tracksuit bottoms and a faded T-shirt. He looked as if he hadn't closed his eyes all night.

"You're a writer, Erin. Could you not have come up with a less clichéd line than that?"

"There are only so many ways to say it's not what you think," I said, watching as he sat down. I wanted to hold his hand – to have him hold mine back and for the both of us to be very much assured that things were not going, spectacularly, tits up.

"You could tell me exactly *how* it was?" he said. "Because my version isn't pretty. My version involves my fiancée, the woman I am set to marry in two months' time, telling me she was going out with a drink with the girls from work. It then involves a friend of mine calling me and telling me that my fiancée is cosied up to some man eating pizza and drinking wine and occasionally holding hands. Is that not what happened, Erin?"

His eyes were pleading and I wanted to tell him straight away that of course that hadn't happened at all and that his friend had been wrong. But to an outsider . . . of course it was different. Actually, even to me it was different.

"Well, it is . . ."

He stood up and made to leave the room.

"But let me explain, Paddy. It's not as simple as that."

"You lied. That's simple. You were with someone else. That is simple."

"I didn't want to upset you."

"Well, that's flipping big of you," he said, continuing to the kitchen.

I stood up to follow him, my head still swimming. I was meant to be getting ready for work. I was already running late but I couldn't leave it like this.

"Paddy, it was Ian," I offered, hoping that he would realise it was nothing more than a little bit of laying some ghosts to rest.

He stopped, turned to look at me but didn't speak. He grabbed his jacket from the worktop and his keys and while I stood there, waiting for the signal that it was okay to keep talking and to tell him exactly what had happened, he brushed past me.

"Go to work, Erin," he called over his shoulder. "Just go to work."

He left, slamming the door and I stood, rooted to the spot, unsure of what move to make next. I knew this was bad. I knew I should go to work. I knew I needed a long hot shower and a huge mug of black coffee. But more than all of that I knew that somehow I had to make it all better. I just didn't have the first notion how.

31

Kitty

"The first thing you have to do is change the locks," Ivy said, lifting the Yellow Pages from under the hall table and beginning to search for a locksmith.

"Okay," I replied.

"Then you text him and ask him to return the key he does have – even though it will be useless. This will give him the very clear message that it is entirely unacceptable to visit someone else's home without their permission."

"Okay," I said, lifting my phone with my hands still shaking.

"You'll have to text Mark as well, just to let him know."

"About James?" I baulked. The thought of telling Mark about James and what had happened with James – *everything* that had happened with James – made me feel a little woozy and not in a good way.

"Well, you can if you want, but I was thinking more about the keys. Technically it's still his house as well. He should probably know if you have changed the locks."

"Okay," I mumbled, thinking that I would need to talk to James face to face – to tell him he had the wrong idea – that perhaps I had given him the wrong idea, that this had to stop and now. "Jesus, Ivy," I said, feeling sick and making a mental note to check my underwear drawer and do an inventory of my existing quota of knickers so that I would know how many I had in the future and be able to monitor if any went missing. Feeling slightly sick I ran upstairs to where I had been sleeping so very peacefully an hour before and I didn't feel secure and comforted any more.

Ivy followed and sat on my bed beside me.

"It's a bit scary, isn't it? I mean, if you want you can come and sleep at my house for a few nights, or I'm sure Rose and Dad wouldn't mind you staying with them."

"This is my home, Ivy, and this is my mess. I'll text James now, arrange to meet. Tell him we need to talk. I know I led him on but I'll put him straight."

"You haven't spoken to him before now? About this? About what happened?" She tried and failed to hide the look of horror on her face.

I shook my head, feeling embarrassed. "I didn't know what to say. I . . . my head was just up my arse and I thought if I let it go he would get the message. I thought it would just go away."

"And how's that working for you?" she said with a sly grin.

"I know, I know," I muttered. I thought of the jacket thrown so casually on my sofa. He must have left it deliberately – he couldn't have just forgotten it. And I thought of the dirty coffee mug. It was like he was marking his territory.

"Do you want me to come with you?" she asked, more softly this time.

"I think I need to do this on my own, but maybe, you know, if you could perhaps watch from nearby . . ."

"In case he turns out to be a complete nutcase?"

I thought of James and of all the years I had known him. He had never displayed any nutcase behaviour before. He had always been very nice to me. He had always been there for Mark. In fact it was only in the weeks since Mark's departure that I had thought any of his behaviour odd at all. And, honestly, it had only been in the last few days since the whole sleeping-together mistake that his behaviour had started to make me uneasy, but I couldn't deny that I had made him think he was in with a chance.

"Yes, please," I said, because at the end of the day I was a coward.

"I'll do it."

"Thanks," I said, squeezing her hand.

"Now," she said, "why don't you go to work and get on with that whole living-your-life thing that we talked about last night and I'll stay here and wait for the locksmith?"

"Are you sure you would be okay on your own?"

"Would you mess with this?" she said, pulling a face and mock-punching me. She had a point.

"I'm sure Rose would be fine at the shop without me . . ."

"Kitty, you have a bridal photo shoot to plan for a glossy magazine. You have dresses to choose and locations to scout. Such opportunities do not present themselves all that often. I believe you may also have some lovely brides wanting to buy frocks. Go on with yourself and text me and tell me when we are all meeting for the Big Showdown."

I nodded and set about getting ready for work.

"It's like a mad house in here today," Rose said, flustered, as I walked through the door and straight into a huge bouquet of flowers which had just been delivered from James.

I sat them behind the counter (I say 'sat', I mean 'threw') and looked back at Rose. Her cheeks were flushed and she looked a little flustered. Her glasses were sitting on the end of her nose as she stared at the computer screen on the cash desk and handed me several slips of paper.

"I know you like your messages in emails but this silly computer is acting the bollocks. Now, I'm giving you these messages, but from the top of my head we have had two appointments booked in for midweek. Your three-thirty has cancelled – says she has a stomach bug and doesn't want to boke all over her dress. She wants to rearrange for the same time next week but we're booked up so you might have to call her and see what suits you both as it's a fitting. I've had two calls from suppliers – shipments have been sent out. Deliveries should be here on Tuesday. It's orders and a few new samples that you ordered. James called. Your mother called – asked if you could give her a ring. *Northern People* have been on the phone checking the best time for the photographer to call down for a preliminary scout and asking what size your samples are so they can book the models. Oh, and this one is important, Jane Kelly called. She needs a last-minute alteration. Her wedding is at two."

"But the dress was fine on Thursday?" I said.

"Yes, but it appears one of her bridesmaids may have had a minor falling-off-the-wagon incident with her diet and may need a little help before she busts at the seams."

"Oh, right – well, Rose, my lovely, you'd best grab your trusty repair kit and scoot on over there."

"We have an appointment due in twenty minutes. Will you manage on your own?"

"Course I will," I said, thinking it really was about time we hired another member of staff. I'll just have to close the door and get on with it."

"I'll be back as soon as I can," she said, hurrying upstairs for her sewing box.

When she came back down she kissed me on the cheek.

"Those are lovely flowers," she said, glancing at the discarded bouquet behind the desk. "You should put them in water."

I smiled at her but as soon as she left lifted them and rammed them as far into the bin as I possibly could. Then, returning to the cash desk, I set about replying to my emails (unsurprisingly the computer worked perfectly for me – Rose never was good with technology) and setting up the photo shoot. I arranged for Liam to call down at three thirty to check out the location for the photos and he told me he would bring Erin with him, which was perfect because one of the dresses due to arrive on the following Tuesday would be hers. I'm sure she had more than enough on her plate to be worrying about without worrying if her dress would arrive on time. This would make things just that tiny bit easier. Oh, and I could show her the dress I thought would be perfect for her to wear for the photo shoot.

I was about to text Mark and James both when my ten thirty appointment arrived, nervously shuffling in the door and glancing around as if she wasn't really meant to be there.

"I booked an appointment," she said nervously. "Justine Duffy?" A woman I assumed to be her mother and two similarly nervous-looking bridesmaids stood behind her.

"Ah Justine!" I said. "Welcome to The Dressing Room! Why not have a seat and we can chat about what you have in mind?"

She perched nervously on the edge of the chaise longue. It never failed to surprise me how some women could be so very nervous about choosing their wedding dresses. They came in almost pale with nerves as opposed to buzzing with excitement. I sat down opposite her and smiled my best professional smile.

"Now I know this can be a little nerve-racking, but let's try and make it fun. We cater for a wide range of tastes and budgets here. We have an in-house seamstress who can do any last-minute adjustments and we carry a wide range of accessories. I know that can sound a little overwhelming – but I can assure you now we don't do the hard sell. I'm not happy unless you are one hundred per cent happy with the gown you choose and I will always recommend you go away and consider your decision before you place an order with us. So please try and relax."

Justine looked at me, and breathed out, exhaling a knot of tension she had obviously been holding within her. "I never thought I would ever get to this day," she said. "I just want to look my best."

I looked at her, her fine, glossy blonde hair, her small frame, her delicate cheekbones. I had no doubt whatsoever we could make her beautiful.

"You will be stunning. You really will. At The Dressing Room we aim to take your breath away and that of your husband-to-be as you walk down the aisle."

She smiled broadly, and her mother and bridesmaids smiled too as I reached for my notepad and pencil.

"Are you married yourself?" her mother asked as three sets of eyes glanced down at where my wedding ring used to live.

I glanced myself. The indentation was still there. I baulked – not sure how to answer. Yes – legally I was. No – technically the vows of our marriage had been broken. Emotionally – yes, I hadn't quite made that leap yet. I opted for a smile and a "Sort of" and hoped they weren't the nosy kinds. Clare's mother blushed and I laughed a little too loudly to show I was fine and then we set about choosing a dress.

In the end Justine's dainty doll-like figure worked best in a figure-hugging dress with stunning lace detailing. They all cried. I may even have shed a tear myself – and when they were gone I looked once more at my finger and vowed to go out and purchase the biggest, flashiest cocktail ring money could buy, to wear at the earliest opportunity.

I picked up a text from Ivy to say the locks had been changed and she would give me the keys when we met for the big old James meeting, which reminded me that I hadn't texted James yet. To be fair, I didn't really know what to say to him. Was I simply to say we needed to talk without giving him any idea what we would talk about? I didn't want to give him any notion whatsoever that 'needed to talk' was code for 'needed a quick shag' or 'I need to tell you I love you' but I didn't want to be so cold as to tell him how I really felt over a text. My fingers hovered over the buttons on my phone before I typed out a quick **Can we talk? Starbucks at 6?** message. It had barely been sent before a message pinged back to me with **YES** written in capital letters complete with a smiley face afterwards. It was fair to assume he had probably taken the message to mean more than it did. I phoned Ivy to fill her in on this latest development and ask if I should text him back just to clarify that this was not a booty call of any description but her advice was to leave things be. "No point in digging any deeper," she said.

Next I texted Mark. **Locks have been changed. Have new set of** keys for you. I hoped this would adequately convey that I was not being a hard-hearted bitch – not yet anyway. Of course, being that texts are very much open to being misconstrued he came back with: To the shop? Is all okay?

Quickly I replied: To the house. All okay. Just being cautious. Which, because when he wasn't being a cheating horrible bastard he was actually quite protective, prompted him to text back telling me he was worried and that I could talk to him if I needed to. Which I thought was a bit ruddy rich considering his recent behaviour. Slamming the phone down on the cash desk in a fit of rage I swore loudly just as Rose walked back in, followed by our twelve o'clock appointment who was looking mildly terrified.

Rose raised her eyebrows at me and made a strange series of facial contortions I took to mean "Are you okay?" and even though it was the very worst thing I could do in the situation I could not stop myself from barking back: "Oh, just the usual. Men! Being feckers. Big lousy cheating feckers."

My bride-to-be, who thankfully was only coming in for a fitting and not to choose a gown, looked on horrified.

"I think I'll come back another time," she said slowly. "Call me to rearrange," she added as she started to back out the door.

I should have called her back, of course, but I just stood there limp while Rose flapped a bit and then stepped in to the save the day.

"Please, pet," she said. "Never mind Kitty here. She's upset. Come in and I'll sort you out. I've seen your dress and it is beautiful! Kit, why don't you take a tea break and I'll take it from here."

I nodded and blushed. Turning to our customer and apologising like a petulant teenager, I then went up to my office and said a long stream of bad words out loud where no one could hear me and I wouldn't make a holy show of myself.

32

Erin

I showered quickly and dressed badly before leaving for work. I didn't apply any make-up, thinking I could just lift some of my stash from my drawer in the office to fix myself up a bit. My skin was blotchy and my hands were shaking ever so slightly – which wasn't so much about the drink as it was about a sinking sense that things had just gone horribly wrong with Paddy. Being the type prone to catastrophising, I had already plotted how horrible this would be for everyone. Rightly or wrongly (and it was very much wrongly as far as I was concerned) I would be labelled the girl who had cheated on the man who had cancer. Paddy would tell his entire family and they would decree I was a bitch of the highest order. I would have to tell Sinéad and Grace who would throw the shittiest of shit-fits ever at the thought of the lost revenue for their forthcoming features and would probably sack me on the spot. And on top of all that, the worst thing imaginable, I would lose Paddy.

Biting back tears I stalked through the office head down until I reached my desk, and kept a low profile as I switched on my computer and checked my emails. There was one from Liam confirming we were going to The Dressing Room at three thirty to plan the photo shoot. I had to fight the urge to open my desk drawer, put my head in and slam the drawer shut repeatedly. As that would more than likely draw a whole heap of attention to me, I just put my head on my desk and prayed that a meteor would crash directly into Derry at that very moment and obliterate life as we knew it.

I still had my head on my desk when Grace walked past, tilted her head sideways to look me in the face and demanded I follow her into her office.

"You look like shit," she said as I sat down. "Are you sick?"

I put my hand instinctively to my forehead, perhaps hoping there would be some form of fever, making all this horribleness an hallucination of sorts.

"No," I said, feeling the clammy coolness of my own temple.

"Time of the month?"

"No."

"Hung over?"

"A little," I admitted, looking up at her.

"Was it at least a good night?"

I snorted and laughed and suddenly couldn't stop laughing even though it was probably the least funny thing in the world ever.

"I'll get you a glass of water," she offered, her face more than a little alarmed.

"I'm fine," I said, straightening myself in my chair. "I'm absolutely fine. I'll get a bacon sandwich and a bottle of Lucozade and put some make-up on and no one will be any the wiser."

"Are you sure? You have been under a lot of pressure."

"Oh Grace, if you only knew the half of it! But shag it. Sure the show must go on. I've a wedding dress to try on and a photo shoot to plan. No bother at all." And then I started laughing again.

"I always come here when I'm stressed out," Grace said, stopping the car at Buncrana beach and looking out over Lough Swilly. "It keeps me grounded. When things were really bad – when I had post-natal depression after Jack was born – we would escape down here and watch the sunset. I know this sounds awfully twee – but sometimes it was just nice to know I was part of something bigger – that the whole world didn't centre around what was going on in my house."

After my second laughter fit Grace had ordered me to her car, saying I was in no state to be in the office and she didn't want me to be the talking point for the office gossips. She had been there herself, she said, when she had agreed to undergo a life makeover several years ago and she knew it wasn't a nice place to be.

In the car on the way to the beach I had told her about meeting Ian. Very kindly she managed not to swerve the car off the road and into a ditch. And I had told her about how Paddy knew we had dinner and how he wasn't happy about it – but in fairness to him he thought it was more than dinner. I told her – admitted out loud – that things weren't perfect between us.

"Things are never perfect between anyone," she said. "Anyone who says they don't occasionally want to throttle the living daylights out of their partner is lying. I love Aidan, I really do, and I consider us to be a fairly strong couple, but there are times when I would gladly do time for cracking a vase over his head."

I laughed and she smiled and I knew that she meant every word.

"People expect a lot from you, Erin. Your situation – it's not one anyone would envy. I imagine the minute that cancer diagnosis walked in the door the reality of who you and he were to each other changed there and then."

"I didn't think it had."

"How could it not? I'd hate to live like that," she said bluntly. "It must feel like walking on eggshells all the time. I hate walking on eggshells. Can I be brutally honest? When you said you were getting married part of me thought that was absolutely lovely and another big part of me thought, and don't get offended, that you were completely off your head."

Her honesty made me smile, even though it should have felt like a sucker punch to the stomach.

"A cancer battle is hard enough without throwing a wedding into the equation."

"Seemed like a good idea at the time," I said wryly.

"I'm not saying it was a bad idea . . . just . . . you know . . ." she trailed off.

"I know."

"Will Paddy listen when you talk to him?" she asked as we walked along the beach, my feet burrowing into the warm sand.

"I don't know. Probably. Hopefully."

"You have to do what is right for the pair of you," she said. "Don't worry about anyone else. Don't worry about the wedding planners or the florist or his family or your family. Don't even worry about the magazine – although I would give Sinéad some distance. Talk it out – do what suits you both. Do you want to marry him?"

"I've probably always wanted to marry him, or at least to be with him. I just didn't want the wedding. I've tried to convince myself over the last few weeks that it's all grand and it will be a great day. I actually do love the dress I've chosen, but the faff and the pressure and the expectation . . ."

"All anyone really expects is that the pair of you get through this, in whatever way you can and how you choose. I'm really sorry if I pushed the whole thing a little bit too hard. I should have known something was up . . ."

I stopped and turned to look at her. "Grace, you have been a huge support to me these last few months. Don't feel bad. It was just one of those things which spiralled out of control."

We walked along the beach a little more, chatting as we went. We even stopped for lunch on the way back.

Eventually I glanced at my watch and realised the time.

"We should get back," I said. "I need to tidy myself up before the meeting at The Dressing Room."

Grace raised an eyebrow. "You still want to go?"

"It's arranged. It's work and, until I know differently, it's all still going ahead. So yes, I'll go."

"If you're sure?"

"Never ask me if I'm sure. I'm not sure about anything any more."

Standing in the changing room in The Dressing Room I looked at the bride in front of me. My hair hung loosely around my face, still windswept from the walk on the beach with Grace. My make-up was scant, only barely covering the excesses of the night before. I could most definitely do with a light smattering of spray tan before the proposed photo shoot. My eyes looked tired, bloodshot even. But the dress was beautiful – very chic. Kitty had outdone herself once again – handing me a dress almost as elegant and flattering as the one I had chosen for myself but different enough so that it gave no clues to as to my actual gown. The lace-covered dress, with delicate lace-capped sleeves and a satin sash under the bust, was beautiful. It clung in all the right places and it would look amazing in the pictures. Liam had been more than happy with the setting on the city walls and the shop for the pictures. We talked about bringing a few props onto the walls, and trying to convince the tourists to stay back for a bit. Liam had wandered out with his light gauges making all sorts of frames with his fingers while Kitty and I had looked on. She seemed distracted and I most certainly was distracted. The whole experience felt a little surreal – Liam with his imaginary cameras, Kitty looking on a little bewildered. Rose was smiling and, if I wasn't mistaken, flirting just a little bit with Liam as Kitty and I looked on.

"Is she always like that?" I asked.

"What, nuts?" Kitty laughed. "Yes. She kind of is."

I watched her pose in front of Liam in more and more theatrical and provocative poses and I laughed. "I'd best tell Liam to get his coat," I laughed. "I'd say he's pulled."

Kitty laughed uproariously. "I don't think my dad would be too happy about that. She's married to him."

"She's not your mum, is she?" I asked in shock, which caused Kitty to laugh more.

"Now there's a story and a half. It's the kind of story I could sell to one of those real-life magazines and make myself a few quid. Rose is my step-mum. I could tell you about my actual mum but it would make your eyes water."

She laughed as she spoke but her eyes were a little dull. Not for the first time I felt like giving her a hug. That would be entirely inappropriate so I settled for a quick roll of the eyes and a "Families, eh?" which made me feel like a total plonker.

"Yes, well. It's not what today is about, so why don't we go inside and try that dress on you. It's not as gorgeous as your actual dress, of course, but beautiful all the same. You must be getting excited now?"

I smiled. "What's that you were saying? I could tell you the full story but it would make your eyes water?"

"One of those days all round then?" she said, putting her arm around me and guiding me down the stone steps and back through the purple doors of The Dressing Room.

And so I stood there in the dress that was not mine, looking at a face that did not look like a happy bride to me.

"Can you pass my bag in, please?" I called to Kitty who was outside the curtain.

She did as I asked without asking what I was at, and I delved in my bag and pulled out my phone and called Paddy. I prayed he would answer – but not even a little bit of me was sure that he would. "Please," I whispered to the phone and to my reflection in the mirror, "Please answer."

My heart leapt when I heard his voice. He couldn't have been that angry. He had answered the phone. That had to mean something.

"Paddy," I started, "I'm standing here, in a wedding dress, not knowing what the hell is happening with us any more. Please, can we talk? Cards on the table, no bullshit talk? Because I swear to you nothing happened with Ian last night. And I know

I was a stupid bitch and didn't tell you I was meeting him but that was the only mistake I made. I swear."

He didn't answer immediately and I swear to God my own heart stopped, waiting for his response.

"Just come home, Erin. Come home and we will talk."

"I'll be there soon," I said, hanging up and putting my phone back in my bag.

I pulled open the curtain to where Kitty was standing, inspecting a pair of shoes and trying to pretend she hadn't heard a word of what I had just said.

"The dress is perfect," I said. "It will be stunning on the day. But I have to go – so if you could help me out of it that would be perfect."

"Of course," she said, and as she unzipped me I wondered what on earth she made of me. Every visit to her showroom had involved some level of high drama or other – she probably thought I was a complete nutcase. Then again, at the moment I did feel like a complete nutcase.

"I'm not usually this flighty or emotional," I offered as she took the dress from me to hang it up.

"Don't worry. I'm not usually this distracted and bitter."

"Shit happens?" I smiled.

"It certainly does," she smiled back. "But for what it's worth, and what little I know, I think things will be okay for you."

"Thank you," I smiled. "And for you? Will it be okay for you?"

"The jury is still very much out on that one, but one way or the other I'm sure it will be."

I didn't care if it was professional or not, but I reached out and hugged her and thanked her for being lovely. Then I set out, my heart in my mouth, knowing that the next few hours would change my life one way or the other.

33

Kitty

I found myself arriving in Starbucks in the knowledge that Ivy was ensconced in a corner somewhere.

The ridiculousness of the entire situation at least lifted some of the tension. I still wasn't sure how I was going to approach it. James had been a great support to me in recent weeks and a friend to me over a number of years. I didn't want to flat out trample all over his heart – but I didn't want him thinking it was okay to have free and easy access to my knicker drawer or to bombard me with texts or phone calls. I should have realised how he felt – to be honest, I had done and it was flattering when my heart was in smithereens. I felt sick as I walked through the door, carrying his jacket in a big shopping-bag.

He smiled at me as I walked in and stood, his arms outstretched as if we were long-lost lovers reunited over a Grande Latte and a gingerbread man. I smiled, too, probably more than a little stiffly, and hugged him briefly and awkwardly with as little bodily contact as I could muster.

"James," I said as I sat down. I reached over and put the shopping-bag down at his feet.

He glanced into it. "Oh. You shouldn't have bothered," he said. "I would have picked it up next time."

I didn't know how to respond to that so I said nothing.

He was staring at me – properly taking in every single inch of my face as if it were the most precious thing in the world to him. Had he always looked at me that way? I didn't know if he had. Or if I had been too blind to notice? It seemed very ridiculous. After all, this was James – the man who had grown up alongside the man I considered, until recently at least, to be the love of my life. We had done everything together – surely I would have noticed this before?

"I've missed you," he said and I felt myself squirm more than a little. I was going to destroy him and all he had done was be there for me and love me. It wasn't his fault I was still in love with Mark and that I didn't love him back.

"James," I interrupted him, thinking it was kinder to stop him before he got into full swing. "Please . . . look, we need to talk. This, it has to stop."

He looked around him and back at me, confusion plastered all over his face and I felt like a Grade A bitch.

"This?" he asked, his eyebrows raised.

"Yes. James . . . it's too much. The flowers, the texts, the . . . visiting . . . the taking our wedding picture."

He blushed, ran his hand through his hair and shifted in his seat. "I didn't take the picture – of course not – I just put it in a drawer. I thought it was upsetting for you to be looking at it all the time. And I came to the house because I wanted to see you – I was hoping you'd be there. So I waited a little but when you didn't turn up, I left."

His eyes were so pleading, there was such love in them and I knew I had to just tell him – to say it fast, like ripping off a plaster.

"I'm so sorry if I led you on, James. I'm so sorry if I gave you the impression this could be more than it was."

"*If* you led me on?" he asked, his eyes darkening.

"Yes," I said, squirming in my seat. "You must have known.

All this stuff with Mark. It's not over – it's so up in the air and I may have given you the wrong signals and I can only apologise for that, with all my heart."

"All your heart," he sniffed, sitting back in his seat and stirring his coffee while he tried to gather his thoughts.

I waited.

He leaned forward and stared directly into my eyes. "There is no '*may* have given me the wrong signals' about it, Kitty," he said, his voiced wounded. "You *did* give me the wrong signals. You *slept* with me, Kitty!" His voice was hoarse and angry. "You let me come round to your house every night and be with you, to comfort you, cook for you, hug you when you cried and then you took me to bed. I don't see how that *may* have been the wrong signals."

"I'm sorry," I said, tears pricking my eyes. "This is just a mess. And Mark – I don't know how I feel about what's happened."

"You don't know how to feel about him running off and leaving you and sleeping with someone else?" he sneered and I felt as if I had been slapped in the face.

"We're married, James, and even though it's over it's complicated. What do we do now, where we go from here? All of it is just confusing and messy and I don't have space for someone else right now." I felt a tear run down my cheek, which by now was blazing from shame. How could I have got it so wrong?

"You had space for me in your bed," he said a little too loudly, causing a few heads to turn. "You can't really be thinking about going back to him?"

"When did I say that? I didn't say that. All I said was that it was complicated and I don't know who I am any more so perhaps it's not the best time to throw myself headlong into something else."

"So you want to throw yourself in but you are holding back?" There was a faint smile on his face which didn't quite distract from the look of increasing desperation in his eyes.

"No." I shook my head, not wanting to hurt him but not wanting to lead him on either. "I don't know what I want. But this, you, it's too much, James. You sending flowers and texts and coming to my house. It's too much."

"I'll back off," he said and I sagged with relief. "We'll slow things down. I'll cool it with the flowers and the texts, but Christ this is the first time I've had a woman ask me not to send flowers and texts."

The tension that had drained from me just moments before jumped right back in, hunching my shoulders and making my neck seize up. I had to make this as clean a break as possible. I couldn't give him any ideas that this would go anywhere. It wouldn't. It couldn't.

"This isn't about slowing down," I said, trying to stay calm, aware of the public setting. "James, it just isn't right. It can't go anywhere. I'm sorry."

He sat back and sucked air in through his teeth, pulling his hair back from his face and looking at me. I waited for him to talk, for a response of sorts, but he just stared. Then slowly, carefully, in a measured manner, he started to shake his head and he started to laugh. It wasn't a nice laugh. It made me feel uneasy and I felt the tension in my body ramp up another notch.

"You are some *craic*, Kitty Shanahan," he said. "Leading me on. Inviting me to your house – I was good when you needed someone to talk to, someone to hold your hand, someone to sleep with. But, Christ, then you just walk out!" He was spitting the words out, his eyes like flints, his fist clenched. I could see the spittle gather in the corner of his mouth and it made me feel sick to my stomach. His voice was loud and I was sure I heard someone tutting behind us and I felt my face blaze and tears spring to my eyes. I knew he was hurting but, Christ, this was a public place. This was vitriol. This was not fair.

"James," I said, "Please . . . I'm sorry."

He shook his head and pushed his coffee cup away from him. I wasn't entirely sure he wasn't just going to throw it over me. "I don't know what I ever saw in you – no wonder he left. He should have run faster."

My face was now blazing, and there was a slight buzzing in my ears. There was no doubt now that we were being watched – that people were drinking in this soap opera playing out in front of them. "You think you are just so amazing!" he spat. "You and your fancy shop – but you've nothing really, Kitty. You *are* nothing."

I tried to find words to bite back. I really did. I tried to find some way to jump in and defend myself but I was so utterly floored by his anger – by his vicious words. I looked at him, trying to find some trace of the person I had known over the last weeks. I wondered where Ivy was – what she was making of it – why she wasn't jumping in – and I wanted to turn to find her but I was afraid to look around, afraid it would draw more attention to me. I opened my mouth to speak – hoping the words would find a way out. Hoping I could quiet him in some way. I hoped but he just looked at me, goading me with his eyes and he came as close as he could to my face.

"*Nothing*," he said and I closed my eyes to escape his stare.

"That's enough!" a gruff voice spoke above me.

It was my father. I don't know where he had come from, but I was glad he was there. So glad – and yet so completely humiliated. How much had he heard? That I had slept with James?

"No one speaks to my daughter like that. No one should speak to any human being like that. So you, you leave. And you don't come near her again. You don't call. You don't text. You don't wander past the shop. You sure as hell don't try and come anywhere near her house. You leave now – and you go home and hopefully realise what a complete arsehole you have been and you learn to speak to people with more respect and treat them with more respect."

James looked at my father, who had remained calm and even-toned the entire time he had been speaking. Then he looked at me and rolled his eyes before getting up and stalking away, leaving the wretched jacket in its shopping-bag behind him.

I could feel every part of me shaking.

"Thank you, Daddy," I muttered, relieved beyond measure that he had been there to put an end to this horrible confrontation.

He sat down beside me and hugged me briefly.

"Ivy called me. She said you might need back-up. I didn't want to interfere, but I wasn't going to let him talk to you like that."

I nodded gratefully and hastily wiped the tears from my eyes.

"Let's go, Kit," he whispered and I let him lead me outside, aware that Ivy was following us.

It was only when I got to my car and sat in that I stopped shaking. Ivy came to my window and said she would go and leave Daddy and me to have a chat. She gave me an awkward hug through the window and left.

My father got into the passenger seat and held my hand. "All this – it will pass. And one day you will probably laugh about it – hard as that may be to believe now. I know when your mother left I fell apart. But you know that anyway, Kit. You were there to help pick me back up again, you and Ivy. I'm sorry I put you through that," he said softly. "I should have been stronger . . ."

"You were plenty strong," I said, squeezing his hand. "We were all as strong as we could have been. In fairness, I don't think I did much picking up. That was Ivy. You were much stronger than I am now. I'm here blundering about like a headless chicken – not knowing what to do, who to trust."

"You can trust me," he said, "and your sister, and Rose . . ."

"Now Mum wants me to go to her wedding but I just can't."

He squeezed my hand again. "The thing is, Kitty, your mum, she's not a bad person. I thought she was for a long time. I couldn't understand it – how one day she could wake up and just leave – just decide she wasn't in love with me any more." He blushed slightly. "But more than that I couldn't understand how she could leave you and Ivy. That destroyed me more than anything – having to tell you. Having to watch you try and come to terms with that. But, you know, pet, over the years that followed I realised she hadn't been happy. She hadn't been the person she once was and she needed to go – and we're better for it. So much better for it. Sure don't I have two daughters who would lay down their lives for me? Sometimes things change and it's a very hard lesson to learn. Believe me. But in the end . . ."

"I want to believe that," I said. "I'm trying really hard to be positive and to try and understand where it all went wrong. Did you really not know it was going wrong with Mum? Was it wrong for a while and you were protecting us? It seemed like you were happy."

He shrugged his shoulders. "At the time I didn't think there had been any signs, but in hindsight she hadn't been herself. It was hard for her to leave though. She does love you."

"I don't think Mum really loves anyone but herself," I said sadly. "I'd like to say that she does. That she has grown up. And I think she tries, but inherently she is just a selfish person. She will always put herself first."

"Some people are like that," he said. "But Kitty, that is about them. It's not about you. It's not a reflection of who you are. You are one amazing young woman."

"As my father you are morally obliged to say such things," I said, wiping a tear away from my eye.

"Girl, I would tell you if you were a pain," he said softly, laughing. "The biggest lesson you will learn in this life is that you cannot, no matter how much you want to, control another person's actions. You can't be master of whatever is going on in their heads. All you can do – all you *do* do – is to be the best person you can be and be true to yourself. If that's not enough for Mark, or whoever, then it will be more than enough for someone else."

We hugged then, there in the car, uncomfortably and awkwardly, but it was still one of the nicest hugs I had ever received in my life.

"You hold your head up high, my girl," he said as we drove off to my home – ready for some tea and biscuits or something a little stronger.

What we weren't expecting when we arrived was to find a rather desolate-looking Mark sitting on the front step, his head in his hands.

34

Erin

"I understand," Paddy said as I walked in the door. "I get it."

"Get what?"

He looked wretched. Not, you know, cancer-wretched but devastated, heartbroken wretched. The kind of wretched I had felt when Ian had upped and left me to pick up whatever shreds of dignity I had left and try and piece them back together. It made me feel sick to think that I had done this to him. Even though I hadn't. Even though nothing had happened.

"Just give me a week – you know, to get organised. Get my stuff together. I'll do all the cancellations and things. We both know weddings aren't really your thing."

He flashed a pitiful look at me as the words buzzed around my head and my brain, although well aware that things were very bad indeed between us, tried to make sense of what exactly he was saying.

"Paddy . . . I don't . . . you have to listen." I felt my heartbeat quicken. In the last few months I had been so terrified of losing him to cancer I hadn't realised I was hurtling towards losing him, no matter what. That he could leave, by his own choice.

Because of me. Because I had stupidly met with stupid Ian and stupidly ruined it all.

"We can't go on like this," he said.

"Nothing happened. Nothing happened at all. We just met and had dinner and I should have told you and I don't even understand why I didn't tell you. But nothing happened. You are the one for me. I just freaked out." I flopped onto the sofa and put my head in my hands.

Sitting down beside me, he took my hands and I held on to them, tightly. I didn't want to let go. I didn't want to even think about letting go because I was so afraid that I wouldn't get to hold them again. The fear in the hospital, the day he was rushed in, that was one thing – this felt more real, more immediate and scary as hell.

"It's been scary, Paddy – and when Ian got in touch, I just had to see him."

Paddy's face paled.

"But it's not what you think. I just wanted to try and make sense of it all – to have closure for what we had been through and to allow me to move on. I wanted to be able to walk down the aisle with all our ghosts put to rest."

"Our ghosts aren't at rest," he said, his hand squeezing mine again and I held on tight. "It's not just last night. I've lived the last few months wondering – probably knowing, if the truth be told – if the only reason you agreed to marry me was because I had cancer."

I shook my head, lifting his hand and kissing it. He pulled his hand away and continued talking.

"I've lived knowing that you could wake up one morning and realised this was too much responsibility for one person and just decide to clear off. And I would have to be the bigger person – you know the cancer sufferer who says 'Go on and live your life, have those things I can't give you with someone else. Don't let me hold you back.' Because, Erin, I know I am holding you back."

"You're not holding me back!" I said, my eyes trying to find his and my heart starting to crack.

"I've changed you, from the vibrant, confident, carefree, gorgeous woman I fell in love with to someone who has to worry about me, who has to remind me to take pills, who has mopped up my sick and held me while I shook and shivered with the side effects of chemotherapy. I put you in the position where you came home and found me looking half-dead in bed and I've done that to you and I can't undo it."

My heart cracked a little more. "Please Paddy, it's not like that."

"I've thought about this a lot, Erin, you have to let me finish. I want to undo the harm I've done, but I can't."

"You *can*."

He shook his head. "And when this is done, if this is done, it's always going to be there. Isn't it? I mean, when we go to have a family, it's possible we'll have to get doctors involved. The chemo, we know the damage it may have done . . . well, the doctors say it's often temporary, but . . . I have taken away so much from you, Erin, and all I ever wanted was to give you the moon. Not a ruddy sperm ice lolly and an intimate date with the fertility doctor. So if I have pushed, if I have put on a stupid, happy, smiley, wedding-obsessed face it was because I was trying to convince myself and you that this was all normal. That we were doing this for all the right reasons. That you, Erin Brannigan, the love of my life, were doing this for the right reason."

I was sobbing now – trying to find the words to make this better but feeling my cracking, shattering, shredded heart sink further and further.

"You think I haven't seen you struggle? You think I haven't seen you pull a face when Fiona talks all things reception-related. Or that I haven't seen that look on your face, that panic-stricken moment of horror when a doctor walks into the room? And you think that I've not seen how you look at me – like I'm a wounded puppy. No man wants to be looked at like he's a wounded puppy, Erin. No man. The doctors took away a testicle and I was okay with that but I look at you and see the life I had wanted slipping away from me bit by bit by bit and that scares me more than cancer. I'm losing you."

"No," I sobbed.

"You don't even realise it yet, not really. But I'm losing you and for a while now I've been trying to hang on but the thing is, Erin, and this breaks my heart into a million pieces to admit, you can't hold onto something that doesn't want to be held onto. And there you are again, with that wounded-puppy-dog look. So here we are. I admit defeat. I admit that I've lost and that's the price I've had to pay for getting through this cancer."

I didn't know how to look at him. I didn't know how to find the words to tell him that I loved him, that he hadn't lost me. Yes, I was scared. I was so unbelievably shit-scared it made me sick to the very core of my stomach and that wasn't something we had ever talked about. We had never allowed ourselves to admit to each other just how scared we were because that would make it real. Neither of us wanted it to be real – not even a little bit.

It was a bastard because I should have been able to tell him all that – and he needed me to speak then. He needed me to speak without so much as a moment's hesitation but I couldn't. Because there was a part of him that was right. Of course our relationship had changed. How could we ever have been so naïve as to think that it wouldn't or couldn't or that it would make us stronger? What a pile of sanctimonious bullshit claptrap.

He looked at me and I looked at him. I knew I could tell him how I loved him, how I desperately, desperately loved the very bones of him but I knew that I couldn't make his fears go away with just words. I couldn't make it go away no matter how hard I tried.

"I don't know what to say," I sobbed. "I don't know how to make you believe me . . ."

"You can't say we didn't try," he said, sadly. "We did try."

287

"I'm not ready to stop trying!"

"I'm not sure you have a choice."

I looked at him, trying to see some trace of something – anything – which would lead me to believe he didn't really mean what he was saying. That this was just some mad blip to add to the list of blips we'd had over the last few months.

"We have choices," I said, sniffing loudly, trying to recover my composure. "We have choices, Paddy. You know that. You can't give up on me. You *know*, you *know* I love you. I *will* marry you."

"Erin," he said, looking at me, his eyes taking on a steely glare, "I don't want you to marry me for this – because of this. And can you tell me, really and truly, that you didn't say yes primarily because I had this illness hanging over my head?"

"I do love you," I said, pleading with him.

"I know . . . I know . . ." he said, breaking down, the tears flowing freely, making my heart finally shatter into a million pieces. "I know you love me but I'm not sure it's enough. I'm not sure I'm the best person for you. You have been hurt before and the thing is, Erin, I can't promise that I won't hurt you again. I can't be the person you want me to be . . ."

He stood up and I grabbed at his hand, trying to haul him back to me – pulling him towards me, the sob which had been building escaping and mingling with the sob that had just broken free from his throat. He shrugged me off, walking away, lifting his coat and walking out of our house and I knew this time that he wasn't coming back. He was right, I thought, as my world crumpled around my ears. You can't hold onto something which doesn't want to be held on to – no matter how hard you try and no matter how fierce your grip.

I crumpled then, folded in half almost, or maybe in thirds, or maybe even in quarters on the floor. I crumpled as I realised I had never known loss or pain before – not compared to this. It was physical – excruciating – ripping through every cell in my body and I felt my body, from the end of my hair to the tips of my toes ache and scream out.

I loved him. God I loved him – and I had lost him. Jesus, I had lost him by agreeing to marry him – by standing by his side through this cancer. Through being human and having doubts. Through, it dawned on me horribly and painfully, doing things wrong.

And I simply did not know where to go from here. I had no clue – no notion at all.

35

Kitty

"You don't have to talk to him if you don't want to," my daddy said as I sat frozen in the car, unsure of what to do.

I shook my head, then shrugged my shoulders, looking like I had some kind of weird nervous tick. "I don't know . . ." My fragile heart was telling me to run to him, to hug him and make him feel better. He looked awful – just awful. My gut – the part that had already started building up really high, really strong and really quite impenetrable walls since his departure wanted to turn the car around and drive away, just leaving him there to have whatever new mid-life crisis he was having. I'd been on the receiving end of it already – I had no desire to have my heart trampled on any more.

"I don't know," I repeated. "I don't know what to do."

"What feels right?" Daddy asked, taking my hand.

"Nothing," I said slowly. "At the moment nothing, no matter how I try."

"Whatever the outcome may be, you and him, you need to talk at some stage. But it doesn't have to be tonight, pet. You've had a tough enough day. But, believe me, avoiding it doesn't make it go away."

"I know," I said, squeezing his hand. "I need to. I need to be a grown-up about it, don't I? I can't run from it."

"No, but there's no shame in putting it on pause for a day or two."

"I'm stronger than that, Daddy. I can do it. I can really do it."

And there and then it was clear to me – to move on – to really move on I had to face him. It was one thing taking off my wedding ring. It was another thing changing the locks. It was another thing completely and altogether to tell James I needed a break from him and the time to find myself. But the one thing I knew I would have to do, to really break free, was to hear my husband tell me why I wasn't good enough for him, why we didn't work and why he needed to not be with me. Even if it would hurt and even if I thought my heart couldn't break any more.

I let go of my father's hand and stepped out of the car. I walked towards the man who had been my heart and soul – my everything – and steeled myself for the final break in what had been the biggest, and greatest, love affair of my life.

Mark Shanahan had captured my heart the very first time we had met. We had shared our very own Jerry Maguire moment that day, except he hadn't had me at hello, he had me at "Excuse me," as he brushed past, arms laden with drinks in a busy bar. He had spilled some Guinness on my far too expensive shoes and I had called him a bollocks even though, really, I didn't mind as it gave us chance to talk. I just knew, you see, in the way you know – the way you know someone is meant for you.

He was gorgeous. Dark-haired, lean, tall – well, taller than me anyway. He had dark, deep eyes, a smile that was as a wide as it was gleaming. He had a keen business head – was there by my side when The Dressing Room opened, offering what advice he could. He had a wicked sense of humour, a quick-wittedness that could make me laugh so hard that my ribs would ache and I would beg him to stop. He was, without doubt, the best kisser

I had ever encountered. And we had never stopped kissing – properly kissing. We weren't one of those couples who had at some stage started just pecking each other on the cheek or simply avoiding any physical contact. We had kissed – properly kissed – at least once a day and there was not a single day where I felt as if we were going through the motions, where it didn't feel real or it felt wrong. It felt right – we felt right. He was the one. He had been the one, always.

He followed me into the house, sheepishly, knowing perhaps that he wasn't meant to be there any more. This may well have been his house – his name was still on the deeds – but this was not his home. He stood awkwardly in the hall – not wandering straight to the kitchen as he would have done. Not slumping on the sofa in the living room, kicking off his trainers and switching on Sky Sports. There was no grabbing me in the hall and leading me upstairs to our bedroom. He just stood behind me, his head stooped. I turned and looked at him and heard a strange noise come from his throat. It took a few seconds to realise he was crying – his shoulders shaking, his body tense. It winded me – I had never seen Mark cry like that before. Not even at his own father's funeral when he had insisted on doing the great stiff-upper-lip routine and had ended up comforting me as I sobbed at the graveside. I stood, watching him shake, his body judder, listening to the strange sounds from his throat, fighting the physical urge to either hug him or hit him. How could he stand here in front of me now, crying? He had been the one who ruined it. He had been the one who had walked – no, actually, run at the speed of light – away. He was the one who had slept with someone else when we were still married. When he was still coming home to me and kissing me every day like he meant it. My head started to hurt and I just wanted to make it stop. I squeezed at my temples, felt my arms twitch, not sure what to do or what to say. I decided just to wait until he spoke – wait to see where he was coming from. By now he was hugging his arms

– a pose I realised I was now copying. Hugging ourselves and not each other – me feeling pathetically useless and powerless.

"Sit down, Mark," I said, thinking he might feel a bit better at least if he was seated comfortably in his misery. He led the way into the living room – instinctively walking to his favourite seat and sitting down. I sat across from him, listening to him sniff and snivel.

"I'm so, so sorry, Kitty. I'm so sorry I ruined it all."

Did he expect me to say it was okay? There was a part of me that wanted to. But a bigger part of me knew that he was right. It had been ruined. So I nodded, sitting forward and wringing my hands, noticing he was wringing his too. I waited for him to say more. He didn't. He just sat there, staring at his hands, glancing at me. Maybe he was waiting for me to make it all better – good old Kitty.

"I can't believe I was so stupid," he said eventually.

"I can't believe you were so stupid either," I replied.

"I didn't mean for things to get so out of control," he said. "I didn't want to hurt you. I would never hurt you . . ."

I snorted. Was I really supposed to believe that he didn't think his actions would hurt me? How could he? "You walked out, Mark. You went away to 'find yourself' – you didn't talk, you didn't call, you didn't care a damn what I was going through."

"I didn't know what to say. I knew, I knew as soon as I left that I had made the biggest mistake of my life. I knew I had messed everything up – handled everything so badly. And I knew I had lost you."

"You didn't lose me. You threw me away. You made those choices, Mark, and yet you're here now – crying and looking miserable and none of this makes sense."

"I only came to pick up the new key," he said, with a very weak smile. "But when I got here, it hit me. Everything that I'd lost."

"You say you lost it like you just casually misplaced it or something."

"Okay," he said, sitting back. "Everything I threw away.

Everything I arsed up and destroyed. Does that make you feel better? Would me throwing myself at your feet or self-flagellating make you feel better?" His voice was sharp and horrid.

"No! Funnily enough there's not a whole lot between me and you at the moment which would make me feel better. I appreciate you have apologised – that is a definite step up from twee letters about things being wrong for a long time. Things weren't wrong for me, Mark. I had no warning – and I phoned your work to find you not there – you having walked out. And then came home to find you not here – and a letter. A bloody letter, throwing away whatever we had . . ."

"I didn't walk out of work," he said, cutting me off mid-rant. "I didn't just pack it in, Kitty. They didn't give me any choice in the end."

I looked at him blankly. They didn't give him a choice.

He sat forward – his head in his hands again. "They fired me. Said I wasn't getting the results I once had. Said they needed to downsize."

"They can't just do that – just fire you?" I said, my brain spinning. Fired? Mark had been fired – Mark who loved his job and worked damn hard. Mark, who had left me a letter telling me he had left his job. This didn't make sense – none of it.

"Things hadn't been right for a while. I'd had a few warnings – falling targets, missed sales pitches. They would have done whatever they could to get rid of me in the end – anything to save them a redundancy package."

"You didn't tell me . . . any of this . . ."

He snorted. "I couldn't, Kitty. My pride was in shreds – and there was your business booming despite the recession and I was sinking like a stone. I thought I would turn it around – that the next month would be better. I wanted it to be better – I wanted to give you what you wanted – security, the baby we wanted."

My heart lurched at the mention of the baby we had wanted. The baby we wouldn't have. Tears pricked at my eyes but I was determined not to let them fall.

"It just got too much," he said, his eyes pleading, and I tried to imagine what it must have been like for him – to have his world fall apart and think he couldn't talk to me about it. We must have been more broken than I thought.

"I would have helped," I muttered. "We would have managed."

"I didn't want to 'manage'. I wanted to make you happy."

I couldn't help but laugh – a weird, strangulated laugh. "Well, well done on that score. I've never been happier. Tell me this, Mark, were you thinking of happiness when you were sleeping around at work too?"

"What?" He jolted upright.

"When you were sleeping around. At work. Before or after your verbal warnings – I'm not sure."

"Kitty, what are you talking about?"

"Sex, it would seem. You know – that thing we used to do together and which traditionally, once you are married, you only do with your partner?"

"I didn't have sex with anyone else," he said.

"Did it not get that far?" I asked. "Was it only, you know, third base or whatever?"

"Kitty, you have lost the run of yourself."

"You are one to talk, Mark!"

"I didn't sleep with anyone else. I didn't get to third base with anyone else, or second base, or first base for that matter. There is no 'someone else'. I haven't the first notion what you are talking about."

"James told me. He told me you told him."

"James? What?" He looked genuinely confused – genuinely thrown. There was not a hint of guilt, of back-peddling, of covering up in his demeanour.

"James told me. He said you had spoken when you came back from wherever it was you had run off to."

Mark shook his head. "He told you that? Why would he tell you that? I didn't . . . I never did . . ."

"He told me. He told me that there was someone and that

you always had your doubts about me." Saying the words brought the tears I had been hiding flooding forward.

"He wouldn't do that. He's my best friend. Why would he lie?"

I felt my stomach lurch. I thought of the big mistake I had made myself – the mistake I'd made with James who, if Mark was to believed, had been lying to me. James who, just a short while before I had been feeling so very sorry for. James who had made me feel guilty – but who had reacted with such anger when I told him I didn't love him. Had we been pawns in his game? The thought winded me. I needed air – the room was starting to spin around me – so I got up and walked to the garden, not sure if Mark would follow me and not sure if I wanted him to. Where on earth did we go from here? It had been shattered – everything we had. If only he had told me – if only I had known. If only I hadn't been so quick to trust James – to let him in. Christ, this was unbearable. If he was telling me the truth, it was me who had cheated. And if that was the case how on earth did I tell him?

I felt him behind me and felt him gingerly put his arms around me, clasping my hands and pulling me close.

"I messed up," he repeated. "But I never stopped loving you. I'm sorry I said I did. I thought if I put enough distance between us, it would be okay – that I could move away. But I realised I couldn't do that. I couldn't just let you go. I don't know what James is playing at – I just don't understand, but please believe me."

My heart, which I thought had been bruised and battered enough, lurched again.

"You shouldn't have," I said, still staring away from him. "You should have told me. Oh Mark . . . you don't realise. I thought you were gone. I thought you had never really loved me – that you had been sleeping with someone in work – that you had been lying to me for months, for years even. And James . . . he was there. He was pushing his way in, filling my head with stories of how you didn't care. I slept with him, Mark. Just once and I regretted it the minute it happened and I don't want anything to do with him – even before now, even before knowing he was lying and I'm so sorry, so very sorry."

His grip loosened and he turned and walked away. I stood in the garden and heard him storm through the house.

He turned to look at me just before he left, his eyes blazing: "I never, ever had doubts about you. Never for one second. And I swear to you on my life that I never so much as looked at another woman, never mind kissed another woman. I just messed up, Kit. I just couldn't bear to let you down – and I was stupid and in some weird, horrible place and I needed space and some stupid part of me thought it would make it easier if I said I just had to go. If I had known, what would happen, what he was doing . . . The bastard."

I listened as the front door slammed and his car door slammed, his engine turned on and he sped away and then I sat down, numb and exhausted. I sat there in the garden for a long time – I'm not sure how long exactly but the sun was starting to fade when I went in, and then resumed my sitting position on the sofa, staring into space and not knowing what the hell had just happened. I lifted my phone and texted James. **Why did you lie about Mark?** I typed and hit send, even though I already knew the answer.

Because I needed you more than he did, he replied and it all felt so horribly real and horribly wrong.

I woke on the sofa just as the sun was starting to rise. I noticed Mark was sitting beside me and my heart leapt and then it sank. He was awake, looking at me, watching me. I was suddenly concerned that, God forbid, I might have been drooling or otherwise making a god-awful eejit of myself by snoring or the likes.

"Mark," I stated, as if he didn't know his own name.

"You look so peaceful when you sleep," he said, "I used to

love to watch you. I know you might think that is a little, you know, mental . . . but, God, when I watched you sleep I fell in love with you time and time and time again."

My heart sank with the words 'I used to'.

I sat up and looked at him. My eyes were still heavy with sleep. My heart still heavy with longing and with regret.

"I did this," he said, "All of this. I should have known . . . I should have thought. James, he was always in love with you. I knew that. I just thought we were so strong that it never would be an issue. It never crossed my mind . . . That bastard."

He looked away and I didn't know where to put myself. James was at fault but maybe I was too. Maybe it was down to Mark. Poor, messed-up Mark. Poor messed-up me. Poor messed-up us.

"I loved you," I said "I love you. I just thought you had given up on us."

"I'm sorry," he said again and I found myself reaching for his hands, revelling in feeling the warmth of his skin on mine. God, I had missed his touch. I missed how we fitted. And we were here, holding onto each other by the very tips of our fingers but wanting more.

"I'm so sorry too," I said and pulled him into a hug – a hug that felt so right, but also felt so very bittersweet. Where would we go, where could we go, from here?

36

Erin

What Becomes of the Broken Hearted?

I typed the title five times . . . and deleted it five times.

There clearly was not going to be any further 'Countdown to the Big Day' articles. Nope, they, like me, were on the scrap heap. But we couldn't just leave it hanging there, Sinéad had said. We needed to give our readers closure, she said. I had smiled weakly and nodded, noting the sympathetic expression from Grace who had come with me when I broke the bad news to Sinéad that her proposed advertising revenue was about to go down the pan.

"I know it would easy to walk away from it all now, Erin," Sinéad said. "But you never know, you might find it cathartic and it might help others going through this to cope better."

I wasn't overly concerned about helping others cope better. I just wanted to get through this myself.

In the end he hadn't taken a week to get his affairs in order. He had just gone, back to his mother's house, picking up his belongings – or most of them – while I was at work. Two days after the big departure I had received an email from crazy Fiona the wedding planner to say she was very sorry to hear our wedding would not be going ahead and that she had enjoyed working with us – and of course she was there to meet any other grand big-function demands but that sadly our deposit was non-refundable.

That made it real. If he had been joking or messing or being a hysterical diva he would not have gone ahead and cancelled the wedding. I had forwarded the email to Jules, who had emailed back with a mixed, confused message about how he was a bollocks (a bad choice of words, I thought) and how she was so, so sorry and she had hoped it wouldn't come to this and that her heart was breaking for me, and for Paddy.

Thus followed a series of emails from suppliers. The car hire company, the photographer, the florist. The cake-maker asked, bizarrely, if I still wanted the layer of cake which was traditional wedding cake as it had been made anyway. "It would be a shame to see it go to waste," she said but I could think of nothing less appealing that sitting at home staring at the cake that should have been. And besides, I didn't even like wedding cake.

Each email was a jolt. Sometimes I cursed at the screen and clicked delete as soon as I could. Sometimes I read the messages over and over, trying to get reality to sink in.

Two days had passed when Paddy had got in touch himself, also by email. I sat shaking at my desk, acutely aware that all around me things were going on as normal and I had, workwise at least, pretty much been burying my head in the sand and talking to no one. The great wedding-dress fashion shoot was looming and I couldn't bring myself to tell anyone how awful that would be – until he sent me the email.

It was short and to the point.

I've done as much as I can. You need to sort out your wedding dress and all. I can't believe it has ended like this but perhaps it is for the best, before either of us got hurt any more.

I read the last sentence over and over and looked at the engagement ring still on my finger and I couldn't believe what I had thrown away . . . what we had thrown away.

Telling Grace had been easier than I thought. She allowed me to cry. She even offered to drive me back to the beach. She listened and soothed and never once said it was for the best, or that time would heal or any such cliché. She just allowed me to feel what I needed to feel in that moment without trying to make it better or rationalise it in some way. She did say we had been tested more in the last year than many couples are tested in a lifetime. I simply wondered if we had fallen at the first hurdle.

Telling Sinéad, well – that was an experience and I left with the instructions to write a final article. I didn't absolutely one hundred per cent have to do it, she said, but I knew that what that really meant was I did absolutely and entirely have to do it. If I wanted to stay in her good books.

"Go home. Take the rest of the day off," she said. "Think about it. You might grow to like the idea."

Grace smiled sympathetically in my direction and also nodded at me to go on home. Given that I felt about as fragile as a china doll, I did not need telling again. I just went to my desk – closed down my computer to stop the arrival of any further gut-wrenching emails – and walked out to the car park. But before I could go home, there was one more thing I had to do.

The Dressing Room looked as stunning as it ever did. The sun was shining brightly, a gentle breeze causing the wisteria to sway. The brass door handles were gleaming, the sash windows sparkling. I thought of all the brides who walked in, filled with expectation, giddy with excitement or nerves or both. I wondered how many came back to fulfil the task I was about to. How many wedding dresses were left on the shelves, how many dreams came crashing down? Pushing open the door I saw Kitty standing at the cash desk, diligently filling in paperwork and singing along quietly to a song on the radio.

At the sight of Kitty, in the shop where I had faced my wedding-dress demons and found a dress I loved and which I knew Paddy would love me in, I felt any modicum of resolve not to cry again weaken.

She looked up to me and smiled, just in time for my façade to crumble entirely.

"I'm so sorry," I mumbled. "It's off. And I don't need the dress. And I'm so sorry."

Before my sentence was finished she was beside me, hugging me and ushering me upstairs, away from the public shop floor, and into the privacy of her office and workroom. Rose was there, but as soon as she saw me she nodded to Kitty and said she would go downstairs and keep an eye on things.

"It's okay," Kitty said.

"I'm so sorry," I repeated – feeling that sorry was the only thing I needed to or could say. "I'm just so sorry."

Kitty was wonderful. She assured me that I wasn't the only bride who ever came to her with this sorry task. "It's harder for you than it is for me," she smiled. "Please feel no need to apologise to me."

I thanked her and took her offer of a cup of tea, which I drank while trying to regain my composure. As I drank and she sat close to me, chatting idly, I noticed two tourists walk along the city walls. An elderly couple – American, I would guess by the baseball caps, rain coats and chinos – they stopped periodically to look from the ramparts over the city and each time they stopped, they stood side by side. He would place his arm around her shoulder and she would wrap her own arm around his waist and they would stand and chat for a while, before kissing each other gently, laughing and moving on.

"Do you think that's the exception?" I asked her, nodding towards the Americans on the wall.

"What?" she asked.

"The happy ending? The happy ever after? The growing old with someone you love? You see a lot of romance here, Kitty – what do you think?"

She looked wistfully at the couple as they continued on their way, walking up towards St Columb's Cathedral.

"Honestly? I think we don't know anyone's back story. We

don't know what they have been through to get to this point. We don't know how any of our stories will turn out – but we have to trust our gut."

"Do you trust your gut?"

She laughed. "My gut has led me up a few wrong paths lately. I think it was on the blink, but it's telling me to give things a go – to try and make my own relationship work. I'm going to give my gut one last chance. What does your gut tell you?"

"That I don't want this to be over," I said, simply.

"Then give it one last throw of the dice," she said.

What Becomes of the Broken Hearted?

Did you ever hear the story of the woman who was scared? The woman who was so scared of getting hurt that she ended up hurting herself more than she could have imagined.

It's a pretty sad story. It doesn't end well. It started with a kiss, and a relationship and a proposal which I knocked back. And another proposal that I knocked back. Because I was scared, you see. Of being hurt. Because I had been hurt before and even though I knew he was different — this new man in my life — I was afraid a wedding would break us.

In the end though — cancer broke us. Or I broke us. Or maybe a combination of both — or maybe a whole host of things. But as I write this, we are broken. The man I love and I have parted. Parted is such a nice word for what, essentially, is a horrendous situation.

You see the man I love, he's on this page, in this picture looking at me and smiling. I'm smiling, a wee bit gormlessly it has to be said, back at him. I see that picture, taken just weeks before everything went wrong and I can't believe I'm even writing this. We are in love. You don't look at someone like that if you are not head over heels in love with them.

So where did it go wrong? Was it the cancer diagnosis? Probably not. I think maybe it was because we assumed it wouldn't change us. We decided early on we would be one of those sickeningly twee couples who were made so much stronger by the experience. I agreed, finally, to get married. I knew I couldn't personally cure his cancer but I could do something to help. For a lot of people that would have been making chicken soup and reminding their loved one to take their meds — for me it was agreeing to the biggest, grandest day of our lives.

And we kept up this façade. Laughing in the face of cancer — mocking it in the way it had mocked us. We pretended we were fine. We adopted a keep calm and carry on mentality — showing no fear. We marched forward with our wedding plans, a big day, a big dress — champagne, party, tearful vows.

We stopped talking to each other about how we really felt. The relationship we had, where we could share every fear, every worry, every foible in each other's life disappeared. We walked on eggshells. Afraid to talk, afraid to argue. At times we were afraid to touch each other — to laugh with each other. We were afraid to be honest with each other. The fear just won, every single day. And we thought we were okay because what was so wrong became what we were and we didn't know how to get out of it.

In the end — if this is the end — we broke up. We parted (that awful word again). Did the fear win? Did the cancer win?

There are people out there, I know, who think putting your life out there for everyone to see is asking for trouble. But I'm here — and I have trouble anyway. My heart is broken — broken in a way that it never has been before. Because, despite all we have been through, all that we have been put through, I still love him. I love him so much that I'm prepared to take this chance knowing that I may fall flat on my face. Knowing that there might not be enough glue in the entire world to piece us back together again. But I can't stop trying. Just because it gets hard. You can't walk away. I'm done with being scared and I'm done with walking on eggshells. I am in love with a man I want to spend the rest of my days with. A man I want — need — to marry. A man who I know can make me laugh for the rest of our days, however long that may be. I want to walk the city walls with him — holding hands, smiling and chatting. I want to walk with him forever.

I've titled this article 'What Becomes of the Broken Hearted?' — I don't have an answer yet. I don't know what will become of us — but this is it. A throw of the dice — and a hope that things will work out.

I hit the save key, and then the print key. I walked to the printer, lifted out two copies of the article and walked into Grace's office, placing one on her desk and then walking into Sinéad's office and placing one on her desk. The cards were dealt now. I would just have to see how they fell.

37

Kitty

Wedding season was all but done but we still had enough to keep us busy. Mostly, things had gone smoothly for us that summer – there had been relatively few crises (for the business, that is).

Today had the potential to be the biggest crisis of all though. My mother was marrying her beloved Charles. She was already near-hysterical with nerves when I arrived at her hotel room that morning with her dress and flowers.

"You came," she squealed, delightedly. "I didn't know if you would."

"I had to bring the dress, Mum," I said. "Of course I would be here."

"And Ivy, is she coming?" My mother's eyes were wide with anticipation at my response.

"Yes," I nodded. "She's coming to the ceremony anyway. She needs time, Mum. We all do."

"It's more than I could have hoped for," she said, but now was the not the time to agree with her and tell her how precarious the situation was.

It had been Mark who had persuaded me to talk to her again.

After that night – the night where he had come to the house – we had spent a lot of time talking. Entire days and nights of talking and trying to understand where we stood and what had happened. We knew it wasn't going to be easy – we knew we would need to take it slowly. We decided to look into marriage counselling and we vowed to be honest with each other as much as we could. He was looking for work – had a few leads to go on. His confidence was dented but I knew he would get it back. As the walls we had put up started to crumble we began to talk about other things – I'd told him about my mother. Her return for her wedding, her hope for a big reunion.

"You don't have to spend your whole life being angry at her," he said. "She probably won't change but can you accept her the way she is?"

So I said I would try. And Ivy said she would try and that made my father happy. And made my mother ecstatic.

So when we sat close to her and watched her exchange her vows, we knew we were finally building bridges. When she turned to us afterwards, walking hand in hand with Charles, who was grinning like a cat who got the cream, I knew I had made the right decision. And when Mark took my hand and led me outside, I knew I had made the right decision there too. I wasn't expecting miracles from either of them – but I had more hope for the future and that was as good as anything. I was starting to believe in happy endings.

38

Erin

It was always breezy at **Grianán of Aileach**. Despite the tall stone surrounds of the ancient Irish ring fort, the breeze always seemed to find a way to whistle in through the gates and dance around your legs. I'm sure someone somewhere has some big theory about it being the spirits of ancient Irish souls reminding you this is their land, or something, but to me it was just a place to be. A sanctuary, a calm place that reminded me that when the past was gone history could not be changed.

On that bright September afternoon, I stood in the centre of the fort, feeling the sun shine on my face. This felt right – this step, this moving on from where I had been felt so very right. Jules took my hand and squeezed it and I hugged her back.

"Careful," she said, "You'll squash your flowers."

"It doesn't matter a damn if they get squashed," I said, looking at the simple bunch of lilacs in my hand.

"He'll be blown away, and I'm not just talking about the breeze," she said.

"I hope so, Jules."

"Don't worry, you look stunning," Kitty said as she straightened the soft lace of my train and tucked a stray curl behind my ear. "This is the real you," she said. "You look simply stunning."

She kissed my cheek and went to stand with the other guests who had gathered. There were only ten of us in total. No crowd. No choirs. No huge floral arrangements. Just me in a simple lace gown from The Dressing Room with flowers in my hair and a small posy in my hand. I was wearing flat comfortable shoes under my dress to stop me sinking into the ground. There were no chairs. No fancy wedding cars had brought us to our destination. There was just this small crowd, a small canopy to protect us from the elements and a single harpist. The celebrant, a kind man with a warm smile and a wicked sense of humour, who had helped us embrace everything that was uniquely 'us' about this wedding, smiled at me as things got underway.

"He's here," Jules whispered and I turned to watch him walk through the gates. I know it was a break with tradition but I wanted him to walk to me – for me to be the one waiting for him, showing him that I would always be there for him.

The look on his face gave me all the reassurance I needed – and I felt myself stop shivering and shaking. He was here.

The article had caused a quite a stir in the media when it had gone to print. Every Tom, Dick and Harriet had wanted me to talk about laying my heart on the line so publicly. I had refused – saying I had said all that I needed to say and now, well, I would just have to wait to see how things went.

I hadn't been expecting an immediate reaction so when publication day came and went I congratulated myself on having some fingernails left. I tried not to think about whether or not he had read the piece while fending off sympathetic glances from my colleagues who all jumped about as high as I did whenever my phone rang.

By the time I went home to lay staring at the phone before thankfully falling asleep, I was safe in the knowledge I had done all I could do.

When I woke in the morning I padded downstairs to find him in the kitchen, cooking breakfast with a fixed look of concentration on his face.

I stood there for a moment. I know this sounds beyond cheesy, but I wasn't sure I wasn't dreaming so I stood and watched as he cracked some eggs and started to mix them.

"You're here," I stated and he turned to look at me.

"I'm here," he said, "And we're going to win."

I smiled and watched as he put the eggs down, walked towards me and kissed me. "We're going to win," he whispered in my ear as we hugged.

The wedding Take Two, as it became known – was always to be a simple affair. No flounces. No frills. Nothing that would attract undue attention. We kept it secret from all but those closest to us – this was about us and our future. Nothing else mattered.

As we joined hands, grinning like eejits in front of each other, the rain started to fall softly.

"They say it's lucky if it rains on your wedding day," I grinned at him, pulling him out from under the canopy and turning my head towards the heavens.

"I couldn't be luckier," he said.

If you enjoyed
What Becomes of the Broken Hearted? by Claire Allan
why not try
If Only You Knew also published by Poolbeg?
Here's a sneak preview of Chapter One

If Only You Knew

Claire Allan

POOLBEG

Chapter 1

Ava

Standing in the middle of the fresh-produce aisle in Tesco, Ava took a deep breath and hoped that God would grant her the strength to get all the way around to the tinned-goods aisle – and eventually through the check-out and on her way home – without losing her mind entirely.

Maisie had insisted she was much too big a girl for the trolley and was currently running rings round the carrots, flapping her wings behind her and declaring that she was a butterfly. A few people had smiled indulgently at the child as she twirled while a perfectly preened thirty-something had tutted loudly and muttered that children should be left at home if they couldn't behave well in public.

Ava wanted to bite back with something witty and cutting but she was too busy trying to remember whether or not they needed onions, what it was Connor had asked her to pick up for him and whether or not she had locked up her classroom before leaving work for the day.

Instead, even though she knew it was childish, she pulled a face at Ms Perfect and took Maisie by the arm and tried to persuade her to help by selecting a few apples for their trolley. It was all going so well until Maisie belted off at lightning speed, reaching out one chubby little hand to the most precarious apple on the bottom of the pile and set off an avalanche of Pink Ladies which gave Ms Perfect the chance to do the very loudest tut in her repertoire before stepping over the apples and heading on her way. Ava felt like crying as she wrestled an indignant Maisie back into the trolley and set about picking the apples up and stocking them back in the display before anyone suggested she pay for the lot of them.

She would need a drink when she got home. A big, cold, alcoholic drink. In a big glass. Maybe one of those feckers which held an entire bottle.

Putting the last apple in place, she took a deep breath just as she heard Maisie squeal a momentous "*Mammmeeeeee!*" before toppling head first out of the trolley and landing with a scream on the floor.

A&E hadn't been very busy, thankfully, and they had been whisked through triage and onto X-ray relatively quickly. Ava had been tempted to ask the doctors if there was any chance of some mildly mind-altering painkillers to help her escape from the headache which was building in her head and the coronary she had no doubt was building somewhere around her heart.

She had phoned Connor, while Maisie screamed blue murder in the background, and had tried to assure him it was okay and it was only a mild trolley-jumping accident and she was pretty sure no bones were broken in the process. She didn't tell him that Maisie had saved herself from splitting her head open by breaking the fall with her hand. He had sighed deeply, and said he would meet her at the hospital. The staff at Tesco had been more than lovely, bringing an icepack and telling her not to worry about abandoning her half-filled trolley but she had been mortified anyway. And worried, of course. Maisie's wrist was starting to swell and bruise and she couldn't be consoled. The dream of a glass of wine slipped further and further away. When the doctor returned to their cubicle and said the injury was no more than a bad sprain, which would require strapping and some pain relief, Ava felt herself finally sag with relief and tears sprang to her eyes.

Maisie looked up, now doped up on Calpol with her eyes drooping, and Ava felt like the worst mother in the world for feeling frustrated and angry at how the whole situation had developed.

Maisie had just been overexcited after a day at nursery. She had been excited to see her mammy and had gone into hyper mode. She hadn't been naughty – she was just being a typical almost-three-year-old, but Ava hadn't been in the form for it – not after a long week at work. Maybe if she had paid more attention this wouldn't have happened. She would have to try harder. Guiltily, she tearfully kissed her daughter on the head and assured her she loved her all the way to the moon and back.

Eventually Connor popped his head around the curtain, looking equally as frazzled, tired and fecked-off as she felt.

"I drove as fast as I could," he said, "but you know what it's like trying to get out of Belfast at this time of the evening. Is she okay?"

"A bad sprain," Ava said looking down at a now sleeping Maisie. "She'll be fine. They've given her painkillers and are going to strap her wrist up."

"Thank God," he said, sitting down on the plastic chair beside his wife and sagging with relief.

Both of them eyed a trolley-bed opposite them and Ava wondered what it would be like to just climb under the harsh, starchy sheets and fall asleep. She could tell by the look in Connor's eyes that he felt exactly the same.

"I'd fight you to the death for it," she said, smiling at him and at the bed. And she was only half joking.

A few hours had passed and Maisie was sleeping in her mammy and daddy's bed, her poor bandaged arm cradling her favourite stuffed bunny rabbit. She had thrown a minor fit at the very notion of sleeping in her own big-girl bed and, too tired to argue with her after all that the day had thrown at them, Ava and Connor had agreed and had tucked her in before returning to the living room to sit, nursing cups of tea and staring into space.

"It could have been worse," Connor said. "At least it wasn't serious."

Ava nodded. "I know." She sat back, closed her eyes and was just about to drift off into a blissful exhaustion-induced coma when it struck her that she still didn't have her shopping done and she would need to face the supermarket again. "Fuck!" she swore. "Fuck. Fuck. Fuck."

Saturday mornings were reserved for that special kind of hell that was a Soft Play centre. Even with a bandaged and swollen arm, Maisie could not be dissuaded from her weekly trip to the ball pools and slides of Cheeky Monkeys. Ava couldn't argue – not after the act of wilful neglect which had seen her daughter tumble headfirst out of a trolley the day before. So she had packed a bag, filled with cartons of juice, boxes of raisins, a couple of favourite dollies and a change of clothes and had strapped her strong-willed daughter into the back of the car. Connor had padded out to see them, still exhausted from his week of commuting to and from Belfast for work. "I'll take her if you want," he offered and Ava had wanted more than anything to let him but instead she settled for hugging him and thanking him for the offer – even though she knew he had made it knowing full well she would never take him up on it.

Saturday mornings were when she met her mummy friends who would arrive with their charges and regale her with stories about their wonderfulness. It wasn't that Ava didn't find Maisie wonderful – she was constantly amazed by her daughter's flighty wee personality as it developed – but she wasn't one of those who felt the need to boast about her either.

Saturdays were the days she also met Karen – known as 'Hell-mum' to Ava and Connor in their private conversations. Karen had taken to motherhood like a layabout takes to work. She did it because she had to but she took no joy in it. She also very much enjoyed sharing her horror stories, time and time again, with anyone who wanted to (or in many cases didn't want to) listen. Ava felt sorry for her to an extent – she clearly had issues by the bucket-load. Ava looked at Karen's five-year-old sometimes and felt her heart sink to her boots. She wondered if, in quieter moments, Karen was actually more maternal than she appeared in public.

Sighing, Ava pulled into the car park of the centre and tried to contain Maisie from running in front of the wheels of the 4x4s hunting for a prime parent-and-child parking space. She saw Karen's Land Rover among them and she braced herself for the latest chapter in 'How Hard My Life Is Compared to Yours' from her once dear friend.

"C'mon, Maisie Moo!" she called, injecting a fake sense of cheer into her voice. "It's time to play and meet all your friends!"

Karen sat sipping from a latte while Ava cradled Maisie – suddenly overcome with nervousness thanks to her sore arm.

"Oh God, you poor thing. Still it could have been worse. I remember when Sophie was the same age – took a tumble in the park and needed three stitches. Still, I only thought things were tough then. God, Ava, you've no idea. Now that's she five – and at school and learning the badness from the other ones – it's even tougher. You can't watch her these days. Into everything."

Ava nodded sympathetically, all the while thinking that Karen hadn't given a single glance to where her daughter was since she'd sauntered into the café attached to the play centre half an hour before.

"I'm sure her being five has its good points," she offered, hoping that her friend would assure her that of course she was just having a bad day and living with a five-year-old was a joy day in and day out.

"Hmmm," Karen said with a sly smile, "I'm sure it has – I just can't think of any of them at the moment. It's all just work, work, work with some worry thrown in for good measure." She laughed as she said it and Ava had to fight the urge to pick up the cream bun she was just about to tuck into and ram it right into Karen's face to stop her from talking any more. She didn't want to hear that it got worse. She wanted to hear that it got better – and easier and altogether more pleasant. She wanted her friend to tell her that she was only a couple of months away from an altogether easier existence when she would not feel so tired, and worried and overworked 99% of the time.

Deciding that ramming a cream bun in the face of one of her oldest friends was probably not the best way to relieve the knot of tension which seemed to exist on a permanent basis between her shoulder blades, she smiled sweetly and took a large bite from it instead, allowing the sugary softness of the confectionery to give her a momentary saccharine-induced high. If they had served ice-cold Pinot Grigio in the Soft Play, she would have knocked a couple of those back too.

Karen was just about to launch into her latest rant on the perils of motherhood (this time – Play-Doh and why it was the work of the Devil) when Ava's phone burst into life. Gratefully, she pawed in her bag to find it. She didn't care who was phoning. It could have been a heavily accented salesperson trying to persuade her to part with her life savings for a timeshare but she would have spoken to him.

Glancing down she saw that it was her mother. This was definitely strange. Sure, she was due to see her mother later that day anyway. Saturday afternoons were always spent at Granny's house, where Maisie had the run of the place and her very own playroom to wreak havoc in.

"Mum?" Ava answered as Maisie glanced up at her.

"Ava, thank goodness I got you," her mother said, her voice choking with emotion.

"Is everything okay, Mum? Mum, what's wrong?"

Suddenly, even though she knew this made her a very bad person indeed, the thought crossed her mind that if something was wrong she would have the perfect excuse to get up and leave the play centre without any hesitation whatsoever. She glanced at Karen who was staring into the bottom of her coffee cup, disgusted to be cut off from her rant before she got into full flow, and she felt guilty. She was a bad friend and a bad daughter.

"It's Betty," her mum said, her voice cracking.

The memory came to Ava of a well-spoken woman in delicious purple satin shoes with a delicate floral detail who had held her hand as she sobbed through her beloved granny's funeral. They had gone to sink the better part of two bottles of wine at a restaurant afterwards – talking into the wee small hours. Ava had been very taken with this bohemian creature with wild curly hair and a gentle smile, who looked years younger than her age.

"I love your shoes," Ava had told her, admiring the large sequinned flower, and the flared heels. Betty was a woman who knew good shoes. Ava had eyed her own sensible flats, which she'd bought off a hanging stand in Primark, with a sense of disgust.

"They're vintage," Betty had said, "I picked them up for ten euro in a market in Paris."

"They're amazing," Ava had slurred.

"Tell you what, I'll leave them to you in my will. When I pop my clogs, you can slip them on your feet and keep them warm for me," Betty had said and the pair of them laughed uproariously.

"Oh Ava, pet, can you come over?" Ava's mother sobbed, cutting through her thoughts. "Betty's dead. My baby sister is dead!"

When she arrived at her mother's house, having deposited Maisie back with her still-sleepy father, Ava was shocked at just how bereft Cora was. It wasn't that she thought her mother to be a heartless cow or devoid of feeling, just that she had never really spoken of Betty and when she had it had been in hushed tones. Betty was most definitely the black sheep of the Scott family, having left Derry for a bohemian lifestyle in the South of France. Ava couldn't say she had blamed her one bit for leaving Derry behind – Derry wasn't exactly a fun place to be by all accounts. Ava would have left too – especially if she had found a very handsome man to marry who wanted to take her away from it all. South of France versus the Bogside and tear gas? Who could have blamed her? But it seemed there were elements in her family who had felt betrayed in some way by Betty's departure. Sure they were all meant to be in this together, weren't they? Whatever the reason, Betty was not someone who was spoken about very often. There weren't even family holidays en masse to Provence even though at family gatherings it was agreed it must be lovely out there.

Looking at her mother now, bent double in grief in her armchair, her sobs racking her body, Ava wondered if maybe she just hadn't wanted to let her sister go, knowing perhaps she would never come home?

"Oh Mum," she said, kneeling down beside Cora and pulling her into a hug. "I'm so sorry!"

"I just thought I would see her again . . . there was so much we needed to say –" Cora broke off, sniffing loudly right in Ava's ear which made her shudder – she never liked getting too close to a clatter of snotters.

Pulling back, she looked at her mother. "I'm sure she knew how you felt about her," she soothed, not quite knowing why she was saying that. She didn't, in honesty, know if Betty knew a damn about her mother and how she felt about her. Ava didn't know how her mother felt about Betty. She just didn't come up in conversation that often.

"How could she not tell us she was sick? She must have known for a long time – it was cancer. Were we so bad she would rather die out there without a being belonging to her close by? And then to be told by letter . . . she had written it in advance to be sent to me . . ." Cora gestured to a letter on the side table and broke into a fresh dose of sobbing. "I would have gone. I would have been there. I know we all have our lives and we're all busy but we would have gone, or we would have brought her home . . ."

Ava hugged her mother again. "She's been in France a long time. Longer than she was ever here. Maybe she just considered that home?"

Cora sniffed. "Home is always home," she said. "She should have let us say goodbye."

"I'm so sorry, Mum," Ava repeated. "I'll make you a cup of tea. You've had a shock. Have you spoken to the rest of the family yet?"

Cora shook her head. "I just called you. I just wanted you."

Ava felt her heart swell at her mother's honest emotion. An only child, her widowed mother leant on her heavily at times. Of course she would have called her in the circumstances.

Ava kissed her and stood up.

"She's left you something," Cora said as Ava turned on her heel to go to the kitchen.

"What?" Ava stopped and turned, sure she must have misheard. How could, why would, Betty leave her anything?

"It says so in the letter. You have to go to a solicitor's in Belfast on Wednesday to hear more." Cora spoke softly, her head downwards.

Ava felt absolutely and totally confused. Sure they had spoken for a long time at her granny's funeral – laughing like old friends – but to leave her something?

"Really?" she asked. "Why would she do that?"

"You must have meant a lot to her," Cora said, looking up, her eyes filling with tears again. "Sure don't you mean a lot to us all?"

•—◆—•

If you enjoyed this chapter from
If Only You Knew by Claire Allan,
why not order the full book online
@ www.poolbeg.com

•—◆—•